A Year in
Paris

by
Malaurie Barber

Justice House Publishing, Inc.
Tacoma, Washington, USA
www.justicehouse.com

A YEAR IN PARIS

Copyright © 2001 by Malaurie Barber.

All Rights Reserved, including the right to reproduce this book, or portions thereof, in any form whatsoever. For information contact Justice House Publishing, Inc., 3902 South 56th St., Tacoma, WA 98409, USA.

Cover art by Sheri

Book Design by R Paterson-Reed

All characters and events in this book are fictitious. Names, characters, places and incidents are products of the author's imagination or are used fictiously. Any resemblance to actual events, locales or persons, living or dead, is entirely coincidental.

The typeface is Garamond. The paper is Book Opaque.

ISBN 0-9708874-1-8

2002 printing

PRINTED IN THE USA

Dedication

I dedicate this book to those of you who have the guts to stand up for yourselves and live your lives as you see fit, not as you are told.

Also, to my sister Elodie, for being one of the strongest people I have ever known.

Acknowledgements

I would like to thank my husband Steve for his constant support and input...not to mention the proofreading. Thanks also to my friend Jennifer for her help and guidance, and to all my internet fans for making me feel special. Thanks to my cousin, Frederic, for being my inspiration for the character of Clément.

Chapter 1

"Promise me you'll call when you get there?"

"I will, Dad."

"Okay. Be careful—you know those French people can be a little crazy sometimes."

"Dad!"

"Bye, sweetheart, see you at Christmas time," he said as he grabbed her in a hug.

A voice over the loudspeaker announced, "Last call for flight 667 to Paris."

"Dad, let me go! I'm going to miss my plane!" Chloe disengaged herself from her father's embrace. "I promise I'll call as soon as I land." She kissed him on the cheek. "Love you."

"Love you too, pumpkin...please be careful." His words were lost to Chloe, who was already making her way toward the hostess, boarding pass in hand. She turned one last time and waved before disappearing through the door.

I can't cry, I won't cry, I won't cry, Chloe mumbled to herself. *Come on, Chloe, you wanted this opportunity to leave good old Washington behind and this is your chance, so stop feeling sorry for yourself and go sit down.*

Chloe made her way down the aisle toward 14C. "Here it is." She stood on her tiptoes trying to put her carry-on into the overhead luggage space. "Damn, why do these things have to be so high?"

"Let me help you, mademoiselle." Chloe turned toward the voice and was faced by two smiling brown eyes.

"Sure, that would be great. These things are not made for people vertically challenged like me," she said with a smile before sliding into her seat.

The stranger put her carry-on away with ease and looked at Chloe. "Well, you and I are going to spend some time together—I'm 14B."

"Great, I hate flying, so having someone to talk to always helps me." She softly tugged a lock of blond hair behind her ear. "Where are my manners? I'm Chloe." She extended her hand to her travel companion.

"I am Vincent," he replied, shaking her hand.

"Well, Vincent, nice to meet you." She smiled at him. As soon as all the passengers and crew were seated, the plane pulled back from the gate and started taxiing toward the runway. "Oh boy, here we go," she muttered nervously. "Have I mentioned that I hate flying?" As the plane started to gain speed, Chloe grabbed her armrest and closed her eyes.

"But you should not close your eyes, the take-off is the best part!" Vincent teased her.

"Speak for yourself. It scares me senseless," Chloe said with clenched teeth. "Just tell me when we're high enough that I can't see the ground anymore."

"All right." Minutes went by and Chloe started to relax. "Okay, it is safe to open your eyes now." Vincent told her.

"Sure?"

"Yep."

She opened her eyes and glanced cautiously out the windows where only clouds were visible. She let out a heavy sigh and slowly let go of her armrest.

"So, how long are you going to stay in France?" Vincent asked.

"What? Oh, sorry, you startled me." She slowly opened and closed her hands to bring back the blood circulation.

"I was just wondering how long you will be in France?"

"Oh, yeah, sorry...one year."

"Pretty long time for someone so young to be away from home."

"Hey, I am 18, and perfectly capable of handling myself," She answered with irritation. *Damn, why does everyone just assume that I am this young kid who knows nothing and can't take care of herself?*

Vincent interrupted Chloe's musings. "I'm sorry, I didn't mean to offend you," he apologized. "I'll shut up and leave you alone now." Reaching for his bag tucked under the seat in front of him, he took out a book.

Chloe carefully took a glance at him. *Okay girl, put your pride in your pocket and make peace. Curly hair, baby face... Come on, he can't be older than 19.* Chloe sighed. "So how old are you anyway?"

"Oh, now you're talking to me, huh?"

"Yeah, well, eight hours is a long time to be silent."

Vincent smiled. "I'm 22, and before you say anything, I know I look much younger."

Chloe laughed. "Why don't we just drop the age thing for a while. I guess from your accent you are French, right?"

"Yes. So, what are you going to do for a year in France?"

"Au pair."

"You are kidding."

"No, look." She grabbed her backpack from under her seat and took out a folder.

"These are pictures of the family I'm going to stay with." She showed Vincent the pictures of a little boy and his parents. "This is Clément—he's two—and those are his parents, Beatrice and Jean."

"Who is that?" Vincent asked, pointing to a picture of Clément in the arms of a tall woman with long black hair and clear eyes. "Wow, whoever that is, I wouldn't mind being her au pair!"

"Hey!" Chloe poked him in the ribs. "This is Clément's half sister, Laurence."

"Why do they need an au pair when they obviously have someone old enough to take care of the little man when the parents are busy?"

"I don't know, they didn't really explain in their letters. I don't think the sister lives with them all the time."

"So, are you going to stay in Paris?"

"No, Versailles."

"That's not too far. I am from Vincennes."

"Where is that?"

Their conversation went on for hours. Vincent gave Chloe dos and don'ts about her future life in France. They talked about everything from music to politics, and when the flight attendant announced that the plane was starting its descent towards Paris, Chloe and Vincent were chattering like old friends.

The landing was not as hard on Chloe, thanks to Vincent, who distracted her by pointing out some Parisian monuments discernable from high above.

"Mesdames et Messieurs, vous pouvez maintenant détacher vos ceintures et procéder vers la sortie," the flight attendant announced.

"Well, I guess it's time to go." Chloe started to get up.

"Here, I'll get your carry-on," Vincent offered.

"Thanks. It was really great to meet you."

Vincent handed her the bag. "Listen, here is my phone number. You can call me anytime, and I'll show you around."

"Okay, great. I'll do that. Thanks."

They slowly made their way toward the exit, and walked out.

"This is where we go our separate ways. I don't have to go through immigration, so I'll talk to you later."

"See you. Talk to you later," Chloe answered.

Vincent walked away, turned around, waved one last time, and was gone.

As Chloe stood in the immigration line, the nervousness she felt earlier in the plane came back. *Come on, we're not flying anymore, so why I am so nervous? New country, new people, new language. Yeah...that'll do it,* Chloe thought. *Okay, what's the sentence in French for nice to meet you...damn, I can't remember!* A tap on the shoulder interrupted her thoughts.

"Hey lady, it's your turn, are you going or what?"

"Oh, sorry."

She walked up to the immigration officer and handed over her passport.

"Have a nice year," the officer said while stamping it.

Well, that wasn't too painful. She tucked her passport back in her jacket pocket and made her way toward the luggage area.

Okay, all the suitcases accounted for. Oh boy, I should have listened to Dad and not brought so much with me. Chloe piled her luggage onto the cart and pushed it toward the exit.

When she emerged into the waiting area her eyes scanned the crowd for the faces she only knew from pictures. *Okay, let's not panic, I'm sure they haven't forgotten about me.*

"Ouch!" Chloe exclaimed when a cart ran into the back of her legs. "Hey, watch where you're going!"

"Well, get out of the way!" an old man answered before shoving her aside and walking away.

Welcome to Paris, City of Love! thought Chloe sarcastically.

"Chloe Jones?"

"What?" Chloe barked, irritated for not finding her host family and by the old man's rudeness. She looked up to find a tall woman with sunglasses staring at her.

"Are you Chloe Jones?" the woman asked.

"Yes, I am."

"Good, follow me," the woman said before turning away.

"Wait a minute, I am not going anywhere with someone I don't even know."

The woman sighed and took off her sunglasses, revealing a pair of clear blue eyes. "I am Laurence Glairon."

"Oh...sorry, I didn't recognize you with the glasses...I wasn't expecting you here," Chloe apologized.

Laurence didn't answer, instead grabbing the cart away from Chloe and pushing her way out of the crowd.

Chloe was almost running to keep up with her. The exhaustion of the eight-hour flight took its toll, and she found herself unable to keep up. Soon she was far behind, finally losing sight of Laurence Glairon.

Chloe stopped and tried not to panic. *She has to realize that I am not following anymore.* She stood alone in the middle of the crowd and tried to fight back the tears that threatened to fall. *Not bad for your first day Chloe, almost run over by an angry old man with a cart and now lost in the airport.* Not able to contain them anymore, tears started falling down her cheeks.

Suddenly a hand grabbed her shoulder. "What are you doing? I told you to follow me." Laurence looked at Chloe angrily.

"I lost you in the crowd, and..." Chloe's tears started flowing even more. She felt helpless, lost, and homesick.

Laurence reached for something inside her leather coat pocket and handed a tissue to Chloe. "Here," she said.

"Thanks," Chloe said sniffling.

Laurence nodded and grabbed Chloe's hand with one hand and the cart with the other and proceeded to make her way out of the crowd.

Once they reached the parking lot, Laurence let go of Chloe's hand. No words had been spoken between the two women since inside the airport. Chloe felt exhausted and numb. She was ready to break the silence when Laurence spoke first.

"Here is the car. Good thing I took Dad's car with the number of suitcases you have," Laurence stated with annoyance.

Chloe was starting to really get irritated with this woman who was less than welcoming and rude beyond words.

"Try packing light for a whole year," Chloe snapped back.

Laurence looked coldly at Chloe. She opened her mouth as if she was going to speak, but instead just turned her back and opened the trunk of a gray Mercedes station wagon. She grabbed the first suitcase and put it in the trunk. Chloe started moving to help her.

"I can handle your suitcases. The car is open; why don't you just go sit down," Laurence said while reaching for another piece of luggage.

"Fine," answered a frustrated Chloe. *What is her problem? Boy, if all French people are this way than I am going to be back home before you know it,* Chloe thought while making her way toward the passenger side. She opened the door and dropped herself onto the seat. Shortly after, Laurence sat behind the wheel and started the car.

Chloe glanced over at the clock. *8 a.m. No wonder I'm so cranky; I've been awake for over 24 hours.* She yawned. *But I wonder what her excuse is,* Chloe thought while looking at the woman sitting next to her.

She doesn't look French at all. Jet black hair, blue eyes, high cheekbones, very tall, Chloe mused. *I bet she never spends a Saturday night without a date.*

"Stop staring."

"What?"

"You have been staring at me for the past five minutes. Stop staring," Laurence said coldly.

"Uh...sorry...I didn't realize I was staring...I..."

"We'll be there in twenty minutes."

"Okay," answered Chloe, relieved at the change of topic. Silence settled once again in the car. Chloe looked out the window and could see Paris lights on her right while the car went down the highway at high speed. Chloe felt some of the excitement she first had when hearing that she had been accepted in the au pair program. *I am not going to let some rude stranger ruin my first day in France. I've been waiting for this moment for too long.* Chloe smiled to herself. *Okay, time to see if Miss Queen of Rudeness can utter more than two words in a row.*

"So, your English is really good, and you barely have any accent. Where did you learn English?" she asked Laurence.

Laurence glanced briefly at Chloe before looking back at the road. "At home."

Oh boy, I see that I am going to have to drag the words out of her. Chloe sighed. "That's interesting, how come?"

"My mother was American," Laurence answered. "Why in the world do you need to know anyway? You're here to take care of Clément, not me," Laurence said angrily.

"Wow, calm down. I was just trying to make conversation."

"Then don't bother," Laurence said flatly.

"Fine."

The rest of the trip passed in silence. Chloe had started to drift off when the car stopped in front of a high iron gate. Laurence reached out the window and dialed a code, opening the gate. The car drove in and stopped in front of a beautiful red brick house with flowers on the front porch. It sat in a row of similar houses that ended with what looked to Chloe like garage doors.

Laurence got out of the car. *I guess that's my signal to move,* thought Chloe. She extricated herself from the comfort of the Mercedes seat and made her way toward the trunk.

"Leave it. You can get it later," Laurence said while walking up the steps to the door. Laurence took her keys out of her left coat pocket and open the door. While stepping inside she yelled in French, "We're home!" Chloe, who was close behind her, heard tiny footsteps running toward them and a toddler's voice screamed. "Lo!"

The toddler came running into Laurence's arms. She picked him up and launched him high above her head and back into her arms. She had a huge grin on her face and was whispering words in the child's ear.

That's a change from what I have had to deal with for the past two hours. Chloe was amazed at Laurence's change of attitude. She was so happy, yet minutes ago she seemed ready to kill Chloe just for talking to her.

Chloe's thoughts were interrupted by the arrival of a woman wearing a green business suit and high heels. Her face looked severe and tired, and her hair was still damp from the shower.

"Hello, I am Beatrice," the woman said while smiling at Chloe. "And I see you have already met my son, Clément, and of course Laurence since she picked you up from the airport." Beatrice walked toward the kitchen and poured herself a cup of coffee. Chloe felt compelled to follow her. "I hope Laurence didn't give you too much of a hard time. She can be very rude sometimes, and God only knows how upset she was this morning to have to get up so early to drive to Roissy."

Chloe debated how to answer this question. *Do I say that she was extremely rude, or do I just pretend nothing happened? I guess if I have to be part of the family for a year I'd better not get on anyone's bad side.*

"No, ma'am, she was really nice."

"Oh good, well, that's a first." Beatrice lit a cigarette and finished her coffee. "Listen, you must be exhausted. Laurence will show you up to your room because I have to go to work. Today just relax, and we'll talk when I get back." Beatrice turned towards Laurence who was still holding Clément. "Clément, viens dire au revoir à maman." Clément jumped from his sister's arms and ran to his mother. Beatrice continued talking as she picked him up.

"We speak English as well as French in this house. I want you to speak English to Clément, so he can learn, and we'll speak French to you so you can also improve. It worked really well with the last au pair, so it shouldn't be a problem." Beatrice gave Clément a quick kiss and put him down before grabbing her coat. "Laurence will take care of Clément for today. Ask her if you need anything." Beatrice opened the door. "Oh, I almost forgot. Laurence, your dad called. He won't be home until the beginning of next week because he had to prolong his trip."

Laurence's eyes didn't betray any emotion, but her voice was quivering when she spoke. "He knows that I'm leaving at the end of the week. He said that…"

Beatrice interrupted her. "Yes, he said to tell you to have a good beginning of semester. Okay, I have to go." With those words, Beatrice was gone.

"Bitch," Laurence mumbled to herself before locking the door behind Beatrice.

"I take it you weren't expecting him to stay away so long," Chloe said sympathetically.

"None of your damn business." Laurence stared coldly at Chloe, defying her to speak again. Chloe stood her ground and stared back into Laurence's eyes, not willing to give this woman another victory. Their staring contest ended when Clément screamed for his mother. Laurence bent over to pick him up.

"Shuh, shuh, don't cry. We are going to have tons of fun today." She rocked him and mumbled nonsense in his ears until his sobs finally stopped. Chloe hadn't moved, not knowing where to go in this unknown house.

"I'll show you to your room. Just get from the car what you need for today. I'll get the rest later."

"Okay, thanks." Chloe made her way to the door. "I need the..."

"The car is unlocked."

"All right then, I'll be right back." Chloe exited and slowly closed the door behind her.

"Well, pumpkin, what do you think of your new babysitter?" Laurence asked her little brother. "If she is as lazy as the one you had previously...well, you are in for a surprise." Laurence moved toward the family room still carrying the child. "Maybe I should transfer to a closer university, so I could come and stay with you...huh, what do you think?" The child gave Laurence a grin and started playing with her necklace.

"Lo, stay. Lo, stay." Laurence distracted Clément's attention from her necklace by showing him a Fisher Price red fire truck. "Tuk," said Clément happily.

"Truck, not tuk," Laurence explained.

"Tuck," Clément repeated.

Laurence sighed. "Okay, sweetie, let's leave the phonetic lesson for another day, and go see what Mary Poppins is doing outside."

At that moment the door opened to reveal Chloe struggling with a large suitcase. "Sorry it took me so long, but I couldn't remember which suitcase I had put my toilet kit in, so I had to open everything. Well, finally I found it, so I figured I would take the entire suitcase in because who knows what I might need today, and...."

"I'll show you your room." Laurence made no move to pick up the suitcase and started up the stairs with Clément still in her arms.

"Could you give me a hand? I mean, it's so heavy I don't think I can carry it upstairs by myself." Laurence did not answer, but she made her way back down the stairs and softly put Clément down.

"Up! Up!" Clément started to scream.

"Clément, chill out, I'll pick you up in a minute. I have to carry your babysitter's suitcase." Laurence seemed annoyed and snapped the suitcase out of Chloe's hand and marched up the stairs as if she wasn't carrying anything more than a simple briefcase. Clément started whining. "Lo, Lo!"

Oh boy, if he can't be away from her for even a single minute, I'm going to have a grand time with him next week when she leaves. Chloe knelt in front of Clément. "Hey, want me to carry you upstairs?" Clément looked at Chloe with teary eyes, and raised his little arms up toward her. "One victory for Chloe Jones," mumbled Chloe.

The wooden stairs of the house creaked as Chloe made her way upstairs. Once at the top of the stairs she looked around for any sign of Laurence. *Wow, this floor is a total maze.* In front of Chloe was a long corridor leading into two more corridors. *One, two, three...damn, four doors. I wonder if they're all rooms. Well, none of them are open, so I guess mine must be somewhere further down,* Chloe walked slowly down the corridor admiring the high ceiling and the antique paintings on the wall.

"Hey, what's taking you so long?" called Laurence.

"Where are you?" Chloe heard a heavy sigh.

"Take the first corridor on your left, second door on your right." Chloe followed the directions and found herself in a large room with an enormous bed sitting in the middle. "Wow, quite a house you guys have," exclaimed Chloe with excitement.

"Well, yeah, I don't really live here," answered Laurence.

"Your parents live here, so that makes it yours too, and boy, it's a great house."

"Whatever." Laurence reached for Clément who was still in Chloe's arms. "Come on babe, time to let your babysitter get some rest."

"Chloe...my name is Chloe, I'm not just 'the babysitter!'"

"Well, there's not much use learning your name. Usually babysitters don't stay very long in this house." Laurence waved toward a door on the far left of the room. "The bathroom is over there." She left the room and closed the door behind her.

What the hell was that about? Never mind, I'm too exhausted to think about it now. She walked to the bed and sat down. *Okay, shower and bed.*

Maybe after some sleep I can think clearly. Chloe got up and opened her suitcase in search of her toilet kit.

"Come on, I know I saw it in here…damn, where in the world did I…oh, here it is." She grabbed her toilet kit and walked to the bathroom. The bathroom had a large tub and warm blue tiles on the floor, a mat was spread out in front of the tub, and the walls were white with paintings of exotic fishes. "Wow! Nice bathroom." Chloe took her clothes off and stepped into the tub. "What I need is a hot bath."

A half hour later a clean and relaxed Chloe walked back into her room. She ruffled through her suitcase to find a pair of boxer shorts and a t-shirt and lay down on the bed. As sleep started to claim her, she suddenly remembered the promise she made to her dad at the airport. "Man, I gotta call him before he panics." Chloe sprang off the bed and looked around the room for a phone. "No phone. Okay, I guess I have to go downstairs." She put on her University of Maryland sweatshirt and left her room.

As she reached the family room at bottom of the stairs, Chloe found Laurence and Clément asleep on the couch. Laurence had a protective arm wrapped around Clément. *I shouldn't need to wake her up to find a phone…what did Vincent tell me I had to dial to reach the States? I knew I should have written it down.* As Chloe walked across the family room the wooden floor creaked, freezing her in her tracks. She glanced at Laurence, but the noise didn't seem to have woken her up. Chloe let out a relieved sigh. *Good, I really don't want to deal with her right now.* She finally spotted a phone at the other end of the room on an antique wooden desk. *This place is a real museum. I can't wait to see the rest of the house.*

"What are you doing?" said a voice from behind her.

Chloe spun around to find Laurence right behind her.

"I…I was just looking for a phone to call my dad…I promised him before I left."

"Why didn't you ask?"

"Uh…I didn't want to wake you up, plus I seem to annoy you every time I open my mouth, so…"

Sudden screams stopped the two women from continuing what seemed to be the beginning of another argument.

"Great, now you woke him up," Laurence barked while running toward Clément.

Chloe was fuming. "I did not wake him up, I was trying to be as quiet as I could, so don't blame me."

Laurence ignored Chloe and rushed back to Clément. "Hey, it's okay. I'm here. No need to cry." Laurence picked him up. "You've been crying a lot today. What's wrong, huh? Wanna go play with your cars?" Clément sniffled and nodded. "Okay, let's go." Laurence turned to Chloe. "Do you know the number?"

It took a second for Chloe to realize that Laurence was speaking to her. "What...what number?"

"The number to dial out of the country."

"No...I can't remember it. Someone gave it to me in the plane, but I didn't wr...."

"001," Laurence interrupted.

"Oh, thanks."

"Yeah," Laurence answered before walking out of the room with Clément.

"Hi, Dad?"

"Hey sweetheart, I was starting to get worried. How was your flight?"

"It was fine."

"I bet you must be exhausted. How is your family?"

"I've only met the mother and the stepdaughter so far...." It suddenly dawned on Chloe that she was thousands of miles away from home, and that so far her impression of her host family was far from pleasant. *No way I can tell Dad about Laurence or he'll want me back home on the next plane.* "Great, Dad. They seem really nice."

"Oh, good."

"Okay Dad, I'm really tired so I've got to go, but I will call you this weekend."

"Love you."

"Love you too, Dad." With those words the line went dead, leaving Chloe to stare at the phone, wishing she could be home right now instead of trapped here in this house with the most complex woman she had ever met.

Chloe went back to her room and got into bed. She glanced at the alarm clock on the night table next to her bed.

It's only 11 a.m. I feel like a truck ran me over. I wonder if Paris is as beautiful as everyone says it is. With those thoughts, Chloe fell into a deep sleep.

Chapter 2

Chloe woke up to the sun shining on her face. She yawned. "Wow, it's 5 p.m. already. Boy, I slept for 6 hours." Chloe stretched, and pushed the covers away from her. She got out of bed, and went to the bathroom to splash some cold water on her face. She passed her hand through her hair rapidly, grabbed a pair of sweat pants from her suitcase and decided to go downstairs. She opened the door to her bedroom to find herself in front of her pile of suitcases. *She told me she was going to bring them in later on...Okay, let's put stuff away.*

Chloe dragged her suitcases in one by one. She was busy trying to find a place for everything when someone knocked at the door. "Come in."

The door opened to reveal Laurence wearing bike shorts and a sports bra covered in sweat, her long black hair up in a ponytail. She obviously had been working out.

"Beatrice is calling for you," said Laurence flatly.

"Oh, she's back. Okay, I'll be right down...I just have to brush my hair, and I'll be right there."

Laurence had already started closing the door.

"Hey, Laurence," called Chloe.

"What?" asked an annoyed Laurence.

"Thanks for bringing my suitcases up for me...I know I have a lot..."

Laurence was patiently waiting for Chloe to finish her sentence, but showed no sign of answering.

"Well, yeah...anyway, thanks," finished Chloe.

"You're welcome," said Laurence before leaving the room.

Wow, she was in a better mood! Good, maybe she was just having a bad day earlier, or maybe it was way too early for her...who knows. Chloe quickly brushed her blond hair, put on some socks and was out the door.

Chloe entered the family room.

"Ah! Chloe, there you are. Did you sleep well?" asked Beatrice.

"Yes ma'am."

"Please call me Beatrice. I really hate being called ma'am or madame...makes me feel old."

"Okay," answered Chloe agreeably.

"Did my stepdaughter show you around the house or was she a bear as usual and only talked to you in monosyllables?" Beatrice asked sarcastically.

Chloe looked at Laurence who had just stepped into the family room. She kept staring at Laurence while answering. "No, she was nice. I was just too tired to take a tour of the house, but I'd love to now."

Laurence was surprised by Chloe's answer. *You'd think I'd given her the royal treatment the way she said it...nice...that's funny. I've been called many things lately, but nice isn't one of them.*

"Laurence?" Beatrice called. Not getting an answer, she raised her voice slightly. "Laurence!"

"Uh...what?" said Laurence.

"Haven't you been listening?" Beatrice sighed. "I was asking you to take Chloe on the nickel tour."

"I have to take a shower. I just came down to get a drink. I'm not your tour guide, Beatrice!" barked Laurence.

"Young lady, as long as you are under my roof you will do as I say," answered Beatrice angrily. "Now, you will show Chloe the house, and when you come back I want you to have a better attitude. Is that understood?"

Laurence was obviously fuming.

"Fine," she said between clenched teeth. "Come on, we'll start upstairs."

Once upstairs, Chloe reached for Laurence's arm to stop her.

"Hey, listen, if you don't have time to do it, no big deal. I'll learn my way around the house soon enough."

Laurence sighed, and her eyes softened a little. *Gotta give her that, she is trying,* thought Laurence.

"It's okay. I'll hear about it for days if I don't do it." Laurence looked at Chloe. *She looks so young. I really hope she can stand up to Beatrice, otherwise her life is going to be a living hell!*

"Oh, okay, I just want you to know that I won't hold it against you."

Laurence gave her a half smile. "Come on, it's a big house, it'll take a while."

Chloe followed Laurence from room to room, admiring the antique furniture and the care with which each room had been put together. After being shown Jean's and Beatrice's bedroom with its rich draperies, its king-size wooden sleigh bed, and its beautiful porcelain doll collection, Chloe was in awe.

"Wow, what do your parents do for a living? This is amazing," she exclaimed.

"They are both antique dealers. My stepmother runs the stores, my father travels around to find rare paintings or furniture or...well, anyway, you get the picture."

Chloe realized that Laurence had put a strong emphasis on the word "stepmother." *From the scene I just saw downstairs, I can guess they don't like each other very much...Okay, Chloe, remember that, don't call Beatrice her mother, but stepmother.*

They slowly made their way to the end of the corridor.

"The rooms in the right corridor are nothing but storage rooms for the antique business."

They walked down the left corridor where Laurence showed Chloe more bedrooms and bathrooms.

"That's it for the upstairs."

"Wait. What about you?" asked Chloe.

"What about me?"

"I mean...where is your room?"

"Right corridor."

"You just said that there were only storage rooms over there."

"Yeah, and my room." Laurence was getting really annoyed with all the questions.

"I would be scared to death to sleep all alone on this side of the house surrounded by antiques."

"Well, I'm used to it."

"Why is your bedroom there anyway? It's not like there isn't enough room."

"Why do you care? Have you ever thought that maybe I wanted to have the bedroom the furthest away from this family?" Laurence answered with anger.

"Sorry. Please don't get upset, I didn't mean anything by it."

"Let's finish, so I can get some peace and quiet." Laurence walked away from Chloe.

Wow, another mental note: avoid personal questions or she'll go off.

The main floor was as grandiose as the upstairs, but the room that really caught Chloe's attention was the library. Thousands of books lined the wooden shelves.

"Amazing. How many books are in this room?" asked Chloe. She walked up to a shelf and picked up the nearest book. "Look at that, this book is so old its binding is made of thread and its pages are yellow. *Les Fleurs du Mal* from Baudelaire. I've heard of him, he was my French teacher's favorite poet. Wow, it's from 1898!" Chloe softly ran her hand over the leather cover and traced the engraved title with her fingers. She turned toward Laurence who was still standing in the door. "Do you ever come here and spend hours just reading and relaxing?" she asked Laurence.

Laurence could not help but crack a smile. Chloe's enthusiasm was contagious.

"No, I don't have time for that, but yeah…it's a pretty amazing room. Come on."

Chloe followed Laurence out of the library and was still digesting everything she saw when Beatrice appeared.

"Here you are. Chloe, do you like pizza?"

Chloe laughed. "Hey, I was raised on pizza!" Beatrice looked at her with surprise.

"It's a joke! We eat lots of pizza in the States," Chloe added.

"Oh! Well, our cook is on vacation, and I must go back to the office, so I ordered pizza for the three of you."

"Wait…wait a minute, I am not babysitting tonight. I have plans," said Laurence.

"Well, cancel, because there is no way I can get out of this meeting."

"I told you last week that I was going to a concert tonight," said an irritated Laurence.

"Well, your dad was supposed to be back, but you don't see him here, now do you? So, who do you think is going to take care of Clément?"

"Uh, I can do it," interrupted Chloe.

The two women turned toward Chloe.

"I can. Really! I'll take care of Clément, so you can go to your meeting and Laurence can go to her concert."

"I don't know. Clément doesn't know you yet," stated Beatrice.

"Yeah, I know, but what better way for him to get to know me than to be left alone with me? After all, that's what I'm here for, to be his babysitter." She said the last word while staring intently at Laurence.

"Okay, I guess that's fine by me. He goes to bed by 8:30 p.m., so give him a bath around 8. For the pizza, I left money on the kitchen table. Emergency numbers are on the fridge." Beatrice grabbed her coat and called her son, who was quietly watching a *Sesame Street* videotape.

"Clément, viens me donner un baiser." When Clément didn't seem to answer, Beatrice walked to the family room. "Maman doit partir, mon cheri. Bonne nuit." She bent over to kiss him on the forehead. If Clément heard his mother, he never made any move to say goodbye, and barely looked at her when she walked away.

"Okay, Chloe. Ask Laurence if you have any more questions. Bye."

"Bye."

During the entire exchange, Laurence had not moved. After Chloe closed the door behind Beatrice, she faced Laurence.

"Would you tell me a little more about Clément? Does he have a favorite bedtime story? Does he mind water in his eyes? Does he use regular..."

"No need to, I'm not going."

"Why?"

"I'm not leaving you alone with him."

"Laurence, I'm going to have to be left alone with him sooner or later. What's wrong with tonight? I thought you wanted to go to this concert."

"He's more important than some concert." There was no anger in Laurence's voice, and Chloe detected a hint of sadness.

"You have to trust me. I can do this. You don't know me, so how can you judge me so fast?" Chloe was now pacing.

"You said it yourself: I don't know you. That's why I don't want to leave you with Clément."

"Your stepmother didn't see any harm in it, so I don't know why you…"

"She doesn't care. She would have left him to the first guy on the street if it meant that she could go to her so-called meeting!" snapped Laurence.

"Okay, okay, we're not getting anywhere by arguing." Chloe sighed. "I'll make you a deal. What time were you planning on leaving?"

"Why do you…"

"Just answer." Chloe was getting more than irritated with Laurence's irrational behavior. *I am not going to let her step all over me, no way.*

Laurence was surprised by Chloe's abrupt tone of voice, and found herself answering the question. "Eight o'clock."

"Good, Beatrice said that Clément takes a bath by 8. Well, we give him a bath earlier, you put him to bed by 8 instead of 8:30, and you leave me in charge."

Laurence did not answer.

"He'll be in bed; what could go wrong?" said an exasperated Chloe.

"Okay, but you have to call me if he so much as wakes up. Got it?"

"Yeah." Chloe smiled to herself at the small victory. "One more thing."

"What is it now?" asked an annoyed Laurence.

"I do everything with you. I want to be there when you bathe him, when you feed him, when you put him to bed…"

"Okay, okay, I get the point."

"Thanks. It's the best way for me to learn what he likes and doesn't like."

"Fine."

The doorbell stopped the conversation.

"Pizza is here," said Chloe.

Laurence opened the door to be faced by a young boy carrying two pizza boxes.

"Vous avez commander deux pizzas?" asked the delivery boy.

A Year in Paris 25

"Ouais, c'est nous," answered Laurence.

"Quarante-huit francs, s'il vous plait."

"Attendez, je vais chercher de l'argent."

"I'll get it," said Chloe as she ran to the kitchen to pick up the money. "Here it is." She handed the money to Laurence.

"Merci, et bonne soiree."

Laurence closed the door. "You understood what he said," said Laurence.

"I had three years of French in high school, and also took classes my first year of college."

"How old are you?" asked Laurence.

Boy, here we go again. "I'm 18."

"Good," answered Laurence before walking away.

Chloe looked puzzled. *"Good?" What kind of answer is that? This girl is a real enigma.*

①   ①   ①

Dinner was a quiet affair. Clément ate his piece of pizza, or at least the toppings, and declared himself done with dinner.

"Done, Lo. More TV?" Clément asked while pulling off his bib and wiping his hands on his sweatshirt.

"Clément, how many times have I told you not to use your clothes as a napkin?" said Laurence while bringing her face closer to him. Clément sized the opportunity to grab Laurence's bangs with his dirty hands.

"Clément, let go."

Clément giggled and let go of his sister's hair. Chloe could not restrain a laugh.

"You think it's funny?" asked Laurence.

"Sorry..." Chloe could not stop herself from giggling, "...but you should see yourself in the mirror."

Laurence got up to go look in one of the mirrors in the entrance. She took one look at herself and understood why Chloe was laughing. Her bangs were glued together with some gooey substance and a piece of melted cheese hung from the right side of her forehead. *How in the world did the little monster manage to do that?* She walked back to the kitchen to find that Chloe had taken the initiative to extract Clément from his high chair and was helping him wash his hands at the kitchen sink.

Chloe heard Laurence walk back in, and she gently put Clément down.

"I'm sorry…I shouldn't have laughed at you, but it was too funny," Chloe apologized.

Laurence grabbed a napkin to wipe her hair.

"Nah, it's okay. I looked funny." Laurence smiled at Chloe and ran toward Clément.

"You little monster… I think… it is …tickle time!"

Clément took off running with Laurence right behind him. She caught him and proceeded to tickle him. Clément was laughing really hard when Chloe heard, "Damn it!" from where she was in the kitchen. She came running into the family room.

"What? What's wrong?"

"He peed on me."

"What?"

"You heard me. I forgot that he's just starting potty training, and when I tickle him too hard he can't hold it."

"Oh." Chloe was trying very hard not to find the situation amusing.

"You can laugh, but it'll happen to you before you know it," smiled Laurence.

Chloe finally burst out laughing.

"Come on, I thought you said you wanted to be there when I give him a bath."

"I'll follow you." Chloe was finally starting to calm down.

"Come on munchkin, bath time. You are climbing up the stairs yourself, little man. I'm not picking you up after what you just did." Laurence took his hand, and led him up the stairs with Chloe close behind.

After the bath, Chloe was waiting downstairs for Laurence to finish saying goodnight to Clément. She had observed Laurence's interactions with Clément the entire evening, and the tenderness and patience Laurence showed puzzled her. *Wow, it sure is different from the way she was with me this morning,* thought Chloe.

Upstairs, Laurence kissed Clément one last time, and slowly walked out of the room.

"Lo," whined Clément.

Laurence sighed and reopened the door. "Sweetie, you've got to go to sleep now."

"Lo, stay," Clément cried.

Laurence walked back and knelt next to his bed. "Listen, I'll sing you a song, but you have to close your eyes and go to sleep."

"'kay," sniffled Clément.

Laurence started singing a lullaby her mother used to sing to her.

"Dors Seraphine
Tu seras marine
Dors Sebastien
Tu seras marin
Les bateaux poussent
Graines sous la mouse
Leurs voiles sont
Grandes comme un liseron

"C'est les reves…" Laurence stopped and gently caressed Clément's cheek before lightly kissing him.

"I love you," she whispered in his ear.

Stepping out of the room she came close to colliding with Chloe, who had been standing behind the door.

"What are you doing?" growled Laurence.

"I…I was wondering what was taking you so long, so I came up to see if everything was all right. I heard you sing…wow, you have a great voice, you know that? Is he asleep?"

Laurence was furious. She grabbed Chloe by the arm and dragged her down the corridor without saying a word.

"Hey, let me go. What are you doing?" demanded Chloe.

Laurence stopped and backed Chloe against the wall. She lowered herself to eye level with Chloe and put her hands on the wall on either side of Chloe's head.

"I'm going to say this once. Bedtime with Clément is sacred. I let you stay while I told him a story, and you had no business spying on us after that. Get it?" Laurence said in a very sharp voice.

"Okay, okay…let me go now. Man, you are a total loony."

Laurence looked at Chloe straight in the eyes. "Maybe I am. You don't want to find out, now do you?" she asked with a sickening smile. She turned around and headed toward her bedroom. "I'm going to go take a shower. There's a monitor in your bedroom. Plug it in so you can hear if Clément wakes up," Laurence said as she walked away. She then disappeared into the right corridor.

Boy, this girl is a nutcase! Okay, today is Tuesday and she said she's leaving at the end of the week. Yikes, five more days with her!

Chloe went into her room looking for the monitor, found it and plugged it in. *Now what? It's only 8. I guess I can watch some TV. I don't have a phone, but I have a TV...weird.* Chloe sat on her bed and turned the TV on. She surfed through the channels. *Damn, no cable and only 6 stations...that's great.* She settled for an old rerun of *Bewitched*. *It is so weird to see Elizabeth Montgomery and hear someone else's voice dubbed in French.* Chloe laughed to herself. *Look at that! Her lips don't even match what she's saying. Ah well, maybe it'll help me learn the language better.*

There was a light knock at the door.

"Come in."

Laurence poked her head through the door.

"Hi, uh...I've got to go. Did you find the monitor?" she asked.

"Yeah," Chloe answered shortly. She was still irritated by Laurence's previous reaction, and intended to let Laurence know that she was upset.

"Okay, I wrote my cell phone number down so you can call me if there are any problems." Laurence walked in the room holding a piece of paper.

"Just put it next to the TV," said Chloe, not taking her eyes off the screen.

Laurence did as told. "Okay, don't hesitate to call," she said before leaving.

Chloe didn't even bother answering and did nothing to show Laurence that she had heard her last comment.

A couple of minutes later, the sound of the gate opening was heard, followed by the loud noise of a motorcycle. Chloe ran to her window and gazed outside to see Laurence putting on a helmet and riding off into the streets of Versailles.

① ① ①

A scream woke Chloe. "What? What the hell was that?" Another scream was heard followed by sobs. "Oh damn, it's Clément!" Chloe ran to his bedroom.

"Hey, it's okay. I'm here." She picked up Clément and hugged him, whispering calming words in his ears. "It's okay, you just had a bad dream...shush..." Chloe's words only made Clément cry louder. *Oh, boy, what am I gonna do?*

Chloe walked to her room with Clément screaming in her arms.

"Look, Clément, TV. You like TV. Isn't this special? You're gonna get to watch TV past your bedtime. Now, you have to stop crying." Clément's screams slowly turned to soft sobs. "Okay, sweetheart, you and I are going to lay on my bed and see what's on, 'kay?" A teary Clément nodded. "Good, now I'm going to put you down on the bed, and I'll get in next to you." As soon as Chloe had laid him down, Clément started screaming again. "Oh boy, you aren't going to make it easy for me." Chloe quickly climbed into bed next to Clément and pulled him into the comfort of her arms. Instantly, Clément stopped crying.

Chloe let out a sigh of relief. "Okay, let's see what's on the French tube late at night." *Come on, please let me find some cartoons,* thought Chloe. "Thank God for Bugs Bunny," said Chloe when she saw the famous rabbit on the screen.

"What do you say, munchkin? Is Bugs Bunny all right with you?" She looked at Clément, who was tucked against her shoulder, to find him with his eyes closed. "So much for Bugs, eh?" She smiled and tenderly wiped away a few remaining tears from Clément's cheeks.

What time is it? Man, 1 a.m. I guess nobody is back yet. Chloe yawned. *Somebody should be coming back soon. Come on, Beatrice. How long does a meeting last? I guess I'll keep him here with me and watch TV until someone comes home.*

①   ①   ①

Laurence unlocked the front door and stepped into the silent house. She hung up her leather jacket in the hallway, and went upstairs to Clément's room. She softly peeked through the open door, and panic rose when she discovered an empty bed.

"What the hell?" She ran to Chloe's room and burst in.

"Where is...." She stopped dead in her tracks. In front of her were Chloe and Clément, fast asleep. Clément was still gently secured in Chloe's arms. Chloe's head had dropped sideways and was resting against Clément's.

Laurence just stood there for a few minutes, unwilling to disturb their rest. *I can't believe Clément let someone he barely knows hold him that way, and on top of it he fell asleep!* Laurence was surprised; it had taken the past au pairs weeks before getting Clément to let his guard down and show any sign of affection toward them. *Maybe...maybe this one is going to stay*, thought Laurence. She quietly turned off the TV and tried to pick up Clément without disturbing Chloe.

Chloe stirred and opened her eyes. "Hey, you're back." She released her hold on Clément so Laurence could pick him up.

"Yeah." Laurence managed to pick up Clément without waking him up.

"What happened?" Laurence whispered.

"Nightmares...I'm sorry, I didn't know what to do, so I took him back here with..."

"No, no...that's fine," Laurence smiled. "Thanks."

"No sweat," said Chloe, smiling back.

"See you in the morning," mouthed Laurence.

"G'night," whispered Chloe.

Laurence walked carefully out of the room.

"Hey, Laurence!" Chloe called softly.

"What?"

"Can you wake me up in the morning? There's no alarm clock in this room." Chloe asked.

"You got it," answered Laurence. She then shut the door behind her.

Chloe slumped back on her pillow and shook her head in disbelief. *I've been here less than 24 hours, and I've never seen someone with so many mood swings. Earlier she was ready to kill me, now I'm her best friend.* Chloe yawned. *Gosh, I'm beat.* She pulled the covers up and in a few minutes was asleep.

①   ①   ①

Chloe woke up and stretched. *Boy, I really needed a good night's sleep. I wonder what time... Shit! 10 a.m. Why did she let me sleep so long?* Chloe jumped out of bed and grabbed a pair of sweatpants and a t-shirt and ran downstairs.

"Laurence?" she called.

"In the playroom," Laurence answered.

Chloe hurried. "Why did you let me sleep so long?"

"Good morning to you too," said Laurence sarcastically. "I thought you might still be jetlagged," she stated simply.

"Yeah...well...thanks, I guess."

"You're welcome," smiled Laurence.

"What time did you get up?" asked Chloe.

"6 a.m. This little man right here doesn't know what sleeping in means," said Laurence, pointing at Clément, who was absorbed in a Lego construction.

"Oh," said Chloe, giving an understanding smile. "I guess Beatrice never made it back home, huh?"

"Good guess."

"Does that happen a lot?"

"Her not coming home?"

"Yeah, I mean…does she often not sleep at home?"

"Yeah, especially when my dad is out of town."

Chloe found it better not to ask where Beatrice was spending her nights.

"Listen…" Laurence sighed before continuing. "You didn't get assigned to the easiest family in the program. We've been through four au pairs in the past two years."

Chloe's attention was riveted on Laurence.

"I can't hide from you that the main reason they left was that Beatrice overworked them and drove them crazy…" continued Laurence.

"What about Clément?" interrupted Chloe.

"What do you mean?"

"Weren't those girls attached to him? He ought to be enough to make it bearable."

Laurence smiled happily. *Girl, you are earning points with that answer.*

"Obviously not. Not everyone comes here because they love children. Most of them come to France as an au pair because it's a cheap way to live here for a year."

"Does Beatrice know that there are rules she is supposed to obey?" asked Chloe, sitting down on the floor next to Laurence.

"Like what?"

"Before I left the U.S. we had an au pair meeting, and they gave us a booklet about our rights."

"I don't know if she does or not. I guess you'll have to take it one day at a time." Laurence looked at Chloe straight in the eyes. "That's only if you think you can handle it. It's not too late for you to back out. I'm sure the organization would find you another family very quickly."

"Are you kidding? And miss all the fun living with you and your family will bring?" answered Chloe jokingly. She realized that Laurence was extremely serious in her offer. "Listen...I know you don't really know me. I also know that we started out on the wrong foot yesterday, but the reasons you gave me are not good enough for me to leave," Chloe said seriously.

Laurence let a sigh of relief escape. "Okay."

"Plus..." Chloe paused and looked deeply into Laurence's eyes. "...I think Clément needs to have someone around he can trust when you're not here." She added shyly, "I think you need to leave someone you can trust in charge of him...and I hope I can be that person."

Laurence looked intensely at Chloe. "Well...Clément let you hold him last night, and he never does that with anyone he doesn't trust, so who am I to deny him anything?" smiled Laurence. "But don't worry, when my dad is here you'll never have to babysit at night. He is crazy about Clément."

Laurence got up. "What do you say I show you what's going to be expected of you when I'm gone?"

"Sounds great, but do I have time to go shower first?" asked Chloe, standing up.

"Yeah, sure...Clément isn't even dressed yet," answered Laurence, picking up Clément.

"Okay, I won't be long," said Chloe while running back upstairs.

The morning passed quickly. Laurence showed Chloe where everything was located in the house. They even went for a quick ride around town and Laurence pointed out to Chloe the closest supermarket, the boulangerie, and the place where Clément would start pre-school next week. Chloe took notes to be sure she remembered everything Laurence said. After lunch Laurence put Clément down for his nap, but this time she let Chloe stay in the room while she tucked him in.

"Chloe, would you mind if I go for a run while he is napping? He should be out for at least two hours, and I should be back in 45 minutes or so."

"No, go right ahead."

"Okay."

"Hey, Laurence? Can I borrow some books from the library or your dad will kill me if I touch anything?" asked Chloe.

"Nobody ever uses the library...go right ahead. I'll see you when I get back." Laurence went up to get changed. *She is absorbing informa-*

tion like a sponge, and Clément really seems to like her...good. She is kind of cute also – I'm sure that if Beatrice gives her any free time she is going to break some hearts, thought Laurence as she changed into spandex shorts and a sports bra.

Chloe opened the library door and was once again mesmerized by the number of books. She left the door open behind her so that she could hear Clément if needed. She ran her hand lightly over the lowest shelf of books. *Wow, there are titles in everything from Russian to Chinese. Okay, where was that Baudelaire I spotted yesterday?* She picked up the book and sat in one of the leather chairs distributed around the room. She slowly opened it to reveal worn yellow pages. *There is nothing like the smell of an old book,* thought Chloe as she inhaled deeply. She lost herself in the poems.

"Hey, what're you doing?" asked Laurence, popping her head through the open door an hour later.

"Damn, you scared me!" said Chloe while trying to calm down her racing heart.

"Sorry," apologized Laurence with a smile.

"This is amazing," said Chloe pointing to the book lying on her lap.

"What's amazing?" Laurence walked up and propped herself on a desk.

"I have been reading for almost an hour...I don't understand a word of what I'm reading, but the language is so beautiful and the atmosphere of this room...I think Baudelaire is going to become my favorite poet."

Laurence laughed, "Yeah, I like him."

"You like poetry! Somehow I have trouble believing that," joked Chloe.

"Hey, I go to college, I'm not ignorant," said Laurence, feigning hurt.

Chloe smiled. "Oh, yeah I forgot."

"Page 41."

"What?"

"Open the book to page 41."

Chloe did as told and let her gaze wander over the page. "What's on page 41?" she asked.

Laurence did not answer, but instead proceeded to recite a poem. Chloe listened in awe, and even if she didn't understand what Laurence was saying, she could easily make out the sounds and match them to the poem printed on the page. When Laurence stopped, Chloe swallowed hard.

"You know it by heart! It was beautiful."

"Yeah, thanks...it's my favorite poem...*Le Serpent Qui Danse.*"

"What do you study?"

"Journalism."

"Neat, it must be very interesting. Are you almost finished?"

"I would have been finished in June if I didn't have to pull out to come and take care of Clément in the middle of the semester. I missed the final exams."

"You mean that you postponed everything to come here and take care of your little brother?" said Chloe in disbelief. She abruptly stood up and starting pacing. "Couldn't they get another au pair faster? I don't get it. How could they do that to..."

"Hey, slow down, I didn't say that I regretted anything."

"Still, it infuriates me to think that you..."

"Listen, stop fuming over something that's not your problem," Laurence said with annoyance.

Chloe stopped her pacing. "Sorry, I guess I got carried away," she apologized while tucking a loose lock of hair behind her ear.

"Yeah, you did. And trust me, I'm not worth getting angry for."

"That's my decision to make," Chloe answered. "But Laurence, why couldn't you work something out with them? Come on, it's your life we're talking about!"

"Listen, that's my problem and no one else's, get it? Stop asking so many damn questions!" said Laurence furiously as she stormed out of the room.

"Wow, what was all of that about?" said Chloe aloud. *I forgot...avoid personal questions...Mental note: you've got to get better at remembering your mental notes.*

Chapter 3

Chloe went in search of Laurence. *We got along too well this morning. I am not letting her spoil that.* She found Laurence in the dining room staring out the window.

Chloe walked slowly through the dining room and came to stand beside Laurence.

"I'm sorry," she said in a soft voice. "I should have known not to push you."

Laurence's eyes were filled with unshed tears when she looked at Chloe. She sighed. "It's all right. Let's not talk about it anymore."

"Okay," Chloe agreed with relief.

"Tell you what. As soon as Clément wakes up we'll go take a walk, and I'll show you more of the town."

"That'd be great."

"Good. Can you keep an ear out for Clément while I take a quick shower?"

"Yeah, sure," said Chloe, realizing that Laurence was still wearing her running clothes.

"Thanks. I won't be long."

Half an hour later, they took a walk down to Boulevard de la Reine. The boulevard was lined with trees and benches. The sidewalk was busy with bikers, runners, and people simply taking a walk.

"Don't you guys have bike trails around here?" asked Chloe after barely avoiding a collision with a bike.

Laurence smiled. "It's an historic town, we're lucky we have paved roads!"

"What's the name of this road?" Chloe asked, so she could start orienting herself.

"Boulevard de la Reine."

"It means, 'the Queen's road', right?"

"Impressive!" joked Laurence.

"Any reason why it's called that?" Asked Chloe, always curious about historic.

"The boulevard brings you to the Queen's gardens. I guess that's why."

"Is there a boulevard du…"

"…Roi? Yeah, it's parallel to this one on the other side of the castle. And before you ask, no, I don't know why it's called that."

Laurence turned left before reaching the end of the boulevard, bringing them in front of the castle. *Wow, I can't believe I'm standing here in front of this great monument,* thought Chloe.

The large U-shaped castle stood glowing in the afternoon sun. Chloe and Laurence stopped in front of the black iron gate with golden trim. Everything seemed shiny and bright, reflecting the name of its first owner, The Sun King.

"Wow, I didn't realize that we lived so close to the castle," exclaimed Chloe.

"Yeah, you should really go visit it."

"I'm planning on it," answered Chloe, admiring the far-away white castle with its paved courtyard. "Is that Louis XVI?" asked Chloe, pointing to the statue of a man on a horse in the middle of the courtyard.

"No, it's Louis XIV."

"Oh!"

"Big difference, he was popular. Trust me, his grandchild wasn't."

"Yeah, no kidding. If I remember right he got his head chopped off."

Laurence smiled. "Yeah, and thousands of nobles too. Okay, enough history for today, we've got to get back before it starts raining."

Chloe had not realized that the sky had become extremely cloudy. "Man, it was sunny when we left."

"Let's hurry. We'll cut through town, so we can take cover if it starts raining too hard." Laurence grabbed the stroller and started walking.

They had barely reached la Rue du Marché when the rain started falling.

"Wet, wet," said Clément, laughing. He had thrown his head back and was trying to catch raindrops in his mouth.

"Let's go in here," said Laurence as she made her way into the indoor market.

Once inside Chloe was taken aback by what she saw. Shopkeepers were behind their stands yelling about their products; the shouts were echoed, everywhere making the place extremely noisy. Chloe picked up different smells. *Hmmm... Fresh bread, cheese, fresh fruits...*

"This is incredible," she said.

"What's incredible?" asked Laurence while pushing the stroller through the crowd.

"This place. It's so exotic."

"Yeah? Don't you guys have markets where you come from?" asked Laurence.

"Not like this. Ours are more...I can't explain. Everything seems so alive here."

Laurence looked at Chloe with a mock smile on her face.

"Come on, don't look at me as if I'm stupid or something. I'm serious, this place is great."

"Maybe. I guess I'm just used to it."

"Can we walk around for a little while?"

"As long as it's still raining, yeah, why not? Lead the way."

Chloe made her way through the crowd looking around in awe.

She is like a child in a toy store. Unbelievable! And this isn't even clothes or jewelry, thought Laurence.

Chloe stopped in front of a cheese stand.

"Ma petite demoiselle, vous voulez acheter quelquechose? Regardez moi ce beau roblochon," said the stand owner pointing at a cheese.

Chloe turned to Laurence, "What is he saying?"

"He wants to know if you want to buy some cheese?" explained an amused Laurence.

"Oh, okay." Chloe looked back at the man. "Non merci," she said with her best French accent.

As they walked away, Laurence joked, "Very good accent you have there."

"Hey, don't make fun. I'm here to learn," said Chloe, pretending to be offended.

"Oh, look at that," she said, stopping in front of another stand. "Those are the biggest strawberries I have ever seen," exclaimed Chloe pointing at the fruit.

"Let's get some," said Laurence.

"Really?"

"Yeah, why not? Hey, Clément? Want some strawberries?"

"Stawbe'ies. Yeah," said Clément happily.

"Okay, so let's get some."

Laurence purchased the fruit. "Come on, let's get out of here."

"But it's still raining," said Chloe. The rain could be heard tumbling onto the roof.

"I know. Trust me."

Laurence pushed the stroller toward the other end of the market and turned into the right aisle. At the end of the aisle was an opening leading to what seemed to Chloe to be another market.

"Yikes," she said while going through the opening.

"Fish market," said Laurence.

"Yeah, I can smell," said Chloe wryly.

Laurence led her to the outside of the market and stopped under a big awning.

"Now, what do you say we try those strawberries?" asked Laurence.

"Now? Without washing them? Gross."

"Okay, suit yourself," said Laurence while grabbing a strawberry and biting into it. "Hey Clément, here you go." She handed Clément a piece of fruit. Clément took the fruit and bit into it, laughing when the juice started running down his chin.

"Oh, boy, you're gonna be one sticky little boy, aren't you?" laughed Laurence.

Clément giggled. "Good, Lo."

"Yeah babe, you're right. These are really good. I think I'll have another."

"Fine, you got me. I'll try, but if I'm sick tomorrow, I'll blame it on you," said Chloe, admitting defeat.

"I knew you couldn't resist." She handed Chloe a strawberry. "Here."

"Thanks." Chloe took a bite. "Wow, these are good."

"Told you," winked Laurence.

A companionable silence settled between them. They both gazed out at the empty street and at the pouring rain.

"Damn."

"What? What happened?" asked Laurence. She then took a good look at Chloe and started laughing.

"That'll teach you to laugh at me when I have pizza in my hair," said Laurence, chuckling. Chloe had juice dripping down her chin, some of which had already found her shirt.

"Very funny," said Chloe while trying to wipe the juice away from her chin. "Arrghh, I can't do that, I have as much juice on my hands as on my face."

"Wait, let me help." Laurence reached in her pocket and got a tissue out. "I swear it's clean," she said. She lifted Chloe's face towards her and dabbed at her chin and the corner of her mouth with the tissue, wiping away the last of the juice.

Chloe was caught off guard by the gentleness of the taller woman. She suddenly felt very awkward.

"Thanks," she said, taking a step away from Laurence.

"You're welcome. I always have tissues handy with Clément around. Hey, seems like the rain is slowing down. Do you feel like braving some little droplets? We're not that far from home."

"Lead the way."

☞ ☞ ☞

When they got home, Beatrice was waiting for them.

"There you are. I was getting worried. You didn't leave a note or anything…"

"I don't remember you leaving a note to tell us you wouldn't come home last night," said Laurence sarcastically.

"You know how meetings go…." answered Beatrice defensively.

"No, I don't," answered Laurence dryly.

Chloe could feel the tension building between the two women. Laurence had her arms crossed on her chest and was staring at Beatrice challengingly. *Come on girl, find something to say before they kill each other.*

"Uh…hi…I learned everything I need to know to take care of Clément today. Laurence even showed me where his pre-school is," said Chloe.

"Oh, really? Good, because I have a full day tomorrow and the day after, and on Friday I'm taking Clément to my parents' for the weekend. I didn't know when I would have had time to show you anything," said Beatrice, relieved for the changed of subject.

Beatrice looked at Clément, who was still sitting in his stroller chewing on a strawberry.

"Gosh, Clément you're a mess. Come on, let's get you washed up before dinner." She picked up Clément. "Oh, I ordered Chinese food for dinner. I hope you like it, Chloe."

"Yes, I do," answered Chloe.

"Oh good…it should be here by 7. Come on, sweetheart, let's take you upstairs and give you a bath."

As soon as Beatrice was out of sight, Chloe turned to Laurence, who was taking her coat off. She was obviously upset.

"Hey, are you okay?" asked Chloe, lightly touching her arm to get her attention.

Laurence passed her hand through her long black hair in frustration.

"Yeah, I'm fine. Nice save earlier."

Chloe blushed. "Thanks, I guess. I'm sorry. I didn't mean to interrupt you and your stepmother, but you seemed ready to kill each other."

Laurence gave Chloe a weak smile. "Yeah…sorry you had to witness that…again."

"Why don't you get along?" As soon as the question left her lips Chloe realized what a mistake she'd made. *Dumb, dumb, dumb… remember, avoid personal questions.*

"Wait, forget I even asked," said Chloe apologetically before Laurence had time to answer anything.

Laurence's eyes had darkened with anger when Chloe asked the question. *Come on, cut her some slack… She's trying.* Laurence took a deep breath to calm herself down.

"It's okay. It's just a long story. I don't want to get into it right now. Ask me some other time. Listen, I'm going up to my room. Tell Beatrice I'm not hungry. See you tomorrow." Laurence left the hallway and went up the stairs, leaving Chloe behind.

Chloe decided to go and spend some time in the library until dinner. She went in search of Baudelaire's poetry. *Okay, page 41. Let's see if I can understand the poem that she recited earlier. I need a dictionary; that would make it easier.* Chloe looked around and spotted a dictionary lying on one of the desks in the far-left corner of the room. *Come on, let it be a French/English dictionary,* thought Chloe while making her way to the desk.

"Yes!" she exclaimed. "Okay, Baudelaire, here I come."

Time flew by, and she was surprised to hear the doorbell. *Gosh, 7 p.m. already.* She went to answer the door but Beatrice had already gotten there.

"Chloe, can you hold Clément for me while I answer?" asked Beatrice.

"Sure. Come little man," said Chloe, taking a very willing Clément from Beatrice's arms.

"Hey, you're all clean! Wanna go and play?"

Clément smiled. "Playroom," he said pointing toward it.

"Okay, you got it."

"Don't get him too wound up, Chloe, or I'll never get him to go to sleep tonight. I'll cook up something fast for him and we can eat."

"Okay, I'll go explore the playroom with him."

Once in the playroom, Chloe looked around with amazement. *Wow, I didn't pay attention earlier…this child is spoiled. Look at these toys!* Hundreds of toys, everything from puzzles, to Legos, to cars, to electric trains were lying around the room.

"Clément, boy, you've got tons of toys. Want to play with your trains?"

"No, Lego."

"Legos, huh? Okay, you're the boss. Let's build."

After ten minutes, Clément was so engrossed in what he was doing that Chloe took the opportunity to walk around the room. She stopped in front of a shelf stacked with children's videotapes and books.

"Kids' books…yeah, that's what I need to improve my French vocabulary." Chloe picked up a book and flipped through the pages. "Cool, better than a dictionary. Hey, Clément? Wanna read a book?"

Clément looked up. "'kay."

"Come on, then," said Chloe, sitting on the floor. Clément flopped himself in her lap, and Chloe began to read.

"I'm probably destroying the pronunciation! What do you say? Is my French accent really bad?" she asked Clément jokingly.

Clément clapped. "More…j'veux encore!"

"Now, no mixing French and English, otherwise your mom's not going to be too happy about that."

"Clément, Chloe…dinner!" yelled Beatrice from the kitchen.

"Speaking of her…come on, Clément, dinner awaits."

In the kitchen, the smell of Chinese food engulfed Chloe as she installed Clément in his highchair.

"Chloe, would you tell Laurence that dinner is ready?" asked Beatrice.

"Uh…she told me earlier to tell you that she wasn't hungry."

"Well, her loss," said Beatrice, actually relieved to not have to deal with her stepdaughter's attitude for the rest of the evening.

During dinner Beatrice told Chloe what would be expected of her in more detail.

"You'll have one weekend free per month where you won't have to take care of Clément at all. The other weekends, you'll be asked to babysit Friday or Saturday night, sometimes both. You'll have Sundays off unless something comes up. My husband and I are never home before 7 or 8 p.m., but Clément is starting preschool next week, and he'll be gone from 9 to 3:30 p.m. every day, so you'll have plenty of free time."

Sounds like fun, thought Chloe sarcastically.

"Do you have any questions?" asked Beatrice.

"No. I might as we go along, but none right now."

"Good then, it's settled. Clément, what are you doing?"

Clément was playing with his mashed potatoes as if they were Play-Doh.

"Clément, this is not proper. Look at you, you are a mess again," Beatrice sounded exasperated and her voice was slowly rising.

"I'll get him cleaned up if you want," said Chloe, trying to get Clément away from his mother's wrath.

Beatrice sighed. "Why don't you do that. Thanks. This child will do anything to drive me insane."

Chloe picked up Clément. "Would you like me to put him to bed also?"

Beatrice seemed to consider the offer for a second. "Yes, that would be great. I'm exhausted from my day of work." She stood up and placed a peck on Clément's cheek.

"Good night, sweetheart."

After washing Clément and putting him into his pajamas, Chloe set him down in his bed.

"Now what? I can't carry a tune so don't ask me to sing, but I'll tell you a story if you want."

"Story with tuk?" asked Clément.

"What's tuk?"

Clément made a vibrating noise with his mouth and pretended to be driving. "Big, big tuk," he said, trying to explain.

"Oh I get it, truck!"

"Yeah," said Clément happily.

"Okay, I don't really know one, but I can make it up."

Chloe wove the story of a truck that wanted to become a fire truck. Her soft voice slowly put Clément to sleep. She kissed Clément good night, and lightly brushed his hair behind his ears.

"Your mom doesn't really seem to understand that you're just a little two year-old boy. That's too bad, because you're really cute," whispered Chloe.

She quietly exited the room, leaving the door half-open. She went downstairs to look for Beatrice, who was nowhere to be found. *She must have retired to her bedroom already. I wonder if...* Chloe open the fridge and looked for the Chinese leftovers. She quickly made up a plate and put it in the microwave to warm up.

"Still hungry?"

Chloe jumped and turned around to find Beatrice wearing a bathrobe and slippers.

"You scared me...yeah...the Chinese food was really good. I thought...I mean, I hope you don't mind," stuttered Chloe.

"No, not at all. Be my guest. Is Clément asleep?"

"Yes, he fell asleep right away."

"Oh, good. Thank you for doing that for me. I get so tired in the evening. It's nice to have someone to take over sometimes."

"Doesn't Laurence help you with that?" asked Chloe.

"Laurence? Well...yeah, I guess she does, but she is not really good with children. At least not as good as you are."

"Thanks, I guess," answered Chloe, not believing what she'd just heard. "I'm going up to my room now. G'night, Beatrice."

"Good night."

I can't believe what she just said. Laurence not good with children! She adores Clément. What the hell is she talking about? Chloe carefully carried her plate upstairs, but instead of going toward her bedroom she went down the right corridor.

Okay...moment of truth. Now, where is her room? Soft music came out of the third door. *I guess that must be it.* Chloe knocked at the door and waited for an answer. *Maybe she is asleep.* She waited few more seconds in front of the door before giving up. She was half way to the end of the corridor when she heard the door opened. She turned around and walked back. Laurence had the door half open and was wearing a pair of boxer shorts and a t-shirt.

"What do you want?" Laurence asked, annoyed.

"I'm sorry, I didn't think you'd be asleep…I…I thought you might be hungry, so I brought you some food since you didn't eat dinner and all…."

Laurence reached for the plate Chloe was holding.

"Thanks. You didn't have to do that."

"Yeah, I know, but I wanted to." Laurence made no move to invite Chloe in, nor did she seem ready to start a conversation.

"I guess I'll leave…uh…good night," said Chloe, turning away.

"Wait!" Laurence sighed. "Do you want to come in for a bit? You can keep me company while I eat."

"Sure. I would love to," answered Chloe more eagerly than she wanted to.

Laurence opened the door wide to let Chloe in. Her room was pretty much a replica of Chloe's, but for the difference in the paintings on the wall.

"Wow," said Chloe while looking around. "These paintings are great. Who are the artists?"

"They're all by the same person."

"They are so full of color and life, you can almost see what mood the painter was in when he painted each one of them."

"She," said Laurence.

"What?"

"I said it's a she," answered Laurence while putting her plate down on an oak desk in the corner of the room.

"So, who is she?"

"Me."

"What? You've got to be kidding!" said Chloe in disbelief.

"Why should I be?"

Chloe stared at Laurence. Her eyes reflected nothing but honesty.

"That's the truth, isn't it?"

"Yep," said Laurence with a smile.

"You're really talented, you know that?"

"Thanks. I like painting. It relaxes me."

"Have you ever thought of selling your work?"

"Come on! I'm not that good. It's just a hobby, nothing more."

"You're full of surprises," mumbled Chloe.

"What did you say?" asked Laurence.

"Nothing, just talking to myself," answered Chloe quickly. "Wow, who is that?" Chloe asked, pointing to the portrait of a woman. The woman looked to be in her forties with light brown hair and very piercing blue eyes. Her smile was bright and seemed to illuminate her entire face. Chloe came closer to the painting and found herself staring at the woman's eyes. *They remind me of...oh my gosh...they're the same as Laurence's eyes.* "She has the same..."

"My mother...it's my mother," interrupted Laurence. She had moved and now stood directly behind Chloe.

Chloe stood staring at the painting. "She is beautiful," she said softly.

"Was...was beautiful," answered Laurence with a quivering voice.

Chloe turned around and faced Laurence. "I...I'm sorry I had no idea...nobody..."

"It's okay," said Laurence, walking away and sitting at the desk.

Chloe didn't know what to do. The conversation was taking a turn she hadn't expected. She just stood there waiting for Laurence to decide if the conversation should go on or not.

"She died seven years ago."

Chloe still didn't dare say anything.

"Car accident...drunk driver." Laurence passed her hand through her hair. "Anyway, it was a long time ago." Laurence stood up abruptly and walked toward the bathroom. "Want something to drink?" she asked.

"You've got a fridge back there?" Chloe asked, surprised and relieved for the change of topic.

"Yep. So you want something?"

"I'll take a Diet Coke if you have one," answered Chloe.

"Coming up."

Laurence walked back toward Chloe and handed the can to her.

"That's weird, it says Coca Light on the can, and not Diet Coke."

Laurence shrugged her shoulder. "Same thing," she said before drinking from a Perrier bottle.

"Weird, it tastes like Coke," said Chloe after taking a drink from her can.

"What do you mean? Coke doesn't taste like Diet Coke."

"French Diet Coke tastes like American Coke."

"I take it you don't like it, huh?" asked Laurence with an amused smile.

"Sorry, but I always thought Coke was too sweet. Can I have something else?"

"I only have Perrier."

"I'll try that."

"Okay. Do you have siblings back in the States?" asked Laurence while walking back to the fridge.

"No, I'm an only child."

Laurence came back with Chloe's drink. "Here. Listen, I'm going to eat my food while it's still warm. You don't have to stand, you can sit on the bed."

"I don't want to disturb you…"

Laurence laughed. "That's a good one coming from the person who woke me up half an hour ago."

Chloe blushed. "Well…I didn't know you'd be asleep."

"I'm just playing with you. Come on, sit down while I eat."

"Okay," said Chloe, sitting on the large bed. "Laurence? Can I ask you a question?"

Laurence looked at Chloe as she bit into her spring roll. She waited to swallow her food before answering.

"You can ask, but I might not answer."

"Okay, fair enough." Chloe gathered her courage and asked, "Do you remember earlier when I asked you why you didn't get along with Beatrice?" Laurence nodded slightly. "You said to ask you later, and …I think it could be important for me to know what's going on since I'm going to live in this family for a year and all. I think maybe it's later and you could explain it to me." Chloe waited expectantly for Laurence's to answer. *Oh, boy…what the hell did you just do?* Chloe thought as she watched a whole range of emotions flash across Laurence's face, giving her only a hint of the battle raging inside Laurence at that moment.

How much can I tell her? How much do I really want to trust her with? Laurence wondered. *It's too soon…*

"Listen. Really, you're reading too much into it. We just don't get along. There isn't much more to it," said Laurence.

"Nothing I should know?" asked Chloe.

"Not really. You already know that Beatrice sleeps around. Besides that, there isn't much."

"What?" exclaimed Chloe.

"Don't tell me you didn't guess? Come on! Do you really think those meetings of hers are real?"

"I thought it was a little weird that last night's meeting lasted that long, but I never thought… Wow, I'm sorry."

"No sweat, really."

"That's why you don't like her," said Chloe matter-of-factly.

"Yeah, partly," answered Laurence.

Chloe looked up at Laurence, realizing there was more to it, but deciding to not push it for tonight.

"Listen, thanks for the food. It's late and…"

"No, no, I should go. I didn't realize it was so late." Chloe got up from the bed. "Can you knock on my door tomorrow morning? And this time don't let me sleep in," Chloe asked as she walked to the door.

"I tell you what, why don't you take my alarm clock?"

"What about you?"

"Don't worry, I have something better than that," said Laurence while pointing at the monitor on the bedside table.

"Wait a minute…do you always leave this thing on?"

"Not always, I only turn it on when Clément is asleep. By the way, you tell nice tuk stories," joked Laurence.

"You heard? I can't believe it!" said Chloe feigning indignation.

"Yeah, I heard. Thanks for putting him to bed."

"You're welcome," said Chloe smiling. She opened the door and was ready to take her leave when Laurence spoke.

"You're right, you know."

" 'bout what?"

"Beatrice doesn't understand that Clément is only two."

Chloe smiled. "No, she doesn't, that's for sure. G'night, Laurence."

"G'night."

Chloe stepped out of the room.

"Hey, Chloe?" called Laurence.

"Now who is keeping who awake," joked Chloe. "What?"

"If you want, on Friday since Beatrice is leaving with Clément early in the morning, I can give you a tour of the castle and its gardens."

"Wow, that would be great! Are you sure? I don't want you to feel like you've got to entertain me."

"I wouldn't be offering if I didn't want to do it. Plus, I'll give you the unofficial tour."

"What do you mean?"

"You'll see. Good night, Chloe." Laurence slowly closed the door.

Cool, what better way to explore than with someone who really knows the area? thought Chloe with a smile as she walked to her room.

Chapter 4

The next two days flew by without incident. Clément was getting used to Chloe, and Laurence slowly gave Chloe more responsibilities, so by the end of the week the roles of spectator and caregiver had been reversed.

On Friday morning, Chloe was awakened by light taps on her door.

"Come in," she answered, still half asleep. *8 a.m.... I thought I didn't have to work today.*

Laurence opened the door and stood in the doorway. "Hi."

"Hi, is something wrong? I thought I didn't need to be ready before 10," asked Chloe.

"No, nothing is wrong. I'm sorry I woke you. I just wanted to let you know that Clément and Beatrice are gone already. I need to change our plans for today."

"Oh, did something come up?" asked Chloe, disappointed.

"Nothing important. There are a bunch of errands I have to run, and I don't think I'll be back by 10…is noon okay?" asked Laurence.

"Yeah, sure. I got scared you were going to ditch me," said Chloe, reassured.

"Nah, I keep my promises," said Laurence. "So, see you at noon?"

"'kay."

Laurence flashed a smile. "Go back to sleep. See you in while," she said softly, closing the door behind her.

At noon, Chloe was waiting for Laurence in the family room, flipping through TV channels.

"Ready?"

Chloe jumped. "Man, have you ever heard of announcing yourself? You've got a bad habit of scaring me half to death."

"I know, and it's so much fun," kidded Laurence.

"Yeah, yeah, make fun of me."

"Chloe, you might want to put on a pair of jeans before we go."

"Why? What's wrong with shorts? I thought it was warm outside?"

"Just trust me on this one."

"You're the boss. I'll go change."

"Put on some tennis shoes also," yelled Laurence from the bottom of the stairs.

① ① ①

The day outside was warm and sunny, a perfect day for the end of August. They walked to the castle taking the same roads as earlier in the week. Once they reached the iron gate, Chloe stopped.

"What are you doing?" asked Laurence.

"Wow! I just can't believe that I'm going to set foot in such an historic place."

Laurence laughed. "Well, you're not if you don't get past these gates. Come on," she said, grabbing Chloe by her shirt sleeve and dragging her inside.

"I'm coming, I'm coming!"

They made their way across the huge cobblestone courtyard, and Laurence headed toward the entrance.

"We've got to get tickets."

"Okay," answered Chloe, taking a place in line.

"I thought we'd visit the main part of the castle today, and you can do the King and Queen's bedroom some other time."

"They're not together?" asked Chloe.

"Technically they are, but to make more money they divide the visit into three sections. So, you've got to buy three different tickets if you want to see everything."

"Oh, I get it."

Their turn in line came. Laurence refused to let Chloe pay for her admission.

"Come on, I should be the one paying for you. I'm sure you've seen this place thousands of times."

"Don't worry about it. Come on, are you ready for a visit into history?"

"Oh yeah!"

"Good, let's go."

They passed through the metal detector and started their visit.

"Metal detector? That's not very historic," joked Chloe.

Laurence smiled. "Better safe than sorry. Okay, let's start with the right wing."

"You're the guide!"

They walked through a long large corridor with paintings depicting different royal families. Laurence was walking very fast.

"Lo, hey! Slow down, we're not racing." If Laurence realized that Chloe had used her nickname, she made no comment.

"I know, but I want to beat this tour group ahead of us. Plus, there isn't really anything interesting until the children's apartments."

"Okay, but don't lose me in the crowd, " said Chloe, picking up the pace.

Once they reached the tour group, Laurence took hold of Chloe's hand. Chloe looked at her with a funny expression on her face.

"I don't want to lose you in the crowd," said Laurence as she pressed through the crowd. Once past the group she let go of Chloe's hand.

"Is that a habit of yours, holding people's hands through crowds?" asked Chloe jokingly. To her surprise Laurence blushed. *I can't believe she's blushing. Did I manage to embarrass her?* Chloe decided to take advantage of the situation and continued to tease Laurence.

"Maybe you just reserve it for Clément and I."

"Okay, okay, drop it."

Chloe laughed. "You're funny when you blush."

"Hey! I don't blush."

"You do too," answered Chloe teasingly.

"Do not!"

"Do too."

Laurence let out an impatient growl. "Fine, whatever. Are we going to visit this castle or not?"

Chloe smiled. "Lead the way."

"Hey! Wipe that smile off your face, miss."

"I'm not smiling."

"Are too." Suddenly Laurence put her hand on Chloe's mouth. "Forget I even answered that." Chloe tried to protest. "Ah ha! !hat did I just say? Come on, let's call it a truce, and go." Chloe's eyes were sparkling with amusement. She nodded.

"Okay." Laurence took her hand off Chloe's mouth.

Chloe bit her lower lip to keep from laughing. *This is a side of Laurence I've never seen, almost playful. I like it.*

"Are you coming? The tourists are going to catch up with us."

"Yeah."

They made their way to the dauphine's apartment. The halls were decorated with rich draperies with faded colors. The bedroom had the same faded drapes, but its bed cover was of bright red velvet. A hairbrush made of gold sat on a dresser. Paintings of the dauphine and her family decorated the walls.

"Wow, that's quite a bedroom. I guess there were some advantages to being Louis XIV's daughter," exclaimed Chloe.

"Yeah."

"I guess it doesn't faze you anymore. You've seen it too many times."

"I guess. Come on, we still have plenty to see."

They walked into a room that Laurence explained had been the Duchesse D'Angoulême's bedroom.

"I don't get it," said Chloe.

"What?"

"I wasn't sure if it was because the dauphine was a child, but it's the same here."

"Stop speaking in riddles. What are you talking about?"

"The beds are they really small or is it just my imagination?"

"Good eye. Yes, you're right, they're smaller than what we're used to."

"Why?"

"You and your historical facts, huh?" joked Laurence. "Back then people thought that you should only be lying down if you were dead. So, they slept sitting up."

"They were really superstitious."

"Yeah, let's keep going."

They made their way through the castle. Laurence pointed out details to Chloe and recounted the many stories about the castle and its residents. The Hall of Mirrors had Chloe in awe. Its hundreds of crystal chandeliers reflected into the mirrors on the walls and its shining marble floor.

"What was this room for?" asked Chloe.

"Receptions. The peace treaty of the first World War was signed in this room."

"Wow, I really can't believe that we're walking on the same floor Louis XIV walked on."

They crossed the Hall of Mirrors into the coronation room.

"Stop!" ordered Laurence in a friendly tone.

"What, what's going on?"

"You see where you're standing?"

Chloe looked around and noted that she was standing next to the furthest window in the coronation room.

"At this exact place ten years ago, two English teachers disappeared in front of their students," said Laurence.

"What? They just vanished?"

"Yep."

"Come on, cut it out. What really happened?"

"I told you, one minute they were walking in front of their group of students, the next they were gone." The intensity with which Laurence was telling this story made Chloe nervous, and she didn't feel too good about standing in the same spot. *Come on! It's just a story, it didn't really happen,* thought Chloe to reassure herself.

Laurence continued her story. "They were discovered two hours later in the left wing."

"Did they explain where they were?" asked Chloe, giving in to the story.

"Yep, they said they had just been walking along when suddenly they started seeing people wearing strange clothes. People asked them in old French if they were coming to the ceremony. The two women realized that they were also wearing strange clothes, and when they looked behind them, instead of their group of students was a large crowd wearing what they identified as 18th century clothing."

"What the hell? Don't tell me that these two women pretended to have gone back to the past."

"They sure did. They said that the ceremony they were asked to go to was the baptism of the dauphin. They also claimed to have spent more than two years living in the 18th century."

"That's crazy!"

"That's what everyone else thought. They got fired for abandoning their students for so long."

"Wow, that's quite a story. Do you think these women could have been telling the truth?" asked Chloe.

Laurence shrugged her shoulders. "Don't know. Some scientists say that a bridge between the future and the past is possible. Personally I think it's bull, but hey! Who am I to say?"

"Yeah, well I don't know, but I don't want to stand here anymore. It's creepy."

Laurence laughed. "All right. Let's move on."

After another hour of touring, they went back to the ground floor using the left wing stairs. They had been following a group for a while now, and Laurence hadn't seemed to mind, but now she was slowing down and looking around as if it was the first time she had seen everything. They stopped in the room of the King's Guard. Laurence bent over slightly and whispered in Chloe's ear.

"Once this group is gone, follow my lead."

"What? What's..."

"No time for questions. Now come on!"

Laurence jumped over the cord separating the public from the room. *What the hell is she doing...Oh brother!* thought Chloe as she followed Laurence.

Laurence grabbed Chloe by the sleeve and dragged her behind three standing suits of armor.

"Duck!" whispered Laurence.

Laurence reached for a small handle on the floor and lifted a wooden trap door.

"After you," whispered Laurence.

Chloe looked down to see a ladder. She seemed hesitant.

"Come on, we don't have much time before one of the guards comes. Go already."

Chloe grabbed the ladder and slowly made her way down. Laurence followed closely, closing the trap door behind her.

"Laurence, I think I've reached the bottom. It's really dark down here."

A Year in Paris 55

Not getting an answer, Chloe called again, "Laurence, you're scaring me."

A hand suddenly grabbed Chloe, making her scream.

Laurence laughed. "Got you."

"Very funny! Are there any light switches in here?"

"No, but I have...." Laurence reached inside her backpack and felt around for a flashlight. "I know I put it here...ha, here we go," she said, turning the light on.

"Laurence, what is this place?" asked Chloe looking around, but only seeing dirt floors and walls.

"Follow me, and I'll tell you."

They walked slowly down the underground tunnel. Chloe, still not reassured, stayed at arm's length from Laurence.

"This place was built under the reign of Louis XVI. It was supposed to be an escape route for him and his family in case the palace was ever overpowered."

"His plan didn't work out very well, uh?"

"Not really. They were stopped from escaping by some of the royal guards before the people of Paris got here."

"Weren't the guards supposed to protect their King, not betray him?"

"Yeah, in theory, but I think they were scared senseless of what would happen to them if the people got to the castle and the royal family was gone. Okay, here we are," said Laurence, stopping in front of a door. "You've got to close your eyes before you go in."

"Why?"

"Chloe, please humor me," pleaded Laurence.

Chloe closed her eyes, and Laurence gently took her hand and led her through the door.

"Okay, now keep your eyes closed until I tell you."

Boy was I right when I said she's full of surprises! thought Chloe.

"Okay, open them up."

Chloe opened her eyes and looked around. Candles had been lit around the room, casting their shadows on tables, sofas, beds, chairs.

"Wow, what is this place?" asked Chloe.

"I'll tell you in a minute, but first I want to show you something else. Come."

They walked through the long room into another room.

"My gosh, this is incredible," exclaimed Chloe. The room had more furniture, paintings were piled against the wall, and faded and ripped draperies hung from the wall.

Laurence reached for something behind a sofa.

"I thought you might be hungry." She walked to a hand-carved wooden table and set a basket on it. She started emptying it.

"We have Perrier, baguette, cheese, dry sausage, and fruit."

"When did you...how did you...?" Chloe was speechless.

"This morning. That's why I picked you up late. There is another entrance along the canal."

"Why didn't we use the other entrance?"

"I thought you wanted to see the castle," kidded Laurence.

"Yeah, but we could have been caught."

"What's life without a little danger?" Laurence joked.

Laurence sat on a wooden bench and sliced herself a piece of bread before spreading cheese on it.

"Is that Brie?"

"Mmm," mumbled Laurence with a mouth full of food.

Chloe looked at Laurence and smiled. "Thanks for bringing me here."

"You're welcome," answered Laurence.

"Lo, how do you know about this place?"

Once again, Laurence ignored the use of the nickname. "My dad. He was born at the end of the second World War. Thousands of Versaillais were left homeless after the war. The bombs also destroyed my dad's house. Anyway, my grandpa was a carpenter, and he got a job restoring furniture for the castle. In exchange for his services, he and his family were allowed to live in the basement of the castle."

"In this room?"

"Yeah, it's been more than 40 years, and they piled up lot of crap through the years, but from what my dad describes it was really roomy."

"That's such a great story."

"Yeah, I think it's cool. My dad spent the first six years of his life running around the park and the castle, so he knows every part of it. He showed me this place."

"That's incredible," said Chloe, taking a bite of her cheese sandwich.

"Do you think all this furniture is from the 17th century?"

"Don't know. Those draperies, definitely yes."

"Do you think I can look at those paintings over there?" asked Chloe.

"Sure. Don't you want to finish eating first?"

"I'm hungry, but this is so exciting I can't sit still," she said, getting up.

Laurence laughed. "Okay, go ahead."

Chloe picked up one of the paintings. It showed the face of a young child with tears rolling down his face. Chloe suddenly felt overwhelmed as if the painting was having an effect on her.

"Laurence!" she quietly called. "Who do you think this child is?"

Laurence got up and stood behind Chloe, looking over her shoulder. "I don't know." The next few minutes passed quietly as they both stared at the painting.

Chloe put the painting down. "Wow, I don't know why I feel like getting all mushy on you suddenly, but this painting is just so real. The tears are just..." Chloe was speechless.

"Yeah, I agree with you. It's really well done," said Laurence, squeezing Chloe's shoulder to let her know that she understood her feelings.

"Do you think it's as old as the 17th century?" asked Chloe.

Laurence slightly scratched the corner of the painting with her thumbnail.

"No extra layer of paint. It's not a fake. Yeah, it might be from back then."

"Wow! Why isn't it on display upstairs?"

"Could be many reasons. They have too many portraits, or the child cannot be identified and consequently is not important, or the painter is totally unknown, or nobody knows about it. Personally, I vote for the last one."

"You think nobody knows about it?"

"Come on, look at this room. Ninety percent of it is filled with antiques, but nobody seems to care about them."

"Your dad is an art dealer, right?" Laurence nodded. "Then why doesn't he tell them, or just take everything if he knows about this place?"

"My dad is too honest to take anything that doesn't belong to him, and he doesn't want anyone to know about this place."

"You mean, nobody knows about it."

"The castle was renovated and opened to the public thirty years ago. I think since then whoever knew about it has retired or is dead."

She stopped and then added softly, "My mother knew, but she passed away, and now you know."

Chloe walked around the room thinking and passing her hand over pieces of furniture, trailing her fingers along the wall, touching draperies.

"It's magical," she said.

Laurence smiled at her and took a sip of her Perrier. "I come here sometimes when I want to think and be alone."

Chloe stopped and sat next to Laurence on the bench. "I realize how much this place means to you, and I want you to know that I promise not to tell anyone about it." Chloe looked intently into Laurence's eyes, and briefly touched her hand to convey her sincerity.

"I know you won't. Otherwise I would have never brought you here."

"Overly confident, aren't you?" teased Chloe.

Laurence didn't answer, but stood instead. "We should get going. It's almost four o'clock, and I want to show you something else."

" 'kay. So, let's go."

"Follow me." Laurence walked out of the room into the tunnel. "You're not afraid of spiders, are you?"

"Um… Why?" asked Chloe.

"You're about to find out why I asked you to wear jeans," answered Laurence.

"Oh boy! I don't like the sound of that."

Laurence chuckled. "Don't worry, they're just little spiders."

They walked through the dark tunnel with only Laurence's flashlight to light the way.

"It's really creepy," said Chloe, her voice echoing through the tunnel.

"Yeah, but I have been here enough times to tell you that there aren't any ghosts running around."

"Are you purposely trying to scare me?" asked Chloe.

Laurence smiled, her white teeth showing in the darkness. "Okay, here is the part where it gets messy." She stopped and pointed her flashlight to the floor illuminating a huge mud puddle.

"Okay, we have to walk around this thing, but as you see there isn't much room. The goal is to walk as close to the walls as you can. Now, remember the spiders?"

"Yes." answered Chloe, suddenly not too sure about this place anymore.

Laurence pointed the light to the walls, which were full of spider webs and crawling spiders.

"No way, I'm not going through that," said Chloe.

"They won't do anything. The annoying part is that the webs get all over you and in your hair."

"Great, that's just great," Chloe said, pacing around.

"Come on, let's get it over with." Laurence walked to the left of the puddle and flattened herself against the wall facing the mud.

"Why can't we go through it? I don't care about getting messy," asked Chloe.

"Because I have no idea what's in it right now, it's really deep, and last time I tried I lost a shoe, but be my guest if you want to try it."

Chloe sighed. "I see I don't really have a choice."

"Nope," said Laurence cheerfully from the other side of the large mud puddle.

"Okay girl, you've done worse than this," mumbled Chloe to reassure herself. "...except for the spiders," she added.

Chloe copied Laurence's moves and started to cross over. Halfway through, she felt something crawling in her hair. She screamed. "Ah!"

"What...what's wrong?" asked Laurence worried, the flashlight not giving her enough light to see what was happening.

"Something is crawling in my hair!" she shrieked.

"Forget about it. You're almost there. You can do it."

Chloe arrived on the other side covered with spider webs. "Argh, it's everywhere," she said dusting herself off and wiping her hands on her jeans.

"Do you still have something in your hair?" asked Laurence. "Here, let me look."

"Get them off me!" yelled Chloe. "I hate spiders, I hate you for taking me here. I..." A sob escaped her. She turned around and kicked the wall. "Arghh! I hate spiders!" she yelled between tears.

Laurence slowly made her way to Chloe and grabbed her by the shoulders, turning her around to face her.

"Calm down. It's okay. I didn't know you'd be so scared."

Chloe hit her on the chest twice before going limp in Laurence's arms. Laurence put her arms around Chloe to comfort her.

"I'm sorry. I swear I had no idea. Why didn't you tell me when I asked you earlier?"

"That wouldn't have changed anything, we still had to get out this way," Chloe sniffled.

"Yes, but I would have crossed with you."

"Now you tell me," said Chloe, trying to regain her sense of humor.

"Are you okay? Can we keep going? We're almost there," asked Laurence, not daring to move until she was sure.

In response Chloe tightened her grip around Laurence. *I can't believe she got so scared*, thought Laurence as she held Chloe.

Chloe let go of Laurence slowly. "Sorry about that," she said, embarrassed.

"Hey, it's okay. Really. Are you ready to get out of here?"

"You bet. I'm glad the spider incident is over."

"Uh, there are spiders all over the walls in this tunnel. I didn't point it out before now because I didn't need to."

"I guess we're going to be walking far away from the walls. After you," said Chloe gesturing to Laurence to lead the way. "What are the walls made out of?" she asked.

"Mostly dirt and sand."

"Ah, that explains it." Chloe got closer to Laurence and held on to her elbow for guidance. "So, what else do you want to show me when we get out?"

"You'll see. Hey, look there," said Laurence, pointing to the glimpse of daylight ahead of them. "Come on," she said as she took off running.

"Hey, wait up!" shouted Chloe. Laurence was already yards away from her. *This girl has too much energy.*

Laurence was waiting for her at the end of the tunnel in front of an iron gate. "How do we get out with this thing in the way?" asked Chloe, pointing at the gate.

Laurence winked at Chloe and smiled. She crouched and started removing two of the left bars by just untwisting them.

"Wow, that's cool!" Chloe squeezed herself through the gap in the bars.

"I aim to please," kidded Laurence as she joined Chloe on the other side and carefully replaced the bars.

They silently walked around the canal toward the park of the castle. They had almost reached it when Chloe stopped.

"Can you hear music or am I going crazy?" asked Chloe.

"They do that every weekend. You can walk in the park along with music from the 17th century. They also turn on every fountain in the park, and they have a major finale in front of Apollo's fountain at 5 p.m.," answered Laurence.

"Can we go?"

"Yep, but we better hurry, it's going to start in a few minutes."

"So what are we waiting for?" said Chloe, breaking into a run.

"Hold on Chloe, you don't even know where it is," Laurence laughed.

Good point, thought Chloe, letting Laurence catch up with her.

Shortly thereafter, Chloe and Laurence were sitting on the grass in front of Apollo's fountain listening to the Requiem from Mozart coming out of the speakers. The fountain was more like a large pond. In the middle was the sculpture of Apollo's horse and carriage jutting out of the water. Statues of Apollo surrounded the pond. At 5p.m. on the dot, water erupted from the center sculpture, pulsing in rhythm with the music. The beauty of it all took Chloe's breath away.

"Hey, are you okay?"

"Yes, I, I'm fine. It's just so beautiful."

"Yes, it is," said Laurence, staring at Chloe for a few moments before bringing her gaze back to the spectacle. After the finale, she turned back to her companion. "Are you ready to go home?"

"Yeah, I guess," answered Chloe, reluctant to wrap up such a magical day.

Laurence got up and extended her hand to Chloe. Laurence pulled Chloe to back on her feet and gently wiped dirt off her forehead. "You must have gotten it in the tunnel," she said softly.

Chloe smiled shyly and lightly leaned into Laurence's hand for a brief second.

"I tell you what. I'll take you out to dinner to make up for the spider episode," said Laurence.

"Really? Cool! I mean, I'd love to. First can we go home and change?"

"Yeah, restaurants don't start serving before 7. Let's go."

They walked home in a silent companionship, Chloe's thoughts filled with memories of the day.

"Are you allergic to any food?" asked Laurence as she unlocked the front door.

"No. I eat pretty much anything," answered Chloe. "Why? What do you have in mind?"

"Hey! I'm not telling since you eat everything. You'll see," teased Laurence.

"Okay, okay, but can I wear jeans or should I wear something more dressy?"

"Hmm. I don't know because I haven't decided where we're going yet. Why don't you just wear something you're comfortable in?"

"Okay, I'll go change."

"Yeah, be ready by 7, and..." Laurence was interrupted by the phone. She rushed to pick it up.

"Allo...P'pa! Comment ça va?" Laurence walked away from Chloe into the family room.

Chloe decided that was her cue to go change and give Laurence some privacy.

As she passed by, Laurence pointed at her watch and mouthed "Seven." Chloe smiled and nodded.

Once in her room, Chloe set about the task of choosing something to wear for dinner.

"She didn't give me many clues about what to wear...hmm...it's kind of warm out...yeah, that will do."

Laurence knocked at Chloe's door at 7. "Are you ready?" she called through the door.

"Coming," yelled Chloe from the other side.

The door opened to reveal Chloe wearing a white tank top with a white long sleeve shirt thrown on top and black jeans. She wore her blond hair up with a touch of makeup accentuating the green of her eyes.

"You look great!" said Laurence, releasing a breath she didn't know she had been holding since Chloe stepped out of her room.

"Thanks. You don't look bad yourself." Laurence was wearing a well-fitted pair of black jeans with a red long-sleeved shirt, slightly open and revealing her tan skin.

Laurence flashed her a smile. "Shall we?" asked Laurence. She offered her arm to Chloe.

"We shall, my dear," said Chloe, catching on to Laurence's little game and taking her arm.

"Where are we going?" asked Chloe.

"It's a surprise."

"Come on, I've had enough surprises for the day. You've got to tell me."

"I'll give you a clue. It's in Paris."

"Oh gee thanks! That's a great clue."

"That's as much as you're going to get," said Laurence as she put on her leather jacket. "You might want to grab something warmer. Do you have a jacket?"

"Only a winter one."

"Wait here," said Laurence, running back upstairs.

"What are you doing?" yelled Chloe, but she got no response.

Laurence came back downstairs as fast as she had left. "Here," she said, handing Chloe a leather jacket.

"Do you really think I need it?" asked Chloe.

"Oh yes; we're going on my bike. The air can get really chilly."

"Cool, I love bikes," exclaimed Chloe putting on the jacket. "It fits almost perfectly. It can't be yours, it's too small for you."

"It used to be mine ages ago. My dad gave it to me for my birthday when I was thirteen. I've outgrown it. Good thing you're a dwarf," Laurence laughed as she opened the door.

"Yeah, yeah, make fun of my 5 feet 2 inches, Miss I-could-out-play-any-basketball-player-in-the-NBA," answered Chloe.

"Oh, touché!" joked Laurence, pretending to have been mortally wounded.

"Come on, cut the drama," laughed Chloe.

"Your carriage is ready, my lady," said Laurence, jokingly bowing and pointing to her motorcycle.

"I'll choose to ignore that one," said Chloe with a pretend frown on her face.

Laurence climbed on the bike. "Get behind me," said Laurence, handing Chloe a helmet.

Chloe did as told and Laurence started the bike and revved it a few times until the idle smoothed out.

"Lo? Where should I hold on?" asked Chloe, raising her voice to make herself heard above the roar.

"To the saddle or to my waist. Whatever feels safer to you," she answered, pointing the bike out into the streets of Versailles.

Chloe held on lightly to Laurence's waist and watched the houses go by as they made their way toward the highway. Once on the highway Laurence sped up, and the wind blew harder in Chloe's face forcing her to scoot closer to Laurence and eventually wrap her arms securely around Laurence's waist. *Sure beats driving in a car,* thought Chloe, smiling to herself.

Laurence drove her bike smoothly, weaving between cars. She slowed down once she reached Paris. Chloe had been lost in thought when suddenly Laurence poked her hands, which were still attached to Laurence's waist. Chloe looked up to see Laurence pointing at something ahead of them.

"Arc de Triomphe," yelled Laurence through her helmet.

"Wow!" exclaimed Chloe. The arch was lit up, and what seemed to Chloe like hundreds of car lights surrounded it. "Are we going there?" asked Chloe.

"We have to go around it. We're going down Les Champs Elysées."

"Okay."

Once they got closer to the Arc, Chloe heard honking and people yelling. "What's going on?" she asked Laurence.

"Nothing. You've got to circle around the Arc, and it's always a mess."

Laurence brought the bike into the traffic circle. Three lanes were painted on the pavement, but there were up to five cars abreast and chaos reigned. Some cars were perpendicular to other cars while trying to exit. It truly was a mess.

"Now you find out why I like driving my bike in Paris," said Laurence. She expertly maneuvered out of the circle, the small size of the motorcycle letting them weave though the creeping traffic without problem.

"Wow, the Eiffel Tower!" exclaimed Chloe, pointing at the tower.

Laurence went around the Champ de Mars and parked her bike on the waterfront.

"Come on, we're running late and we've got five minutes before the boat leaves," she said as she grabbed Chloe's hand and ran toward the dock. They climbed onto a boat.

"Bonsoir. Nous avons des reservations pour Glairon," said Laurence.

"Par ici, mademoiselle," said the hostess.

"Are we going to eat on this boat?" asked Chloe.

"Yep. Hope you don't get sea sick," Laurence said with a smile.

They were seated at a table next to the window. Fancy silverware, a white table cloth, napkins, and candles decorated the table.

"Wow, it's great," exclaimed Chloe.

"They also have great food," answered Laurence.

The half moon reflected on the river making the surface glitter with silver. The Eiffel Tower loomed over the river. The boat slowly started to drift down the river. Musicians played violins and the gentle lapping of the water combined to create a beautiful melody.

"This is so beautiful, so peaceful," said Chloe.

Laurence smiled. A waiter came to the table to take their orders.

"Can I order for us?" asked Laurence.

"Hmm...should I trust you?" joked Chloe.

Laurence winked and turned to the waiter.

"What did you get?" asked Chloe once the waiter left.

"You'll see."

"I get it, more surprises."

The waiter came back with a bottle of sauvignon blanc and poured some in their glasses.

"Merci," said Laurence, reaching for her glass. She lifted it as a toast.

"To you, Chloe. I hope you have a great year, and that you actually stay the entire year," said Laurence with a smile.

Chloe took a sip of her wine. "So, you're leaving on Sunday?" asked Chloe.

"I have to," answered Laurence.

"Too bad, I kind of like having you around," Chloe said smiling.

"After the way I treated you the first day, I don't know how you're even talking to me right now," said Laurence sadly.

Chloe shrugged her shoulders. "Everyone deserves a second chance," said Chloe. "Plus, you didn't turn out to be such a bad person after all." She picked up her glass and drank some more. "Why were you acting so bitchy the first day?" she asked shyly. *Maybe she's going to bite my head off, but I've got to know.*

Laurence sighed. "I told you we had so many au pairs before you. I thought you were another one of those pompous little Americans only here for fun."

"What made you change your mind?" asked Chloe, looking into Laurence's eyes.

Laurence finished her glass and poured herself another before answering. "Don't know...I guess you just seemed so honest and eager to know Clément. You also seemed to be able to handle Beatrice and not everyone can do that."

Chloe registered what Laurence said about Beatrice but decided to not pursue the topic. "I think Clément likes me," she said.

"Yeah, I think so too," answered Laurence. "He is a great little guy, you'll see," Laurence added. Her eyes shone with affection every time she spoke of Clément.

"The food is here," Laurence announced as the waiter approached.

He deposited a plate with a dozen of escargot in front of each of them.

"Is that..."

"Yep, escargot...snails, whatever you want to call it," answered Laurence laughing at the face Chloe was making. "Trust me, it's really good. It's cooked in garlic and butter."

"I'll try, but how do you get them out of their shell?"

"You use the little tiny fork next to your plate," Laurence demonstrated by popping one in her mouth.

"Okay, here goes nothing," said Chloe, closing her eyes, holding her nose and uncertainly placing the escargot in her mouth. "Hey, it's really good!"

"Told you," smiled Laurence.

Chloe decided that tonight she was going to learn more about Laurence. "What are you going to do when you graduate?"

"Move back to Paris. Get a job."

"What's your dream job?" asked Chloe.

"I'd like to work for a magazine like *Premiere*."

"Yeah, I love reading that magazine. All their offices are in the States, though. Hey, you could move to the States; your mom was American, it should be easy for you."

"Hey, hey, hold your horses. Yes, I can move to the States if I feel like it because I have dual citizenship. But there is no way I'm doing that because I have to think of Clément. I'll have to make do with what's around here."

"Okay," said Chloe, sensing that she would not get more out of Laurence on the topic. "What do you do for fun?"

"You like asking questions, don't you?" kidded Laurence. "I like to paint, go to the movies, sometimes go dancing."

"I love dancing!" said Chloe with excitement.

Laurence smiled. "Do you go clubbing a lot back home?" asked Laurence. *She wants to play twenty questions with me; we'll see who wins,* thought Laurence.

"Sometimes. I'm not twenty-one, so there aren't many places I can go."

"Right, I forgot you have to be twenty-one in the States for most clubs."

"Yeah, it's a pain."

"Did you just graduate from high school?" Laurence asked, suddenly eager to learn more about Chloe.

"No, last year. I went to college for a year, but I don't really know what I want to do."

"Where did you go?"

"University of Maryland. It's a great school. My dad wants me to study computers. I tried for one year…I hated it. I need to find my own path." Chloe finished the sentence more for herself than for Laurence.

"Okay, forget about your dad. What do you want to do?"

"You'll laugh if I tell you. Everyone before you has," answered Chloe.

"Come on, cut me some slack. I promise not to laugh."

Chloe pondered the issue for a minute or two. "Okay. I want to major in theater."

"You want to act."

"Not just act. I love plays. I want to learn more about what's going on backstage, what it takes to put on a play. It just fascinates me," explained Chloe. She had started speaking with her hands, which she always did when speaking about something she was passionate about.

"Chloe, you should do it. It sounds great."

"Really?" asked Chloe, not believing that somebody was actually encouraging her.

"Yes. Why don't you?"

Chloe sighed. "It's complicated."

"Try me," said Laurence, briefly squeezing Chloe's hand to encourage her.

"My dad pays for my college. He told me that he won't pay for a theater degree," explained Chloe. " 'Sweetheart, I won't waste hard-earned money on a useless degree. Study computer or law. Those are degrees with great jobs,' " said Chloe, imitating her father.

"What does your dad do?" ask Laurence as she finished her last escargot.

"He's a lawyer."

"I figured," answered Laurence. "What does your mom say about it?"

"My parents got divorced when I was thirteen. I see my mother for Christmas and sometimes during the summer. She's too busy traveling around the world with her job," said Chloe, suddenly deflated.

"Sorry, I didn't know. What does she do that keeps her so busy?"

"She's a news reporter for a TV station in D.C. She covers the crazy things. For example, when the U.S. was bombing Kosovo, she was right there."

"Dangerous job," commented Laurence.

"Yeah."

"Listen, Chloe, I think you should do what you want with your studies. It's your life, not your dad's. You don't want to wake up in ten years and think, 'if only I had known.' "

"I know, but I really can't afford it."

"Ask your mother. She doesn't do much for you–she might help out of guilt. Get a loan. I don't know, just follow your dreams."

Chloe looked at Laurence intently. "Maybe. We'll see," she said, indicating she wanted a change of topic by waving her hand.

They made small talk throughout the rest of dinner, slowly learning more about each other.

"Boy, I'm stuffed," exclaimed Chloe after finishing the last bite of her chocolate mousse.

"No kidding, Miss I-have-to-sample-everything-on-the-dessert-cart," laughed Laurence.

"Hey, you said I could!"

Laurence smiled. "Tell you what, when we get back to the dock we can take a walk around the Eiffel Tower."

"That would be great."

"I also think I had too much wine to drive back right away."

Half an hour later, the boat came to a stop and Laurence and Chloe got off. They walked away from the dock in a friendly silence. Chloe was the first to speak.

"Uh...I want to thank you for today and dinner...you really didn't have to. Well, anyway, thank you."

"No need to thank me. I had a great time. Do you want to walk some more or go home?"

"I wouldn't mind walking for while if you want to."

"Fine by me. Let's go to the Eiffel Tower and come back."

"The Eiffel Tower? That big thing over there?" asked Chloe jokingly. She stopped and turned to Laurence. "I tell you what I'll race you." And with that, she took off running.

"You little..." Laurence took off behind her. Her long legs gave her an advantage, and once she was at arm's length, she pounced on Chloe, dragging her down on the grass.

"Hey!" Chloe yelled as she fell. Laurence twisted her body between the ground and Chloe to soften their fall. They were both out of breath and laughing hysterically. Chloe rolled off Laurence. "I can't believe you...you're..." she stopped trying to catch her breath. She then turned on her side facing Laurence. She propped her head up and asked with a smile, "Why did you do that?"

"Hey, you challenged me," smiled Laurence, turning on her side to face Chloe.

"Yeah, I challenged you to a race, not to a football game," Chloe kidded, poking Laurence teasingly in the ribs.

"Sorry, I got carried away. It was fun." She softly brushed off some dirt from Chloe's sleeve. She looked up to see Chloe looking at her with wonder in her eyes. They stared at each other for what seemed an eternity, neither Laurence nor Chloe willing to break the spell. Chloe's hair had loosened up during the run and was delicately falling in a cascade on her shoulder, the moonlight giving it a slight shade of red. Laurence could not take her gaze away from Chloe. She was mesmerized by the color of her eyes, the shape of her nose, the slight movements of her eye lashes. *Wow, Laurence, get a grip. What is wrong with me˜ must be the wine I had for dinner.* Laurence broke the silence. "I think we should get up," she said, almost whispering.

Chloe nodded and slowly sat up. *What's wrong with me? I'm never speechless.*

"Lucky us, there aren't that many people out tonight; otherwise, we'd have been the entertainment of the evening rolling around in the grass like that," joked Laurence, trying to regain her composure.

"Yeah, lucky us," answered Chloe, still not sure of what had just happened between them.

They got up and decided to call it a night and walked silently back to the dock. *What the hell just happened back there? She's Clément's babysitter for God's sake? What's wrong with me? I really have to get a grip*, thought Laurence. Once they reached the bike, Laurence handed Chloe her helmet and climbed on. Chloe got on behind her and without a second thought grabbed hold of Laurence's waist tightly, leaning forward to rest her head on Laurence's back.

Chapter 5

They got back to Versailles shortly after midnight.

"I'm beat," said Laurence, opening the front door and stepping in.

"Yeah, me too. I think I'll call it a night. Thanks again for today. I really had a great time." Chloe took her jacket off and handed in to Laurence. "Thanks for letting me borrow your jacket."

"I tell you what. You keep it. It doesn't fit me anymore, and I'd rather you have it." Laurence walked into the kitchen and poured herself a glass of water. Chloe followed her.

"Really? Wow…thanks. I don't know if I should accept this…"

"Why not? I'm telling you, it's no sweat." Laurence finished off her glass of water and put the dirty glass in the dishwasher. "I'm going up. I'll see you tomorrow."

"Good night."

Laurence stopped in the doorway and turned to Chloe as if she was going to say something, but instead she shook her head and went upstairs. *What the hell was I thinking? I was going to get all mushy again and tell her I had a great day. I said that already. Once is enough. I think I just need a good night's sleep. Yeah, that's it, I'm just tired.*

Chloe stood alone in the kitchen staring at the door where Laurence was just a few minutes ago. She slowly shook herself out of her reverie and went up to her room.

The following morning, Chloe woke up around 10 a.m. and went downstairs to have breakfast. She found Laurence in the kitchen wearing her usual spandex shorts and t-shirt, reading the newspaper.

"Good morning," said Chloe while entering the kitchen. "What time did you get up?" She took a seat at the kitchen table.

"Around 9. I went for a run and got us some breakfast."

"Really? What is it?" asked Chloe, suddenly realizing that the kitchen was smelling of fresh bread and coffee.

Laurence got up and opened the oven, reaching inside for a tray filled with croissants and bread. She set it on the table and opened up the fridge, getting out three jars of jam.

"Wow…maybe I'll have to start running also. If I keep this up I won't be able to get into my jeans. It smells great…thank you."

Laurence smiled. "Breakfast is served," she said, bowing mockingly. They made small talk throughout breakfast. Laurence tried to teach Chloe some French words, but each time Chloe would repeat them with her best French accent, Laurence burst out laughing.

"Hey, stop making fun of me…I'm trying here," said Chloe, becoming offended by Laurence's behavior.

Laurence calmed herself down. "I'm sorry, but you're just so cute when you speak French. You concentrate so much your nose wrinkles." Laurence started laughing again just thinking about it.

"Fine…we'll stick to English."

"No, no…okay, I won't laugh anymore," said Laurence sincerely. She got up and started cleaning up the table.

"Hey, I'll do that. You got breakfast. I'll clean up. Go take a shower." Chloe pushed Laurence away from the sink.

"Are you saying I smell?"

"Well, now that you mention it…"

Laurence picked up the jar of orange jam and filled a spoon with the sticky substance. "I'll show you stinky." She slowly approached Chloe, spoon in hand.

"Did I say stinky? I meant that you smell great…come on Laurence, what are you doing?" Laurence grabbed Chloe and wiped the spoon across Chloe's face.

"Laurence, stop it…stop it," yelled Chloe, trying to get away from Laurence's grip.

"Who is stinky and sticky now? Uh..." Chloe ran to the table and reached inside the jar, picking up a handful of jam.

"See if you laugh when I'm done with you." She pounced on Laurence and tried spreading the jam on her face only resulting in getting the back of her head. They suddenly stopped and looked at each other. Jam ran down their faces and hair stuck to their foreheads. Chloe started to laugh, soon followed by Laurence.

"Boy, I'm glad Beatrice's not here. She'd have a heart attack," said Chloe.

"No kidding. I think we both need a shower now."

"I'll clean up the mess... you go ahead." Chloe picked up some paper towels and wiped some of the jam off her face.

"Are you sure?"

"Yeah...go ahead."

"Thanks." Laurence left the kitchen, and Chloe started cleaning up.

① ① ①

Chloe finished her chores and got ready for the day. She decided to wear a pair of jeans and a short-sleeved shirt. She was getting ready to go downstairs when she heard a knock at the door.

"Who is it?"

"Laurence. Who else is in this house? Can I come in?"

"Sure."

Laurence opened the door and stepped in. She was wearing blue jeans and a white t-shirt, her hair was up in a pony tail, making her look much younger. "Uh...I'm going downtown to meet a friend...want to come?"

"Sure. I have to call my dad, though. Do I have time?" Laurence nodded. Chloe put on her watch and tied her tennis shoes. "Car or bike?"

"Bike."

Chloe picked up her leather jacket and stuffed her wallet inside. "Give me five minutes to call my dad and I'll be ready."

"No rush."

Chloe ran downstairs and dialed. The answering machine picked up. "Hey Dad. It's me. Just wanted to say hi. I'm doing great. I'll call next week. Love you." She hung up and yelled, "Okay, I'm ready."

Laurence appeared in the doorway. "Let's go."

① ① ①

The ride to Paris was faster than the night before. Laurence had explained to Chloe that they were going to see a friend she had not seen in a long time. The meeting had been set for 4 p.m. in front of the fountains at Les Halles market. At 4:15, Laurence parked her bike on a side street and took off her helmet.

"Okay, here we are. We're not too late. Hopefully Tony is still there."

The street was crowded with artists painting portraits, jugglers putting on a show, and guitarists playing, hoping for some pocket change. The ensemble created a very busy atmosphere full of music and laughter.

Laurence and Chloe walked into a brasserie called "A la Crêpe." Laurence scanned the room for Tony and spotted him in the far corner reading a newspaper. She called across the room. "Hey, Tony!"

Tony waved and got up to meet them.

"Te voilà. Toujours ponctuelle à ce que je vois," said Tony, grabbing Laurence and planting two kisses on her cheeks.

Laurence laughed and moved aside to introduce Chloe.

"C'est mon amie Chloe. Elle ne parle pas très bien le Francais." She then turned to Chloe and introduced Tony to her. "Chloe, this is Tony, a longtime friend."

"Bonjour," said Chloe, shaking Tony's hand.

"My English isn't as good as Ms. Perfect over there, but I will try," said Tony with a heavy accent as he sat and gestured to seat next to him. Chloe smiled and took the offered seat.

The conversation started in English, but as it got more animated French took over. Chloe tried to follow the conversation but soon gave up. Her mind drifted back over the past few days and how much time she and Laurence had spent together. *She is quite something. I'm really going to miss her. Boy, I wish she could stay. I wonder if Tony is one of her ex-boyfriends.*

This last thought somehow bothered Chloe. *I can't imagine her with him...or with anyone for that matter. Come on, Chloe! What is wrong with you, girl? She probably has boyfriends left and right. Look at her, she is stunning.* Chloe looked at Laurence from the corner of her eye. She was engaged in animated conversation with Tony. The heat of the restaurant had given Laurence a nice pinkish shade on her cheeks, highlighting her clear blue eyes. Her red t-shirt showed muscular arms tapering to very elegant hands. For the first time Chloe saw the tiny scar on Laurence's left hand. *I wonder where she got it. It looks like a bad cut...I guess I'll ask her. Boy, I'm going to miss her...* Chloe sighed and took a bite of the chocolate crêpe she had ordered.

"Are you okay? I'm sorry, it must be really boring for you," said Laurence, looking at Chloe with concern.

"No, I'm fine. I was just thinking."

Tony watched the exchange between the two women and smiled to himself.

"Girls, I have to get going anyway. I tell you what. I'm going dancing with some friends tonight. Would you like to come along?"

"Wow, Tony, that would be great," answered Chloe with enthusiasm. "Well...that is, if Laurence wants to," she added.

Laurence had thought of staying in because she still had to finish packing and wanted to have an early start in the morning. She glanced at Chloe, who was looking at her expectantly. "Yes, but we can't stay late."

"Awesome," exclaimed Chloe, giving Laurence a quick squeeze on the hand across the table. Tony's smile grew even larger at the display of affection.

"Great. We'll meet at 11 p.m. at La Joconde, Porte de La Chapelle," said Tony, smiling.

"Tony..." growled Laurence.

"What?" asked Tony innocently.

"You know what. Don't even think about it!" Laurence was looking menacingly at Tony.

"What's wrong? What's going on?" asked Chloe. If Laurence heard her question she didn't flinch, but instead kept her gaze on Tony.

"Laurence?" asked Chloe again, not understanding the situation.

"Be there at 11...I promise you, no set up," smiled Tony.

"You better be true to your word, my friend," answered Laurence.

"I will, I will... Okay, bye Chloe...see you guys tonight." Tony left the restaurant.

Laurence was fiddling with her napkin, avoiding Chloe's questioning gaze.

"Hey, earth to Laurence. What just happened here?"

"Nothing to worry about...want to walk around before we go home to change?"

"Don't change the subject on me. Come on, what happened?"
"You don't take no for an answer, do you?" said Laurence, smiling.
"You know I don't. So, are you going to tell me?"
"You asked for it...Tony always tries to set me up when we go to clubs."
"Okay, but I don't see where the problem is. You're a big girl, you can say no."
"Chloe, do you know what kind of club we just got invited to?"
"Nope. I figure your clubs can't be that different from ours."
Laurence laughed out loud. "Chloe, you're so innocent. We just got invited to a gay club." Laurence took the last bite of her strawberry crêpe and waited for Chloe's reaction.
"What?"
"La Joconde is one of the biggest gay clubs in town." She finished her drink and took her wallet out of her jacket.
"Is Tony gay?" asked Chloe, hesitantly.
Laurence dropped 40 francs on the table. "What do you think? Come on, don't tell me you didn't see it."
"Uh...no, I didn't. I don't think I've ever met anyone gay." Chloe, suddenly feeling shy, reached for her wallet and busied herself counting her cash.
"No need to, I took care of it," Laurence said, pointing to the money on the table. "Maybe we shouldn't go tonight..."
"No, I want to go," exclaimed Chloe.
Laurence sighed. "Okay, but you might be in for a shock."
Chloe nodded. "Laurence, you said that Tony always tries to set you up when you go out with him. If it's a gay club..." Chloe's voice trailed off.
Laurence looked intently at Chloe and waited for her to finish her sentence.
"...he sets you up with other women?" asked Chloe shyly, finishing her sentence.
"He tries."
"Oh," answered Chloe. Not looking at Laurence she asked, "Is he ever successful?"
Laurence smiled at Chloe's shyness. "Chloe, look at me." Chloe slowly brought her eyes to level with Laurence. "The answer is no. He has never found a match for me."

A Year in Paris

"Oh...can I ask you a question?" Laurence nodded. "Are you…"

"…gay?" asked Laurence, finishing Chloe's question.

"Yeah...are you?"

"If being attracted to women makes you gay, then yes I am. But, if having ever had a relationship with a woman is what makes you gay, then no, I'm not."

"I don't get it," said Chloe sincerely.

"Tony thinks I should get involved with another woman because every guy I've been involved with so far has been a jerk. I don't really care at this point if the next person I'm with is a man or woman, I just want them to love me for who I am."

"Oh...that makes more sense."

"I'm surprised you haven't left screaming yet," said Laurence ruefully.

"Why? You're my friend. It doesn't bother me...and thanks."

"For what?"

"For telling me."

"You're welcome," said Laurence with a smile.

They left the restaurant and walked around Les Halles for a little while. It was close to dusk, and the heat of the day dissipated, giving way to the cooler air of the evening. The streets were less crowded than earlier during the day. A couple sat next to a fountain murmuring soft words to each other, the artists were packing up their palettes and pencils, and the musicians were putting away their instruments.

"Wow, it's true what people say," whispered Chloe to herself.

Laurence's acute hearing picked up on Chloe's remark. "What do you mean?"

"I read somewhere in a magazine that everything stopped in Paris around 7 p.m."

Chloe looked around her and took it all in: the orange and red color of the sunset reflecting on the pavement, the smell of fresh bread being baked, the sound of the city getting ready for the evening, and the way Laurence's hair shone with the last sun ray of the day. Chloe shyly smiled at Laurence. "I wish you didn't have to go tomorrow."

"I wish I didn't have to go too," Laurence answered softly.

"Lo, would you do me a favor?" asked Chloe, stopping and facing Laurence.

"Anything...just ask."

"I know you probably are going to be really busy once you get back to school, but would you...." Chloe stopped, suddenly feeling timid.

"Would I what?"

"...call me once in a while...I mean...I don't really know anyone around here. Well, I did meet this guy in the plane, but I mean, I like you and..."

"Yes," answered Laurence, speaking over Chloe's mumble.

Chloe, oblivious to Laurence's answer, kept on going. "...we spent so much time together. I understand if you don't think you'll have time. It's okay, really..."

"Chloe, didn't you hear?" asked Laurence, grabbing Chloe by her shoulder.

"Hear what?"

"Yes, of course I'll keep in touch. Of course I'll call you."

"Really?"

Laurence nodded, not releasing her hold on Chloe's shoulder. "I'll do my best...I...really like you, Chloe. I wonder how you put up with me, but I'm glad you do," said Laurence sincerely.

Chloe looked at Laurence, feeling relief wash over her. *I don't know why I care so much, but I'm glad she didn't turn me down.* "Thanks."

Laurence let go of Chloe's shoulder and teasingly poked her in the ribs. "You're welcome. We're friends, you said so yourself." Laurence looked at her watch. "Listen, we probably should get going. By the time we get home and get ready it'll be time to drive back."

"Okay, let's go. I like this part of Paris. It's so exotic."

"I've never heard anyone call it that, but if you say so." Laurence led Chloe back to the bike.

As soon as they got home, Beatrice called to see when Laurence was leaving, and if she would still be there by the time they got back. It turned out that she hadn't planned on coming home before late evening, and Laurence's train was in early afternoon. Laurence argued a long time with Beatrice about not seeing Clément before she left, but nothing could coax Beatrice into coming home earlier. After the phone conversation, Laurence slammed the phone into its receiver.

"Damn—damn her! ARGHHH!" Laurence paced the living room floor, kicking the furniture in her way. "I can't stand it anymore!"

yelled Laurence at a picture of her dad and Beatrice displayed on top of the entertainment center. She picked up the picture and sent it flying across the room, breaking the frame in pieces. The noise the picture made when it crashed stopped Laurence in her tracks. "What am I doing?" She looked around the room. The phone was on the floor near the door, pieces of glass covered the wooden floor, cushions had been thrown around the room, and the coffee table legs carried the mark of Laurence's boots.

Chloe, who had left Laurence to her privacy after the phone rang, rushed back downstairs after hearing loud crashes. "Laurence, are you alr…" She stopped in the middle of the stairs, seeing the disaster in the living room. "What happened?" she asked, making her way cautiously to the bottom of the steps.

Laurence was kneeling on the floor picking up pieces of glass. "Don't walk in here if you don't have any shoes on," said Laurence, ignoring Chloe's question.

"Laurence, what the hell happened here?" Laurence stood up and sighed, passing her hand in her hair. "My God! Laurence, your hand…you're bleeding." Laurence looked at her hands and realized that the left one was covered with blood.

"It's nothing…just a small cut."

"Small cut! Let me look at it," said Chloe, walking toward Laurence.

"It's nothing really, just leave it," said Laurence, suddenly embarrassed about the situation.

"It could be deep…it looks deep. Where is your first aid kit?"

Laurence stepped away from Chloe. "I told you it's okay," she said forcefully.

"Listen, you're bleeding all over. We need to do something about it."

"Fine…in the bathroom near the library."

"Thanks, now you sit down and let me go get it." Chloe pushed Laurence into a leather chair and ran to get the first aid kit.

She walked back to the living room to find Laurence wearing a defeated look on her face. She chose to ignore it and first take care of the cut. She grabbed a chair from the dining room and positioned it so she could have a clear look at Laurence's left hand. She gently picked it up and started cleaning the wound.

Laurence stared at Chloe. *Why did I let my temper get the best of me? She hasn't even asked me why I trashed the room.*

"It's going to sting a little." Chloe carefully, almost tenderly, tapped some antiseptic on the wound. Laurence didn't flinch; her eyes were still riveted on Chloe. She was taken by her kindness and could not take her mind away from the softness of her hands. *Laurence, you have to get a grip.* She shook her head. "Thanks...it didn't hurt at all...you'd make a good nurse."

Chloe smiled and brushed her blond hair back. She lightly touched Laurence's knee. "Laurence...what happened?"

"I'm sorry...Beatrice...she really has a way of getting to me." Laurence suddenly felt ashamed of her behavior.

"Laurence, she must have done a little more than 'get to' you...you messed up this room pretty bad." Chloe looked around the room, assessing the damages.

Laurence looked at Chloe and got up. "Yeah...well, I'll clean up...no sweat."

"Laurence, please talk to me. What did she say to put you in such a mood?"

Laurence sat on the couch in defeat. "She's not coming back before late evening tomorrow. I won't see Clément before I go...it'd be okay if she wasn't doing it purposely, but she is."

"Are you sure?"

"Yeah...trust me." Chloe sat next to Laurence on the coach.

"Why would she do that?" asked Chloe, lightly touching Laurence's newly bandaged hand.

"Many reasons. Don't want to discuss them now." Laurence abruptly got up and started cleaning the room, indicating clearly that she wasn't going to answer any more questions. Chloe sighed.

"Fine, have it your way. Do you still want to go tonight?"

"Yeah, it should be a good distraction. Why don't you go get ready? We should get going in an hour or so."

"'kay," said Chloe, going back upstairs. Once in her room, she tried to shake off the incident, but her mind couldn't help going back to Laurence and how violent she had gotten after Beatrice's phone call. "You're being silly, she'll never do anything to you," she spoke aloud to herself while choosing her outfit.

Laurence cleaned up the family room and went upstairs to change. Once in her room, she shed her clothes and stepped into the shower.

A Year in Paris 81

The warm water soothed her nerves, and Laurence made a pact with herself that she was not going to let anything ruin her last evening with Chloe. She turned the water off and got out, grabbing a towel to wrap herself in. She wiped the fog off the mirror and stared at herself. Her black hair hung wet on her broad shoulders, and her tanned face looked relaxed and younger than it had in years. Laurence smiled at her reflection, and lightly brushed her fingers under her eyes. *No more bags...wow. I guess I have been sleeping better lately.* She grabbed a brush and started fighting with the knots in her hair. *I bet Chloe doesn't have knot problems. Her hair always looks so silky.* Laurence smiled at the thought. She finally combed through the last knot and ripped the now wet bandage from her hand. The cut had stopped bleeding, and it didn't look too deep.

"I really have to learn to control my temper," sighed Laurence, walking to her bedroom. She looked through her closet and opted for a pair of black jeans and a pale green silk shirt. She put on a light touch of makeup, grabbed a Perrier from her personal reserve and left her room.

Chloe was already waiting. Her eyes settled on Laurence.
"Here you are. You took forever."
"Sorry, I don't usually take so long," apologized Laurence.
"I'm teasing. I just got downstairs. Are we taking your bike?"
"No, I want to be able to drink something. We're taking the metro." Laurence looked at Chloe. She wore light brown eye shadow that intensified the green of her eyes. She had on tight black leather pants and a sleeveless red turtleneck. Her hair was up but some loose strands of hair had fallen around her face, and her ears bore golden earrings in the shape of a sun.

"Laurence, you're staring," exclaimed Chloe.
"Oh, sorry...I...didn't mean..."
Chloe laughed. "It's okay. Are we going or what?"
"Yeah...yeah, we are," answered Laurence, embarrassed. "It's a short walk to the metro."

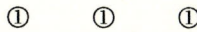

They got off at Porte de La Chapelle. Chloe had been surprised and outraged by the number of homeless people begging for money inside the train. They would climb on at a stop, give a little speech, and go down the aisle with their hands extended, expecting money from people. Chloe's heart had been broken when she saw a young mother entering the train with her newborn to beg for food and money. She had reached for her wallet, but Laurence had stopped her.

"Don't. If you start giving you'll never stop."

They were now walking out of the metro station. The polluted air of Paris seemed almost fresh compared to the smell of sweat and unwashed bodies found in the metro.

"Yuk," said Chloe once they were outside. "God, your metro is gross and dirty. Do all those homeless people sleep in there?"

"For the most part, yeah. It's dirty, but it gets you where you have to go. Not all stations are this bad."

"Glad to know that."

"The club is a few blocks away. Chloe, it's not the best area, so stay close to me and keep one hand on your wallet." Laurence crossed the street, followed by Chloe.

The walls were covered with graffiti and a trashcan had been tipped over, its contents spilled across the pavement. The remains of a burned car stood next to the sidewalk.

"I'm glad I'm not here alone," said Chloe, getting closer to Laurence.

"It's creepy, but I've walked those streets alone, and nothing has ever happened. Don't worry."

"Okay, I'll take your word for it," Chloe answered, speeding her walk.

They took one last turn and found themselves in front of La Joconde. A large crowd was waiting in line, and two bouncers were letting people in after searching them.

"What are they doing?" Chloe asked, taking her place in the line.

"Checking for drugs and weapons."

"Boy, and I thought Paris was the city of love, city of peace."

Laurence laughed. "Come on, Chloe, aren't there any bad areas in Washington?"

"Yeah, I guess so."

"Same here. We just happen to be in one of them."

"Why put a club in a place where people are scared of walking alone?" asked Chloe sarcastically.

"Because French people are very narrow minded and would never put a gay club in a fancy neighborhood, that's why."

"Oh..." Chloe had not thought about that. She had always been told that the French were very promiscuous and open to any kind of sexuality.

"I know what Americans think of the French, that we sleep with everyone and cheat on our partners. Isn't that true?" asked Laurence.

"Well... It's what I heard."

"Chloe, you can't believe everything everyone tells you. I know that my family is not the best example because of Beatrice, but trust me, people don't make a habit of cheating on their spouses. Also, the French are very old fashioned, so the gay movement is not very popular." Laurence pushed Chloe forward. "Go on, it's our turn."

Once the bouncer opened the door, the music burst out, enveloping Laurence and Chloe in its rhythm. They entered a large room with people dancing in the middle, bars surrounding the room on each side.

"Tony is upstairs. Come on," said Laurence, shouting to be heard above the music. Wooden stairs stood at the extreme right of the room, leading up to a series of balconies overlooking the dance floor below, off of which several open rooms were accessible. Laurence pushed Chloe toward the furthest room on the right. Tony was sitting with three of his friends on a couch at the end of the room. The room was small but nicely decorated. Black and white photographs of men and women hung on the walls, and a leather couch and black coffee table complemented its atmosphere. Tony spotted Laurence and Chloe.

"Hey, girls! Over here," he yelled.

They made their way to Tony. Laurence kissed Tony lightly on the cheek and shook hands with his friends.

"Guys, this is my friend Laurence and her family's adorable new au pair coming straight from the States. Honey, what's your name again?" Tony asked, putting his arm around Chloe's shoulders.

"Chloe."

"Chloe, Laurence, those are my friends Sylvain and Marc, and this is my special friend Clovis." Tony plopped himself back on the couch and grabbed Clovis's hand to drive his point across. Laurence smiled and pulled over two chairs from a nearby table. She offered one to Chloe, who sat down, smiling her thanks.

The room was far enough from the dance floor that conversation was possible. The music was still loud, but screaming was not necessary anymore.

"Do you girls want to drink something?" asked Tony.

"Yeah, but I'll get it," answered Laurence. "Chloe, would you like something?" asked Laurence, getting up.

" A Coke, please."

"J'croyais que les Americains étez élever à la bière," said Sylvain sarcastically while sipping his drink. He had bleached blond hair, an earring in his left ear, penetrating brown eyes, and was wearing a white t-shirt and a simple pair of blue jeans. Chloe looked at him. She understood what he had said, and knew he was probably joking, but she could not find the words in French to answer.

"Hey, play nice," said Laurence. "Chloe doesn't speak much French, so the rule is that if you want to make fun, you have to do it in English so you guys are on equal ground. Get it?" Laurence's face bore a smile, but her eyes were intensely fixed on Sylvain, leaving no doubt that her request had better be agreed to.

"I was just joking," answered Sylvain.

Laurence ignored him and turned to Chloe. "I'll be right back."

"'kay."

"I'll keep an eye on her," joked Tony, smiling at Laurence. Laurence left the room glancing one final time at Chloe. "Boy, she sure is protective," commented Tony.

Tony lit a cigarette and offered one to Chloe.

"No thanks. I don't smoke," she answered.

Tony nodded. "So, Chloe, how do you like your stay so far?"

"I like it. Laurence took me to the castle of Versailles yesterday. It was great." Chloe smiled at the memory.

"You're here for one year?"

"Yeah."

"Beatrice hasn't driven you crazy yet?" asked Tony with a smile.

"You know about her?" Chloe was somehow surprised.

"Yeah, Laurence and I go back a long way." Tony took a puff from his cigarette and seemed to be contemplating his next question. "You guys seem to get along very well."

"I think so. We didn't start out that way, but we have come a long way." Chloe looked at Tony, wondering where this round of questions was taking her.

"She's been through lots of crap, so treat her well." Before Chloe had time to ask what he meant by that, Laurence had made her way back to the table with their drinks.

"Here you go." She handed Chloe her drink and sat down. "Tony, I hope you haven't been bothering Chloe," she said half jokingly, half seriously.

"No, I've been a perfect gentleman." Tony suddenly stood up and grabbed Clovis's hand. "I love this song. Come on, let's go dance." Clovis got up and laced his fingers with Tony's. "Are you girls coming?" asked Tony.

"Let's go, Lo," said Chloe getting up.

"No, go right ahead. I'm just going to sit here for a while."

"You're such a party pooper," said Tony, putting his free arm around Chloe's shoulders. "Come on babe, let's go boogie. Are you guys coming?" he asked Sylvain and Marc. Without further delay, he led Clovis and Chloe out with Sylvain and Marc following close behind. Chloe glanced back briefly at Laurence before being dragged out. Laurence sat back in her chair and let her gaze wander over Chloe's form until she was out of sight. She slowly lifted her glass to her lips and let the cold liquid go down her throat, the bitterness of the alcohol making her frown.

Meanwhile, the others had made their way downstairs. They forged a path through the crowd of dancers and started moving to the music. Chloe let her gaze wander around the room and stopped it on two women locked in a kiss, dancing to their own rhythm, oblivious to the crowd. She had expected to bolt or at least feel disgusted, but instead she was riveted and could not take her eyes away. Tony followed Chloe's gaze and smiled to himself.

Chloe finally turned her focus back to Tony and his partner, and she smiled faintly at Tony. The crowd of dancers had gotten larger and space was more and more limited. Tony and Clovis were dancing closer and closer, their bodies almost rubbing against each other. Couples were forming and the throbbing lights were pulsing to the increasing rhythm of the music. Chloe started feeling oppressed, her movements were restricted and breathing was becoming difficult because of the hot smoky air. She suddenly stopped dancing and brought her hand to her forehead to wipe the sweat off.

"Chloe, are you okay?" asked Tony, touching Chloe on the shoulder.

"I feel a little dizzy…I…I think I'm going to go sit down for a while. I'll be back." She abruptly pushed Tony out of the way and headed for the stairs, elbowing people out of her way. When she arrived in the room, she stopped dead in her tracks at what she saw.

Laurence was sitting on the couch sipping her drink and talking to some woman. Chloe knew she should be making herself known, but something told her to stay back. Laurence threw her head back and her laugh reverberated through the room, reaching Chloe's ears. The stranger scooted closer to Laurence and caressed her knee with one hand while she turned Laurence's face towards her with the other. Chloe's heart sped up at the sight and the dizziness she felt earlier came rushing back. She passed her hand through her hair and propped herself against the wall to keep her balance. She bravely looked in Laurence's direction, expecting to find the two women in an intimate position, but instead found herself staring into Laurence's eyes.

Chloe broke the gaze, turned around and ran down the stairs. She elbowed her way through the dance floor, passing Tony and Clovis, but ignored them.

"What the h…go get Laurence, I'm going to go make sure she is all right," Tony said to Clovis. Clovis nodded and hurried upstairs. Tony went in search of Chloe outside. He opened the exit door and stepped into the fresh night air. Chloe was sitting on the sidewalk, her back against the wall, her eyes closed.

"Hey, you're okay?"

She recognized his voice and kept her eyes closed. "Yeah, I just needed some fresh air."

"What happened back there?"

"Don't know." She didn't want to answer and just wanted to be left alone. Yes, the throbbing lights and the smoke had been part of her sudden nausea, but what had pushed her to run was the sight of Laurence almost being kissed by a woman. *I don't get it. Why should I care what she does? I'm not attracted to women… I'm not supposed to be attracted to women. Oh shit, what is wrong with me?*

"Clovis went to get Laurence. Can I get you a glass of water?" asked Tony.

Tony, I just wish you could go away right now, so I can sort out my emotions…as if bringing Laurence here is going to help.

"No, thanks, Tony. I'll be fine in just a minute." The door opened suddenly and Laurence came rushing out, followed by Clovis. She knelt next to Chloe.

"Chloe, what's wrong?" She had gotten frantic with worry when Clovis had told her to come quick because Chloe wasn't feeling well. Laurence touched Chloe's forehead, her cheeks, and finally grabbed her hands. Chloe had opened her eyes at Laurence's first touch and was now looking at their joined hands. She felt warmth going through her and a sense of security.

"I just felt a little dizzy inside. Nothing to worry about. Probably the smoke, I'm not used to it."

Laurence brushed the back of her hand against Chloe's cheek and kept one hand intertwined with Chloe's. "You feel warm to me. I think I should take you home."

"No. I don't want to spoil your last night in town. If you call me a cab and give him the address I can go back by myself. Please don't cut it short because of me."

"No way I'm letting you go back alone." Laurence stood up suddenly and extended her hand to Chloe. "Can you get up?"

"Yeah, I think so." She grabbed Laurence's hand and let herself be yanked to her feet. As soon as Laurence let go of her hand, she started to crumble. Laurence caught her and held her up. "We're going home."

"Okay," said Chloe weakly.

Laurence turned to Tony and Clovis who were still standing outside. "Guys, we are going to call it a night. Thanks for everything."

"Okay, call me when you get back to school." Tony lightly kissed Laurence on the lips. "Bye, Chloe, I hope you feel better." He gave her a quick squeeze on the arm, grabbed Clovis's hand, and left.

"I have to hail a cab. Do you want to sit back down?"

"No, I'm okay. Go ahead." Laurence slowly let go of Chloe. She stepped off the sidewalk and starting waving at cabs passing by. After a few minutes, one stopped. She went back to Chloe and helped her get in the cab. Once Chloe was secured, she got in the other side.

"Versailles, rue de Provence."

"Oui madame," answered the cab driver. "Voulez vous prendre l'autoroute ou le periferique?"

"J'm'en fiche, le plus rapide."

"D'accord."

Laurence turned to Chloe who was propped up against the door, her eyes closed.

"How are you feeling?" asked Laurence.

"I'm okay. Really, we could have stayed longer."

"Come on, Chloe, cut the crap. Five minutes ago you could barely stand up." Laurence's reply was made with more animosity than she intended.

"Please, Laurence, don't be mad...I'm sorry," Chloe said softly. For a brief moment she thought she had been reacquainted with the Laurence she first met, abrupt, rude and constantly annoyed with her.

Laurence's annoyance vanished as soon as Chloe spoke. Chloe looked so miserable, her hair hung in her face, and she was staring at her hands lying on her lap.

"I didn't mean to sound bitchy. I'm sorry. You're not feeling well, and I'm being obnoxious," said Laurence, scooting closer to Chloe.

Chloe looked hesitantly at Laurence who was now only a few inches away. "Sorry I ruined your evening, and I didn't mean to spy on you earlier."

"Don't worry about it. I was trying to find a way to get rid of this person, so it was perfect timing."

"I still feel bad."

"Please don't... I was worried about you," whispered Laurence.

"Really?"

"Yeah." She pulled Chloe towards her, so she could lay her head on her shoulder. "Use me as a pillow, I'll wake you up when we get home." Chloe let Laurence wrap her arm around her shoulder, and softly put her head down. She tried to fight sleep, but her eyelids felt heavy.

"Don't try to stay awake. I promise I won't leave you in the cab," kidded Laurence, her breath softly brushing against Chloe's hair. So, as the car went down the highway and Paris was left behind, Chloe closed her eyes and surrendered to sleep.

Laurence sat in the cab with Chloe asleep in her arms and watched the street lights go by, adjusting her hold on Chloe. *I don't know what's wrong with me. I was so worried for her. Why? Less than a week ago we were strangers. Going away is going to do me some good. I'll*

go back to school and forget about this week. Forget...yeah, that's probably the safest...

The cab pulled up to the gate. Laurence softly shook Chloe awake. "Hey, sleepyhead, we're home...come on, wake up."

Chloe opened her eyes, and sat up. "Are we there already?"

Laurence chuckled. "Yeah, you slept all the way. How are you feeling?" she asked while handing the cab driver his fare and opening the door. She stepped out and turned to help Chloe.

"I'm okay."

Laurence slammed the cab door. "Good. A good night's sleep, and you'll be as good as new."

"Hope so." Chloe yawned and followed Laurence who had just opened the gate. They stepped inside the courtyard. The high brick walls made it a nest away from the city noise. A light was still burning on the second floor of the house next door.

"Guess our neighbors are burning the midnight oil," remarked Chloe.

"Yeah, looks like." Laurence opened the front door and walked into the dark house. She felt around for the light switch. "Damn, where is it? I can never find this damn...here we go," she exclaimed turning the light on.

Chloe walked past Laurence into the kitchen and poured herself a glass of water. "Want some water?"

"No, I'm going to call it a night."

Chloe walked into the family room and sat down on the couch, sipping her water. The dizziness of earlier had disappeared. *Must have really been the smoke,* she thought, putting her glass down on the coffee table and unlacing her shoes. "Lo, when are you leaving tomorrow?"

"Since I can't see Clément, first thing in the morning."

"Will I see you?" asked Chloe, her heart suddenly beating faster with anxiety.

"Don't think so." Laurence started up the stairs. "It was great hanging out with you. Bye."

Chloe sat dumbfounded for a few minutes. *What? That's it? Great hanging out with you, bye? What the hell?* Tears started slowly falling down Chloe's cheeks. *She can't just walk away like that after everything we shared.*

"Damn her. I'm not going to let her get away so easily." Chloe got up angrily and ran up the stairs, decided to at least get a proper goodbye out of Laurence. *Who the hell does she think she is?*

Laurence's door was closed, but Chloe didn't even bother knocking. She barged into the room in a fury. "Laurence, what the hell was all of that about? 'Great hanging out with you, bye.' I thought we had a little more going on than just the usual great to meet you," yelled Chloe, walking toward Laurence, who was standing at the window with a surprised look on her face. "What was all this fuss about being worried about me earlier if you feel like you can just turn your back on me and leave? Were you just lying?" Chloe stopped to catch her breath, tears rolling down her cheeks, her eyes a deep dark green, her face red with anger.

Laurence had not moved. She was standing near the window, not knowing what to do, not knowing if she should let herself do what she really wanted to do. Her fists were clenched and she was staring intensely into Chloe's eyes, her heart melting at the view of the tears she had caused. Suddenly she made a decision and stepped forward. She reached for Chloe's face and gently wiped her tears, not once looking away.

They spent what seemed an eternity staring into each other's eyes. Chloe's tears had stopped, and she could only feel the warmth of Laurence's hands on her face. Slowly, Laurence took a step forward and drew Chloe into her arms, wrapping them tightly around her. Chloe let go of the tension she had been holding and started crying again. Not a word had been exchanged. Laurence tightened her grip on Chloe and lightly kissed the top of her head.

"I'm sorry. I don't know how to let you go. It scares me, Chloe. I thought that by just walking away, it would be easier. I was selfish, I only thought about myself. I never thought you cared. I'm sorry; please don't cry. I really was worried earlier, and it scares me to think I could care so much."

Chloe's tears had dried, giving way to soft sniffles. She lifted her head up and looked at Laurence with red puffy eyes. "I'm sorry I burst into your room like that, but the thought that you could leave without really saying goodbye horrified me. I could not believe after what we shared this week that you could walk away so easily."

Laurence sighed and squeezed Chloe one last time before releasing her. She walked to her bed and sat down, patting the area next to her for Chloe to sit down. Once Chloe was settled next to her she spoke again. "I don't know what's happening to me, Chloe. When I'm not with you, I think about you. When I'm with you, I can't stop looking at you. I..." She stopped, at a lost for with words.

Chloe reached for Laurence's hand. "Please...go on."

Laurence looked at Chloe and nodded. She took a deep breath and tightened her grip on Chloe's hand. "Do you remember what we spoke about this afternoon? About what Tony believes about me?" Chloe nodded. "I think he might be right." Chloe suddenly withdrew her hand. "I'm sorry, Chloe. That's mostly the reason I thought it would be better to just leave tonight without properly saying goodbye." Laurence stared at the door, not daring to look at Chloe.

Chloe had been surprised by Laurence's statement, but still wasn't sure about one thing. "Laurence, do you think you like me...I mean do you think you..."

"Yes, I think so... Oh, I don't know, I'm confused. It's all new to me," interrupted Laurence, roughly passing her hand through her hair.

"What about earlier at the club? That woman..."

"I told you I didn't know how to get rid of her. I've been battling with the feeling I have for you for a while, and maybe I wanted to see if it was just you or...I don't know what I'm talking about." Laurence passed her hand through her hair nervously.

"What do you want from me?" asked Chloe hesitantly.

"Nothing," exclaimed Laurence abruptly. "Chloe, I'll deal with it. I know that until today you had never even been in touch with a homosexual...I...I'm not asking you for anything except your friendship. I'll go away for a few months and deal with that on my own. You'll see, it'll be all gone by the time I come back," said Laurence, rushing through.

"What if I don't want you to?" whispered Chloe, fiddling with the blanket.

"What?"

"What if I don't want you to?" repeated Chloe loudly.

"What do you mean?"

"What if I didn't want you to stop thinking about me this way?" asked Chloe timidly.

"Chloe, you don't know what you're asking."

"You assumed I want to run away from this. Why? Because I had never been exposed to homosexuality before today? Why do you assume you're the only one having those feelings?"

"Chloe…"

"No, let me finish. The smoke wasn't the only reason why I was sick earlier. Confusion was a big part of it. While I was dancing I saw two women kissing and wondered what it felt like. I couldn't help thinking about you. My brain was telling me no, but my heart was saying yes, then I went back upstairs and I saw you with that woman, and it hurt. I'm as confused as you are Laurence, but I know one thing."

"What's that?" asked Laurence, swallowing with difficulty.

"There is something strong between us, and I'm not willing to just brush it away and pretend it's not here."

A long silence established itself. The only noises in the room were those of far away cars and a barking dog. Laurence broke the silence. "What do you suggest we do?"

"I don't know," answered Chloe, suddenly feeling drained. "I don't know how much I'm ready for or what I can give you."

"Let's take it slow. No strings attached. I don't know what I'm ready for either."

Chloe nodded. "I guess I should get going." She got up and slowly walked to the door.

"Chloe, wait…please stay…" Laurence got up and extended her hand to Chloe.

"Lo, we just said let's take it slow."

"I just want to hold you through the night. I'm leaving tomorrow, and I want to know I was with you until the last minute." Her hand was still extended. Her blue eyes were almost begging. Chloe paused a few moments and looked at Laurence's hand, and she reached for it. Laurence smiled and walked toward the bed. She removed the top cover, took her shoes off, and lay on the bed. Chloe removed her shoes and climbed in bed next to Laurence. She lay down next to her, not daring to touch. Laurence scooted closer and shyly grabbed Chloe's hands. "Is that okay?" she asked, unsure.

"I have a better idea," answered Chloe, moving up on her side and laying her head on Laurence's shoulder. "Is that okay?"

"Yeah, it's great," answered Laurence. She reached for the switch, turned the light off, and pulled the blanket over both of them. "Good night, Chloe."

"Good night, Lo." Chloe snuggled closer and closed her eyes. She quickly drifted off to sleep, feeling safe and secure.

Laurence lightly kissed the top of Chloe's head. Her last thought before falling asleep was, *What do we do now?*

① ① ①

Laurence finished brushing her hair and looked at the clock. *7:30. I should get going if I want to get the 8:30 train.* She silently put her jacket on and walked to the bed where Chloe was still fast asleep, holding the pillow Laurence had been sleeping on. Laurence contemplated the idea of just leaving her a note but decided against it. *No more running away.* She quietly sat on the bed and tenderly brushed her fingers over Chloe's forehead. Chloe mumbled something and buried herself deeper into the pillow. Laurence gently shook Chloe to wake her.

"Chloe, I have to go," whispered Laurence.

Chloe opened her eyes and looked around the room, disoriented. Her gaze settled on Laurence and a smile lit her face. "Good morning."

"Good morning. I have to leave, but I wanted to say goodbye."

Chloe sat up in the bed. "Do you really have to go so early?"

"Yeah, my train leaves at 8:30." Laurence looked at Chloe, not knowing what to do or what to say next. "I...I guess I'll call you." She got up, straightened her jacket and turned around, but was stopped by a hand on her arm.

"Wait," said Chloe, forcing Laurence to face her. "You forgot something."

"What's that?"

"This," answered Chloe, stepping forward and hugging Laurence. Laurence buried her face in Chloe's hair.

"You should go back to sleep, it's very early. You can use my room when I'm gone, you know."

Chloe released her hold on Laurence, squeezed her hands and stepped back. "Thanks, I probably will. At least you have a phone," she smiled.

"Yep, and cable too."

"Oh yeah, this room is mine," laughed Chloe. Laurence brushed a strand of loose hair behind her ear and picked up her suitcase.

"I should go." She stood for a few moments looking at Chloe, not knowing what to do. She opened the door and turned to Chloe one last time. Chloe had not moved from where she stood after the hug. Her hair was disheveled, black streaks of make up covered her cheeks and her shirt was wrinkled. Laurence took it all in as if trying to store Chloe's picture in her mind. "I really should go."

Chloe nodded and swallowed hard. "'kay."

"I'll call," said Laurence before abruptly walking out of the room and closing the door. Chloe stood staring at the door for a few moments. She heard the front door close behind Laurence and looked out the window. She yanked it open and shouted to Laurence, who was already walking down the sidewalk. "Laurence!" Laurence turned around and looked up at Chloe. They both smiled. No words were needed; their smiles held the promise of the future.

Chapter 6

Chloe closed the window and walked back to the bed. She contemplated going back to sleep, but decided against it. She showered and got dressed before going downstairs for breakfast. Sitting alone at the kitchen table sipping her orange juice, Chloe felt lonely, and her mind kept drifting back to the evening Clément had slathered Laurence's hair with pizza sauce. She tried to shake the images away, but everywhere she looked something reminded her of Laurence.

"Boy, that's not good. I wonder how long her train ride is..." Chloe mused to herself. She rose and cleaned up the remains of her breakfast. She thought of going for a walk, but the fear of missing Laurence's phone call kept her in the house. She decided to settle in the library and read some more of Baudelaire's poems.

The morning went by slowly. Chloe tried to concentrate on her reading, but the task was almost impossible. Shortly after noon, the phone rang. Chloe jumped to her feet and ran to the family room. "Hello?"

"*Bonjour, c'est Beatrice.*"

"Oh, bonjour, c'est Chloe," she answered, the disappointment obvious in her voice.

"*Hi Chloe, you seem somewhat surprised. Were you expecting someone else to call?*"

"No...no."

"Has Laurence left already?"

"Yes, early this morning."

"Hm...too bad...I'm getting off the highway, and we should be home in the next twenty minutes. See you then." Beatrice hung up.

"You witch. You're not sorry at all that Laurence has already left," said Chloe after hanging up.

Twenty minutes later, Chloe heard a car pulling in through the gate. She opened the front door and stepped out to welcome Beatrice. Beatrice opened the door of her Mercedes, and Chloe heard the sound of Clément crying.

"Oh good, Chloe, you're here. Would you mind getting him? He has been crying on and off since we left my parents'...I can't stand it anymore." She left the car doors open and walked into the house, assuming her request would be obeyed. Chloe opened the back door and reached for Clément, who was still strapped into his car seat.

"Hush, hush...what's wrong babe? Huh? Had a bad trip?" She picked him up and closed the car door. "It's okay." Clément's cries became hiccups mixed with tears. "Boy, I think I know why you're crying...you need a change of diaper...Come on." She carried him upstairs to his bathroom. Beatrice could be heard from her room, talking on the phone. Chloe lay Clément down on his changing table and started pulling off his pants. "Geeze, Clément! When was the last time you were changed? Look at this mess."

Clément's cries stopped as soon as his diaper was off. His discomfort had obviously been the cause of his screams. "Sweetheart, would you like to take a bath? It would probably help you feel better." Clément nodded between sniffles. "Okay, then. Let's get these clothes off you."

"Chloe?" called Beatrice from her bedroom.

"In Clément's bathroom," yelled Chloe.

Beatrice popped her head through the door. "Listen, I would really appreciate if you could take care of Clément. I have to go out...some business I have to take care of. Is that okay?"

Boy, if I let her get away with that, she is going to ask me to take care of him at the last minute all the time. Chloe was ready to say that she had already made some plans, but one look at Clément's tear-stained face made her change her mind. "Sure, no problem."

"Thanks. If it runs late I might stay in a hotel since I have to drive back to Paris tomorrow for work. Anyway, don't worry...bye." Beatrice's high heels were heard clicking down the stairs, the door opened and closed, and the car left the courtyard.

"Well, big guy, it's just you and me." For the first time since Beatrice had stepped out of the car, Clément smiled. Chloe finished undressing him and stood him up on the floor while turning the water on. "Ready to go in?" She grabbed him under the arms and picked him up high in the air, making him fly above her head. Clément started giggling. "That's better than crying. Come on little airplane, into the tub." She sat him in the tub and grabbed a bunch of toys from the toy-net attached to the wall. "Here you go."

Chloe let him play for a few minutes and started washing him. "Hey, buddy, you've got to get up so I can wash your legs." Clément stood up, splashing water everywhere. "Hey, little monster, be careful."

"Funny!" laughed Clément.

"Yeah, yeah, funny. You're the one taking the bath, not me," smiled Chloe. "Wow, what happened to your hip, you've got a huge bruise right here." She gently brushed her fingers on the purpled area. Clément flinched. "It still hurts? You must have fallen pretty hard. Are you ready to get out?"

"No...no..." said Clément, sitting back in the tub.

"Come on babe, I'll go play Legos with you."

At the mention of his precious Legos, Clément stood up and opened his arms to Chloe so she could pick him up.

While dressing him, she took a look at his bruised hip again. "There isn't much I can do for it, babe. I wonder what you did to hurt yourself so badly." She finished dressing him—making the decision not to put a diaper back on since they were trying to train him—and brought him down from the changing table. "Here you go."

"Lego?"

"Yeah, lead the way." Clément grabbed Chloe's hand and dragged her downstairs to the playroom. For more than an hour they built castles and airplanes out of Lego blocks. Clément seemed to have the mind of a future architect, building complicated patterns and being very careful to match colors, even taking apart a wall Chloe had just built because she had mixed blue and red blocks.

"Hey, sweetie, you want a snack?" asked Chloe.

"Yes," said Clément excitedly, getting up and running to the kitchen.

"Boy, he doesn't waste any time." She followed him to the kitchen. In the kitchen Clément was already sitting at the table, his little legs dangling from the chair. He smiled at Chloe when she walked in and started banging his hands on the table.

"Coe, drum."

"Yeah, yeah, drum...noisy too. Come on, stop that. Wait a minute, did you just call me by my name?"

"Coe," repeated Clément.

"No, no, Chlo-e," repeated Chloe, enunciating her name to Clément.

"Coe!" said Clément again.

"Okay, okay, forget it. Coe it is. At least for the moment. What do you want to eat?" Chloe opened the fridge and gazed inside. "What about a fruit cup?"

Clément grimaced. "No. Cookies!"

"I tell you what. You eat half of the fruit cup and you can have a cookie. Deal?" she said, giving her hand to Clément to seal the deal.

Clément laughed and slapped her hand. "'kay."

"Good, here you go." She placed the fruit cup and the cookie in front of Clément. He started reaching for the cookie, but Chloe stopped him. "No, no, what did we just say? Fruit first and cookie last." Clément looked at Chloe and grabbed his spoon. "Good, much better. Now you eat, and we'll go for a walk after. What time is it?" Chloe looked at the clock hung on the kitchen wall. "4:30. Yeah, we'll have time for a walk." *Why hasn't she called yet?*

Clément finished his snack and jumped off his chair. "Catch me, 'loe." He took off running toward the family room.

"Boy, he is going to kill me." She took off behind him. "Here I come." She heard giggles coming from the family room, but Clément was nowhere to be found once she got there. "Where are you? Oh, I get it, now we're playing hide-and-seek. Guess I'm it." She looked briefly behind the couch and spotted Clément but decided to prolong the game. "I wonder where Clément is? Clément?" Suddenly keys were heard in the front door and someone stepped through the door. Chloe ran to the entrance. "Who's there?"

"Hello," said the voice. At the sound of the voice, Clément burst out of his hiding place and ran to the door. "Papa, papa!" He jumped into the stranger's arms.

"Hey, p'tit gars. Regarde moi. Comme tu as grandi!" He picked up Clément and hugged him tight, kissing him profusely. "Tu m'as manqué. Je t'ai ramené quelque chose."

"Un jouet?" asked Clément.

"Hum...peut-être," he joked. He put Clément down. "You must be Chloe. I'm Jean."

"Oh, hi," said Chloe, shaking his hand. "I wasn't expecting you before next week."

"Some of my meetings got cancelled. Has Laurence left already?"

"Yes, early this morning. I'm sure she would have stayed longer if she had known."

"That's too bad. I was hoping she'd still be here," said Jean, disappointment obvious in his voice. "I guess I'll call her later on tonight. What about Beatrice?"

"Uh, she left. She said she had some business to attend to."

"Hum...okay," answered Jean, dismissing the topic. "Listen, it's still nice outside, I want to take Clément for a walk in the park. Would you like to join us?"

"I don't want to bother you."

"No, really, I wouldn't have asked otherwise. So, is that a yes?" smiled Jean.

"I'd love to," smiled Chloe. Jean's good mood was contagious, and she found the loneliness she felt after Laurence's departure slowly go away.

"Great. I'll go change for some more suitable clothes, and we can get going."

Chloe looked at Jean. He was wearing a dark blue business suit and his tie was loose around his neck. *I understand where Laurence's height comes from*, thought Chloe. Indeed, Jean was tall, his lean body enlarged by broad shoulders, and his face was slightly tanned. He had a large forehead with dark black eyebrows guarding eyes as black as a crow's. A few wrinkles circled his mouth, and hair that must once have been dark as night now bore silver streaks around the temples. *I guess Laurence gets her blue eyes from her mother. I wonder who Clément gets them from...must skip a generation.*

Jean picked up Clément, who was still clinging to his father's leg.

"Come on, big guy. Want to come upstairs with me so I can give you your present?" Jean walked upstairs carrying Clément.

"Boy, that's quite a change from Beatrice," murmured Chloe. She rushed to her bedroom to put on a sweatshirt. On her way back down, she heard Clément giggle. *Yep, definitely a change.*

They went to the castle park. Jean had brought a ball and ran around with Clément teaching him how to play soccer. Clément proudly wore his gifts from Jean, a pair of toy binoculars and a baseball hat, and he looked adorable. After a few minutes of running around, Jean stopped and ran to Chloe who was sitting on the grass watching the game. "Come on, I shouldn't be the only one getting tired here." Chloe got up and joined them.

An hour later, Chloe and Jean collapsed on the ground exhausted. Clément ran to his dad and tried to get him to get up. "Jouer enco'e papa. Allez."

"Non, j'en peux plus," laughed Jean.

The sun had started to set, and the previously crowded park was almost empty. "I tell you what. I'll take you guys to McDonald's. It will be just like home for you, Chloe," joked Jean.

"Hey, we eat other things besides burgers," exclaimed Chloe with a good-natured grin.

"I know...I was just joking," answered Jean, smiling. "Hey sport, you can get a happy meal. They have toys inside."

Clément started jumping around. "Toys...Coe come?" he asked, grabbing her hand and looking at her expectantly.

"I think so," she answered, getting up and brushing the grass off her pants.

"I think he really likes you. Good, because we had bad luck with the other au pairs," remarked Jean.

"Yeah, Laurence told me."

"I know Beatrice left you guys alone when she went away to her parents' with Clément. Was Laurence nice to you?" Jean grabbed Clément's hand and walked back to the car parked outside the gates.

"Yes sir, very. She showed me tons of things around Versailles. I had a great time."

"Oh good. My daughter has been known to have quite a bad attitude sometimes," said Jean as he started the car. "Okay, let's go. I'm famished."

① ① ①

Over burgers, Jean told Chloe stories about Laurence as a child, and how strongly Clément resembled her. Chloe was fascinated to learn that Laurence took riding lessons for ten years; how, like Clément, she always tried to get her way with everything; and how at the age of five she took off by herself and managed to get to the metro and ride to Paris while her parents were frantically looking for her at home. Her father was obviously crazy about her, and the tone of his voice reflected great pride.

"Yes, she is quite something," he added, finishing his food. He adjusted Clément's napkin and wiped the corner of his mouth with it. "Clément, you're a mess."

"She is also a very talented painter," added Chloe.

"She let you up in her room...wow," said Jean surprised.

"Why is it that surprising?"

"I can't remember the last time she let anyone up there, let alone me!" exclaimed Jean. "She likes you. Good, my daughter is a very lonely person, and she doesn't have many friends. I'm glad you guys get along." Jean got up and picked up Clément. "I'll go wash his hands and we can get going." He left in search of the bathroom.

I really hope she hasn't called while we were out...I wonder if I could pry her phone number out of her dad, thought Chloe.

Once home, Chloe asked Jean if she could check the phone messages using the excuse that her dad may have called.

"Sure, the answering machine is near the phone."

Chloe pressed the flashing red light, but to her disappointment she heard Beatrice's voice instead. *"Hi Chloe, my meeting lasted longer than planned, and some of my co-workers invited me out for dinner. Don't wait up. Thanks."* Beep, and the answering machine went quiet.

"Damn, she hasn't called," mumbled Chloe for herself.

"What is it? Did your dad call?" called Jean from the family room where he was reading a book to Clément.

"No, he didn't. I...I was also hoping that Laurence would call to say she made it," answered Chloe.

"Probably not...my daughter is not big on phones and even less on keeping in touch. I'll call her later." Jean looked up to see a very disappointed Chloe. "What? Did she promise you she'd call?"

"Well...sort of...I just wanted to know if she got there safely," fumbled Chloe.

Jean shook his head. "I'm sorry if she said she'd call and hasn't. As I was saying, she is not very reliable for that. I wouldn't expect hearing from her until next time she comes down here."

"Oh, okay," answered Chloe softly.

"Hey, don't worry about it, you'll meet plenty of people during the year. I can give you her number if that makes you feel better." Jean didn't wait for Chloe's answer. He moved Clément off his lap and grabbed an address book from one of the coffee table's drawers. He scribbled a number on a torn piece of paper and handed it to Chloe. "Here you go."

"Thanks. I guess I'll go upstairs now if you don't mind."

"No, of course. I'm going to put the monster to bed in a few."

"I gave him a bath this afternoon already."

"Oh, okay. Thanks."

"Goodnight."

"Could you come down around 7 a.m. tomorrow? I have to go to the office, and who knows about Beatrice."

"Sure. Oh, I almost forgot, Beatrice left a message." Chloe went up the wooden staircase, holding the piece of paper tight in her hand.

She first walked to her bedroom and lay down on her bed in the dark. "Damn, what do I do now? Call her or not?" Chloe sat up and reached for the remote control and flipped the TV on. The brightness of the screen lit up the room, making her squint. She flipped through channels for a short time and settled on a game show. After a few minutes of trying to concentrate on translating, Chloe gave up. She stood up, grabbed the piece of paper with Laurence's phone number and left her room. She stopped in front of Laurence's door, took a deep breath and entered. The unmade bed still carried the shape of their bodies. Chloe gently smoothed out the blanket and grabbed the phone.

"Here goes nothing..." she said while dialing.

"*Allo?*"

"*Oui, bonsoir, je voudrais parler à Laurence*," asked Chloe with her best French accent.

"*Laurence*," yelled the voice. "*Téléphone.*"

"*D'accord, merci...allo?*"

"Laurence?" asked Chloe, her voice almost shaking.

"*Chloe, is that you?*"

"Uh...yeah...I just wanted to know if you made it back home." Chloe sat on the bed and fumbled with the telephone cord.

"*Yeah, I'm fine. How did you get my number?*" Laurence's voice sounded cold, almost harsh.

"Uh...your dad gave it to me."

"*My dad? Is he back?*"

"Yes, he was sorry he missed you."

"*Yeah, I bet. How is Clément?*"

"Good, very good. We all went to the park this afternoon and played soccer...it was fun."

"*I'm sure it was.*" A voice was heard in the background. "*Yeah, yeah, I'm coming... Okay, Chloe, I have to get going. Thanks for calling.*"

"Uh...okay...when will I talk to you again?"

"*School starts again tomorrow, and I'm going to get really busy...I'm rarely home...*"

"I see your dad was right..." said Chloe sadly.

"*What did my dad say?*" asked Laurence, a hint of anger in her voice.

"That you weren't very big on keeping in touch or calling people. I'm sorry if I thought that after last night..." her voice trailed off.

"*Listen, I really have to go...I'm afraid you're expecting too much from me here. I don't know what I can give you...we talked about that...we agreed...*"

"Yeah, we did," sighed Chloe. "Go and have fun, Laurence. Bye." She hung up, not waiting for Laurence to answer.

In Lille, Laurence hung up the phone and sighed. *I have to give her a chance to back out...* She walked slowly to the door, picked up her keys, and looked one last time at the silent phone before leaving the apartment.

In Paris, Chloe sat dumbfounded on the bed, her fists clenching the covers over and over again, tears falling slowly down her cheeks. She got up, taking one last look at the bed that held the memory of the night gone by, and left, closing the door slowly behind her. She walked down the corridor leading to her bedroom, her sadness slowly giving way to anger. She flung open her bedroom door and stamped inside.

"Who the hell does she think she is? How could have I been stupid enough to think that Miss Ice Queen could care about anyone besides herself? Stupid…stupid!" She walked into her bathroom. "I need a cold shower, so I can clear my head and stop fooling myself."

Chloe took off her clothes and stepped into the shower, turning the cold water on, letting it clear her mind. Shortly after she added hot water and slowly rested her forehead on the shower stall, the warmth relieving the tension. After a while she turned the water off and stepped out. She dried herself and put on a pair of shorts and a t-shirt before getting into bed. The emotional stress of the day slowly took its toll, and Chloe let exhaustion take her to dreamland.

Chapter 7

Chloe spent the next few weeks babysitting Clément and learning her way around town. Her day was fairly simple. She would get Clément ready in the morning, and walk him to school around 9 a.m. She then had until 3 in the afternoon to do as she pleased. She had walked back to the castle many times and stood at the same spot where she and Laurence had stood weeks before. The sadness and melancholy from being deceived by Laurence were slowly wearing off, and she sometimes wondered if everything had just been a figment of her imagination. Chloe had not spoken to Laurence since their last phone call, but she knew that she regularly called and talked to her dad and Clément.

Chloe enjoyed her life at the Glairons' house, but often wished she could get to know more French people of her own age. One Sunday while cleaning her room she found Vincent's phone number lying behind her bed table.

Must have fallen when I was unpacking. I wonder if I should call him. I don't even know if he remembers me. Oh, what the hell! What do I have to lose?

She ran downstairs to the family room. The house was quiet; Jean, Clément, and, surprisingly, Beatrice, had gone out to the park. Chloe had declined the offer to join them, not wanting to spend more time than necessary with Beatrice. She quickly dialed the number and waited for someone to pick up.

"Allo, je voudrais parler a Vincent, s'il vous plait."

"*Oui c'est moi*," answered the voice.

"Vincent, this is Chloe. From the plane. Remember me?"

"*Yeah, of course. My gosh, I wondered what happened to you.*"

"I'm fine…settling in."

"*How is life with your family?*"

"It's okay. The kid is great."

"*Good. Do you like it here? Not too homesick yet?*"

"I was for a while, but I'm starting to like it, plus I'm crazy about the kid."

Vincent chuckled. "*Listen, what are you doing right now?*"

"Nothing really…I was cleaning my room and found your number, and I thought I'd give you a call."

"*I'm glad you did. Want to go and have some coffee? It's only four, and I'm half an hour away from Versailles. I know a great coffee place…*"

"Huh…yeah, sure I'd love to."

"*Great. Give me your address, and I can be there in 45 minutes.*"

They exchanged addresses and Chloe hung up. *Okay, good. I need to get out a little.* Chloe looked at her reflection in the mirror hung on the family room wall, readjusted her ponytail, and straightened her shirt. The weather had gotten cooler as September went by, even though today was particularly sunny. Chloe rushed to her bedroom to pick up something warmer to wear than the simple linen short-sleeve shirt she had on. She rummaged through her closet, and her hands brushed past the leather jacket Laurence had given her. A rush of sadness passed through her, and she took the jacket off its hanger and brought it to her face, smelling the leather and the lingering scent of Laurence's perfume. She shook her head and threw the jacket on her bed, grabbing a University of Maryland t-shirt from the closet. She put on a pair of white sneakers and hesitantly picked up the leather jacket. Chloe stared at it for a few moments and made a decision. "It's going back," she said aloud. She ran and bolted into Laurence's room, throwing the jacket on the bed. She took one last quick look around the room and left.

While waiting for Vincent to arrive, Chloe went to the library, a place that had become her favorite retreat over the past few weeks. She had spent numerous hours looking through books trying to improve her French. Sometimes, she would just sit in the high-ceilinged room and enjoy the silence. The room was built with thick walls that stopped any unwelcome noise from intruding on the peace and quiet of its occupants. Chloe picked up *Madame Bovary*. She had been trying to read at least one chapter each day and was really enjoying the story. It also helped that she had previously read it as a class assignment a few years back. As she got comfortably settled in the large leather chair, the phone rang. *Damn, what now!* Chloe had lately starting feeling at ease with her French capacity and was less reluctant to pick up the phone.

"I'm coming...I'm coming..." she yelled at the phone.

"Allo," her voice annoyed from being disturbed.

"*Chloe?*" asked the voice.

"Oui," she answered, daring not to hope she recognized Laurence's voice.

"It's Laurence."

"Oui, je sais." Instead of the excitement Chloe expected to feel, she felt numb and partially angry. She purposely kept the conversation in French. "Ton père n'est pas là."

"*I know, I spoke to him this morning, he told me he would be taking Clément to the park this afternoon...Chloe, I wanted to speak to you.*"

"What?" Chloe forgot about her intention to keep speaking French, and her mind was filled with thousand of angry thoughts. *What the hell?*

"*I've been thinking a lot, and I'm sorry I've been ignoring you for the past weeks...*"

Chloe interrupted her. "Sorry? Why Laurence? Because you lied to me or because you treated me like shit last time we spoke. Or maybe just because..."

"*Okay, okay, you made your point. I never promised you anything, Chloe. We said we didn't know what was going to happen, and I needed to think,*" Laurence sighed. "*Listen, when is your next weekend off?*"

"Why?"

"*I'd like you to come over to Lille for the weekend.*"

"You...you want me to come visit you?" asked Chloe, dumbfounded.

"*Yeah...I'd like to...*"

"You know what the problem is, Laurence? I hate being told what to do, and what I hate even more are people who think they can just jerk me around whenever they feel like it..." The door bell rang. "I have to go. Goodbye, Laurence, and please, in the future, keep any lame requests you have to yourself." She angrily hung up and took a deep breath to calm herself down. The bell rang again. "I'm coming," she yelled.

She opened the door to Vincent. He stood tall in the doorway, wearing a light summery jacket and a pair of blue jeans. His hair had grown and brown curls surrounded his face, giving him a babyish look. "Hey, my directions weren't too bad, huh?"

"No, they were fine. It's great seeing you again," Vincent said with a smile.

"You too…so, where are we going?"

"You'll see. Let's go?"

"Yeah, let's." She closed the door behind her and stepped into the fresh air. "Chilly outside today," she said more for herself than as a mean of conversation.

"I parked my car on the street a few blocks away."

"'kay." They walked silently down the sidewalk.

Vincent broke the silence. "Are you okay? I mean on the plane you talked non-stop, and you haven't said much yet."

"I'm sorry. I just had an argument with someone I know, and I'm still upset about it."

"Oh…here is my car. Are you sure you want to go? Because we don't have to if you're not in the mood for it."

"Don't worry about it. I'm glad we're doing this."

"Okay." Vincent opened the door of a blue Golf GTI for Chloe. "It's not very far from here. It's on the other side of the river."

"Still in Versailles?"

"Yeah, but rive gauche." Vincent started the car and carefully drove off into the busy streets of Versailles.

Fifteen minutes later, the car stopped in front of a café facing the river.

"Here we are. We can sit outside if you want. It's protected from the wind, so it shouldn't be too cold."

"I'd love to." They chose a table on the far left corner of the patio. The small round tables each had only two chairs, both facing the street. "This is weird, why are the chairs this way?"

Vincent chuckled. "Didn't you know that French people were nosy? They like to see what's happening in the street…you should see in Paris, it's a ritual to sit down at a café and talk about the people walking by."

Chloe sat down. "Well, I guess we should do as everyone else then. When in France…"

"Yeah," smiled Vincent, taking a seat next to Chloe. "What do you want to drink?"

"Perrier."

"Perrier? Wow…never met any American who likes Perrier."

"Yeah…well, I do," stated Chloe with a hint of sadness in her voice, remembering that it was Laurence's favorite drink.

"Tell me, what have you been up to?" asked Vincent, waving the waiter over. They quickly placed their order.

"Just getting settled, I guess. Nothing much, really."

"Have you been to the castle yet?"

"Yeah, I love it. It's so beautiful."

"If you haven't seen everything yet, I'd love to take you there sometime."

"I got a very detailed tour, thanks. I'd love to see more of Paris, though."

"We should do that sometime." The conversation stopped as the waiter came back with their drinks. Chloe settled back comfortably in her chair and took a sip of her Perrier. She let her gaze wander along the river. The late afternoon sun was slowly going down, casting its last rays on the river, where couples were strolling hand in hand tenderly whispering in each other's ears.

Vincent's voice broke Chloe out of her reverie. "Earth to Chloe!"

"What? Sorry, I was just watching those couples," apologized Chloe. "I'm sorry I'm not the best company today."

"It's okay. We all have our days. What did you find so fascinating in those couples?" asked Vincent, waving at the space where a few moments ago lovers just stood.

"They just seem so happy…I know it might sound stupid, but it seems as if the world could have collapsed, and they wouldn't have realized it because they were so lost in each other."

"Ha, l'amour," joked Vincent.

"You're such a guy!" answered Chloe, a slight hint of hurt in her voice.

"I'm sorry. I was just joking. I know what you mean. Do you have a boyfriend in the States, Chloe?"

"Wow, that's a personal question. Is that a come on?" she joked, trying to lighten the mood.

"Don't know. Depends on your answer," said Vincent, jokingly flirting with Chloe.

"Hum...I see." Chloe scooted forward on her chair and looked at Vincent. "No, I don't have anyone in the States."

"Okay, so let's say that was a come on. What do you say?" he asked with a smile.

Chloe considered the question for a minute. Her mind was torn between her need for a friend and her uncertainty about Laurence. She sighed deeply. "I don't know, Vincent. What about we become friends first?"

Vincent stared at Chloe, his brown eyes reflecting amusement. He picked up his glass of Coke and clinked it with Chloe's as if to seal a pact. "You got it."

After the drinks, they went for walk along the river. The ease they had felt with each other in the plane had come back, and they were chattering away like old friends. Vincent spoke of his studies at La Sorbonne, and how he wanted to go to law school.

"Boy, you'd get along great with my dad," said Chloe smiling.

"Why?"

"He's a lawyer."

"Hey, if I have the father on my side, do I get the daughter?" kidded Vincent.

"Hum...we'll have to see about that," Chloe answered jokingly.

As the afternoon wound down, they made their way back to the car. "It was great seeing you again. We've got to get going, though; I have an exam tomorrow morning," explained Vincent, opening the door for Chloe.

"No problem. It was nice." She sat down and buckled herself in.

"It was. We should do that more often," Vincent looked at Chloe and smiled tenderly.

Before she had time to control it, Chloe's cheeks turned crimson. "Yeah, we should," she answered very fast.

"Hey, you're blushing. Do I have an effect on you, Chloe?" teased Vincent.

A Year in Paris 111

"No, you don't; you're openly flirting with me. I'm not used to it, that's all." Vincent laughed.

"Come on, you're kidding me, right? A girl like you never gets hit on. That's a good one."

"No, I'm very shy. I guess I just don't pay attention. Can we drop it?" She pleaded, feeling more and more embarrassed.

"Yeah. Sorry, you're so easy to tease," joked Vincent while starting the car.

Half an hour later, the blue GTI pulled in front of the Versailles house.

"Here we are. Can I have your number or is that too big of a come on?" teased Vincent again.

"You are impossible," answered Chloe.

"Yep, I like it that way. So can I?"

"Do you have a pen?"

Vincent pulled a pen out of the glove compartment and handed it to Chloe. She picked it up, slowly took hold of Vincent's hand, making sure she prolonged the contact, and wrote her number on his palm. *Two can play this game*, she thought while putting the cap back on the pen and giving it back to a surprised Vincent.

"Give me a call," she said while exciting the car. She dialed in the code to open the gate and walked into the courtyard. Vincent honked and waved one last time before disappearing into the streets of Versailles.

① ① ①

Chloe opened the front door and barely had time to take her shoes off before Clément came running towards her, screaming her name. "Hey, slow down little man, you're going to knock me over." She picked him up and softly kissed him on the cheek. "Did you have a good time at the park?" Clément nodded and wiggled himself out of Chloe's arms before taking off running to the family room.

"Hey Chloe, come on in here," called Jean.

"Did you guys have a good time?" she asked.

Beatrice was lying on the sofa, looking exhausted. "A good time? I broke two nails and had to run after a plastic ball for two hours!" she answered sarcastically.

"Honey, stop complaining. For once, Clément got to spend time with both of his parents. I don't want to spoil that," said Jean harshly. "Chloe, where did you go? Did you have a good time?"

"I went to a café on the left side of the river with a friend of mine."

"Hum...does this friend have a name?" smiled Jean.

"Vincent."

Jean chuckled. "Good, I hope we get to meet him very soon."

For the second time today, Chloe blushed. "He is just a friend. I met him on the plane ride over here."

Jean looked at her, and got up to start a video in for Clément. "By the way, there is a message from Laurence on the answering machine for you."

"Really?"

"Yes, she is asking that you call her back."

"I'm surprised she called at all," mumbled Beatrice.

Jean gave her a warning look. "Go on. You know where the answering machine is."

As the music of *Sesame Street* came on and Clément yelled, "'ookie monste'!" Chloe walked to the answering machine and pressed play. "*Hi, Chloe, it's Laurence. Call me back, would you? Here is my number: 03-04-78-97-45. You can call until very late. I'll be up.*" Beep... Chloe erased the message and shook her head. *I'm not calling. I'm tired of being a plaything.*

Chloe decided to grab something to eat from the fridge and go up to her room for the evening. As she was standing in front of the fridge with the door open, trying to make up her mind on what to eat, Jean sneaked up behind her. "Don't be too harsh on her."

Chloe jumped. "Wha... You startled me. What are you talking about?" She snagged some leftover pasta and put it in the microwave.

"Laurence. I know you're mad. I can tell. I don't want to tell you what to do, but I know my daughter, and she thinks she's not good enough for anyone's friendship. I don't know why. I'm just saying that maybe you're a little too fast to judge her."

Chloe didn't know what to say. She was still pondering her answer when Jean interrupted her thoughts. "Listen, you don't have to be friends with my daughter, I'm not forcing you here, but I was under the impression that you like her."

Chloe removed her plate from the microwave and sat at the table. "I do," she said while reaching for the salt.

"Just think about what I said, okay?" Jean looked at Chloe expectantly. She slightly nodded, making Jean smile. He left the room to go back to Clément, who could be heard giggling in front of the TV.

I guess Sesame Street *is funny*, thought Chloe, taking a bite of her food.

① ① ①

The night went by slowly, sleep a word almost foreign to Chloe. She couldn't keep the images of her time with Laurence away from her mind, and her will to keep her out of her life was slowly faltering. She tossed and turned the whole night, hearing Jean's voice telling her, *"She thinks she's not good enough for anyone's friendship."* Around 5 a.m., Chloe gave up on getting any decent sleep and got up, deciding to go for a run. She put on a pair of sweats and a t-shirt and left the house. The air was extremely chilly and the sun was starting to rise. Streetlights were still lit, and only a few cars were passing by. Chloe started a slow jog down the street.

Gosh, I'm really out of shape, she thought after turning onto Boulevard de la Reine. She kept her run steady for another ten minutes before stopping at an intersection, totally out of breath. A few morning joggers passed her, their paces light and their heads high. She dropped her hands to her knees and lowered her head, trying to bring her heartbeat back to normal until she was able to start jogging again. This time she paced herself, and she made it around the block and back to the house without falling over.

She walked into the silent house, making sure not to make any loud noises. She silently took off her shoes and went into the kitchen for a glass of orange juice. Surprisingly, Jean was sitting at the table, reading the newspaper.

"Good morning, Chloe. You're up early."

"I went for a run."

Jean smiled and picked up the coffee pot. "Coffee?" he offered.

"No thanks. I'll have some orange juice." Chloe opened the fridge and poured herself a glass.

Jean folded his newspaper and got up. "I'm going to be gone at least until the end of the week. Here is the hotel I'll be staying in." He picked up a piece of paper and scribbled a number on it, handing it to Chloe.

"What kind of number is that?" asked Chloe, surprised at the eleven-digit number.

"It's in China."

"Wow, you're going there on a business trip!"

"Yes, it wasn't planned really, but I got a phone call this morning very early, and one of my associates located an antique I have wanted to buy for a very long time."

"So, you're taking off for China," said Chloe, incredulous.

"That's where the piece is." Jean walked into the hallway, followed closely by Chloe who was still holding the piece of paper. "Listen, please don't hesitate to call if you need to. I don't want to wake up Clément, but hug him for me, would you?"

"'kay." Jean walked to the family room and picked up his suitcase next to the door. "Have a good trip."

"I will." He opened the door and turned around. "...and Chloe?"

"Hum?"

"Don't forget what I said last night." Jean closed the door slowly behind him to minimize the noise.

"I haven't," she whispered to the closed door.

① ① ①

Chloe finished her orange juice and headed for the shower, almost bumping into Beatrice on the stairs.

"Bonjour, Chloe."

"Oh, sorry, I almost knocked you over here."

Beatrice slightly smiled and patted Chloe on the shoulder. "It's all right, just be careful in the future. I have to get going. I'll be late tonight. So don't wait up." She went down a couple of steps and turned around. "I almost forgot. There is a parent-teacher conference this afternoon at Clément's school, I forget what time exactly. Could you go? Just let me know what happens." Beatrice turned and went down the remaining steps, picked up her handbag, and headed for the door.

"Wait," called Chloe.

"What is it?" Beatrice seemed annoyed that Chloe stopped her, and her impatience was showing.

"Why can't you come back for the parent-teacher conference?" asked Chloe, dumbfounded.

"I have to work, Chloe."

"Come on. What can be more important than talking to your child's teacher about his well-being?" spat Chloe, not even trying to hide her anger.

"First of all, young lady, watch your tone of voice. Second of all, there are many things you don't know."

"What do you mean, many things I don't know? I know one thing is that I have never met anyone who ignores her child more than you do." The words came out of Chloe's mouth before she had time to stop them. *Boy, if that doesn't get me fired, nothing will.*

"Chloe, I do not ignore my child, I have a busy life. As I said, there are many things you don't know." Beatrice didn't wait for Chloe's answer and stepped outside. Before closing the door, she looked at Chloe. "I think the conference is at 3." She closed the door and left.

As the door closed, a little voice called from the top of the stairs. "Papa?"

Chloe rushed upstairs and stopped Clément from trying to go down by himself. "Hey, little monster. Good morning. You want to go down and have breakfast?" Clément nodded. "Well, remember how I taught you to go down the stairs? Turn around and go down backwards." Clément did as he was told. "Good boy." He stopped halfway down and looked up at Chloe before opening his arms to be picked up. Chloe picked him up and he wrapped his arms around her neck, holding her tight. She stopped in the family room and sat on the couch, Clément still in her arms. "Are you okay?" Clément nodded and tightened his hold on Chloe's neck. They stayed this way for what seemed an eternity, Chloe whispering tender words in his ears, Clément holding on to her as if life depended on it. *Gosh, Clément, how much of my conversation with your mom did you hear?*

After a while, Clément went limp in Chloe's arms. She moved slightly and realized that he had fallen back asleep. *Okay, it's only 7 a.m., and he doesn't have to be in school before 9.* Chloe kept her arms around Clément and gently lay down on the coach, Clément's head pillowed on her chest. She adjusted herself to be more comfortable, and closed her eyes, joining Clément in the land of dreams.

She woke up suddenly and frantically looked around at the clock. *Damn, it's 9:15!* Chloe shook Clément, who was still asleep in her arms. "Hey babe, come on wake up." Clément slowly opened his eyes and sat up. "Come on, let's get you some breakfast, and dress and go to school."

Half an hour later, Clément and Chloe were walking down the street, almost running to get to the school. *Damn, they really have to let me use one of the cars.* They got to the school shortly after 10. Chloe handed Clément to his teacher, apologizing profusely for his lateness.

She managed to ask for the parent-teacher meeting schedule, hugged Clément, and left. On her way back home she stopped by the boulangerie and got some fresh bread and pain au chocolat for Clément's snack.

She walked into the house and took off her sneakers. *Boy, maybe I'm going to finally be able to get a shower.* She walked to the family room and spotted a dozen beautiful roses laying on the coffee table. The flowers' aroma filled the room, giving it a summery feel. "What the hell? How did they get in here?" She picked up the roses and discovered an envelope with her name on it carefully tucked into the wrapping. She put the flowers down and delicately opened the envelope. She was surprised to find a train ticket to Paris/Lille for this coming weekend; a note accompanied the ticket.

I am sorry. Please come. Love, Laurence

Chloe looked around, expecting to see Laurence. After scanning the room for a few minutes, she came to the conclusion that Laurence must have had the roses delivered by a neighbor, and went in search of a vase to put the flowers in. She discovered a crystal vase in the dining room buffet. "That will do." After putting the flowers neatly into the vase, she hesitated a moment before grabbing the note and ticket and making her way upstairs.

She walked in her bedroom and set the flowers on her night table. She sat down on her bed, staring at the ticket, her mind in turmoil. She could not decide if she wanted to give in or stand up for herself. *She can't treat me like crap and then send flowers and be forgiven. I won't let her treat me like that.* Chloe threw the ticket on her nightstand and lay down, covering her eyes with her arm.

"What's your decision?"

She sat up in a rush, her heart racing, her eyes scanning the room for the voice. She discovered Laurence standing up against the far wall, wearing worn out blue jeans, a white t-shirt. Her face, half in the shadow and half in the morning sunlight, showed uncertainty her voice had not held a few minutes ago. Chloe got up and looked at Laurence, speechless. "What are you doing here?" she whispered.

Laurence took a few steps forward, careful to stop far enough from Chloe so she didn't startle her. "I wanted to see you."

Chloe nodded, finding it hard to speak.

"You never called back last night, and I wanted you to know that I really meant it when I said that I was sorry, and I wanted you to come over."

"So, you just jumped on the first train this morning and came here," stated Chloe, incredulous.

"Pretty much," smiled Laurence.

"You shouldn't have bothered," said Chloe flatly.

Laurence took a deep breath. "You have every right to be upset, but doesn't anyone deserve another chance?"

"Another chance? Isn't what I have been giving you ever since we first met—another chance?" barked Chloe.

Laurence looked at Chloe sadly. "Yes, maybe you're right."

"Now, I'm going to ask you the question again. What are you doing here?"

Laurence looked deeply in Chloe's eyes and started speaking "I have been acting like a selfish brat, and I hurt you. I don't want to apologize for my actions, Chloe, but please know that I'm sorry I hurt you. I never meant to. I spent the past few weeks telling myself that it was for the best that you will go back home hating me…but it's not. I don't want you to hate me. The time I had with you here was the best time I've had in years. I'm not always a nice person, Chloe, but I want to be nice to you. You make me want to be nice to others. I still don't know what I can give you or how much, but I know one thing…" Laurence took a deep breath. "…I really care about you, so much it's almost scary, and I don't want to lose you."

The room suddenly darkened and rain started falling outside, thunder only few miles away, the turmoil on the outside similar to that in Chloe's head. A crash of thunder broke their gaze, and Chloe walked to the open window to close it and block the outside noise, leaving only silence. She propped herself against the edge of the window and looked at Laurence whose only movements had been to follow Chloe with her gaze.

Chloe sighed. "What if I say, yes, I forgive you. Do you take my heart and break it again? This whole thing is new to me. Being attracted to a woman is new to me." She paused and raised her hand stopping Laurence from replying. "No, please let me finish. You're probably going to say I won't do it again, I promise, and we both know it's bullshit. I don't want any false promises; I only want the truth. I want to know what's happening in this thick head of yours, and I want you to tell me when you think you want to run away. It's only under those conditions that I can forgive you."

"I accept," answered Laurence very seriously.

Chloe took a few steps forward stopping at arm length from Laurence. "No more running away?"

Laurence shook her head and grabbed Chloe's hand, bringing it to her chest. "I promise." Her heart skipped when a tear rolled down Chloe's face.

"This is the chance you were asking for, Laurence. Don't blow it." The rain beating against the window made Chloe's voice barely audible. Small steps were taken, arms wrapped around slender bodies, and hearts beat faster, the rain suddenly forgotten.

① ① ①

They stayed wrapped up in each other's arms for what seemed an eternity, neither of them willing to let go. Slowly, Laurence released Chloe. "Does that mean you're coming this weekend?" she smiled tenderly.

Chloe nodded and stepped back into Laurence's arms, burying her face in Laurence's t-shirt, taking in the smell of her perfume, the way her body felt under her hands. "That is if I can have the weekend off. Your dad left for China this morning."

"You're kidding!" She stepped back from Chloe and took her hand, leading her to the bed. She sat down and kept Chloe's hand in hers. "Business trip?"

"He said that a friend of his called him about an antique. He didn't say how long he was going to be gone for. Sorry I didn't ask him."

"No, no, you have nothing to be sorry for. Chloe, I came here to see you today, not my dad, not anyone else, just you." She gently rubbed Chloe's palm, sending chills all the way down Chloe's spine. Chloe jerked her hand away, and rushed to explain her action when she saw the look of hurt on Laurence's face.

"I can't concentrate when you do that," she explained with a smile.

"Am I distracting you?" laughed Laurence tenderly.

"Yeah, you are."' Chloe paused and looked in Laurence's eyes. "I'm happy you're here. I missed you."

Laurence smiled, her smile brightening her face. The cloud of tension she felt over the past week was suddenly gone. "I missed you too." She reached for Chloe's hand again, gently resuming her previous movement. Chloe swallowed with difficulty, flinching slightly under Laurence's ministrations. Laurence looked up at Chloe and spoke softly. "Am I scaring you? You flinched when I touched you."

"No, no you're not," Chloe breathed, taking both of Laurence's hands in hers to make her point. "It's just that it's new to me, and…and when you caressed my hand…" Chloe stopped at loss with words, not knowing how to explain how she felt.

Laurence smiled. "I won't rush into anything, I swear. If I ever make you uncomfortable, please tell me."

Chloe nodded and released Laurence's hands. "I will."

They just stared at each other, their eyes holding the promise of things to come.

"I should probably go shower. I went for a run this morning, and never got a chance to clean up ever since," said Chloe, breaking the spell.

"Okay. Would you like to go grab some lunch after that?"

"Sure. I have to be at Clément's school at 3 p.m. for a parent-teacher conference. When are you going back?"

"My train is at 8 p.m. I'll come with you to the meeting. I can't believe that Beatrice is not doing it herself."

"We had an argument about it this morning," said Chloe, getting up.

"I'm sorry she is such a bitch. You know you haven't been here that long. You could really ask for another family."

"Lo, we've been over that. I'm not going anywhere. I think Clément needs me…somehow I get the feeling that Beatrice's attitude toward him is affecting him more than we think."

Laurence passed her hand through her hair, tucking it back behind her ears. She sighed. "I wish I weren't so far away," she stated, sadness in her voice. "Thanks, Chloe."

"You're welcome. The Glairon family is stuck with me, whether they like it or not." She smiled and tenderly stroked Laurence's cheek. Laurence grabbed her hand and lightly kissed the palm, making Chloe blush intensely.

"Huh…well…I think I'd better go shower." She slowly pulled her hand from Laurence's grasp.

"I'll wait for you. I'm going to go to my room, there are a couple of things I might want to take back with me tonight."

"I won't be long." She turned around and walked into her bathroom; closing the door behind her.

①   ①   ①

The first thing Laurence saw when walking in her room was the leather jacket lying on the bed. She picked it up and put it on the chair next to the door. She started looking through her paintings and canvasses. She packed up a few blank canvasses in a large bag and a dozen paint tubes. She then looked through a pile of paintings propped up against the wall. Finding what she was looking for, she left the room, picking up the jacket on her way. She walked back to Chloe's bedroom, knocking at the door before entering. Not getting an answer, she slightly opened the door and called.

"Chloe, it's me. Are you dressed? Can I come in?" *I guess she must still be in the shower.* She walked in, dropped the jacket on the bed and went to open the window. The rain had stopped, and the sun could be seen piercing through the cloud. *Il y a probablement un arc en ciel quelque part*, thought Laurence. The bathroom door opened, and Chloe came in, wrapped in a towel, her wet hair hanging over her shoulders.

"Oh, hey…I wasn't expecting you back so soon," she said, embarrassed to have walked in only wearing a towel.

"I…I knocked and called, but you didn't answer, so I figured you were still in the shower. Sorry."

"Let me grab some clothes and get dressed." Chloe looked through her dresser and picked up a long sleeve t-shirt with the Maryland Terrapin logo on it, grabbed a pair of jeans from her closet, and went back to the bathroom.

She came back in brushing her hair. "Give me five minutes to comb through this mess, and we can go."

"No rush. I found something that belongs to you," she said, pointing to the leather jacket on the bed.

"I…I was mad, I also missed you, and this jacket was a constant reminder of you…I'm sorry," apologized Chloe, the brushing forgotten.

Laurence smiled and walked closer to Chloe. "I know. I understand. I acted like a jerk."

"Yeah, but it's all behind us now, isn't it?"

"Yes, it is. I have something I want you to have." Laurence handed Chloe a small painting.

"Lo, this is beautiful." The painting represented a mother and child playing in a flower garden. Everything from the affectionate look on the mother's face to the child's playful demeanor had been captured. The flowers looked so real, Chloe could almost smell their perfume.

"This is the first painting I did after my mother died. I stopped painting for a while after her death. I couldn't find the inspiration. I had therapy sessions after she passed away…I…I didn't cope with losing her very well. Anyway, one day my therapist asked me what was the best memory I had from my mother…you're holding it right now."

"The people in the painting are you and your mom?" asked Chloe, staring at the painting.

"When I was six, we went to visit my grandparents in the south. They had this beautiful garden. My mother explained to me that she always loved this place because she could always find peace and comfort. She looked so serene and happy…" Laurence's voice trembled slightly. "Over the week we stayed there, she and I played so many games in this garden. It was a happy time." Laurence stopped for a second to get her emotion under control. "I want you to have this painting because it is one of my most precious possessions, along with the portrait of my mother I have in my room."

Chloe looked at Laurence, understanding the gesture and value of it. Giving her her most precious belonging was a way for Laurence to show she wasn't going anywhere.

"Thank you. You know you can always take it back…"

"I know."

A silence hung for a few minutes. Laurence stepped closer to Chloe and gently stroked her cheek. Chloe felt riveted in her spot, her eyes glued on Laurence, her senses aware of the gentle stroking. Laurence tenderly kissed Chloe's forehead, and brushed her lips across her eyelids. At the first feel of Laurence's lips on her skin, Chloe closed her eyes, the sensation almost too much. Laurence stopped for a second and looked at Chloe to reassure herself. The sight of Chloe standing with her eyes closed, breathing faster, made Laurence's heart leap. She pushed away any voices telling her it was the wrong thing to do and softly brushed her lips on Chloe's. Chloe felt Laurence's lips against hers, and this simple act made her body tingle. She slowly opened her eyes and was met by the sight of Laurence's blue eyes. No words were necessary to explain what had just passed between them; the flush of their faces and their ragged breathing was enough.

"I...I think I should finish brushing my hair and...we can go," said Chloe, trying to get her breathing under control.

Laurence nodded. "I'll wait for you downstairs." She exited, softly closing the door behind her. Chloe sat abruptly on her bed, hugging the painting, only one thought going through her mind: "Wow."

① ① ①

They walked to a nearby café called Chez Paul and got a table in the far corner. Old wine, beer and coffee advertisements hung on the wall, and waiters walked around heads held high, wearing black pants, white shirts and white aprons. Old French men stood at the bar, almost staggering, their faces red, sipping glasses of wine.

"Those people at the bar seem to have had way too much to drink," said Chloe, munching on some bread the waiter brought.

"Yes, they sure do. Would you be interested in seeing a movie Saturday night?" asked Laurence, picking up her knife and spreading butter on her bread.

"I don't know if I can understand it, but yeah, that would be fun."

"Good. I'll see what's playing."

"'kay."

Laurence waved the waiter over, and they placed two orders of ham sandwich and salad. They made small talk until their food arrived.

"Wow, this is a huge sandwich," exclaimed Chloe, looking at the half-baguette sandwich on her plate.

"Yes, but it's very good," said Laurence, taking a bite of hers, soon followed by Chloe.

"Yuk...what's in it?" asked Chloe almost spitting out what she had in her mouth.

Laurence laughed at Chloe's face. "What do you mean what's in it?"

"I mean it tastes weird."

"It's ham and salty butter."

"That explains why. Don't you guys know about mayonnaise?"

"We sure do, but we don't use it on sandwiches," explained Laurence, amusement in her voice. "If you really don't like it, we can order something else for you."

"No, that's fine. I'll scrape off the butter." She opened her sandwich and proceeded to remove the butter with her knife. "Much better," she pronounced after taking a bite.

After lunch, Laurence proposed a walk in the park of the castle since they still had time before going to Clément's school. They entered the park from an entrance Chloe had never seen before.

"Is that really part of the castle? We don't even see it."

"The park is enormous. This part has more trees and hiking trails, it's less touristy."

"Fall is upon us," said Chloe, looking at the leaves falling from the trees. They walked slowly, getting deeper into the park, fewer and fewer people crossing their path. Once she felt that they had gone far enough into the woods, Laurence gently took hold of Chloe's hand.

"Is that okay?" she asked, unsure.

Chloe tightened her hold on Laurence's hand and interlaced their fingers. "Yeah, it's more than okay."

They walked for another few minutes in silence. "Would you like to sit down for a while?" asked Laurence.

"Sure." They sat on the grass, their backs propped up against a tree, their hands still linked together.

"I like this place," said Laurence.

"Let me guess—another one of your retreats," joked Chloe.

"No, not really. I just like it because it's quiet, and you don't see any people when you go very far in."

"Must be a great place to paint when spring comes, and everything is blooming."

"I never painted here, but you're right. I should try it."

Chloe looked up at Laurence and took a deep breath. "Can I ask you a question?"

"Sure, what is it?" asked Laurence, turning her head and looking into Chloe's green eyes.

"You...I mean you kissed me earlier...I..."

Laurence interrupted Chloe. "I'm sorry. I should have asked you before. I just went with my instincts, I..."

"Hey, hey, did I say anything about having not enjoyed it?" smiled Chloe, shifting closer to Laurence.

Laurence swallowed with difficulty and shook her head. "So, what's your question?"

Chloe looked away suddenly embarrassed. "Hey, you can tell me," said Laurence softly, turning Chloe's face back towards her, she gently let her hands brushed down Chloe's arms and grabbed both her hands.

"When you kissed me I felt...." Chloe stopped for a moment, trying to find the words to described the way she felt. "I felt...as if electricity was passing through my body. That's probably not the right description, but I can't find the words...it was just so..."

"Shh," whispered Laurence, tenderly putting her finger on Chloe's lips to stop her. "I know what you mean, I felt the same way."

"I wish it hadn't been so brief," whispered Chloe, her eyes suddenly finding the fabric of her jeans very interesting.

Laurence smiled. "Hey, please look at me. There is no reason to be ashamed. I didn't want to scare you off, that's why it was so brief. Right now, there is nothing I would like more than to kiss you again." The last part almost a murmur in the wind.

Time seemed to stop, leaving only Chloe and Laurence staring at each other. Chloe took a deep breath and scooted closer to Laurence, their foreheads almost touching, their breaths mingling. "I don't know if I know how to do it right," whispered Chloe. She softly kissed Laurence's nose and eyes before lightly kissing her lips. Uncertain of the effect she was having, she withdrew, only to have her face caught by Laurence.

"Please don't stop," spoke Laurence softly.

By way of answer, her voice and hands trembling, Chloe tenderly brushed her lips over Laurence's and felt Laurence's hands gently tugging her closer. Taking it as an invitation, she softly deepened her kiss. Laurence let herself feel the sensations, the taste of Chloe's lips, the gentle pressure. She gently combed her fingers through Chloe's long hair, making Chloe quiver each time she brushed her fingertips against her neck. The kiss ended as softly as it started. Forehead against forehead, fingers intertwined, they both tried to catch their breath.

"And you said you didn't know how to do it right?" Laurence joked shakily, her hand lightly squeezing Chloe's fingers.

Chloe smiled, she lightly passed her fingers on her lips, not believing what she had just done. "I didn't do too bad then, huh?" she asked, uncertainty in her voice.

"That was...amazing," said Laurence sincerely. "Anytime you have this kind of impulse, please don't fight it," she joked.

"Okay, but the same goes for you."

"Okay," echoed Laurence, getting up and giving her hand to Chloe to help her up. "We probably should get going. It's almost 2:30."

"Already? Yeah, we should go."

① ① ①

They spotted Clément in the playground going down a slide. About 20 kids were running around under the supervision of a few teachers. Chloe walked into the playground followed by Laurence.

"Hey, Clément!" she called.

Clément waved at Chloe and ran towards her, screaming her name. "Cloe." She picked him up and hugged him tightly. "Hey, sweetheart, I have a surprise for you." She pointed at Laurence who had taken a step back during Clément and Chloe's interaction. Clément looked at Laurence and his face lit up with an enormous smile.

"Lo!" He extended his arms to Laurence. She took him from Chloe's arms and kissed his cheeks, holding him tight.

"Look at you, you've grown so much." Clément tightened his grip around Laurence's neck. "Tu m'as manqué p'tit gars."

"I tell you what, I'll stay here with Clément while you go and talk to his teacher," offered Chloe. "Anyway, it'd be easier since my French is still so-so."

"Okay, it shouldn't take too long." Laurence put Clément down and knelt in front of him. "I'm going to go and talk to your teacher. You stay here with Chloe, okay?" Clément nodded and grabbed Chloe's hand. "Good, that's settled. I'll be back in a few."

Half an hour later, Chloe was starting to wonder what was taking so long when Laurence stepped out. She picked up Clément from the swing and walked up to meet Laurence.

"What did she say?" asked Chloe. Laurence's face was serious and worried. "Lo, what did she say?" asked Chloe again when not getting an answer.

"I can't tell you right now," she said, pointing at Clément discreetly. "When we get home."

The walk home was quiet. Laurence carried Clément all the way, her walk fast and determined. Once they got home, Chloe got the pain au chocolat she had bought for Clément earlier and gave it to him as a snack.

"Hey, little man, would you like to watch a video while you eat?" asked Laurence.

Clément ran to the family room. "Sesame, Lo!"

"Okay, *Sesame Street* it is." Laurence plugged the video in and mouthed "kitchen" to Chloe. Chloe nodded and followed Laurence to the kitchen.

"What's going on? Come on, you're worrying me."

Laurence sighed and sat at the kitchen table, passing her hand through her hair in frustration. "Have you ever seen any strange bruises on Clément?" asked Laurence, her voice quivering.

Chloe sat down and thought for a minute. "Once. The day you left, when Beatrice came back. Clément had a huge bruise on his hip. I didn't think much of it because you know how he is, he runs and falls all the time." Chloe softly brushed Laurence's hand. "Come on. Tell me what's going on, please."

Laurence got up to get a Perrier from the fridge. She offered one to Chloe, who refused. "His teacher said that Clément is very scared of people touching him…"

"We hug him all the time, what is she talking about?"

"…let me finish. She said that a week ago, he started screaming when the teacher's assistant came behind him while he was drawing, and patted him on the head." Laurence stopped and took a sip of her drink. "She also said that she has seen bruises on his legs and back, but not that much in the past month."

"Is she insinuating that we beat Clément? This is insane." Chloe got up angrily, only to be yanked back on her chair by Laurence.

"Listen for a minute. She said that the kind of reaction Clément has to people touching him is common to abused children."

"It just doesn't make sense. He is with me all the time, and I swear I would never do anything to him…I…"

"Chloe, stop it. I know you wouldn't. Think—she said that she hasn't seen but one for the past month. You have been here for a month."

"I thought he didn't go to school before. How does she know what happened to him before that?"

"She is the school principal, and she also runs the camp over the summer. Clément went to her morning camp July and mid-August. That's where she knows him from."

"Didn't you take care of him during the summer?"

"I did most of the time, but I usually went away during the weekend."

"He is a child. Children hurt themselves…"

"I agree, and it's why I never paid too much attention to the bruises he would get during the weekend because I know how active he is. Now, I can't help think that he never had any bruises when my dad was home, but always when Beatrice took care of him."

"Are you saying that she …" Chloe couldn't even finish her sentence; the idea of what was implied horrified her.

"Yes, that's what I'm saying," said Laurence, her hands clenching into fists.

"Okay, let's say it's true. How do we prove it? Clément is too young to speak up." Chloe passed her hand in her hair in frustration. "We should talk to your dad…"

"No. Come on, Beatrice is his wife. He refuses to admit that she cheats on him! Do you think he is going to believe that she is abusive? No way," said Laurence, her tone harsh, her eyes black with anger.

"Hey, cool off, okay? I'm just trying to help here," answered Chloe gently.

"I'm sorry…It's just that I don't know what to do."

"We don't leave Clément alone with her ever again…that shouldn't be too hard since she is gone most of the time." Chloe got up and starting pacing around.

"Okay, but we can't keep on doing that forever, Chloe." Laurence got up suddenly and threw away her empty bottle of Perrier as Clément came running into the kitchen, his face covered with chocolate. "Hey, I see you haven't learned yet that food goes in your mouth, not on your face," said Laurence, picking him up and turning on the faucet. She grabbed a paper towel and cleaned up his face and hands. "Is your tape finished?"

"Oui…fini," answered Clément, wiping his wet hands on Laurence's white t-shirt.

"Hey, stop that…I tell you what, go and play in the playroom, and we'll be there in a minute." Laurence put Clément down and tenderly ruffled his hair. Clément took off running.

Chloe waited to make sure that Clément was out of earshot before continuing the conversation. "Listen, I think you don't give your dad enough credit. Maybe you could just talk to him and see what he says. What do you have to lose? If he doesn't believe you, then we're back to where we are now."

Laurence looked thoughtful for a few moments. "Maybe you're right, I'll call him as soon as he comes back from China." Laurence picked up an apple and took a bite. "Maybe we're just imagining everything, and Clément just really fell."

"I don't know, Lo. I hope so." Chloe's voice was almost a whisper. She grabbed Laurence's hand and squeezed it to show her support.

"Thanks," softly said Laurence, a hint of sadness in her voice.

"We're together in this mess, okay?"

"Okay," answered Laurence, a slight smile on her face.

Chloe let go of her hand. "Come on, let's go see what he is building."

① ① ①

They spent the rest of the afternoon playing with Clément. Around dinnertime, Laurence went to McDonald's to get dinner for the three of them. The happy meal was a huge success with Clément, and he insisted in taking the little plastic toy he got with it into the tub with him. Laurence helped out with Clément's bath, but shortly after 7, she had to get ready to go. She went up to her room to retrieve the bag she had packed earlier and walked back downstairs where Clément and Chloe were watching TV.

"I think I have everything." She knelt in front of Clément. "Hey, babe. I have to go. You be a good boy, and I'll see you soon." She kissed Clément on the forehead and brushed his cheeks with her hand. Clément threw his arms around her neck and hugged her tight. She slowly unwrapped herself from his grip and kissed him one last time. "Love you, babe." She walked to the entrance followed by Chloe. "I'll see you this weekend, right?" asked Laurence, a hint of uncertainty in her voice.

"What if your dad is not back? I can't leave Clément with Beatrice. Not after what we discussed," said Chloe, her eyes tearful, her voice trembling.

"Then, you take him with you. I know she won't object." Laurence came closer to Chloe. "Chloe, coming here today was the smartest thing I have done in a long time. No matter what, I want you to come this weekend…I've missed you too much over the past weeks to bear not seeing you for a long time." Laurence looked at Chloe, her eyes only reflecting honesty. Slowly, she drew Chloe into her arms and held her tight.

"I'll be there," said Chloe, her voice muffled by Laurence's shoulder. Laurence kissed Chloe's hair and released her. She lightly kissed her cheek and grabbed her bag.

"I should get going. I'm going to miss my train." Her words saying she should go, her heart screaming for her to stay.

"Thanks for the flowers," smiled Chloe.

Laurence smiled back and softly touched Chloe's cheeks. "I'll call you when I get home. Remember, you can use my bedroom." She playfully winked at Chloe and closed the door behind her.

A little while after, Chloe put Clément to bed and went back to her room. She sat on her bed not believing what had happened that day. Memories of Laurence's lips on hers made her heart beat faster and her face flushed. She decided to spend the night in Laurence's bedroom since Laurence said she would call. She grabbed her nightclothes, toothbrush, her book, and the monitor and left her room. She checked on Clément and found him peacefully asleep. She made sure his monitor was on and went to Laurence's room.

The room was quiet, the only sign of Laurence's earlier stay the paintings scattered on the floor. Chloe picked them up and propped them back against the wall. She looked around the room and lightly passed her hand across the furniture as if trying to memorize places that Laurence might have touched. She broke out of her reverie and went into the bathroom to get ready for the night. On the sink stood an almost empty bottle of Calvin Klein perfume; she smelled it and recognized it as Laurence's. Dirty towels had been thrown on the floor weeks before and still remained where they had landed. Chloe laughed, thinking that obviously cleaning was not a number one priority for Laurence. She picked up the towels and put them in a hamper under the sink. She quickly got ready for the night, crawled under the covers, and picked up her book. As the hours went by, Chloe couldn't help thinking of the last time she waited for Laurence's phone call, and it never came.

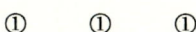

A loud ring woke Chloe. "What? What is it?" It took her a few moments to get her bearings and remember that she was in Laurence's bedroom. Once she got her thoughts together, she realized that the phone had woken her. "Damn, I must have dozed off." Chloe picked up and answered with a sleepy voice.

"Allo."
"Hey, it's me."
"Laurence?"
"Who else were you expecting?" she answered jokingly.
"I fell asleep. What time is it?"
"A little after 11."
"How was the train ride?"
"Pretty boring."
"I'm sorry."
"It's okay...the trip was worth it," said Laurence sincerely. *"How is Clément?"*
"Thanks. He fell asleep right away. What time is your first class tomorrow?"
"8 a.m."
"That's early!"
"Yes, I don't know why I always end up with the early morning classes. Listen, I can't talk too long because I'm really tired, but I just wanted to make sure you knew I was thinking about you."
"Are you?"
"What?"
"Thinking about me," asked Chloe teasingly.
"Yes." Laurence's answer meant more than a simple yes. It was a promise. *"Are you?"*
"Thinking of you?"
"Uh-huh."
"I haven't been able to think of anything else since you left."
"Are you in bed right now?"
"Yeah, I was reading, and I guess I fell asleep."
"Are you spending the night?"
"If it's okay with you..."
"Yes, it is. I wish I could be there." Laurence's voice was only a sensual whisper.
"I wish you could be here too," answered Chloe, suddenly finding it hard to keep her heartbeat at bay.
"I should really go. I'll call you tomorrow... Good night."
"Good night, Lo."

Chapter 8

Chloe slept very little and was woken up by the phone again around 6 a.m. by Jean, calling to tell her that he should be back by Thursday. Chloe hung up and lay in bed for a while, her mind still sleepy, but happy to know that Jean would be around this weekend to take care of Clément. She had a strong feeling that Beatrice never came home the night before. Shortly after 7 a.m., Chloe heard the sounds of Clément waking up. She got out of bed and went to get him. Clément seemed refreshed by his night of sleep and in a very giggly mood. He asked for Laurence and his dad, but never mentioned Beatrice. Chloe put on a sing-along tape for him while she quickly showered. She fed him, dressed him and walked him to school. Clément's teacher handed her a note saying "Clément's parents."

Chloe slowly walked back from the school, enjoying the fresh autumn breeze, and the early morning sun. She stopped by the boulangerie as she did the day before, and bought a croissant for Clément's snack and one for her breakfast. On her way home, she waved at the neighbor, who, as every morning, was sitting on his front step sipping his coffee.

"Bonjour, monsieur Cambier."

"Bonjour, ma p'tite Chloe. Comment vas tu ce matin?" asked the old man, dipping his toast in his coffee and swallowing the morsel.

"Je vais bien, et vous?"

"Oh, tu sais, j'suis plus tout jeune." He slowly got up and walked up the steps. "Bonne journée ma grande."

"Oui, vous aussi."

Chloe enjoyed her morning small talks with Monsieur Cambier. She didn't always understand what he was talking about, but he was always very nice and polite to her. She had learned a few weeks back that he was a veteran of World War II and had worked all his life in the mines in the north of France before retiring and moving to Versailles with his wife. His wife was an aristocrat, and her marriage forty years ago to a commoner had broken any bonds she had with her family, except with an old aunt who, when she died, had left her the Versailles house. Monsieur Cambier was quite a character, with his old overalls and constant cigarette hanging out of his mouth. He spent most of his day sitting on his front steps watching the traffic and people walking by.

Chloe opened the gate and was surprised to find Beatrice's car parked in the courtyard. She found Beatrice lying on the couch wearing her robe and covered by a blanket. "Hi, I wasn't expecting you home before tonight," said Chloe, entering the family room.

"Hello, Chloe. I don't feel very well, so I decided to spend the day at home," explained Beatrice, her voice low and almost shaking. Chloe felt absolutely no compassion for the sick woman.

"Okay, I'll go up to my room and let you rest."

"Chloe, wait. Could you bring me a cup of tea?"

Chloe looked at the woman lying on the coach, ready to tell her to do it herself, but instead nodded and left for the kitchen. She warmed up water in the microwave and dumped a tea bag in it. "Here you go," she said, handing Beatrice the beverage.

"Thanks. I don't know what's wrong with me. I never get sick." Beatrice took a sip from the warm beverage. "Hum…this is good. What did Clément's teacher say yesterday?"

Chloe looked at Beatrice, trying to evaluate how much she was willing to tell her at the moment. She sighed and reached for the note Clément's teacher had just given her. "She gave me that this morning."

Beatrice took the note and opened it, scanning quickly over it.

"She wants to see Jean and I as soon as possible." Beatrice fell back on her pillow and threw her arm over her eyes. "Oh, God, what has this kid done now?" she said, exasperated.

"It's not what he has done she is concerned about, it is what you have done to him." The words flew out of Chloe's mouth before she had time to react. *Damn, why can't I just shut up?* Chloe froze and waited for Beatrice to react.

"What do you mean?" asked Beatrice, sitting up.

"I don't think it's my job to tell you. Why don't you discuss it with her?" Chloe slowly backed up towards the stairs.

"What did she say yesterday, Chloe?" asked Beatrice, her voice almost menacing.

Chloe sighed. "She said that Clément reacts strangely to people touching him. She said that she has seen strange bruises on him." Chloe held Beatrice's gaze, refusing to back down.

"She said that. Interesting. Well, we'll have to see what she is basing her convictions on," said Beatrice, lying back down.

"To the bruises she has seen on Clément, Beatrice," replied Chloe angrily.

Beatrice propped herself in her elbow and looked at Chloe. "Well, well, young lady. Are you insinuating that we hit our child?"

"I'm insinuating that you hit your child, Beatrice. Not Jean," barked Chloe, slowly losing her temper.

Beatrice laughed sarcastically. "You know, young lady, you are not irreplaceable. You have done a good job so far, but I'll not tolerate any insults in my house. Is that clear?"

Chloe looked at Beatrice coldly. "I don't know what this child has done to you, but I swear if you ever…ever touch him again…"

"What? Are you threatening me?" Beatrice asked amused.

"Take it as you will," answered Chloe. "And for your information…I might not be irreplaceable, but I'm your only choice. Nobody wants to come and work for you, Beatrice. Also, if you call the organization and ask them to send me back, I'll explain to them what your idea of being a good mother is." She stared into Beatrice's eyes for a few seconds and walked away. Before she had time to reach the stairs, Beatrice's voice stopped her.

"This argument would work if I were really his mother, Chloe."

"What?" said Chloe loudly, turning around to face Beatrice.

"Don't tell me you didn't know," smiled Beatrice, clearly amused.

"Know what?" asked Chloe incredulously.

"Come on, Chloe. Does Clément look anything like me?" laughed Beatrice.

Chloe walked back toward the couch. "No, but I don't look anything like my mother, and it doesn't mean that... Are you saying that Clément is not yours?"

"Yes, that's what I'm saying. Now, please, I'm really tired, and I'd like to rest."

"Wait a minute. You cannot tell me that and expect me to walk away. What do you mean he is not your son?"

"What do you think I mean? I'm not his mother."

"Is Jean..." Chloe could not finish her sentence almost scared to hear the answer.

"No, he isn't either."

"So he's adopted. Big deal. It still doesn't give you the right to mistreat him. He is legally your son." She abruptly stood up, her anger suddenly back.

"Oh, Chloe, you are so naïve," laughed Beatrice. "Who does Clément look the most like? Come on, think a little." Beatrice had sat back, obviously thinking the situation was quite entertaining.

Chloe thought for a minute, and suddenly the answer dawned in her. "No, it's impossible..."

"And...you probably thought you knew everything about her, didn't you?" laughed Beatrice.

Chloe stared at the coffee table, her mind not wanting to believe what she had just learned. "Laurence? It can't be..."

"Well, it is. Someone has to cover for that brat's mistake. She is lucky Clément is healthy and smart with the drugs she took while she was pregnant with him." Chloe looked at Beatrice, dumbfounded, finding nothing to say. "Come on. Have you nothing to say?" joked Beatrice sarcastically.

"Why did she give him away?" asked Chloe, wanting to understand.

"Jean thought it would be the best thing for the child. Anyway, she was in rehab and really didn't have much say in the situation."

Chloe nodded. "She is fine now. Why is she still pretending to be his sister?"

"Miss Goody-Two-Shoes is too concerned about his well-being. Anyway, the little brat looks exactly like her," said Beatrice spitefully.

Beatrice's last sentence refueled Chloe's anger. "The bottom line, Beatrice, is that Clément thinks you are his mother, and if the reason you mistreat him is because he looks like Laurence, you are even more pathetic than I thought. What I said earlier still stands." She abruptly turned around and ran upstairs.

① ① ①

Chloe's first reaction was to go to Laurence's room and dial her number in Lille. She let the phone ring twice and hung up. Her anger was slowly giving way to disbelief. "Why hasn't she told me? Why?" she asked aloud, the only answer the noise of the cars passing by in the street. The phone suddenly rang, making Chloe jump.

"Allo."

"Hey, it's me. You called?"

"Hey, yeah...I...I didn't think you'll be home. How did you know it was me?"

"Caller ID."

"You're home early," said Chloe, trying to change the subject.

"I only have a class from 8 to 9 a.m. My next class is not before 3."

"Weird schedule."

"Is everything all right?"

"Sure, why are you asking?"

"Because your voice sounds a little shaky."

Chloe found nothing to answer.

"Chloe, are you still there? Chloe, what's wrong?"

"Yeah, I'm here."

"Are you okay?" asked Laurence, her voice showing concern.

"I just had a talk with Beatrice...and..."

"Did she say anything to upset you?" asked Laurence, anger in her voice.

"Why didn't you tell me?"

"Tell you what?"

"About Clément?" A long silence happened before Laurence spoke again.

"What did she tell you?"

"She is not his mother, nor is Jean is father. Why didn't you tell me, Laurence? Why didn't you tell me he was your child?"

Laurence sighed. *"What would it have changed, Chloe? Clément doesn't know, and it's probably for the best."*

"How can you say that? How could you....?"

"Wait, don't be too quick to judge me before you've heard my side of the story. Chloe, please don't do that," asked Laurence, almost begging. When she didn't get an answer, she continued. *"I don't know what she told you, but it's complicated, and I can't explain it over the phone. This weekend?"* she asked, fearing the answer.

"Do you ever regret giving him away?" asked Chloe.

"Every day of my life," answered Laurence, her voice barely audible.

"Your dad is coming back on Thursday. My train gets in at 10 a.m. Be there."

"I will be…Chloe?"

"What?" she asked, her tone harsher than she intended it to be.

"Thanks," said Laurence, her voice slightly trembling.

Chloe sighed deeply. "Together in this mess, remember?"

"Together," said Laurence before hanging up.

Chloe hung up the phone and stared at it for a moment, her anger replaced by sadness. She felt sad for Laurence, and what she probably had to go through alone. She recalled Tony's cryptic comment at the bar. "Explains why she doesn't trust anyone." Chloe lay down on the bed and stared at the ceiling, letting the emotions of the morning wash over her. Closing her eyes, she let images of Laurence playing with Clément invade her mind, and slowly she fell asleep. She woke up shortly before 3:00 and had to run to pick up Clément on time.

The rest of the week passed without any more complications. Chloe tried to take care of Clément as much as she could, always keeping an eye and ear open when Beatrice was in charge. They had not talked any more about the conversation they had, nor of what Beatrice had told Chloe. When Jean came home on Thursday, Chloe felt relieved and for the first time in three days, relaxed. She decided to not tell Jean that she knew about Clément until she got the story from Laurence, and to wait for him to speak to Clément's teacher to voice her suspicions toward Beatrice.

When Chloe told Jean that she was going to spend the weekend at Laurence's, his face lit up with a smile, and he gave his approval right away, even going to the extent of canceling a meeting on Saturday so he could take care of Clément.

Saturday morning arrived very quickly, and Jean dropped Chloe at the train station a little after 7 a.m. As they drove away, Clément waved goodbye to Chloe.

The train ride was smooth, and Chloe slept through most of it. She woke up as the train pulled into Lille's train station.

"Arrêt Lille," called the conductor's voice. Chloe grabbed her bag from the overhead and got off the train. She scanned the crowd for Laurence, but could not see her. "Okay, she said to wait for her and not move," repeated Chloe to herself, planting herself near a ticket booth. Suddenly someone touched her shoulder from behind, making her jump.

"Sorry I'm late."

She turned to find herself staring at Laurence. Laurence was smiling, her blue eyes shining with excitement. She wore her usual blue jeans, white t-shirt and leather jacket, her black hair was pulled back behind her ears, and she wore a small pair of silver earrings representing the moon.

"I thought you had forgotten about me," answered Chloe with a smile.

Laurence bent to pick up Chloe's bag and lightly brushed her knuckles over Chloe's hand. "Of course not. Come on, let's go. I'm only five minutes away."

They stepped out into the busy streets of Lille. After going down a wide boulevard, they turned into an older neighborhood. The houses had a rustic appearance, and the streets were narrower.

"My apartment is in this building," said Laurence, gesturing. She retrieved a key from her back jeans pocket and opened the main entrance door. The lobby was large with high ceilings, and mirrors were placed on each side of it, giving it a larger appearance. Laurence took the stairs two by two, stopping at the first floor and opening the second door. "Welcome to my home," she said smiling, bowing mockingly to let Chloe in. Her apartment was very small, but warmly decorated. The main room was used as a study room, a living room and a bedroom. A large futon was set against the wall, large built-in closet doors were on the left wall separated by a fireplace, and the opposite wall from the futon had big windows half covered with heavy curtains. On the right were two doors, which Chloe assumed were for the kitchen and bathroom. Paintings hung on the walls, some reproductions of Matisse's *By the Sea* works, others original works from Laurence. The carpet matched the blue of the futon, a large TV was placed on a dresser near the windows, a laptop computer had been left open near the TV, and a small table and two chairs stood next to the other window.

"Lo, this is great," exclaimed Chloe.

"Thanks. I'd give you a tour, but trust me, what you see is what you get. The only other rooms are the bathroom and the kitchen."

"Yeah, I figured," smiled Chloe.

"Oh, here, let me take your jacket." She removed Chloe's jacket and put it on the back of one of the chairs. Laurence turned to Chloe and stepped closer, lightly running her hand along her arms. "Thanks for coming," she said softly.

"I wouldn't have had it any other way," smiled Chloe. Laurence only hesitated a moment before slowly drawing her into her arms.

"I wanted to do that at the train station, but I didn't want to embarrass you," explained Laurence, tightening her hold.

"What?" Chloe moved slightly back and looked at Laurence. "Lo, I come from a country where everyone hugs everyone. What are you talking about?"

"Maybe in the States, but not here. It's very rare to see people hug, unless they are…you know, more than just friends."

Chloe laughed softly at Laurence's attempt to protect her. "Lo, aren't we more than friends?"

"Huh…yes…I mean, only if you want to…" Laurence rushed to answer, stumbling over the words.

"Lo, how can you even doubt that we are more than friends after Monday?" smiled Chloe.

"I don't. I know where I stand," she answered seriously.

"Me too, so stop being insecure, and don't ever fight the urge to hug me gain, okay?"

"Yes, ma'am," joked Laurence. "What about we go sight-seeing for a while and grab lunch later on?" asked Laurence, tenderly passing her hand through Chloe's hair.

Chloe took one step back and looked at Laurence. "That sounds great, but before we do anything, I want to finish the conversation we had the other day on the phone." She backed up and sat on the futon, waiting for Laurence to come and join her. Laurence sighed and sat next to her.

"What do you want to know?" asked Laurence with a defeated tone of voice.

"Only the truth. Lo, please look at me. I'm not judging you, but I think I deserve to know what happened." She grabbed Laurence's face and turned it gently toward her. "Nothing you say is going to make me run away screaming. I swear." She looked intensely into Laurence's eyes, trying to convey her sincerity.

Laurence sighed again. "Okay...I don't even know where to start."

"Why don't you just tell me why you let your dad raise Clément, and we'll see where we go from there," said Chloe, lightly stroking Laurence's hands.

"I told you that when my mother died, I didn't accept it very well." Laurence looked at Chloe, waiting for a sign that she remembered talking about it. Chloe nodded. "Anyway, I was impossible to deal with, and my dad could not trust me to stay out of trouble when he was on business trips." Laurence paused for a few moments and ran her hand through her black hair. "He sent me to boarding school, thinking that there they would be able to keep an eye on me...and they did...well, at least for a while. The people in the school were strict, and forced me to calm down and get myself back together. I stayed away from home for six months before coming home for vacation. That's when my dad introduced me to Beatrice...I hated her from the start." Laurence suddenly got up and went to stand by the windows. "After that, I went back to my wild ways, and got expelled from the school. It was only three months before my senior high school exam, so he registered me into a correspondence program, and somehow I managed to pass the exam. By then Beatrice and I couldn't stand each other, and the atmosphere at home was unbearable." Laurence paused and walked through the kitchen door.

"Do you want something to drink? I have Perrier and Coke," she asked from the kitchen.

"Perrier would be great, thanks."

Laurence walked back in with the cold beverages in hand and

handed one to Chloe. She opened hers and resumed her story. "Where was I? Oh, yes…well, Beatrice talked my dad into having me move out. So, during the summer I registered for college in Lille, got a place to live in and left. My dad paid for everything, probably out of guilt I guess…anyway, I got into drugs and alcohol, never went to class and somehow got pregnant." Laurence stopped and finished her Perrier.

"What do you mean, somehow got pregnant?" asked Chloe incredulously.

Laurence stared at the blank TV screen, refusing to look at Chloe. "I don't know Chloe…I was drunk and probably high, and I don't remember." Chloe sat next to Laurence not knowing what to say. "I love Clément more than anything in the world, but I had nothing to give him." Laurence's voice had dropped, and she was playing with her empty bottle.

"What happened next?" asked Chloe, slowly taking hold of Laurence's right hand and squeezing it. Laurence looked at Chloe, her eyes filled with tears threatening to fall.

"When I found out I was pregnant, I took even more drugs until one day I overdosed and passed out. The hospital called my dad, and told him what happened and the state I was in. He came and took me home." Laurence stopped again.

"Lo, if you want to we can stop for now, and you can tell me the end tonight," said Chloe, not wanting to upset her even more.

"No, no, I need to say it…I need you to know."

"Okay," answered Chloe softly.

"There was no way I could have taken care of Clément, so my dad and I struck a deal. He would help me clean up my act, forget that anything happened and try to put me through college again, on the condition that he and Beatrice raised Clément as his parents."

"You agreed?" interrupted Chloe.

"Yes, I had no other choice. I was in no physical or mental shape to raise a child. I thought it would be the best for him.… Chloe, I had nothing, and if I had refused, my dad would have thrown me out in the streets, and then what kind of life would Clément have had?" Laurence got up and started pacing. "It made me feel better to know that I would still be part of his life, even if he was never to know that I was his mother. I thought my dad was trying to do what was best for me…"

"I can't believe he would put such an ultimatum on his own daughter," said Chloe in disbelief.

"That wasn't all his idea."

"Let me guess...Beatrice?"

"Yes, she is the one who had the idea of the ultimatum, and somehow managed to convince my dad. Anyway, the rest is history. I went to rehab, never did drugs again, and went back to school." Laurence sat back next to Chloe and hesitantly looked at her.

"I'm so sorry," said Chloe.

"For what?" asked Laurence, puzzled.

"That you had to go through that alone," answered Chloe, grabbing Laurence's hands and lightly kissing them. The tears that had been in the verge of falling suddenly starting spilling from Laurence's eyes. "Lo, please don't cry," said Chloe, brushing the tears off Laurence's cheeks. "Shh, It's okay." She pulled Laurence into her arms and stroked her hair, whispering tender words in her ears to soothe her. Laurence buried her face into Chloe's neck and wept.

① ① ①

Chloe held Laurence until her tears stopped, and Laurence sat up, wiping the remaining tears away from her eyes. "Sorry."

"For what?" asked Chloe.

"Acting like a cry baby," answered Laurence.

"Lo, don't ever apologize for that. I'm glad you told me, and I'm glad you let yourself go."

"Well, your shirt is soaked now," said Laurence, trying to lighten the mood.

"Oh, big deal," smiled Chloe. "If you're still up to it, I'd love this sight-seeing tour and lunch you promised."

"Sure, let me rinse my face...my eyes must be really puffy...damn, I hate crying," said Laurence, walking to the bathroom. She came out a few minutes later, feeling slightly refreshed, and for the first time in a long time, she felt relieved. "What about lunch first? It's almost noon, and I'm quite hungry."

"Sure. You're the boss," smiled Chloe, getting up and putting her jacket on.

"Okay, do you like Italian food?"

"Huh...not really, but French Italian food might be different than American Italian food," laughed Chloe.

"I'm sure it is. Come on, I don't have a car here, so we have to walk."

They walked back down the same streets as earlier, but instead of turning into the train station, they kept on going. They went through a pedestrian street lined with restaurants and clothing stores. They walked through an underground tunnel to cross a major intersection and arrived at the restaurant. It was a very tiny place with the menus written in French and Italian. Chloe found the food delicious, and at the end of the meal she had eaten more than her share.

"Gosh, I feel like I'm going to explode," she said while rubbing her stomach.

Laurence laughed. "I guess walking around for a little while won't be a bad thing."

"Lead the way," said Chloe, getting up.

Lille was a big city, but the center of town was only pedestrian, helping the crowd to forget the craziness of the traffic and insulating them from the noise. They walked through the street, arms touching, hands sometimes brushing against each other. They walked past the movie theater.

"I can't believe that. They're playing *The Sixth Sense* in French," exclaimed Chloe, pointing at the gigantic poster.

"Have you seen it?" asked Laurence.

"Yes, months ago. I loved it. Have you?"

"No, it just came out here, you know."

"You're kidding, right?"

"No. Would you like to see it again? They have a showing at 3:30 p.m. It's in 20 minutes."

Chloe looked at Laurence and nodded. "Yes, it could be fun to sit through it in French."

"Okay, let's go then."

Laurence bought tickets and led them into a large theater. They chose a row far back and sat down in the center. The room filled up quickly, and at 3:30 the movie started. Laurence waited only a few moments before lacing her fingers with Chloe's and bringing their linked hands onto her lap. Chloe smiled in the dark, but didn't take her gaze from the movie. Although she seemed engrossed in the movie, her mind was on the light stroking Laurence's thumb was doing to the inside of her wrist, and the sensations such a small movement produced in her. Laurence didn't release Chloe's hand until the lights came back on.

"That was a great movie," she said with a smile.

"Yeah, I'm glad I had seen it before because I had trouble concentrating," said Chloe jokingly. "Don't take that innocent look, would you? You know very well that when you take my hand, I can't concentrate on anything else."

"Huh…well…" Laurence didn't know what to reply. "Maybe we should go," she said blushing.

Chloe laughed. "Yeah, let's go. What time is it?"

"Past 6. Do you want to come back to my place? We can order pizza for dinner."

"You are not much of a cook are you?" joked Chloe. "I'd love to go back to your place, but honestly I'm not hungry at all right now."

"I'm sure you will be later on."

They walked back leisurely to Laurence's apartment while talking about the movie.

"I knew there was something wrong after he went to the restaurant to meet his wife, and she never even once looked at him."

"When I first saw it, I had no clue until the end. Isn't this little boy great?" asked Chloe.

"Yes, he sure is. He has such a spooky gaze," said Laurence, opening the door to her apartment.

Chloe collapsed on the futon and sighed. "Gosh, I'm exhausted. Don't know why, we didn't do much."

"You got up very early," answered Laurence. "Hey, I make a mean non-alcohol fruit cocktail, want one?"

"I'd love to." Laurence left for the kitchen, and for the next few minutes the blender noise stopped any possible conversation. Laurence came back and handed Chloe her glass. She sat next to her and clinked their glasses together.

"To this weekend," she said, looking at Chloe and taking a sip of her drink.

Chloe nodded and drank. "Hum, it's good. What's in it?"

"Can't tell," teased Laurence with a wink.

"Secret recipe, I see," joked Chloe. "Wow, you have quite a large number of CDs," said Chloe, looking at the CD tower standing next to the desk. She got up to take a closer look. The CDs were from a variety of French singers, American rock bands and classical music. "Boy, I wouldn't know what to choose. Can I just turn the radio on?"

"Sure," answered Laurence.

Chloe pushed a couple of different radio stations before stopping on one playing songs from the '80s. "I love the '80s. It's still my favorite music period."

"I like it too. They had great bands back then. Not those boys bands crap."

"Hey, hey don't forget New Kids on the Block. I was a big New Kids on the Block fan," smiled Chloe. Outside the sun was slowly setting, darkening the room. "Sweet Dreams" from the Eurythmics came on. "Lo, come on, dance with me," asked Chloe, grabbing Laurence and yanking her to her feet.

"Chloe, come on…not here in my apartment."

"Why not? Plus I never got to dance with you at the club," said Chloe, moving to the music.

"Fine, I'll dance," said Laurence, picking up the beat and starting to move. The next song was from the Pogs, and Laurence started jumping everywhere.

"Hey Lo, what are you doing?" asked Chloe laughing.

"Didn't you guys have this dance in the States? It's called the pogo, you just jumped and smashed yourself against everyone. Brings back memories," laughed Laurence, throwing herself against Chloe.

"Hey…wait a minute, I can do that too," chuckled Chloe. She started jumping and throwing herself against Laurence. A stronger shove sent Chloe flying towards the futon, but she grabbed Laurence in her fall and they both collapsed in a heap, laughing. Laurence ended up on top of Chloe, and her sudden goofiness turned to embarrassment. "Sorry," she said, trying to extract herself, but was stopped by Chloe.

"Lo, stop running. It's okay. I swear you're not scaring me," whispered Chloe. The song ended, and a slower beat replaced it. "I love this song," said Chloe recognizing "Still Loving You" from the Scorpions. "Would you dance with me?" she asked shyly.

Laurence nodded and slowly got up and extended her hand to Chloe. She led her to the center of the room and wrapped her arms around her waist. They stared at each other and started moving to the rhythm of the music. Chloe came closer to Laurence, never leaving her gaze. The room had become darker, casting shadows on their faces. Laurence drew Chloe closer into the circle of her arms and touched their foreheads together. No words were spoken; none were needed. Laurence started rubbing her hands up and down Chloe's back while Chloe moved even closer and buried her face into Laurence's chest. She tightened her grip around Laurence's waist and lightly kissed her collarbone through her shirt. This slight kiss sent tingles all the way down Laurence's spine. She tenderly took hold of Chloe's chin and lifted her face. She scanned her eyes for any signs of discomfort and lovingly brought her lips to Chloe's. Chloe passed her hands through Laurence's hair and softly stroked the base of her scalp while pressing their lips closer together. The dancing was suddenly forgotten as they got lost in each other's kiss. Laurence brought her hands up to caress Chloe's face and gently deepened the kiss. Chloe gasped and stopped her hands' movements on Laurence's scalp, Laurence's lips distracting her from anything else. As the song ended, Laurence slowly moved away.

"Wow," she smiled, opening her eyes slowly. "Are you okay?" she asked, suddenly concerned that she had pushed Chloe too far.

Chloe looked at her, trying to regain control of her emotions. "Would you stop asking me that? I think I was a willing participant, and yeah, I agree...wow," she said with a huge smile on her face.

Laurence smiled back and caressed Chloe's face. "I'm sorry, I just don't want to push you into something you don't want."

"Lo, please stop worrying," said Chloe, leaning into Laurence's hand. The room had gotten really dark, making it hard for them to discern each other. The darkness brought an air of mystery to the situation. Chloe moved toward Laurence and lightly pushed her back until she encountered the futon and had to sit down. Chloe kept on staring at Laurence, the green of her eyes turned to a deep brown with the darkness of the room. She gently straddled Laurence's lap and sat down facing her. "Lo, I know you said that you've never been with another woman, but I'm sure you've been with guys. You probably didn't stop every few minutes to ask them if they were okay and if you were going too far."

"It's different, Chloe," answered Laurence, putting her hands on Chloe's laps.

"How? Why do you assume I'm this fragile little girl who is going to leave screaming as soon as you do anything to her?" asked Chloe, suddenly feeling frustrated with the situation.

Laurence sighed and shook her head lightly. "Chloe, why rush? I don't know what I'm doing here, and I want to make sure that whatever I do, I do it right."

Chloe got off Laurence's lap and knelt in front of her, taking her hands. "Lo, I don't want to rush into anything either, but you have to trust me that if you do something I don't want, I'll tell you. We have to stop wondering if everything we do is right and go with our instincts like I did in the forest on Monday, and like you just did a few minutes ago when you kissed me. Okay?"

Laurence nodded. "Go with my instinct, right?"

"Yeah, no holding back."

"Okay," said Laurence, getting up and pulling Chloe back on her feet. She suddenly picked up Chloe, making her yelp, and laid her down on the couch. She knelt in front of the couch near Chloe's head and lightly kissed her way down to her mouth, where she placed a soft kiss. Chloe brought her arms behind Laurence's neck and drew her closer. The kiss, tender, almost like a dream, sent shivers down Chloe's body, and she gradually closed her eyes. She tucked Laurence closer, and her heart started beating faster when she felt the weight of Laurence's body settling next to her. She opened her eyes to gaze into Laurence's. The blue of her eyes had turned smoky black, revealing passion. Laurence resumed her kissing, and ever so slightly let her hands roam over Chloe's back before pulling her shirt out and running her hands on bare skin. At the feel of Laurence's hands on her skin, Chloe stopped the kiss and buried her face into Laurence's neck. The gentle stroking suddenly stopped, and Chloe looked up.

"Why did you stop?" she asked.

"I...I think we should slow down. Before you say anything, listen to me. We're moving fast, and it's scaring me." Laurence paused and looked at Chloe for some sort of understanding; finding Chloe looking at her very intensely, she continued. "I have never been in any type of serious relationship and honestly...I can't even remember the last time I slept with someone. Neither of us has been with a woman before. I want to make sure that when we do make love, neither of us has any doubts..."

"I don't have any doubts now," said Chloe softly.

"...but I do," whispered Laurence.

Chloe extracted herself from Laurence's arms and got up. "What do you mean you do?"

"You told me you only wanted the truth from me. You said that you wanted to know if I felt like running away. Chloe, I'm only being honest."

"What are you scared of, Laurence? Haven't I showed you enough you can trust me? I don't get it. I thought you cared for me…"

"Wait a minute. Who said that I don't care for you? Chloe, if I didn't care for you I wouldn't care if I slept with you or not. I don't want to be some sort of experimentation or the affair you have while spending a year in Paris…"

"Then what do you want?" asked Chloe harshly.

"Everything." Laurence got up and walked to Chloe.

"What do you mean?" asked Chloe her anger slowly dropping.

"What I mean is I want you to consider having me in your life for a very long time…and unless you are sure, then I don't think we should cross the line," explained Laurence stepping closer to Chloe.

"Lo, I can't predict what is going to happen between us, but I can tell you that I really care for you, and…"

"Chloe, I don't doubt for a minute that you care for me, but what I'm asking from you is a commitment. I want us to be on the same level, so there are no surprises. No one gets hurt unexpectedly, and we know where we stand," explained Laurence, taking Chloe's hands and lightly kissing them.

"You drive a hard bargain," said Chloe with a slight, understanding smile.

"I love you," answered Laurence, looking straight into Chloe's eyes. "No, please, you don't have to say anything unless you really mean it," said Laurence, stopping Chloe from replying. "Just think about what I said, okay?"

Chloe nodded. "Does this mean no more kissing, hugging or dancing?" Chloe joked to lighten the mood.

"Hum…no…I think kissing is required…hugging is a must, and we'll have to see about dancing," said Laurence with a wink.

"Lo?"

"What?"

"I promise I won't make you wait too long for…"

"Chloe, there is no rush. I just want us to be together for the right reasons." Laurence walked to her desk and picked up the phone. "What about that pizza now?"

"Sounds great. I'm starving."

"What do you like?"

"Ham and pineapple?"

"Yuk...I'm a cheese and sausage kind of girl. What about we do half and half?"

"Sure, that's fine." Chloe watched the traffic outside while Laurence placed the order. Her mind replayed the conversation they just had. *Do I love her? Am I just attracted to her?* Chloe looked at Laurence, her black jet hair shined in the darkness, her figure stood elegantly propped up against the fireplace, her hands playing with the telephone cord. Chloe let her eyes roam over Laurence's body, and her heart skipped a beat. *I don't think I could let her out of my life right now... she matters too much. I think I'm in love with her.* Chloe smiled at Laurence who seemed to be in an animated conversation with the pizza place. *I'm going to have to prove it to her; I have to show her that I want to be with her for her and not for sex or anything else.*

"What are you thinking about?" asked Laurence, interrupting Chloe's musing.

"You," answered Chloe honestly. "Do you think we should call home to check on Clément?" asked Chloe, stopping Laurence from answering.

"I was thinking about that. Yes, I think we should." She dialed the number and waited for someone to pick up.

"'pa?"

"Laurence. Comment se passe ton weekend?"

"Très bien. Comment vas Clément?"

"Il coure partout. Nous sommes allés à EuroDisney World aujourd'hui."

"C'est surper," giggled Laurence.

"Est-ce que Chloe est près de toi?"

"Oui."

"Passe la moi pour une minute."

"Chloe, my dad wants to talk to you," said Laurence, handing the phone to Chloe.

"Hi, Jean."

"Hi, is she driving you crazy yet?" he joked.

"Yeah, but I can deal with it," Chloe teased back.

"Are you having a good time?"

"Yes, I am."

"Okay, what time are you getting back tomorrow?"

"My train arrives at 7p.m."

"I'll come get you."

"No, it's okay, I can take a cab. Plus, it's Clément's bath time."

"That's okay, Beatrice can do that."

"No," answered Chloe more forcefully than expected. "I mean, really you don't need to. Lo and I were thinking that I might grab a later train, so you see, we are not sure yet."

"Oh, okay. Call me if you change your mind."

"Sure. Thanks."

"You are welcome. Bye."

"Boy, that was a close call," said Chloe, hanging up the phone.

"What?"

"He wanted to come and get me from the train station tomorrow night and leave Clément with Beatrice."

"He is not going to, is he?" asked Laurence, worried.

"No, I changed his mind. Lo, you have to talk to him."

"I know. I don't want to do that over the phone though. I'm thinking of going home next weekend to talk to him."

"That might be a good idea."

"Do you think you can keep Beatrice at bay for another week?"

"Yeah, it shouldn't be a problem."

"Thanks."

"Lo, can I ask you something?"

"Sure go ahead," answered Laurence. "I'm getting another drink. Do you want something?"

"No, thanks. Maybe later on with the pizza."

"'kay." Laurence disappeared into the kitchen and came back a few moments later holding a glass of water. "What's your question?"

"What are you going to do about Clément?"

"What do you mean? I'm going to talk to my dad…"

"No, I mean, have you ever thought of raising him as your own?" Chloe walked back to the futon and sat down.

"He is not mine anymore. I explained that to you."

"Yes, I know, but you technically could. Think about it…he loves you more than Beatrice, and no offense, but even if your dad is a great dad, he is not around very much." Chloe paused and smoothed out some imaginary wrinkles off her jeans.

"Chloe, can't we drop it? This conversation is going to bring us nowhere," said Laurence, a hint of sadness in her voice.

"But Lo, don't just give up so easily. There is something you can do about it. I'm sure that you could prove to the judge that you were forced to give him up and signed the papers..."

"I never signed anything," interrupted Laurence.

"What?" exclaimed Chloe.

"Drop it," said Laurence shortly.

"No. What do you mean you never signed anything?" asked Chloe insistently.

"I never signed any papers saying that my dad was allowed to adopt Clément, that's it."

"Wait a minute. If the law here is the same as in the US, the mother automatically gets reported as the legal parent unless she signed papers agreeing to have her child adopted. The father is the one who has to go and declare the child, so the child can carry his name. Have you ever looked at Clément's birth certificate?"

"No. Chloe..."

"Come on, hear me out." Chloe got up and started pacing. "To know if your dad ever went and declared himself as the father, you just have to look at the birth certificate. If he did, his name should be on it. If he didn't, it should say *father unknown*." Chloe suddenly made a realization. "Oh, my God. Laurence, you know what that means? Since you never signed anything, it means Beatrice is not legally Clément's mother."

Laurence looked at Chloe not knowing what to say. "Chloe, either way it makes no difference. Clément thinks she is his mother, and I don't want to confuse him."

"Laurence, for God sakes, you have to face the facts. He is scared of her, she beats him."

"We have no proof," answered Laurence, frustrated.

"What is wrong with you? A little while ago, you were ready to talk to your dad about it, now you are throwing this 'we have no proof' crap at me! Come on, what's really bothering you?" asked Chloe. Her voice had raised a notch, and she was getting really animated.

Laurence sat on the edge of the window, her face illuminated by the outside lights. "I can't be a mother to him, Chloe. A sister, yes, I know how to do that, but not a mother."

"That is bullshit, Laurence. You have so much patience with him, and you are so concerned about everything he does. How can you say that?"

The intercom suddenly buzzed. Laurence walked up to it and pressed talk.

"Allo."

"*Pizza.*"

"D'accord. Premier étage. Première porte sur la gauche." She buzzed the pizza guy in and turned to Chloe. "I don't want to talk about it anymore. Can we do that?" she asked firmly.

Chloe sighed. "Fine. Let's drop it."

① ① ①

Laurence paid for the pizza and closed the door. She dropped the pizza on the table and went into the kitchen to retrieve two plates.

"Dinner is served," she said jokingly, sitting down.

Chloe couldn't help smiling. She sat down facing Laurence. "What do you have planned for tomorrow?" asked Chloe, reaching for a slice.

"My friend Jackie who lives next door is leaving for a trip early tomorrow morning, and in exchange of watering her plants, I get to use her car. I thought we could drive up north a little, and we could visit one of the old coal mines. If you are interested, that is." Laurence took a bite of her pizza.

"Sounds like fun. How come you left your bike in Versailles?"

"I don't usually, but I had too much crap to bring back here. If I come next weekend, I'll take it back."

They finished eating while making small talk.

"How did it get to be so late already?" asked Chloe, looking at the alarm clock on top of the TV.

"It's only 10. Do you want to watch a movie?"

"That would be fun. What do you have?'

"One of my all-time favorites is this movie called *La Grande Vadrouille*. It's with this French comic actor, Louis De Funes. He is hilarious...I think you might understand better if it's a comedy." Laurence got up and opened one of the closet doors in search of the tape. "Here it is," she said showing off the tape. "Are you game?"

"Sure, you have to tell me what it's about, though."

"It's hard to explain. What about I stop the tape every once in a while to check if you understand?"

"Okay."

Laurence opened the futon and grabbed two pillows from the closet. She sat down with her back propped up against the wall and patted the area next to her. Chloe flopped herself next to Laurence and adjusted the pillow behind her head. Laurence pressed play and turned the lights off.

They had not touched since the conversation earlier, so Laurence hesitantly took hold of Chloe's hand, interlacing their fingers together. Chloe turned to her side and looked at Laurence. They stared at each other, the movie playing in the background, the only words spoken in the room those of the characters on the screen. At the same time, they moved forward as if drawn by a supernatural force, their lips softly pressed together, their eyes closing. The kiss was gentle, undemanding, just a reassurance that things were still possible between them. It stopped as gently as it started, nose and forehead touching, hearts beating faster, eyes looking deeply into each other and hands linked together.

Laurence lay back on her pillow and opened her arms for Chloe. Chloe scooted forward and put her head down in the crook of Laurence's shoulder, wrapped her arms around Laurence's waist, and sighed.

"What's that sigh for?" asked Laurence, gently running her hand through Chloe's hair.

"Nothing really. It just feels so right."

"What feels so right?"

Chloe sat up. "You, holding me, kissing me…I know you think I'm not ready to make a commitment yet, but you are wrong. I…think…I love you. No wait, that came out wrong. I don't think I love you, I know I love you…please don't say anything. I respect what you said earlier, and I'm not asking you to change anything. I just want you to know, and I'm going to do everything in my power to prove it to you."

"Thanks," whispered Laurence.

"For what?"

"For being so understanding."

"Yeah, yeah, don't get used to it," teased Chloe, lying back down. Laurence chuckled suddenly. "What's so funny?"

"Those guys are too much," said Laurence, pointing at the TV. "I have seen this movie so many times, but this scene still makes me laugh."

"Care to explain?"

"Sorry, I keep on forgetting that you don't understand everything. Those two guys are trying to run away from the Germans. They stopped in a hotel for the night and have to share the same room. Well, the two German officers running after them just stopped in the same hotel and are also sharing the same room."

"I don't see what's so funny."

"Wait, I'm not finished. Okay, The Germans are in room 9 and the French guys in room 6. One of the Germans just got up to go get something to eat, and one of the French guys got up to go to the bathroom. While they were gone, the 9 falls, spins, and now looks like a 6..."

"I get it. The German guy and the French guy are going to walk back into the wrong room. The French guy is going to spend the night with the German guy, and vice-versa."

"You got it!"

"French people have a weird sense of humor. Sorry, but I don't find it funny..."

"We have a weird sense of humor? I recall seeing a movie called *Austin Powers*...that was twisted humor."

"Okay, okay, so we don't agree on movies," yawned Chloe.

"Are you tired?" asked Laurence.

"Getting there."

Laurence reached for the remote and turned the TV off, plunging the room into darkness. She disengaged herself from Chloe and turned the light on.

"You didn't have to stop the movie."

"I know, but I don't want to get up too late tomorrow, so we should probably get some sleep. It's getting late anyway." Laurence got up and grabbed a t-shirt and boxer shorts from the closet. "I'll go change for the night. Be right back."

Chloe was left alone in the room. She went into the kitchen to get a glass of water. "Boy, it's tiny in here," she exclaimed. The small kitchen was barely large enough for a small fridge, a stove and a sink. Chloe extended her arms and laughed when she realized that she could almost touch the walls.

"What's so funny?" called Laurence from the other room.

"Your kitchen," answered Chloe, pouring herself a glass of water. "It's minuscule," said Chloe, continuing the conversation as she came back into the main room.

"It fits its purpose," answered Laurence pulling off the cover and slipping into bed. "Plus, I never cook. I don't have time, and I hate it."

"That explains it." Chloe looked through her bag and retrieved a nightshirt and her toothbrush. "I'll be right back."

"There are clean towels on the rack for you."

"Thanks."

Five minutes later, Chloe came out carrying her clothes and dumped them next to her bag. She suddenly stopped and looked at Laurence who had already made herself comfortable in bed.

"Where do I sleep?" she asked awkwardly.

Laurence laughed. "Are you going to go shy on me?" She tapped the area next to her.

Chloe smiled and got into bed. Laurence reached for the light switch and the room went dark. Chloe adjusted her pillow. "Thanks for inviting me this weekend. I'm having a great time."

Laurence propped herself up on her elbow, her face barely visible in the dark. "Thanks for coming. A week ago, I wasn't too sure you'd be here right now."

Chloe smiled in the dark and softly caressed Laurence's face. "You know when we first met, I used to think you were such a cold b…"

"Bitch?" asked Laurence amused.

"Well, yeah, but I changed my mind very fast."

"I wasn't too easy to deal with, so no offense taken," said Laurence, bringing Chloe's hand to her mouth and kissing them. "We should really get some sleep."

"You're right. I'm beat." Chloe turned on her side facing the windows and closed her eyes. "Good night, Lo." Instead of an answer, she felt the bed shift, and Laurence wrapped an arm around Chloe's waist, drawing her close.

"Is that okay?" asked Laurence.

Chloe scooted back closer and rested her hand on Laurence's arm. "More than okay."

Laurence lightly kissed Chloe's hair. "Good night, Chloe," she whispered before closing her eyes.

Chapter 9

Chloe woke up alone in bed. She grabbed a pillow and covered her face with it to protect herself from the sun rays piercing through the blinds. *I wonder where Lo went.* After a few moments of trying to go back to sleep, Chloe sat up, rubbed her eyes and stretched. She glanced at the alarm clock and realized that it was only 8. *I can't believe I am awake so early on a Sunday morning.* She got up and went to the bathroom to splash some water on her face.

"Hello," said Laurence after opening the door.

Chloe stepped out of the bathroom smiling. "Hi, where did you go?"

"For a run, and I got us some breakfast," she explained showing the bag of croissants she had just gotten from the boulangerie.

"It smells really good. Do you go running everyday?"

"Yes, I try," said Laurence, going into the kitchen and coming back with two plates, the butter and two knives. "Can you get two glasses and the orange juice in the fridge?" asked Laurence while setting up the table.

"Sure." Chloe got what Laurence asked for, and put everything down on the table next to the rest. "Thanks for getting us breakfast."

"You're welcome," smiled Laurence, motioning for Chloe to sit down. Instead of that, Chloe moved and hugged Laurence. "What is that for?" asked Laurence, teasingly.

"It's a good morning greeting," answered Chloe while releasing Laurence.

"I see. Wouldn't this be more appropriate for a good morning greeting?" said Laurence, drawing Chloe back into her arms and kissing her tenderly. The kiss was brief, almost teasing.

"Lo, are you trying to torture me here?"

"What do you mean?" asked Laurence, not understanding the question.

"If you keep on kissing me like that, I don't know if I can keep up with our bargain," answered Chloe, sensually rubbing Laurence's arm.

Laurence blushed. "Well…I…I didn't realize that …"

Chloe laughed. "It's okay, just teasing. Come on, let's eat."

They ate leisurely, enjoying the feel of the warm croissant melting in their mouths.

"What is that?" asked Chloe, pointing at a jar containing a brown substance.

"The best thing on earth. It's called Nutella. It's Roche D'or chocolate with hazelnut."

"How do you eat it?"

"Like this," said Laurence, opening the jar, digging her knife in it and spreading a large amount on a croissant.

"Yuk," said Chloe, making a face.

"Don't knock it before you've tried it." Laurence broke off a piece of the croissant and handed it to Chloe, who took it hesitantly. "Come on, I'm not trying to poison you," joked Laurence.

"Fine." She took a small bite and waited for the taste to register. "Wow, it's really good."

"Told you," smiled Laurence, finishing her croissant and licking the leftover Nutella off her fingers.

They finished off breakfast, and Laurence sent Chloe to go shower first while she cleaned off the table. Chloe showered quickly and put on a pair of jeans and her long sleeved UM t-shirt, dried her hair, brushed her teeth and stepped out.

"How many sweatshirts and t-shirts with a University of Maryland logo do you have?" asked Laurence, jokingly.

"Try living on campus with no car and the closest mall 10 miles away, and you'll see if the bookstore doesn't become your favorite clothing store."

Laurence laughed. "Okay, my turn. I won't be long. We can get going after that."

"Sure." Laurence grabbed some clothes from the closet and closed the bathroom door behind her. She came out ten minutes later dressed in a pair of jean overalls and a white tank top. "Okay, are you ready?"

"As I'll ever be," said Chloe, putting her jacket on. "I like your overalls."

"When I wear them, it means I ran out of clean pants, and I have to do some laundry," smiled Laurence. She opened the door and let Chloe slip by before stepping out and locking it.

They got into a tiny little yellow car that Laurence said was called a Clio.

"Where are we going?" Chloe asked as Laurence started the car.

"To a small town call Leware. It's only half an hour away from here. We'll be back in time for your train. It's at 4:30, right?"

"Yeah. Are we going to visit a mine?"

"That's the plan. Is it still okay with you?"

"It should be interesting."

"It is." Laurence drove through the streets of Lille and got onto the expressway. Chloe relaxed and put her hand on Laurence's lap. Laurence reached for it and stroked it lightly. Ten minutes later, Laurence maneuvered the car into the exit ramp. They drove through the countryside and fields surrounding it.

"What is that?" asked Chloe, pointing at a black mountain.

"This is a coal mountain."

"Wow."

Laurence pulled the car into a parking lot and stopped. "Here we are." They got out and walked into a building where miners' memorabilia was displayed everywhere. After paying for the tickets, they were asked to wait for a bus to take them to the mine, and were handed protective hats.

"Now we are going to look really goofy, wearing those things," laughed Chloe.

Laurence shrugged and put her hat on. After taking a look at her, Chloe started laughing.

"Go ahead and make fun," smiled Laurence.

"Sorry, you look like the perfect miner with your overalls and your hat," laughed Chloe. Before Laurence had time to answer, the bus arrived to take them to the entrance of the mine.

"Lo, is that really a mine or a reproduction?"

"It used to be a real one, but it hasn't been working for over ten years now. It's only for visitors."

They stepped into a room with thousands of lanterns hanging on the wall. The guide explained that this was the room where the miners would come, register for work and grab their lanterns.

"What is he saying?" asked Chloe, not understanding.

"It's very dark down there, so the lantern was the miner's best friend," explained Laurence. As they followed the guide through the visit, Laurence translated everything. What really fascinated Chloe was the wooden elevator, which was more like an open cage hanging from a cable. Laurence explained that sometimes up to thirty people would climb into it to be sent to the bottom. The elevator would descend at speeds up to four meters per second.

"Like a small roller coaster," stated Chloe.

"Worse than that. The guide said that anyone who would go in it for the first time would puke."

"Yuk, that's a pretty picture."

They went through tunnels and were showed how a miner would keep the tunnel from crumbling by reinforcing it with wood. The darkness and suffocating air were oppressive; the mine was silent except for the voice from the guide, making Chloe want to run up for fresh air and light.

"Hey, are you okay?" asked Laurence to Chloe who had stopped.

"Yeah, it's just so hot in here, and somehow freaky."

"We are almost out," answered Laurence, taking hold of Chloe's hand and leading her toward the group.

"How deep are we?" asked Chloe.

"I'm not sure, but I'll guess 80 or 100 meters."

"What's that in feet?"

"I have no idea, sorry. Trust me, though, it's fairly deep."

"It's why we can't hear anything."

"What do you mean?"

"Listen...beside the guide's voice, you can't hear the traffic or the birds...I can't even imagine how people could work in those conditions."

"Children came down here also. They were allowed their first descent at the age of nine."

Chloe looked at Laurence. "It's crazy."

Laurence nodded and let go of Chloe's hand as they caught up with the group. A few minutes later they were back to the surface. "Okay, I'm happy to be back topside again," said Chloe, taking her hat off.

"I agree, and I'm hungry. I tell you what, it's only 11:30, we could go to the local supermarket, get some food and have a picnic."

"Wow, that sounds great." Chloe smiled. "Very romantic."

Laurence smiled back. "So, let's go." They waited for the bus to take them back to the parking lot and got in the car. Laurence drove into downtown Leware and stopped in front of a small grocery shop.

"I don't think we're going to find any major supermarket. Let's check this shop out."

The shop had the minimum necessities, but they were able to buy a baguette and dry sausage to make sandwiches. Laurence drove them out of town, and after they had been driving on a country road for a couple of minutes, turned right suddenly onto a dirt road.

"Where are we going?" asked Chloe curiously.

"You'll see," Laurence answered simply.

They drove down the very bumpy road for a few minutes, and Laurence stopped the car under a tree.

"Come on," she said, grabbing the groceries and getting out of the car. She started walking into a wheat field.

"Hey, Lo, you can't do that," called Chloe.

"Why not?"

"It's private property."

Laurence looked around, amused. "I don't see anyone for kilometers. Come on. Trust me, nothing is going to happen."

"Okay," answered Chlo,e unsure.

Laurence walked through the field, followed closely by Chloe. Once Laurence thought they were deep enough, she started running and jumping in a circle, flattening the wheat so they could sit down. "Come on, help me out."

"Lo, you're crazy," laughed Chloe, joining in.

After a few minutes of jumping around, Laurence took her jacket off and laid the food down on it. "Lunch, my lady," she said, gently mocking Chloe. Chloe sat down and looked around. They were surrounded by wheat, and she couldn't see anything besides the intense blue sky above them. The sound of cars passing by could be heard, but it sounded very far away, almost as if they had managed to isolate themselves from civilization.

"This is great."

"I told you there was no reason to worry," smiled Laurence, cutting the baguette with her pocket knife.

"Pocket knife, huh?"

"Never hurts to be prepared." Laurence handed Chloe a piece of bread and sliced one for her.

"Lo, this field belongs to someone. What if this person comes and catches us?"

"Not a chance. People are very religious around here, and trust me, nobody works in the fields on Sunday unless it's harvest time." Laurence cut off some slices of the dry sausage and put it on her piece of bread.

"What's the name of this thing again?" asked Chloe, pointing at the sausage.

"Saussiçon. It's really good."

"You guys really eat the strangest things," said Chloe, imitating Laurence and putting some slices of the dry sausage on her bread.

Laurence chuckled. "I'm going to drop it this time." She opened the bottle of water they bought and drank from it before handing it to Chloe.

"How did you find out about this place?" asked Chloe before drinking.

Laurence sighed. "One of the guys I used to party with a few years back…his parents own a farm not far away. I got really drunk one night, and somehow woke up here."

"In this field?"

"Where the car is parked…"

"Some party it must have been," joked Chloe.

"I don't remember." Laurence finished her sandwich and lay down with her hands behind her head. She slowly closed her eyes and let herself bask in the sun. Chloe took off her jacket and lay down next to her. She propped herself on her elbow and looked at Laurence. She looked relaxed, her chest rising slowly up and down with the rhythm of her breathing, the wheat slowly casting shadows over her face, her hair shining with red highlights from the sun.

"I can feel you staring at me," smiled Laurence, her eyes still closed.

"Sorry..." said Chloe, embarrassed from having been caught. Laurence sat up smiling. "Don't be. It's okay," she said tenderly.

Chloe looked at Laurence. The blue of her eyes was almost transparent, giving her a very surreal appearance. "Your eye color is so strange. It changes with your mood. Black for anger, deep blue for amusement, green for passion, but right now I can't read it...it's so clear it's almost white," explained Chloe softly.

Laurence smiled and gently brushed a lock of blond hair behind Chloe's ear. She let her hand linger on her neck and drew her in for a kiss. She slowly pushed Chloe back down and lay down next to her. Her hands caressed Chloe's face, her lips tenderly moving against hers. Chloe ran her hands along Laurence's back and pulled her closer, deepening the kiss, making Laurence gasp. Passion slowly started to build and their hands got more adventurous. After a few moments, Laurence withdrew, her breathing ragged, her voice quivering. "I...think we should stop..."

Chloe was going to protest, but one look at Laurence made her change her mind.

Laurence looked flustered, her eyes almost scared. "Sure," she answered softly, sitting up.

"I'm sorry...I started it and I shouldn't have," apologized Laurence.

Chloe reached for Laurence's hand. "Lo, it's okay. Remember, kissing is a must," smiled Chloe.

"Yeah, but how long can we control it?"

"Until you find it in your heart to trust me and let go." Chloe didn't wait for an answer and got up. "I guess we should probably get going."

"You're right, we should." Laurence got up and followed Chloe, who had already started to make her way back. She caught up with her and stopped her. What she was going to say vanished at the sight of tears in Chloe's eyes.

"Chloe, I'm sorry, I..."

"It's okay, you were honest with me. I didn't know how hard it would be. I'm just expecting too much from you," said Chloe with a shaky voice.

Laurence wiped the tears rolling down Chloe's face with her thumbs and brought Chloe's face to eye level with her. For a few moments they stared at each other.

"I love you, Chloe," said Laurence, breaking the silence.

"I love you, too. I thought I would try to prove to you that I love you, and that you can trust me, but the truth is that I don't know how. I can only tell you and hope you'll believe me. I'm not giving up on you Lo, it just hurts me that you can't trust me enough to give me this part of yourself I yearn for."

Laurence dropped her gaze and stepped back. "I'm sorry."

"I know, you've said that already. Lo, I believe you, I'm not mad. It takes time. Please look at me." Chloe touched Laurence's shoulder gently turning her to face her. "I guess I'm also sexually frustrated," joked Chloe, wiping remaining tears off her cheeks.

Laurence smiled and took Chloe into a hug. She buried her face in her hair and whispered, "I love you."

"I know," answered Chloe, her voice barely a murmur.

Chapter 10

They walked back to the car, each lost in her thoughts. Before getting into the car, Laurence tried to apologize again, but Chloe refused to hear her.

"Lo, enough, okay? I don't want to talk about it anymore," explained Chloe, suddenly feeling extremely tired.

Laurence nodded and got into the car, unlocking the door for Chloe. Not a word was exchanged as Laurence drove the car down the dirt road. Her hands were holding the steering wheel very tightly, her knuckles were almost white, her jaw was clenched and her eyes were fixed to the road. Chloe saw Laurence's tension and suddenly felt guilty for the way she reacted. She sighed and shook her head. *She's been through a lot and she has every right to want to wait before taking our relationship further. What has gotten into me?* Not knowing how to apologize for her reaction at the moment—while driving 120 kilometers per hour down the expressway—Chloe decided to wait until they got back to Lille.

Twenty minutes later, Laurence parked the car in front of her building and got out, followed by Chloe. Still no words had been spoken. They walked into the apartment, and Laurence dropped her keys on her desk. She stood at the window, her hands in her pocket, her shoulders slightly hunched. "You should probably pack. Your train is in an hour," she said, breaking the silence.

Chloe came up behind Laurence and forced her to turn around and face her. "Listen, I'm sorry about my reaction earlier. You don't understand how frustrating it is to realize that someone you care so much about just doesn't see it…just doesn't believe you." Chloe looked at Laurence, but Laurence's eyes held no answer, no sign of understanding. "Fine, be mad. Have it your way," said Chloe frustratedly. She walked to her suitcase and stared packing.

"It's true, isn't it?"

"What?" said Chloe, surprised at hearing Laurence's voice.

"You really care for me."

Chloe stopped her packing and came close to Laurence. "When is that thick head of yours going to understand that? I don't just care for you…I love you. It's deeper, more powerful." Chloe stopped and looked at Laurence, whose eyes had lost their anger to be replaced by a hint of hope. "Lo, I don't want to keep going over that with you. Either you believe me or not, it's up to you. I know how I feel and I know what I want."

"I'm being stupid, huh?" asked Laurence.

"No, you're being careful, and I can't blame you, but I don't have to agree."

Laurence nodded and smiled tenderly. "The roles are reversed now. Yesterday, I was telling you to take your time and to make sure you knew what you wanted. Today, I'm asking for more time…"

"You don't know what you want anymore?" asked Chloe, hesitantly.

"No, no I do," rushed Laurence. She stepped forward and took hold of Chloe's hands. "Nothing has changed. I still want you. I guess the physical relationship is scarier than I thought it was going to be…kissing is okay, but more is frightening, more intense than anything I have ever felt. I'll get over it," she smiled.

"But…do you believe me now when I say that I know what I want?" asked Chloe, slowly.

"Yes."

Chloe's face lit up with a smile, and she threw herself into Laurence's arms almost knocking her over. They hold each other tightly for a few minutes before letting go. "We should really get going," said Laurence, caressing Chloe's face.

"Yeah, I know. I'm basically packed."

"Okay, let's go then." Laurence picked up Chloe's suitcase and they left the apartment. Laurence drove Chloe to the train station. In contrast to the day before, when she had not hugged Chloe in public for fear of embarrassing her, Laurence took Chloe into her arms and briefly kissed her on the cheek.

"Call me when you get home, would you?" asked Laurence.

Chloe nodded. "As soon as I get home." She picked up her suitcase and climbed onto the train. Chloe waved at Laurence as the train left the station, and settled back on her seat once Laurence was out of sight. The train ride was uneventful, and shortly after 7, Chloe arrived at her destination. She got out of the station and hailed a cab.

"Rue de Provence, Versailles," she said to the cab driver while climbing in.

The ride back to the house was smooth and fast, the traffic almost non-existent on this Sunday evening. The cab pulled up in front of the house around 7:45, and Chloe rapidly got out after paying the driver. She opened the door and was treated to Clément's screams coming from upstairs. Chloe dropped her suitcase and rushed upstairs calling Jean's name, but got no answer. She burst into Clément's bedroom and rushed to the bathroom where the screams were coming from. There was Clément sitting in the tub, his little body racked with sobs.

"Hey, hey, sweetheart, it's okay. Where is everyone?" she knelt in front of the tub and called again for Jean and Beatrice, once more hearing no reply. "Let's get you out of here." Chloe bent to pick up Clément. "My gosh, you are freezing…oh, sweetheart, how long have you been in this water?" She picked up Clément, whose sobs had turned into quiet tears, and wrapped him in a towel, rubbing him to warm him up. She carried Clément to his room and put him gently on his bed. "Hush, hush, I'm just getting you something warm to wear." She quickly grabbed a pair of pajamas from his dresser drawer and returned to him. She unwrapped the towel from his body and sat him up to put on his top, but suddenly stopped, terrified by what she saw. "Oh, my gosh, Clément!" Clément had a large bruise extending from his lower back to the middle of it, and his legs bore cigarette marks. Chloe contained a sob and took a large breath to calm herself down. *Think Chloe, think. How did I not see that in the tub?*

"Okay, what does Laurence put on your cuts when you fall to

avoid an infection? Come on, damn it, what is it?" Chloe mumbled to herself. She gingerly checked Clément for any other injuries, slowly lay him on the bed, and draped a blanket over him. "It's okay, pumpkin, I'm going to make it all better, just let me get something in the medicine cabinet…hush, hush…I'll be right back." She ran downstairs and opened the cabinet, frantically dumping its contents in search of the medicine. "Yes, Neosporin, that's it." She ran back upstairs and found Clément exactly in the position she had left him.

"Okay, sweetie, this is going to help with your burns." She softly applied the transparent gel to his ankles and put bandages on his burns. "Okay, now your back." She turned him on his side and gently ran her hand over the bruise, making Clément cry. "Oh, babe, I'm so sorry…I think we need to have a doctor see it." Chloe started feeling very angry. "If I ever see your mother again, I swear I'm going to kill her…how could she? How…." Chloe let tears of anger fall and hugged Clément to her chest. "And where is your dad? He said he'd be here when I get back…this is all my fault." After a few minutes, she stopped and got up, carrying Clément with her. "We've got to get out of here. Who knows what she'll do when she comes back." With one hand, she picked up Clément's old diaper bag and threw in some socks, underwear, a pair of sweat pants, a t-shirt and a sweater. She quickly put his pajamas on and wrapped him in the blanket again, being careful of his injured back. Clément was now sniffling and clinging to Chloe. She ran to her room and picked up her address book, as she was rushing out of the room again, she saw a note lying on her bed. She quickly opened it.

Chloe,
Hi, I hope you had a great weekend. I'm sorry I had to leave. I will be in England until Friday. Here is the hotel I'm staying in. Ritz hotel, 21-45-67-89. I'll call with the room number.
Thanks.
Jean.

"Damn you, Jean," she said vehemently, stuffing the note in her pocket and rushing downstairs. She put Clément down on the coach and grabbed the phone.

"Come on, come on…please pick up….Allo?"

"Allo."
"Vincent, this is Chloe."
"Hey, Chloe, how are you?"
"I need your help right now. Please come get me as soon as you can."
"Chloe, what's wrong?"
"Vincent, please," begged Chloe.
"Okay, I'll be there as soon as I can."
"Thanks," whispered Chloe, hanging up the phone.

She then dialed Laurence's number, but got the answering machine. "Lo, we have a problem here. I...I...Call me at this number later on." She left Vincent's number and hung up, thinking it was no use to alarm Laurence for the moment.

Chloe went back to Clément and sat him on her lap. "Okay, babe, I'm taking you out of here. It's going to be all right." Fear suddenly replaced the earlier adrenaline rush, and Chloe tightened her grip on Clément and waited for Vincent to come to the rescue.

Chapter 11

Chloe waited with Clément wrapped tightly in her arms. Clément had stopped crying, and his body was limp in Chloe's arms. Chloe tried to keep herself calm and gently rocked him, whispering a lullaby in his ear. Suddenly the phone rang. Chloe got up, making Clément whimper. "Shush...it's just the phone."
    She gently put Clément down on the couch and ran to the phone. "Allo."
    "It's me. What's happening? What is the problem?"
    "Lo…" Chloe stopped, trying to hold her tears back.
    "Chloe, what's going on? Come on, you're really scaring me."
    Chloe took a deep breath, and glanced at Clément, who was lying on his side in a corner of the couch. His body was folded in the fetal position and his eyes were looking ahead, their expression almost blank.
    "I came home and I found Clément alone in the tub. He had been there for who knows how long, and he was screaming. I took him out, and…." Chloe stopped again, the images of Clément's injuries almost too much to bear.
    "Damn it Chloe, what is it?" asked Laurence angrily, fear taking the best of her.
    "I'm sorry…he has cigarette burns on his ankles and a large bruise going from his lower back to the middle of it…"

"Where is my dad?" asked Laurence coldly.

"He apparently left earlier for England. So, Beatrice was alone with him...Lo..."

"I'm going to kill her," growled Laurence.

"I'm taking him out of here. I called my friend Vincent, he is coming to get us...that's the number I gave you...Lo, I'm taking him to the emergency room..."

"I'm on my way."

"It's no use to rush. You don't even know where I'll be by the time you get here. I'm getting him out of here in case Beatrice comes back. We'll stay at Vincent's...I'll call you from the hospital and give you directions to his house." Chloe felt Laurence's hesitation. "Laurence, this is the best solution. There is no use in having you drive down here like a maniac and get into a car accident. Please," begged Chloe.

Laurence sighed, realizing that Chloe was right. *"You're right, but please call me as soon as you get to the hospital and know what's happening."*

"I promise."

"How is he?"

"In shock."

Laurence's voice trembled over the phone. *"Take care of him?"*

"I will. I'll call you. I love you, Lo." With those words, she hung up the phone.

"Well, well, well, isn't that sweet?" Chloe spun around, looking frantically through the dark room for the voice. Beatrice stepped put of the shadows and faced Chloe. "Planning on going somewhere?" she asked with a deranged look on her face.

Chloe looked at Clément, who hadn't moved from his previous position on the couch, and back at Beatrice. She didn't answer and started walking toward Clément, only to be stopped by Beatrice. With the closeness of Beatrice, Chloe smelled alcohol and cigarettes. "You're drunk, get away from me."

Beatrice laughed. Her laugh resonated through the high ceilings of the house, making her sound crazy, and giving Chloe a chill. Chloe took a deep breath and tried to keep her voice calm and low.

"Beatrice, I think you've done enough damage. Let me go."

The request seemed to register in Beatrice's alcohol-soaked brain, and she moved slightly to the side. Chloe rushed to Clément and picked him up. "Let's go wait outside." Suddenly Beatrice came rushing toward them and tried to grab Clément, barely giving Chloe time to jump out of the way. "Beatrice, what are you doing? You're scaring him," yelled Chloe, losing her cool. Clément started crying again, and hung on to Chloe's neck desperately. "Get away from us. I have to take him to the hospital, and if I were you, I'd make myself very humble because once I tell them who did this to him, you are done for," said Chloe harshly while slowly backing up toward the door and grabbing the diaper bag.

The doorbell suddenly rang, making Beatrice jump. Chloe kept on backing up, her eyes fixed on Beatrice, who was still standing in the family room. Chloe opened the door and Vincent stepped in.

"Hello. What was the emergency?" asked Vincent with a smile. He saw Clément glued to Chloe, Beatrice standing in the family room with her hair disheveled, black streaks of makeup on her cheeks, and Chloe's tense face. "Chloe, what's happening?" he asked with urgency.

"Take us out of here," said Chloe, still looking at Beatrice, waiting for her to make her next move. Chloe stepped out and closed the door. "Come on, hurry, where is your car?" she asked, rushing down the front steps.

"Across the street."

"Let's go," Chloe took off running, throwing the bag to Vincent and tightening her grip on Clément. They got into the car. "To the closest hospital," she said, while climbing in the back with Clément.

Vincent started the car and drove it down the street. "There is one few blocks away. Would you mind telling me what's happening here?"

"Sorry...the woman you saw is Beatrice. We suspected that she beats Clément, but weren't sure...got the proof tonight." Chloe kissed Clément's forehead. "Just a few more minutes, pumpkin."

Vincent parked the car in front of a white building. "Okay, come on."

They rushed through double doors. The smell of the hospital almost made Chloe gag. They walked right up to a nurse, Chloe still holding Clément. Before reaching her, Vincent stopped Chloe. "Listen, what about you speak English and I translate. I know your French is better than it was, but..."

"Fine," answered Chloe, going up to the nurse. The nurse smiled at them and asked what the problem was. Vincent explained that he was going to translate, and Chloe jumped in, explaining everything from the moment she found Clément in the tub to Vincent's arrival.

"Chloe, slow down, I need time to translate." Chloe nodded and Vincent translated everything to the nurse. As the story was told to her, her face showed consternation and sadness. She said something in French and handed Vincent a form to fill out.

"What did she say?"

"To go sit down and fill that out. Someone is going to take care of us shortly."

"What do you mean, fill that out? This is an emergency, damn it, can't they see that?" Chloe asked angrily.

"Chloe, look around. Some people are in worse pain than Clément. Trust me, someone is going to help, but until then doing as she said is our best bet."

Chloe looked around the room. It was filled with moans from people in pain, and the speaker system was going non-stop, calling for one doctor after another. Nurses were rushing around trying to get everyone taken care of. "Okay, let's fill this out."

She told Vincent the information and he wrote it down, writing being an impossible task for her with Clément in her arms. Vincent got up to give the form to the nurse and sat back down next to Chloe.

"Vincent, can you go and call this number for me? It's Laurence…Clément's sister. Tell her not to do anything yet because we don't know how long we are going to be here. Thanks." She gave Vincent the number and settled back on her seat. Vincent came back after a few minutes.

"She said okay, but if she doesn't hear from you in the next two hours, she is coming no matter what…I gave her the directions to my apartment. I'm not letting you guys go back there with this madwoman."

Chloe looked at Vincent, and for the first time that evening she smiled. His attempt at chivalry was sweet, almost funny. "Thanks," she whispered tiredly.

Another twenty minutes went by before they were called. Vincent was told to wait for them in the waiting room. "I need him to translate," yelled Chloe, panicking.

"It's okay, Chloe, they are saying that the doctor speaks English. You'll be fine. I'll wait."

Chloe looked at Vincent, nodded slowly and followed the nurse out of the room, still carrying Clément. They were put into a small white room and told to wait for the doctor.

A man in his fifties with white silver hair and a jovial face entered the room, introducing himself as Doctor Frank.

"I was told that you don't speak French very much."

"True."

"What about…" He looked at the form in his hand. "…Clément?"

"He understands both."

"How old is he?" said the doctor, flipping through pages.

"Two," answered Chloe.

"Okay, let's take a look at him. Could you sit him up on the table, please?" asked the doctor, smiling.

"Sure." Chloe gently put Clément down on the table, but he refused to let her go and started screaming. She picked him back up and soothed him by whispering tender words in his ears. "Shush, it's okay, sweetheart. The doctor is going to help you feel better. I'm right here, I promise. I'll hold your hand, okay?" Clément nodded with teary eyes, and Chloe slowly put him back down on the table.

"I read that his back is injured…I need you to take his top off."

Chloe nodded and slowly removed Clément's pajama top. Every time she moved she made sure a part of herself was in body contact with Clément. Doctor Frank came and stood next to Clément.

"Hi, Clément. I heard you're hurt. I'm here to make you feel better. Would you like that?" he asked, kneeling at eye level with Clément, who sniffled and nodded. "Great. I'm going to have to touch the area where it hurts. I'll be as gentle as possible."

Chloe watched Doctor Frank and how he interacted with Clément. He spoke to him as if Clément understood every word, without babying him, but at the same time with gentleness. Doctor Frank passed his hand lightly on Clément's bruised area, making Clément flinch and whimper. He then removed his socks.

"Clément, I'm going to have to take off your bandages so I can take a look at your burns. It's going to hurt a little, but I'll be as quick as I can." Clément tightened his grip on Chloe's hand while Doctor Frank removed the bandages, but he didn't cry.

"What did you put on them?" asked Doctor Frank to Chloe while examining the burns.

"Neosporin."

"Good. Nothing much could have been done at this point. I need to x-ray his back. I really don't think anything is broken, otherwise you wouldn't be able to pick him up like that, but I want to make sure. I also need to talk to you one on one. Did anyone else come with you?"

"Yes, but Clément doesn't know him at all."

Doctor Frank seemed to think for a minute. "Let's get those x-rays taken care of first, we'll deal with the rest after that."

Chloe explained to Clément what was going to happen, but Clément seemed to have given up any kind of fight and let himself be taken to the x-ray room. Chloe stayed with him every step of the way. After the x-rays, they were asked to wait for the doctor's diagnosis in another white room, this one much larger than the other one, and had a bed and an armchair. Chloe sat on the chair with Clément falling asleep in her arms.

Doctor Frank walked into the room carrying the x-rays. "Okay, it's what I thought, nothing is broken, just badly bruised. We're going to give him something for the pain so he can have a restful night of sleep. Is he sleeping?" asked Doctor Frank, looking at Clément. Chloe nodded. Doctor Frank lowered his voice, and asked. "Can you put him down on the bed?"

Chloe got up and softly put Clément down as to not wake him up. Doctor Frank stepped into the corridor and motioned for Chloe to follow him. She left the door open and made sure she stayed in hearing range in case Clément woke up.

Doctor Frank smiled at Chloe. "We have to keep him in observation until tomorrow morning. We'll set up a bed for you in his room. We also had to call social services and the police."

"What?" exclaimed Chloe.

"What you described to the nurse is a case of child abuse. The police will come and take your statement about his mother, and then tomorrow morning social services will ask you questions. You're not related to Clément, so we can't release him to you ..."

"But, I don't..."

Doctor Frank interrupted her. "I saw the bond you and Clément have. The only reason social services is not here right now, taking Clément away to a foster family for the night, is because I told them he would be fine with you, and I would make you spend the night here. Does Clément have any other relatives besides his mother?"

"Yes, a sister. I called her earlier and told her to wait to hear from me before doing anything. I can call her, and she could be here in a few hours."

"Good. What about a dad?'

"Yes, but he is in England...nothing would have happened if he hadn't left," said Chloe with a defeated look on her face.

"Call him also. You came with a young man, would you like me to tell him to come see you now?"

"Yes, please."

"Okay. We're getting a room ready. A nurse will come to get you." He started walking away.

"Doctor Frank?"

"Yes," he answered, looking at Chloe.

"Thanks for everything."

He smiled and walked away, leaving Chloe standing in the corridor. She walked back into the room. Clément was still asleep. She sat back down on the chair and passed her hand through her hair, feeling the exhaustion and stress of the night.

A light knock at the door brought her out of her daydream; Vincent poked his head through the door. "Can I come in?" Chloe nodded.

"Will he be okay? What did the doctor say?"

"Badly bruised. Nothing serious. We have to stay for the night for observation." Chloe didn't feel like giving more explanation. "Can you call Laurence again and give her directions to the hospital? Tell her to come."

"Sure," answered Vincent, walking out and softly closing the door.

While Vincent was gone, a nurse came in with pain medicine. She had to wake Clément up to give it to him, but surprisingly Clément swallowed the medicine and went back to sleep. Vincent called Laurence and came back to the room to wait with Chloe. Shortly after midnight, they were told that a room was ready.

After tucking Clément in, Chloe turned to Vincent. "Thank you so much. Without you, I don't know what would have happened."

"Are you sure you don't want me to stay until his sister gets here?"

"No, we are fine. I'll call you tomorrow and let you know what's going on."

"Okay." Vincent walked to Chloe and caressed her cheek before bending over to kiss her, but Chloe stopped him before his lips reached their goal.

"No, Vincent," she said feeling exhausted.

"Sorry, bad timing, I shouldn't have. I'll go now. Call me tomorrow." Vincent smiled and left the room. Chloe was too tired to call him back and tell him that nothing between them was possible. *We'll have this conversation later,* she thought.

A small bed had been added to the room next to Clément's, and Chloe lay down on it. She was just starting to drift off to sleep when someone knocked on the door. She got out of bed and opened the door to two policemen. One of them introduced himself as Officer Geret and explained that he was here to translate and his partner would take notes. They asked Chloe to describe everything that happened since she found Clément in the tub and to give the names of people who could prove that Beatrice was a child abuser. Chloe couldn't think of anyone besides herself, Laurence, and maybe Clément's teacher. She also told them about the time that she saw the large bruise on Clément's hip. The officers said that they wished to talk to Laurence tomorrow, and that they would be back first thing in the morning to finish the interview.

Chloe checked on Clément, still fast asleep, and she tenderly brushed his hair back and kissed him before laying back down and falling asleep.

In the middle of the night, she was woken up by a shove on her shoulder. She sat up suddenly and came face to face with Laurence.

"Shush, it's only me," said Laurence, wrapping her arms around Chloe. Chloe buried herself in Laurence's chest and hugged her tight. Laurence held her for a few heartbeats and slowly let her go. She approached Clément and repositioned his blanket, slightly lifting the bottom of it to see the bandages wrapping his ankles. She kissed him and whispered "I love you" in his ear before coming back to Chloe.

"How are you doing?" she asked, passing her hand through Chloe's hair.

"I'm so glad you're here...the police came, they want to talk to you tomorrow. Social services also wants to talk to us. Lo, we have to get in touch with your dad. I have the number in my pocket....I..."

"Slow down, slow down. It's 4 in the morning, we'll call him in a couple of hours. There is nothing he can do at this point. Let's just get some rest, okay?"

Chloe nodded, her eyes becoming teary again. "I don't know why I feel like crying. Clément is the one hurt," said Chloe, unable to stop the tears from falling.

"It's okay," said Laurence, tenderly kissing Chloe's forehead. "I can only imagine what would have happened if you hadn't come in and found him. Thank you." Laurence drew Chloe into her arms again. "I love you," she whispered in her ear.

The last statement made Chloe lose every bit of control she had left, and she sobbed against Laurence's chest. "How could she do that to him?" she cried. "How?"

"It's okay…shhh," said Laurence, trying to calm her. "Trust me. This will not go unpunished."

They held each other for a long time, seeking comfort in each other's presence. After a while, Laurence lay down on the makeshift bed and kept Chloe in her arms. She rubbed Chloe's back, slowly lulling her to sleep.

Chapter 12

Laurence lay on the bed with Chloe asleep on her chest. She tried to close her eyes and rest for a while, but it seemed impossible. Her heart felt heavy with guilt and anger. After a restless hour, Laurence kissed Chloe's forehead and slowly moved from under her. She stretched and moved to Clément's bed. He was still asleep in the same position she had seen him in earlier. Laurence tenderly caressed his brows and went to close the blinds to protect him from the rising sunlight. His breathing seemed heavy and his sleep undisturbed. Laurence brought a chair closer to Clément's bed, took hold of his hand and sat down.

"How is he?"

"You're awake." Laurence smiled at Chloe who had just come up behind her.

"Did you sleep at all?" asked Chloe, rubbing Laurence's shoulders.

"No, I couldn't sleep," answered Laurence, trying to keep her voice as quiet as possible, so as not to wake Clément.

"We should probably call your dad now."

"I know. I'll go." Laurence squeezed Chloe's hand and got up. "I'll be right back."

"Lo?"

"What?"

"Don't you need the number?" asked Chloe with a smile while holding Jean's note.

"That would help," said Laurence, reaching for the piece of paper.

She left the room and went in search of a phone. She found one in the main lobby, and dialed the number on the piece of paper. The conversation with Jean was animated. Laurence explained very clearly what happened and ordered her dad to come home right away. Jean was stunned by the news, and extremely worried about Clément, but still could not believe that Beatrice would do such a thing. His skepticism sent Laurence into a fit, and after telling him that he better come as soon as possible, she hung up on him.

Laurence walked back to the room in a very somber mood. Halfway down the corridor, she heard Clément cry, and started running. She burst into the room.

"What's wrong?" Clément sat on the bed, where a nurse was removing his bandages. "What are you doing to him?" she asked, walking menacingly toward the bed.

"Lo, calm down. Yelling is not going to help. She is only doing her job."

Laurence looked into Chloe's tired eyes, took a deep breath and nodded. "Sorry."

"It's okay. Just go to him."

Laurence came closer to the bed, and sat next to Clément. "Hey, little man. It's me. I missed you. Shhh, stop crying, this lady is just trying to help."

Clément looked at Laurence, his eyes filled with tears. "Lo," he sobbed.

"Shhh....I'm here, it's okay." Laurence scooted closer. "Est-ce que je peux le prendre sur mes genoux?" Laurence asked the nurse. The nurse nodded and let Laurence lift Clément onto her lap. She wrapped her arms around him and spoke to him softly. "You see, she is not hurting you, no need to be scared. She is here to help you feel better." Clément's tears gradually stopped and his body relaxed.

Chloe watched the scene from the window. She had stepped aside, wanting to give them this moment with each other. Seeing their faces so close to each other left no doubts in Chloe's mind of the strong resemblance. Clément had Laurence's clear blue eyes, her thin nose and her black hair.

The nurse finished up and asked Laurence to help her check Clément's back.

"Okay, sweetheart, you're going to have to get off me for a minute. I'm right here, holding your hand." She slowly lifted Clément off her, and sat him down on the bed. The nurse quickly lifted his top and eyed the bruised area. She spoke briefly to Laurence and left the room.

"What did she say?" asked Chloe, stepping back into the picture.

"They are bringing breakfast up. She also heard that social services should be here around 8."

"What did your dad say?"

"He's coming," answered Laurence briefly. From Laurence's tone of voice, Chloe knew that there was more to it, but understood Laurence's reluctance to speak in front of Clément.

"Okay...what now?"

"Now we wait," said Laurence, grabbing the remote and turning on the TV. She flipped through channels and stopped on one playing cartoons. Clément was still sitting in the same position as before the nurse left. "Hey, babe, you can move now," said Laurence softly. "Come here." She picked him up and sat him down next to her, putting some pillows behind him to make him more comfortable. Clément snuggled next to Laurence, and she wrapped her arm around him.

Chloe felt out of place, as if she was intruding on something special. She stood on the left side of the bed with her hands on the back of the chair. Suddenly, the events of the night before came rushing back to her, and she felt nauseous. "I need to get some fresh air." She left the room in a hurry, not waiting for Laurence to answer. She crossed the lobby and rushed out. The early morning air hit her, and stopped her run. She stumbled to the side of the building and crumpled to the ground, her back against the wall, her head between her hands. After a few seconds, she forced herself to inhale deeply, and closed her eyes. "I don't know if I can do this...it's more than what I bargained for," Chloe spoke aloud, tears running down her face and doubts invading her mind. At the same time, memories of telling Laurence that they were together in this mess came back to her. She remembered Laurence telling her she loved her, giving her the painting, the laughs they shared in the past few weeks, and the feel of Laurence's lips on hers. The more the memories came rushing back, the more the idea of leaving Laurence seemed intolerable.

·

Chloe shook her head and wiped the remaining tears off her cheeks. "Mom always told me to go with my heart…never thought I'd see the day where I actually followed your advice, mom," said Chloe, getting up and straightening herself out. She wiped the dirt off her pants and walked back into the hospital and up to the room. She stepped into the room, and was immediately grabbed by Laurence and dragged outside.

"Lo, what are you doing?" asked Chloe, once Laurence let go of her arm.

"Clément fell back asleep, and I didn't want to whisper to talk to you. What the hell was that about?" she asked, her voice on the verge of anger.

"What do you mean?"

"Why did you run out earlier?" Laurence stepped back from Chloe.

"I…I needed some fresh air," answered Chloe, propping herself against the wall.

"Don't lie to me. You felt like running away from all of this, didn't you?" asked Laurence angrily. Chloe didn't answer, and just nodded.

"So why are you here then?" Laurence's eyes had turned black and she looked every bit the Laurence Chloe first met.

"Because I care…because I love you, and the thought of not being with you hurts too much…because I love Clément, and I want to be here for him." Chloe looked at Laurence and tried to convey her honesty with her eyes. She stepped forward and attempted to reach for Laurence's hand, only to have Laurence take one step back.

"Chloe. I never expected things to get so bad, but they are. I can't force you to stay…it's much more than what you asked for…."

"I'm not going anywhere…"

"Let me finish," said Laurence abruptly. "My attention needs to be on Clément. I can't keep on worrying about you, and if you're still going to be here next time I turn around. So, I'm asking you this…" Laurence fixed her eyes on Chloe. "If you even have the slightest doubts, I want you to go now. I'm going to walk back into this room; only follow me if you're sure. This isn't just about us anymore, Chloe. We have a child in the picture…yeah, things just got complicated." Laurence took one last look at Chloe, turned around, and walked back into the room. Her heart was racing, her mind telling her to run back into the corridor and take Chloe in her arms, but one look at Clément's sleeping form stopped her. *I have to do what's right for him.*

Chloe watched Laurence walk into the room. She stood alone in the corridor, the hospital slowly coming to life around her. She waited a few moments to recompose herself, and opened the bedroom door. Laurence was standing at the window, her back to Chloe. She turned around and looked at Chloe, who stood still in the middle of the room. They stared at each other, Laurence's eyes were full of questions; Chloe's were cold, anger visible in them. She walked up to Laurence and stopped inches away from her. She stared at her menacingly.

"Don't you ever, ever, push me around or talk to me this way," said Chloe between clenched teeth. Laurence stared at Chloe, stunned by her anger. Chloe put her hand on her chest pushing her against the wall. She spoke coldly, her voice strong and vibrating with anger. "I love you. This is one thing I've never had any doubts about. Now, I'm tired of having to prove it to you. Yes, I had doubts about wanting to stay, but only for a minute...I'm human too. I know what I want, but I can't promise that I won't want to run away again because I probably will, but you have to trust that my love for you will be enough to stop me." Chloe paused and took a step back. She opened her arms and softly said, "What is it going to be, Laurence? Trust or doubts?"

Before Laurence had time to answer, someone knocked at the door. "Entrez," she yelled, taking a look at Clément, who was still asleep, mindless of the argument that had just happened in the room. A policeman stepped into the room and asked to speak with Laurence. She briefly looked at Chloe, and followed him out of the room.

The interrogation was similar to the one Chloe had experienced the night before. Laurence was informed that the police had tried to go and interrogate Beatrice, but she was nowhere to be found. She gave them the address of Beatrice's office in Paris, and also told them that she could have gone to her parents'.

"Vous avez l'addresse de ses parents?"

"Non, mais mon père l'a."

Laurence explained that her father should be here later on in the afternoon. If Clément was not released they could find him in this room; otherwise, they could find him at the house. The policeman nodded and wrote something down on his note pad very quickly. He thanked Laurence and walked away. She breathed deeply and fought against the fatigue settling in her body. Walking toward her were two women wearing blue business suits and high heels. Laurence turned around and walked into the room, leaving the door open. "Social services is here." She had barely finished her sentence when the two women appeared in the doorway. Laurence greeted them and invited them in. Clément started to stir, and he opened his eyes slowly. Chloe moved to his side.

"Hi, sweetheart. Did you sleep well? Are you feeling better?" she asked while running her hand through his hair. Clément sat up, rubbing his eyes. "I bet you must be really hungry and thirsty."

"I want juice," whined Clément.

"Someone should bring breakfast any moment now, sweetheart," said Laurence. She turned toward the women. "Qu'est ce que je peux faire pour vous?"

The shortest lady walked to the table in the corner of the room and put down her briefcase, opened it and retrieved a note pad. "My name is Sophie and this is my co-worker Jeanne. We both know about the language situation in this case, and we can conduct everything in English," she said with a very heavy French accent. "I need to ask you both questions while my co-worker plays with the boy."

"Clément, his name is Clément," said Chloe, holding Clément's hand.

"Yes, this is right," answered the woman looking at her notepad.

"What are you here for?" asked Laurence, her tone of voice made it very clear that patience was not going to be an option.

"We have to analyze Clément's behavior and decide if we can release him or if he is in any danger."

Laurence sat on a chair and motioned Sophie to do the same. Jeanne sat next to Clément on the bed, sending him straight into Chloe's arms for protection. Jeanne showed Clément a large pad of paper with crayons. "Tu aimes dessiner mon petit?" she asked with a smile.

"You like to draw, Clément, come on… it will be fun," Chloe said to him while grabbing a crayon from Jeanne's hand and giving it to Clément. Clément hesitated, but finally took it.

"I d'aw tuk," he said, reaching for the pad of paper.

"If you want to," smiled Chloe.

"Tuk?" asked Sylvie.

"Truck. He can't pronounce Rs yet."

On the other side of the room, Laurence and Sophie were in deep conversation. Sophie needed to know everything, from how long did Laurence think the abuse had been going on, to whether Laurence thought her father could also be responsible.

Another knock was heard, and two nurses walked in carrying two trays of food. They set one tray on the nightstand, and the other one on the table next to Laurence. One of the nurses smiled at Clément and commented on his drawing. Clément briefly looked up and went back to his drawing. He had picked up a red crayon and was trying with difficulty to draw the shape of a fire truck; he held in his other hand a yellow crayon, and alternated between coloring the truck and the sun he had drawn in the right corner of the paper.

"Clément, you can continue after, what about something to eat right now?"

"Juice?" Clément asked, pushing his paper away and dropping the crayons on the bed.

"I think so. Look, your favorite, cornflakes." Chloe reached for the small package and poured the cornflakes into a bowl. She suddenly remembered Jeanne, who was still sitting on the bed. "Is that okay, if he eats now? Can he continue later?"

"Yes. I think I've seen enough anyway." Jeanne got up and walked up to Sophie. They briefly talked among them, and Sophie turned to Chloe.

"We would like to speak to you now, if you would please follow us outside."

"Why can't we do it here?" wondered Chloe, swinging the bed table and adjusting it in front of Clément. She poured some milk in, and set the bowl in front of him.

"This is our policy, now if you would please…"

"This makes no sense, I—"

"Chloe, please do as they say," interrupted Laurence.

"Fine," Chloe mumbled, getting up and walking out.

①   ①   ①

They walked down to the cafeteria and sat down in one of the far corner booths.

"We asked you to be alone with us, so we know you're speaking the truth," explained Sophie.

"What do you mean?" asked Chloe, annoyance obvious in her voice.

"We have to make sure that you're not under any pressure, and that no one told you what to tell us."

"This is absurd." Chloe felt as if she was being tried for a murder she didn't commit.

"Simple precaution. Now could you tell us everything that happened since you found Clément in the tub last night?"

Chloe repeated the story again. She was then asked to describe Beatrice's behavior toward Clément. She passed her hand through her hair, and sighed.

"She never really took care of him. She spent more time going to so-called meetings than with her…son." Not knowing how much Laurence had told them, Chloe decided to not mention Clément and Laurence's real tie.

"Do you think it was the first time she hit Clément?" asked Jeanne.

"No, and I have no proof." She explained the strange bruise on Clément's hip a few weeks ago, and told them that his teacher was also suspicious.

"What about the father?" asked Sophie, her mispronunciation of the "th" sound making hard for Chloe to understand.

"The father?" asked Chloe to make sure she understood right. Sophie nodded. "What about him?"

"Do you think he could also be abusing Clément?"

"My god no," exclaimed Chloe. "He is crazy about him. He is away a lot, but always plays with him when he is in town. He is a great dad."

"What about Laurence?" asked Sophie, making note on her pad.

"She would never. She loves him so much. You know, I'm tired of you trying to accuse people of something they haven't done," said Chloe, getting up.

"Miss, we're only trying to determine if it's safe to send Clément back. Please sit down."

Chloe looked at Sophie and Jeanne and sat back down. "You're going to let him come home, aren't you?" asked Chloe, fear settling in her voice.

"Only once we're sure Beatrice is getting some help."

"What if they can't find her?"

"We'll see. We still have to talk to the father." They got up and thanked Chloe for her time, and exited the cafeteria. Chloe sat dumbfounded. After a few minutes, she left and headed slowly back to the room.

When she entered, Clément and Laurence were nowhere to be found. Clément's empty bowl and glass were on the bed table; the other tray had not been touched. She sat at the table and opened the box of juice sitting on the tray. *Only 10 o'clock; why do I have the feeling it's going to be a long day?* thought Chloe, sipping her drink. *Where in the world are they?* She waited half an hour and started getting worried; by then she had cleared the tray of all its food. She walked into the adjacent bathroom and splashed cold water on her face, wishing she had thought of taking a change of clothes the night before.

"Hello," someone called from the doorway.

"Who is it?" She walked back in the room, drying her face with a towel and saw Jean standing there, wearing a long blue marine coat and a matching business suit. "Thank God, you're here. We weren't expecting you before late afternoon."

"I flew in, instead of taking the boat. Where are they?"

"I don't know. I just walked back in...I was going to go and look for them."

Jean took off his coat. "Let's go, then. Could you tell me again what happened?"

So, Chloe repeated for the umpteenth time the events of the night before. Jean was confused, not believing that his wife would do such a thing. They spotted Clément and Laurence in the playroom. Clément was playing with Legos while Laurence was speaking with a doctor Chloe had not met yet. Laurence saw them standing at the window, watching them, and came outside the room to meet them. She looked at her dad and spoke sarcastically. "Nice of you to make it." She stared at him.

"Laurence, I know you're upset, I'm sorry about what happened," Jean moved closer to Laurence and laid his hand on her shoulder. She abruptly moved his hand away.

"Don't you patronize me. I trusted you with my son. You let a madwoman raise him," she growled. Jean looked at Laurence and glanced briefly at Chloe. "She knows, " said Laurence, not taking her eyes away from her father.

"You know very well that if I had known, I would have never left him alone with her," said Jean, trying to defend himself.

"For God's sakes, how hard was it to see that he was scared senseless of her? Did you ever wonder why he would never run to her or want her to kiss him? Did you?" Laurence's voice had raised and people walking by in the corridor where staring at them. "You were too worried about keeping up appearances, about pretending to have the perfect family. That was more important to you than facing the truth."

"Lo, calm down," interfered Chloe, only to be dismissed by Laurence.

"Don't you tell me to calm down. This is my son in this hospital playroom, being psychoanalyzed by a shrink because I trusted someone else beside myself to keep him safe!" Laurence's voice cracked, and she was obviously on the verge of tears. She lowered her tone and defeatedly said, "Go on. I'm sure Clément would be happy to see you, and everyone has a lot of questions for you." She stepped aside. Jean hesitantly attempted to reach for her, but withdrew. He shook his head and walked into the playroom. Chloe watched Clément rush into his father's arms through the window.

"Lo…" She stopped, knowing that she couldn't reach Laurence at this moment. Laurence's hands were balled into fists, and her eyes were glistening with tears. Laurence looked at Chloe and walked away.

"Laurence," called Chloe.

"Leave me alone," answered Laurence, not even bothering to turn around. In a few moments she was out of sight. Chloe was considering going after her when the policemen from earlier appeared.

"Miss? We were told we'd find you here. Is that Monsieur Glairon?" asked the policeman, pointing at Jean through the glass window.

"Yeah," said Chloe.

"Good. You'd be pleased to know that we found Beatrice. She is in our custody."

"Where was she?"

"At the house."

Chloe shivered, thinking of what could have happened if they had been dismissed earlier. "What's going to happen?"

"It depends on him," answered the policeman, looking at Jean.

"What do you mean?"

"It depends if he presses charges or not or if she asks for mental help." With a head movement, he sent his co-worker inside the playroom to get Jean. Jean stepped out.

"Chloe, would you stay with Clément?" asked Jean before walking away with the two policemen.

① ① ①

An hour later, Clément and Chloe were sent back to their room, and Jean and Laurence had not yet returned. The doctor stopped by and told Chloe that Clément was free to go as soon as everything with social services was worked out. He told Chloe that Clément should avoid running for the next few days, and that his bandages should be changed twice a day for four days, and to let the skin heal without anything covering it after that. As he left the room, Jean came back.

"What happened?" asked Chloe anxiously.

"We can go," he answered simply, walking to Clément who was watching TV.

"Come on, I'm sure there is more to it. Jean, please, I deserve to know," pleaded Chloe.

Jean sighed and sat on a chair. "Beatrice confessed everything. She asked for mental help. We can take Clément back as long as we agree on a visit from social services every week for the next 6 months."

"Is Beatrice coming back?" asked Chloe, almost fearing the answer.

"I'm going to file for divorce. No, she's not coming back." Chloe released a breath she hadn't realized she was holding. "You know it means more work for you. I would understand if you chose to leave. I'm sure the organization can find you a new fam…"

Chloe interrupted him. "What is it with you guys assuming I'm going to leave screaming? Gosh, I'm sick and tired of it. Read my lips, I am staying. Got it?"

Jean could have been offended by Chloe's tone of voice, but instead smiled in relief. "Good, then let's go home." He picked up Clément and turned the TV off. Chloe grabbed the diaper bag and followed him out of the room, glad this chapter in her life was over.

"Where is Laurence?" asked Jean, walking down the corridor to the lobby.

"I don't know. She left after your argument, and I haven't seen her since."

① ① ①

They took a cab home. Chloe was hoping to find Laurence waiting for them, but no such luck. Jean told Chloe to go and rest for the remainder of the day. She protested that she was fine.

"I've spent the night in a hospital before, so I know you didn't get much sleep last night. Go on, it's only 2. I'll call you tonight for dinner."

Chloe kissed Clément, who wrapped his arms around her and returned her kiss. "I'll see you in a little while, sweetheart."

Once in her room, she took off her clothes and ran herself a bath. She lay down in the warm water, letting it sooth her tired muscles, and closed her eyes. She got out only when the water started getting colder. Chloe put on a robe and quickly brushed her teeth. She couldn't stop her mind from thinking about Laurence. *Where can she be?* She came back into her room and sat on her bed, softly brushing her hair, her hand combing through the locks mechanically, her mind filled with worries for Laurence. A light knock at the door broke her out of her wallowing.

"Come in," she answered, getting up and making sure her robe was properly closed.

The door opened and Laurence entered. She walked up to Chloe and stopped.

"I thought it was your dad," stammered Chloe.

"I never answered your question," said Laurence, ignoring Chloe's rumbling.

"What…what question?"

"Trust or doubts?" Laurence lifted Chloe's face toward her, and stared at her. "The answer is trust," she said simply. Chloe blinked and looked back at Laurence, her face very close, the blue of her eyes almost transparent. Before Chloe had time to speak, Laurence bent and kissed her. Her kiss was not soft as usual; instead, Laurence let the passion in her release, and poured every bit of it into her kiss. Chloe stood stunned for the first moment, but quickly responded. After long minutes, Laurence broke the kiss. "I'm sorry about earlier, I…"

"It's okay," interrupted Chloe, drawing Laurence back for another kiss.

Laurence wrapped her arms around Chloe's waist and slowly directed her toward the bed, laying both of them down. She lay on her side, softly caressing Chloe's face, and brought her lips very close to

Chloe's. "No more fear. No more running," she whispered before rolling them over and lying on top of Chloe. Chloe's face was flushed, her mind finding it hard to form any coherent thoughts. She locked her arms around Laurence's neck and drew her in. Their eyes locked, holding only love and understanding. Laurence gently nibbled down Chloe's neck, slowly undoing her robe and caressing her stomach. Chloe gulped and moaned, drawing Laurence back for another kiss. Their hands started roaming freely on each other's body, and as the passion escalated to the point of no return, this time Laurence didn't stop it, but instead embraced it.

Chapter 13

"Wow," said Chloe, gasping for air as she buried her face in Laurence's chest.

Laurence smiled and kissed the top of Chloe's hair, tenderly tightening her grip around her. "It was okay then?" she said hesitantly.

Chloe looked up at Laurence with glassy eyes. "Do you even have to ask?" she teased, but seeing the uncertainty in Laurence's eyes, she decided to answer more seriously. She lightly kissed Laurence's nose, and looked at her. "It was more than I hoped for, more than I had ever imagined."

Laurence relaxed a little, and kissed Chloe's lips. "Thanks."

"For what?" asked Chloe.

"Letting me be with you," answered Laurence softly.

Chloe let her lips linger on Laurence and whispered, "I wouldn't have it any other way" before kissing Laurence deeply. She broke the kiss and looked at Laurence. "I love you," she said sincerely.

"I know," smiled Laurence, kissing Chloe's forehead and drawing her head to rest on her shoulder. She closed her eyes, and sighed contently. "I'm suddenly very sleepy."

"Me too. We didn't get much sleep last night...actually, you didn't sleep at all." Chloe closed her eyes and put one arm around Laurence's waist. Laurence pulled the covers up over their bodies and settled back with Chloe in her arms.

"Lo, wait a minute. We can't go to sleep. What about your dad? You have to talk to him," said Chloe sitting up.

"Relax, I already did before I came to see you," said Laurence, pulling Chloe back down.

"Are you guys okay?"

"No… but we will be since Beatrice is out of the picture."

"I know she asked for mental help, but did he press charges?"

"No."

"That was stupid," said Chloe, propping herself on her elbow.

"That's what I told him, but he feels that filing for divorce should be enough."

"How is Clément?"

"He was watching TV when I saw him. It seems okay, but he doesn't seem to have as much energy as usual. We should keep an eye on him. The bath experience must have been traumatizing," said Laurence, shivering at the thought. Chloe scooted closer, and caressed her face, tenderly kissing her forehead. Laurence looked at Chloe. "I…I'm glad you didn't run away. I was a real jerk earlier."

"Yes, you were, but I think we're okay now," smiled Chloe.

"I love you," said Laurence, looking deeply into Chloe's eyes.

"I know," teased Chloe.

"Hey, this is my repartee," said Laurence with a mock pout.

"Oops, sorry," joked Chloe. "Was I supposed to answer 'I love you too?'"

"Yes, that would be more appropriate," smiled Laurence.

"Far be it from me to be rude." She giggled and regained her serious look at Laurence. "I love you too."

Laurence kissed Chloe lovingly, drew her against her chest, and ran her hand through her hair. "Let's get some sleep, okay?"

Chloe yawned. "That sounds like a good idea." She closed her eyes and let Laurence's heartbeat lull her to sleep. Once Chloe's breathing became heavy, Laurence tightened her grip and closed her eyes.

A knock at the door woke them up. "Chloe, dinner is ready if you're hungry," called Jean through the door.

"Okay," answered Chloe's sleepy voice.

"Laurence, Clément has been asking for you," called Jean amusedly.

"I…I'll come down in a minute," answered Laurence.

"He knows?" asked Chloe, sitting up.

"I told him earlier."

"You what?" asked Chloe, stunned.

"Come on, he's not stupid. He asked how things were going with you, and I told him that I couldn't answer that until I had a talk with you."

"Okay, friends have talks. He thinks we're just friends, right?"

"No, he knows. I don't want to hide anything, Chloe. I'm not ashamed of loving you," said Laurence seriously.

Chloe sighed and grabbed her discarded robe from the floor, tossing Laurence her clothes at the same time. "I'm not ashamed either, but I work for your dad. Don't you think it's going to be a little awkward?"

"Why? My dad doesn't care as long as it doesn't interfere with your job, and I'm quoting him," said Laurence, putting her shirt on.

"Fine, but I'm still really embarrassed by going downstairs and facing him right now." She grabbed some clean clothes from her closet and walked into the bathroom to change. A few minutes after she stepped out. "Okay, let's go then."

Laurence smiled. "You're priceless, you know that?"

"Yeah, yeah, yeah, come on, lead me to be humiliated."

Laurence grabbed Chloe's hand. "We weren't going to hide forever anyway, were we?" asked Laurence, suddenly wondering if telling her father had been such a great idea.

Chloe sighed and smiled. "No, we weren't. Come on, dinner awaits."

Laurence smiled and led Chloe out of the room.

① ① ①

Clément barely ate, and he whined throughout the entire meal.

"Come on babe, I made you some pasta. It's your favorite," said Jean, trying to force a spoonful of food into Clément's mouth. Clément grabbed the spoon and threw it on the floor, splattering pasta all over Jean's shoes. "Clément!" yelled Jean, sending Clément into tears.

"Stop forcing him. Can't you see he isn't hungry?" said Laurence, trying to keep her anger at bay for Clément's sake.

"He has to eat something, or he is going to get sick," answered Jean, flashing a reproaching glance at Laurence.

"Forcing him is not going to help. For heaven's sake, last night at this time, he was sitting in a tub full of freezing water because your wife left him there after beating him. How is he supposed to feel?" barked Laurence.

"Okay, that's enough, you two," Chloe intervened. She got up and picked Clément up from his chair. "Okay, sweetheart...it's okay. Calm down now."

"I want Lo," cried Clément.

"She's right here," answered Chloe, kissing his forehead and handing him to Laurence who was now standing next to them. She picked him up and left the kitchen, but not before sending a deadly glance toward her father.

Jean sighed. "I don't know if she can ever forgive me." He got up and put his plate in the sink.

"She will. You're not really responsible, Beatrice is."

Jean smiled slightly. "Thanks, but it's more complicated than that...it's her son she's holding right now."

"Yeah, I know, but you're legally Clément's father, aren't you?" pried Chloe.

Jean looked at Chloe for a second and opened his mouth as though to speak, but nothing came out. He turned around and mumbled, "I have to go and make a phone call."

Chloe stood alone in the kitchen, watching the space Jean had vacated seconds before. *Gosh, these people are complicated,* she thought while clearing up the table, and grabbing a paper towel to pick up the mess Clément had made on the floor. Suddenly a thought hit her. *Could it be that Jean's silence means that he never declared himself Clément's dad?*

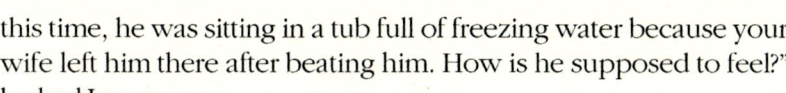

She was just putting the last dish in the dishwasher when Laurence came up behind her. "Hi," Laurence smiled, propping herself against the sink.

Chloe wiped her hands on a dishtowel. "Where is this cook that Beatrice was talking about when I first got here? I hate doing dishes."

"Another one she drove crazy. His vacation was a way for him to get away and never come back...sorry," answered Laurence, opening the fridge and taking out a small box of orange juice.

"Those are for Clément's snack," said Chloe, pointing at the drink.

"So?" answered Laurence, teasingly piercing the top with a straw and sipping from it.

Chloe shook her head. "Where is Clémemt?"

"Upstairs with my dad." Laurence's eyes darkened. "I tried to run him a bath, but as soon as I picked him up to put him in, he started crying."

"Oh, Lo, I'm sorry. It's going to take some time. Hopefully, he is not scared of water now."

"Hopefully...I didn't feel like fighting. We'll try again tomorrow morning."

"Is your dad tucking him in for the night?"

"Yes, he is reading him a story." Laurence finished her drink and tossed the empty container in the trash.

"I'm sorry I interfered earlier at dinner time, but nothing good was going to happen from you guys fighting in front of him."

"I know," said Laurence sadness in her voice. "It'll get better." She picked up an apple and bit into it, making the silent room resonate with the crunching noise. "It's only 7:30; would you like to go for a walk?"

"Now?" asked Chloe.

"Yes, now," answered Laurence, amused.

"Sure, let me go and get my jacket upstairs. Do want me to tell your dad we're going for a walk?"

"Sure," called Laurence, sitting down at the kitchen table to wait for Chloe.

① ① ①

They walked slowly through the streets of Versailles. The streetlights were on, although night had not fallen completely yet. The weather had gotten much colder, and the trees were almost bare. They strolled holding hands through the quiet city; everyone seemed to have already retired for the night.

"Lo, we're walking toward the castle. I thought the gates were closed at night."

"Yes, they are," answered Laurence simply while directing them into a street adjacent to the main entrance of the castle. They followed the gates around to the back, but instead of making a full circle, Laurence dragged Chloe down a small hill, and stopped in front a river.

"Hey, I remember this place," said Chloe, looking around her. Laurence smiled and took out a flashlight from her jacket pocket. "Lo, I'm not going in this tunnel at night. No way."

"Come on, where is your sense of adventure?" She ignored Chloe and flashed her light ahead. The light roamed for a few seconds and settled on a grille.

"Lo, I'm not going. There is no way I'm going through that puddle of mud by smashing myself against a wall full of spiders." Chloe crossed her arms against her chest and stood her ground.

"I know. Trust me, you won't have to deal with that anymore." Laurence unscrewed the bar the same way she had done it a month ago, and stepped in.

"Laurence, don't you leave me here!" called Chloe, looking around in panic.

Laurence's head popped out. "Then come on."

Chloe sighed and stumped her feet. "Fine, but you better be telling the truth about those spiders." She heard Laurence chuckle from the inside, bent over, twisted sideways to go through the small space provided by the removal of the bar, and stepped in. Laurence was waiting for her, flashlight in hand. She extended her hand to Chloe who took it, holding on to it as though her life depended on it.

"If you squeeze my hand that hard, you're going to cut off the circulation," laughed Laurence.

"Sorry," answered Chloe, relaxing her grip.

They walked down the tunnel, and Chloe started slowing down once they got closer to the spider area. "I told you that you don't have to worry." Laurence pointed her flashlight ahead. The mud puddle was covered with wooden planks, making it possible to go across it without having to step in it or go against the wall.

"Lo, when did you have time to do that?" wondered Chloe, stepping cautiously on the wooden planks.

"Earlier, when I left the hospital." She followed Chloe, making sure she stayed at arms' length.

"That's where you were," Chloe jumped off the makeshift bridge. "I should have known you'd come here...it's your retreat."

"Chloe, move up! I can't get off if you just stand there," said Laurence to Chloe who had stopped as soon as she had put a foot on dry land.

"Sorry." She moved to the side. "That's what you wanted to show me?"

"Not really. Come on."

"Lo, can we turn back and do that another day?" asked Chloe. She felt exhausted and the darkness of the tunnel made her really nervous.

Again Laurence ignored her request. "We're almost there."

They walked down the tunnel for a few more minutes, and stopped in front of the room they had explored a few weeks back. "Lo, I love it here, but seriously, I have had enough adventure for one day…"

"Would you stop whining?" teased Laurence, opening the door. They stepped into the dark room with Laurence's flashlight the only light source.

"It's even more messy than I remember," commented Chloe, looking around. Furniture was piled up on top of each other, old drapes and rugs formed a large pile on the floor, paintings lined up against an old dresser and only a small aisle had been left to make the second room accessible. The movements of Laurence's flashlight made the furniture take on a strange appearance.

"Follow me," said Laurence, crossing the room and opening the second door. Chloe sighed and followed closely. As soon as Laurence entered the room, she turned her flashlight off.

"Hey, what are you doing?" called Chloe in the darkness. Instead of an answer, she heard a match being cracked and a candle was lit, followed closely by five others. Once Chloe's eyes adjusted to the candlelight, she looked around in awe. "Lo, this is…" She picked up a candle, and walked around the room, speechless. The room had been cleaned up and organized. A table and two chairs stood next to the left wall; rugs had been thrown on the floor, giving the dirt room a comfortable aspect. An old buffet leaned against the right wall, a wooden tray with two glasses and silverware sitting on it, and next to it were shelves filled with books. Chloe moved closer to the shelves and picked up a book. "My gosh, Lo…this is from Diderot…I can't believe it. This is so old, look at the cover!" She lifted her candle higher, turned around—and froze. There on the corner were two white sheets suspended from the ceiling by ropes, forming a large rectangle. She turned to Laurence, who motioned to her to go in. Chloe lifted the corner of one sheet, and stepped underneath.

"Holy..." Blankets had been thrown on the floor to make a bed, four pillows had been added, a small table with an antique oil lamp stood on the side of the make shift bed, and on the wall a painting had been hung. Chloe stepped closer to the painting. "Oh, Lo..." she whispered, tears in her voice.

Laurence took it as her cue to walk in. "You called," she said teasingly, coming up behind Chloe.

"You remembered?"

Laurence nodded. "How could I not? This painting seemed to move you so much last time we came."

Chloe stared at the painting of the crying child. "Thank you," she whispered, setting the candle on the table and turning to face Laurence. "When did you...how did you..." She found it hard to speak as if everything she had seen was part of a dream.

"When I left the hospital. I wanted to do something nice for you...I thought this room would be our place to get away from everyday problems...a place to come to forget." Laurence brushed a loose strand of hair behind Chloe's ear.

"This is amazing. I don't know how you did it. Where did you find those books?"

"They were in a wooden crate...they are not that old, maybe 60 or 70 years."

"Even so, this is amazing...I love it." She stood on her tiptoes and lightly kissed Laurence. "Do we have to go back soon, or can we stay here for a while?"

"No, we can stay," answered Laurence, drawing Chloe back for another kiss. The kiss was soft and languorous. Laurence drew Chloe closer, gently slid Chloe's jacket off and wrapped her arms around her waist. Tenderly, she lifted Chloe's shirt and ran her hands over the skin of her back, never once breaking their kiss. Slowly, she lowered them down onto the blankets, and nibbled on Chloe's neck before coming back up to look her deeply in the eyes. The candlelight gave Chloe's eyes a golden green shade, and passion shone in them. Chloe sat up, forcing Laurence up with her, and removed Laurence's jacket before diving back for another kiss. She pushed Laurence on her back and lay softly on her.

"I think we're going to be here for a while," smiled Chloe, her voice a murmur.

Laurence laughed heartily and combed her hands through Chloe's hair, stopping to softly massage the base of her scalp. "For a while, huh?" she said tenderly teasing while pulling Chloe back into another kiss. They lost themselves in each other, and when the candle burned out, neither of them realized it.

Chapter 14

Laurence stayed through the end of the week. Together with Chloe and Jean, they tried to help Clément, but although his external scars healed quickly, the damage done to his mind was taking longer to heal. He woke up almost every night drenched in sweat and screaming. He refused to take a bath unless the stopper was removed from the tub and the water left running.

Laurence's heart broke every time Clément had a nightmare. She felt useless and unable to help him. She spent most of her day reading and playing with him. On Thursday, Jean went back to work, but he made a point of calling many times a day to check on Clément. Laurence and Chloe's relationship grew stronger during the week. Chloe showed patience toward Clément and helped Laurence with moral support. She never once complained that Laurence spent all her time with Clément and always tried to make herself scarce and leave them alone.

At the end of the week, Laurence stood with her jacket on in the entrance, her hands balled into fists inside her pockets, her eyes shining with tears, Clément crying in the background and Jean trying to comfort him.

"Lo, he'll be okay. Jean and I will make sure of it. You have to go back to your studies. Come on, you're only a few months away from graduation," said Chloe, trying to persuade Laurence.

"I know, but I feel that I'm giving up on him," she answered, her shoulders hunched and her voice trembling.

"You're not." Chloe stepped closer to Laurence and tenderly caressed her face. "Hey, Lo, come on, look at me," pleaded Chloe. Laurence looked up. "You're coming back next weekend. It's only five days. I'll call you every night and let you know how things are going. Okay? Lo, your dad is here too, and he proved to us this week that he can be really counted on."

"You're right, I'm being stupid," said Laurence, shaking her head.

"No, you're not. You're just being overly protective, and it's normal. Now, go on, it's getting late, and you have quite a drive."

"Plus, Jackie is coming back from her trip tonight, I should bring her car back…gosh, her plants are probably dead."

"I'm sure she'll understand if you explain to her what happened."

"She should." Laurence looked at Chloe and smiled. "Thanks for everything…I'm sorry if I didn't spend much time with you this week…I'll make it up to you."

"Don't worry about it." Chloe hugged Laurence briefly, and stepped back. "I'll see you next weekend."

Laurence nodded, passed her hand trough Chloe' s hair and gently brushed her lips against hers. "I'll call you when I get home."

"You'd better," smiled Chloe.

Laurence looked at Chloe one last time, opened the door and left. Clément's cries had slowly become whimpers. Chloe stepped out onto the front porch and waved at Laurence. As the car went through the gates, Laurence honked and waved and expertly maneuvered the car through the parked cars on each side of the street, and disappeared down rue de Provence.

Chloe walked back inside, lost in her own thoughts.

"Chloe, phone call," called Jean.

"Okay." She rushed to the phone. "Allo?"

"Chloe, it's Vincent."

Chloe realized that they never called him back after Monday's incident and started apologizing profusely.

"I know you had a lot on your plate. Don't worry about it. I know how you can make it up to me though," joked Vincent.

"How?"

"If you're not busy right now, let's go out for a drink."

"I don't know, it's been really hectic here lately…"
"*Come on. You probably need a break.*"
"I'll ask. Hold on a minute."
Chloe went in search of Jean and Clément and found them in the playroom.
"Jean, if you don't need me tonight, I'd like to go out with a friend."
"Please go ahead. We'll be fine," smiled Jean, putting an extra block on Clément's Lego construction. ·
"Okay, thanks."
Vincent happily told Chloe he'd pick her up in 45 minutes and hung up.
"Boy, I think I'm going to have a talk with him," Chloe sighed, after hanging up.
"Are you okay?" asked Jean, coming out of the playroom, followed by Clément.
"Sure," answered Chloe, absently.
"You don't look too happy."
"I'm going out with Vincent. I feel that after Monday, I owe him that much."
"I don't see what's the problem in that?" Jean picked up Clément who was hanging onto his leg.
"He has a crush on me."
Jean stopped and laughed. "That might be a problem. Just tell him."
"I know, I'm planning on it. I just feel bad about it….I never thanked you for being so open-minded about Laurence and I," said Chloe, following Jean to the kitchen. Jean sat Clément at the table, and opened the fridge.
"What am I going to feed you with?" He picked leftover mashed potatoes and a slice of ham and closed the fridge. "Why wouldn't I be open-minded? I haven't seen my daughter that happy and open to anyone since her mother died. You bring out something in her that even we can't," said Jean, motioning to him and Clément.
"Thanks," smiled Chloe. "I guess I should go get changed." She ruffled Clément's hair and left the kitchen.

① ① ①

Exactly 45 minutes later, Vincent rang the doorbell.
"Boy, you're right on time," said Chloe while opening the door.

"I hate being late," smiled Vincent, handing Chloe a bouquet of roses. "These are for you."

Chloe looked at the flowers, surprised. "I...thank you..." Why don't you step in for a minute while I put them in a vase."

"Sure," smiled Vincent, following Chloe.

She went to the dining room buffet and picked the same vase she had put Laurence's flowers in a few weeks back. Chloe smiled at the memories of the flowers and how much Laurence's bouquet symbolized a change in their relationship. She had dried the flowers carefully after a few days, and they were now displayed upstairs in her room. Chloe filled the vase with water and put in the flowers.

"Okay, Vincent. I'm ready," she said, walking back to the entrance where Vincent was waiting.

"Did you have dinner?" asked Vincent.

"No, but I'm really not hungry. Let's just get a drink."

"Okay, what about we go to the same place we went to last time?" asked Vincent, opening the door and letting Chloe go by.

"That's fine."

"We can make it our special place," smiled Vincent.

Oh, boy! I really have to talk to him, thought Chloe, choosing not to answer Vincent's remark.

They drove to the small café on the left bank, the traffic almost non-existent on this Sunday night. Vincent parked his car a few spaces away from where he had previously parked.

"There are no lights. Are you sure it isn't closed?" asked Chloe, pointing at the dark café.

"They've been here forever, I don't get it." Vincent walked up to the door. "There is an eviction notice...I guess now we know why it's closed." He turned and walked back to Chloe who was waiting on the sidewalk. "I'm sorry. I really had no idea. Can we just go for a walk around the lake, or do you want to try to find another place?"

"A walk sounds fine," answered Chloe.

They walked they chatted about the week. Chloe explained to Vincent what happened with Clément, and how her week had been spent trying to help Clément overcome his fears.

"They don't sound like a very good family to stay with," stated Vincent. "You know you could probably find another one...I mean, you've been here for what, almost two months? That shouldn't be a problem."

Chloe laughed. "I don't know why everyone tells me that...I'm not going anywhere. I really like the family. I'm staying."

"Your choice," answered Vincent. They walked silently for a few minutes, slowly circling the lake. "Chloe, can I ask you a question?"

"Sure, what is it?"

Vincent took a deep breath. "I...well, my...I'm stuttering like a teenager," smiled Vincent. "There is this big formal dinner at the University next weekend, and I want to know if you'd like to come with me."

Chloe stopped. "Why don't we sit down for a while?" Vincent nodded, and they walked to a bench closer to the water. "I don't know if I can come with you..."

"It would be fun. Chloe, I'm trying to do things right here. I could be the typical male, and just kiss you and try to get you in bed, but I'm asking you out as a date. I'm trying to be a gentleman here," interrupted Vincent, smiling tenderly at Chloe. He scooted closer to her, and looked into her eyes. "I like you, Chloe. I think you're beautiful, and you have something I've never found in any girl in this country...I think I'm slowly falling for you." Vincent suddenly stopped. "So much for doing that the proper way...I'm sorry, I'm probably scaring you."

Chloe couldn't help smiling at Vincent's attempt to do the proper thing. "Vincent, I appreciate the offer, but there is something I think you need to know..."

"You didn't have anyone in your life last time...don't tell me you've fallen in love in this period of time." Chloe nodded. Vincent sighed. "That will teach me to be so slow. Is it just a flame or are you guys serious about each other?" asked Vincent, testing the water.

"I think it's the real thing," smile Chloe. "I'm sorry. I should have told you at the hospital when you tried to kiss me, but so much was going on..."

"It's okay. Who's the lucky guy?"

"Laurence."

Vincent looked at Chloe, surprised. "You're kidding, right?" he asked incredulously.

"No."

"Why didn't you say something? Why didn't you tell me that no matter what I had no chance?" asked Vincent, a hint of anger in his voice.

"Because this is new to me. I wasn't expecting to fall in love in this country, even less with a woman." Chloe got up. "I think you should take me home."

Vincent nodded. The ride back was filled with tension and unanswered questions. Vincent pulled in front of the house. "Is she Clément's sister?" His words the first spoken since Chloe's request to be driven home.

"Yes, she is."

"I remember her picture from the plane. She is really beautiful."

"Yes, she is," smiled Chloe, images of Laurence dancing in front if her eyes. She turned to Vincent. "Listen…I'm sorry, I should have told you earlier. I like you. You're a great guy, and I want us to stay friends. I owe you for Monday. I'm sorry if I made you believe there could be anything more than friendship between us…"

"You don't owe me anything." Vincent turned and faced Chloe. "I really have no luck with girls," he smiled. "Friends it is," he said, the tension quickly fading.

Chloe smiled, and hugged him. "Thanks. I'll call you this week. Maybe we can do something this weekend, and you can meet her."

"I'd like to meet her…I really feel dumb pursuing you when…."

"Vincent. Don't. I'm flattered, really." Chloe stepped out of the car. "I'll call you."

Vincent nodded and started the car. Chloe waved one last time and disappeared into the courtyard.

Chapter 15

October flew by. Chloe and Laurence's relationship grew stronger as the weeks went by. Sunday night separations were becoming harder and harder, neither of them willing to let go and be apart for five days. Clément had slowly come back to his old self, playful and full of energy. Life was good, and without the dark presence of Beatrice, much more enjoyable and relaxed. Jean had started to travel again, but he always made a point of never being gone more than two or three days at a time.

The only stressful time for Chloe was when social services came over for their weekly visit. She felt judged and was always scared of doing something wrong. Jean always tried to be present during those meetings, but he unfortunately wasn't always able to be. The same women from the hospital had been assigned to what they called "Le dossier Glairon," and each time, one of them would insist on playing with Clément while the other spoke to Chloe or Jean.

On a cold November day, Chloe and Clément were walking home from school. They stopped at the boulangerie to buy Clément a snack and were back on their way. Clément was excitedly explaining to Chloe how a clown came to their classroom today, and how he blew up balloons and made animal shapes with them. Clément ran down the sidewalk with his arm dangling in front of him, pretending to be the elephant the clown had made. Chloe ran behind him laughing, and caught him as he ran through the open gate of their courtyard.

"Caught you," said Chloe, laughing and grabbing Clément by the shoulders. Clément didn't respond; his gaze was fixed ahead, and his body was shaking. "What is it, sweetheart?" asked Chloe, following Clément's gaze. There, at the end of the courtyard, was Beatrice's gray metallic Mercedes. "Okay, babe, no need to panic." Chloe picked up Clément and slowly walked back out. Once out of the courtyard, she rang Monsieur Cambier's bell urgently.

"J'arrive, J'arrive," Monsieur Cambier called. He opened the door, and Chloe almost pushed him out of the way to get in. Clément was still holding on to Chloe trembling. A panicked Chloe rushed to explain why she was there.

"On se calme mon petit. Je ne comprend rien si tu me parles dans ta langue de sauvage."

An older woman's voice was heard coming from the other side of the house. "René, qui est ce?"

"La jeune voisine. Quelque chose c'est passé, mais je ne comprend rien—elle parle Anglais."

A woman with long gray hair pulled into a ponytail came toward them. She carried herself elegantly and was wiping her hands on a kitchen towel. She walked up to Chloe and smiled, warmly extending her hand.

"I speak a little English if you speak slowly," she said with a smile and a thick accent.

Before explaining anything, Chloe took a deep breath, and asked to use their phone. Madame Cambier directed her toward the living room. Chloe tried to put Clément down, but he started crying, so she tenderly kissed him on the head and sat down with him on her lap, one arm holding him, and the other holding the phone.

"Monsieur Glairon, s'il vous plait. C'est une urgence."

"Tout de suite mademoiselle."

"Allo!"

"Jean, it's Chloe. We have a problem. Beatrice is here."

"What? Are you guys okay?"

"Sort of. Clément is panicked. He saw her car first...we were coming back from school..."

"Did you see her?"

"No, as soon as I saw the car, I picked him up and left."

"Where are you?"

"At our neighbor's house. Monsieur et Madame Cambier."

"I want you to stay there with Clément until I come. Let me talk to Monsieur or Madame Cambier, and I'm on my way."

"Okay." Chloe handed the phone to Madame Cambier, who had come back into the living room with two glasses of milk and chocolate cookies. She took the phone from Chloe, and as she spoke with Jean, her expression grew concerned. She hung up the phone and looked at Clément while shaking her head in consternation.

"He said to stay here," she said, gently brushing Clément's hair back. Clément had relaxed a little, but still kept hold on Chloe's arms. "You want cookies?" she asked in halting English. Chloe smiled at her kindness, and picked one up from the tray. She broke it in half and offered the other half to Clément, who refused it. "Children always want cookies…not good, not good," said Madame Cambier, shaking her head once again. She got up and came back shortly after, carrying a box full of paper and markers. She smiled at Clément and set them up on the table in front of him. "Draw?" she asked. Clément looked at her and slid from Chloe's lap slowly, making his way to the box of markers and paper, he looked back at Chloe, silently asking for permission.

"Go on, sweetheart," smiled Chloe, grabbing another cookie.

She got up and walked to the window, trying to see if she could still spot Beatrice's car, but the placement of the window made it impossible to see anything besides the sidewalk. *Damn, what can she be doing inside?* She walked back to her seat and smiled at the sight of Clément drawing away with Madame Cambier happily helping him choose different colors.

An hour went by when suddenly police car sirens were heard coming down the street followed by an ambulance, but instead of passing by, they stopped in front of the house. Chloe rushed to the window, and turned back. Clément was still peacefully drawing, unaware of the outside noises.

"Madame Cambier. The police car stopped at our house. I need to know what's happening. Would you please keep an eye on him for a few minutes?"

"Go ahead." She smiled.

Chloe ran outside. On the sidewalk, a small crowd was starting to form. The front door was open, and Jean's car was parked in front along with the police cars and the ambulance. Chloe pushed her way through and ran up the front stairs but, before she had time to step in, was stopped by a policeman.

"Let me go. I live here," she yelled, not understanding.

"Non, personne ne peut entrer," said the officer, holding her. Another officer popped his head through the family room door.

"Qu'est ce qui se passe?" he asked.

"J'en sais rien, je comprend rien a ce qu'elle raconte."

The officer in the family room came forward. "Hello, I'm Officer Pernat. You can't stay here."

"I live here…what's going on?"

"You live here?" he asked.

"Yes, yes, I babysit Clément, the little boy, I…"

"Where is he now?"

"At the neighbor's house. We were coming back from school…what's going on? Why are you here?" asked Chloe, fear suddenly gripping her. "Jean," she called, snatching her arm out of the policeman's hands and running toward the family room. She was stopped by one of the policeman before she had time to make it up the stairs.

"Jean," she yelled, not getting an answer.

The officer turned her around and looked at her. His eyes held compassion and sadness. "Miss, I think you should sit down." Chloe looked at him and let him take her to the couch. "Miss, I'm sorry, but Jean Glairon was shot less than an hour ago."

"What?" asked Chloe in shock.

"His wife called us to confess…she has already been arrested…I'm sorry."

"If this is a joke, this is sick," said Chloe, getting up angrily.

"Miss, please sit down," said the officer gently.

"No…you liar!" Chloe ran upstairs in despair, tears pouring down her face, calling for Jean. She got to the top of the stairs and was stopped by a paramedic. She pummeled his chest and yelled for him to let her through. He gently but firmly held her at arm's length. Chloe looked past him and froze. A few feet away was Jean, laying under a white sheet, the bottom of his shoes the only thing visible. Before being able to control herself, Chloe screamed.

The paramedic kindly walked her back down and handed her to the officer with a sad smile. Chloe sat on the couch in shock, unaware of the tears falling down her face.

"Mademoiselle?" called the officer. Chloe slowly looked at him, her eyes blank and unexpressive. "You said the little boy is at the neighbor's house. Can you both stay there for the night? Is there any other family we can contact?"

Chloe nodded. "His daughter in Lille. I'll call her...I—"

"No, we'll take care of it. Do you have the number?" asked the officer, making sure his voice was calm and gentle. Chloe nodded and wrote it down on the officer's note pad. "Thank you. I'm going to take you back next door now. Tomorrow we'll come and ask you some questions."

Chloe mechanically followed him. Before reaching the door she stopped. "I want to call her myself."

The officer turned around and looked at Chloe. "Miss, calling someone to tell them that their father was shot is not an easy thing. I think you should let us handle it..."

"No, I need to do it," said Chloe, wiping off tears from her eyes.

The officer sighed. "There are no laws stopping you from doing it, but please, let us handle the details."

Chloe nodded. "I just want to tell her. You can talk to her after I do." She didn't wait for the officer to answer, turned around and walked back to the family room. She stared at the phone for a few moments and picked it up. It rang five times, and Chloe was ready to hang up when Laurence picked up.

"*Allo.*"

"Lo, it's me."

"*Hi. You got me to run, I heard the phone ring from downstairs....wait, you never call in the middle of the day. Are you okay?*" asked a concerned Laurence.

"I'm fine, so is Clément....Lo, there's been an accident."

"*What do you mean?*" Laurence's voice trembled, the worst possible scenario passing through her mind, but she was not prepared for the news Chloe announced. Laurence swallowed hard. "*Is that a joke?*"

"I wish it was, sweetheart," answered Chloe softly.

"Where is Clément?" asked Laurence with tears in her voice.

"At the neighbor's house."

"You go to him, you hear me? Stay with him until I get there....I can't afford to lose him too...I..."

"Lo, he is safe there, I swear. Beatrice has been arrested already."

"I'm on my way."

"Okay," murmured Chloe, hanging up. She walked back to the officer who was waiting for her in the entrance. "She's coming," she said flatly. The officer nodded and walked Chloe back to the Cambiers' house.

In Lille, Laurence stared at the phone still in her hand and slowly put it down. She balled her hands into fists and hit the wall, the pain shooting through her hands, not enough to appease her. She slid down to the floor and sobbed.

Chloe found Clément watching TV with Monsieur Cambier. She silently sat next to him.

"Look, Sesame," laughed Clément, pointing at the TV screen. Chloe looked, almost unable to focus, feeling numb. She heard Madame Cambier close the front door and come back to the room. She motioned for her husband to come, leaving Chloe and Clément alone in the room. Chloe looked at Clément, who was happily giggling at Cookie Monster's last joke, and started sobbing. Clément turned to Chloe, his eyes questioning. She picked him up and squeezed him against her chest.

"I'm sorry, sweetheart, I'm okay," she took a deep breath and tried to calm down.

"Let's go home," smiled Clément, getting up and pulling Chloe's hand.

Chloe's tears started again on Clément's statement. "Oh, babe, not tonight, okay?" she said, sniffling. "Tonight, we stay here...it's going to be so much fun."

"Tomo'ow we go home?" asked Clément.

"Tomorrow," answered Chloe, her voice barely a whisper.

"Okay," said Clément, happy with the answer, and turning his attention back to his TV show.

Chapter 16

Chloe wiped some remaining tears off her cheeks and slowly got up. "Stay here, sweetheart, I have to go and ask Madame Cambier something." Clément looked at her briefly and returned his attention to the TV show. Chloe sighed, wishing she could capture Clément's innocence if only for a minute and forget the events of the past few hours.

As she stepped out, she almost bumped into Madame Cambier. "Sorry, I didn't see you," she apologized.

Madame Cambier smiled. "I made dinner, come and eat. After that I'll show you to your room." She walked into the family room, knelt next to Clément, and softly whispered something in his ear. Clément giggled, clapped his hands, jumped up, and charged toward the kitchen at a dead run.

"Come on, C'oe. Food." He ran back, grabbed her hand, and followed Madame Cambier to the kitchen with Chloe in tow.

"What did you tell him? I've never seen him so enthusiastic about eating," asked Chloe before picking up Clément and sitting him on a chair at the large kitchen table.

"It's a secret," smiled the elderly woman. She picked up a pan from the stove and dropped two spoonfuls of mashed potatoes on Clément's plate and got a slice of ham out of a white package and cut it in little pieces for him. To Chloe's surprise, Clément grabbed his fork and started eating. *When I think that I have to fight with him everyday for him not to eat with his hands...amazing.*

"Would you like some potatoes?" Madame Cambier asked Chloe.

"No, thanks...I really don't have the heart to eat right now."

"You eat," said Madame Clément, putting some food on Chloe's plate. "You'll get sick if you don't eat," she said, her tone of voice indicating she would not take no for an answer.

Monsieur Cambier, who was sitting across from Chloe, winked at her. "Ecoute ce qu'elle dit mon petit," he smiled.

Chloe nodded, put some food in her mouth, and swallowed slowly. Clément finished up his plate hastily, put his fork down and clapped his hands. "More TV now," he laughed.

"Clément, I think it's bedtime for you," Chloe countered, pushing her half-empty plate away.

"This is what I promised him if he ate everything on his plate," smiled Madame Cambier. "Viens mon cheri, seulement 10 minutes." She looked at Chloe for acceptance. Chloe, who was too tired to fight, quickly nodded and let Clément go back to the family room.

① ① ①

Around 8:30, Madame Cambier took Chloe and Clément upstairs to show them the sleeping arrangements. Her house was simple, but nicely decorated. She took them into a large room with a single and a double bed. The walls were covered with light blue wallpaper and a painting representing a picnic by a lake with people wearing bright dresses and children running around playing ball hung on the wall. The wooden floor squeaked as they walked across it. Pajamas that appeared to be Clément's size were displayed on the single bed.

"This is where my daughter and her husband sleep when they come visit. They have a little boy," explained Madame Clément. "The bathroom is..." She stopped, thinking. "I don't know the word. I'll show you." She stepped out and showed Chloe a door at the far end of the corridor.

"Thank you. I don't know how to..."

"I'm happy to help," smiled Madame Cambier.

"His sister should arrive tonight. She knows we're here...I...she might come knocking at the door..."

"You sleep. I come and wake you if she comes."

"Thank you."

Madame Cambier lightly kissed Clément on the cheek and left the room. Chloe looked at Clément, who had discovered a toy chest in the left corner of the room and was happily taking toys out.

"No, no, babe, it's time for bed. Let's get you washed up and in your pajamas."

"No, I play," whined Clément.

Chloe sighed heavily. "Please, no arguments tonight, okay?" she said, almost pleading. Her voice must have held a desperate tone because Clément got up and grabbed his pajamas. "Thank you," Chloe said, relieved.

She quickly got him ready for the night and came back to the bedroom to tuck him in. "You stay with me," asked Clément, patting the area next to him on the bed.

"Just for a minute," Chloe conceded softly. She climbed into bed and draped an arm around him.

"I want papa," said Clément, his voice choking a little.

Chloe's heart skipped a beat at his request and tears sprung to her eyes. "Not tonight, sweetheart."

Clément sniffled a little and cuddled closer to Chloe. "Tomo'ow, papa comes home?" he asked, uncertainty in his voice as if he knew his request could not be answered.

Chloe took a deep breath and got hold of her emotions before answering. "Not papa, but Lo will be here."

"Lo?"

"Yes, so you have to fall asleep very fast so morning comes quickly, and then you can see Lo."

"Okay," yawned Clément. He closed his eyes and took hold of Chloe's hand. Once he was sure she wasn't leaving him alone in this strange room, he let sleep take him.

① ① ①

A soft tap on the shoulder woke Chloe. She sat up abruptly and looked around the room, disoriented. After a few seconds, she got her bearings back and wiped the sleep off her eyes.

"She is downstairs," Madame Cambier said softly.

Chloe nodded and got out of bed. *I must have fallen asleep*, she thought while arranging the covers back up over Clément's sleeping form. She followed Madame Cambier downstairs.

"She's in the living room. I'm going to bed. Goodnight."

Chloe thanked her and stood riveted in her spot, her legs refusing to walk to the door and face Laurence and the grief she knew she must be feeling. After a few moments of uncertainty, Chloe walked up to the door and stopped with her hand on the knob, took a deep breath, and opened it. The room was dark, the only light coming from the fire Madame Cambier must have lit earlier in the evening. Laurence was standing tall at the window, her back to the door. She waited for Chloe to close the door before turning. Her face looked tired, the shadows from the flames making it look almost cadaverous, and her eyes were red, the lack of light not enough to hide the long hours of crying. Chloe walked up to Laurence, but stopped halfway when she realized that Laurence had not moved or even said a word. She looked at her and her heart swelled with pain at the sight of Laurence's torments, and stood there trying to convey her love through her glance.

"Where is Clément?' asked Laurence, breaking the silence, her voice bearing almost no emotion.

"Upstairs sleeping," answered Chloe, shivering slightly from the cold tone of Laurence's voice.

"We have to take him to school tomorrow morning. The police want to talk to us, and I don't want him to be around."

Chloe nodded. Laurence took a step forward, and stopped again. She briefly rubbed her eyes, and her facial features seemed to soften a little.

"They wouldn't let me in the house…those dumb cops wouldn't let me into my own house," said Laurence, her voice quivering, and her need for control slowly slipping.

"I know. It's just a stupid protocol…I'm sorry, sweetheart," said Chloe, stepping closer to Laurence.

"I couldn't see him…they've taken his body away already…they said tomorrow." Laurence's voice was slowly regaining its coldness. Chloe, unwilling to let Laurence go back into her previous mood, gently took hold of her hand. "There is nothing we can do tonight…come with me upstairs," she asked softy. Not getting an answer, she gently guided Laurence out of the room, up the stairs and into the bedroom. Laurence followed mechanically. Chloe indicated for her to sit on the bed, knelt in front of her and removed her tennis shoes, and tenderly stood her back up and removed her jeans and her sweatshirt, leaving her in her t-shirt and underwear. Laurence let herself be undressed like a baby, her gaze fixed on Clément who was sleeping peacefully. Tears started rolling down her cheeks. Chloe looked up at Laurence's face covered with tears, and she quickly shed her clothes and opened up the bed. She gently wiped off Laurence's cheeks and lightly kissed her on the lips. "Come on, let's get you in bed," she said tenderly, dragging Laurence into the bed with her. She propped herself up on two pillows and drew Laurence into her arms. Laurence had stopped crying. She put her head in the crook of Chloe's shoulder and wrapped her arm around her waist. Her brain rushed with thousands of things to say, but fatigue took over, and her eyelids became heavy. She tried to fight sleep, an effort not lost on Chloe.

"Don't fight it, Lo. Go to sleep. You'll have to deal with a lot tomorrow." Chloe lightly massaged Laurence's scalp.

"Thank you," said Laurence emotionally, speaking for the first time since the living room.

"Together in this mess, remember," answered Chloe, kissing Laurence's forehead and tightening her grip. "I love you, Lo," she whispered before closing her eyes.

"I know," answered Laurence, bringing a smile to Chloe's face. The image of a little girl playing with her mother in a garden full of flowers under the loving watch of her father flashed into Laurence's mind; tears swelled up in her eyes, and she tightened her grip on Chloe, burying her face even further into her shirt. She forced herself to stop thinking and closed her eyes, willing to surrender to what she knew would not be a restful sleep.

Chapter 17

Dawn crept slowly through the parted blinds. Chloe opened her eyes and smiled tenderly at the sight of Laurence sleeping peacefully. They must have moved during the night because Laurence was now on her side facing her. She propped herself up on her elbow and tenderly passed her hand through Laurence's hair. She watched her eyes flutter open, still foggy with sleep.

"Good morning," said Chloe softly.

Laurence didn't answer, but instead looked at Chloe and gently drew her in for a kiss. The kiss was tender, their lips softly moving against each other, only conveying the love they felt for each other. Chloe broke up the kiss and caressed Laurence's face.

"Do you still want Clément to go to school today?" she asked. Laurence nodded. "Okay, then I should probably get him ready, it's already 7:30," said Chloe, sitting up. Laurence stretched, got out of bed and put her jeans on.

"If you don't mind I'm going to let you walk him to school. I... have to call my dad's business partners and tell them what happened. I also have to make some arrangements for the funeral, and we have to talk to the police…."

"Lo, slow down. One step at a time. Yes, I'll take Clément to school, but after that I can help you…"

"I appreciate it, but he was my father, and it's my job to handle things," answered Laurence. She had reverted to the aloof attitude of the night before. Chloe realized that she was now facing the businesslike Laurence, and even if she didn't like this side of her, she understood Laurence's need to be in control of her emotions.

"Very well. You know I'm here if you need help," answered Chloe, wishing Laurence would let her help.

Clément's voice suddenly stopped their conversation. "Lo," he called.

Laurence rushed to his side, and picked him up. "Hi babe. Happy to see me?"

Clément smiled and hugged Laurence. "Today we go home?" he asked.

"I hope so," answered Laurence, putting him down. "Listen, Chloe is going to get you ready and walk you to school. I'll see you when you get back, okay?"

"Okay," answered Clément smiling and running to Chloe, who was putting her sweatshirt on.

"Let's get you ready." She picked up his discarded clothes. "I wish I had something else to put on you beside the clothes you had on yesterday."

"How did he get those pajamas?" asked Laurence, pointing at Clément.

"Madame Cambier has a grandson who is Clément's age."

"Then ask her if she has clothes for him to wear today," said Laurence, sitting up on the bed and tying her tennis shoes.

A light knock at the door surprised them. "Come in," called Laurence, getting up.

Madame Cambier's head popped through the door. "Breakfast is ready," she said, opening the door completely.

Chloe nodded. "Madame Cambier, do you by any chance have clothes for Clément to wear today?"

Madame Cambier smiled and walked up to a large dresser in the corner of the room. She opened a drawer and took out a pair of sweatpants and a matching top. She then opened another drawer and retrieved socks, underwear, and a t-shirt. "I like to be prepared for when Frederic comes...it's my grandson's name," she said, handing the clothes to Chloe.

"Thank you," smiled Chloe.

①   ①   ①

An hour later, Chloe and Clément were walking through the kindergarten school's courtyard. Mothers whispered between them as they walked by. Clément's teacher came rushing toward them.

"Bonjour…hello, I didn't think you would come today."

"You speak English," exclaimed Chloe, not believing it.

"Well yes, I do," smiled Clément's teacher.

"Why didn't you say something earlier? You've seen me struggling trying to put a sentence together, so I could speak to you…you could have said something," said Chloe, still astonished.

"You're here to learn our language, Mademoiselle; I thought I was helping."

Chloe sighed, unwilling to let her temper get the best of her. "I guess in a way you might have been."

The teacher gave a polite smile and looked at Clément. She spoke briefly to him, asking him to go and play with his friends in the playground.

Clément turned to Chloe. "You come get me?"

"Of course, sweetheart," smiled Chloe, kissing him and gently pushing him toward the playground. "Go play now." Clément waved and left running.

"I heard what happened," said Clément's teacher.

"How?"

"The news on TV. I'm sorry. What is going to happen to Clément?"

"His sister will take care of him…I suppose."

"Yes, he has been through a lot lately…I think she will be a good mother to him."

Chloe smiled briefly at the truth of the statement. "Yes, I agree. Now, if you'll excuse me I have to get back."

"Of course."

"One more thing…Clément doesn't know, and we'd appreciate if it could stay this way for now."

Clément's teacher nodded. "Of course. We'll see you at 3," she said, turning and walking away.

Chloe left the school under the scrutiny of every parent who had come to drop their kids off. As she walked by them, she felt like screaming at them to mind their own business, but instead she chose to ignore them. The sky was overcast and a cold wind grabbed her when she turned at the corner of the street. She zipped up her jacket and put her hands into her pockets, unconsciously speeding up her walk. The streets were busy; pedestrians walked fast, their heads low and their shoulders hunched to protect themselves from the wind, and cars weaved between lanes trying to get through the morning rush hour traffic. As Chloe walked, lost in her thoughts, she barely felt the rain start to fall. She walked with her eyes fixed on the pavement, her body in cruise control mode, her mind miles away. Suddenly a loud bell brought Chloe out of her trance. She looked up just in time to jump aside and avoid a bicycle coming down the sidewalk at full speed.

"Et fait attention," yelled the cyclist at Chloe as he passed her.

Chloe shook her head in disbelief and tried to stay focused on the activities around her. Shortly after, she turned onto rue de Provence. Four police cars were parked in front of the house, the gate was wide open, and Laurence was talking with a policeman on the sidewalk. Chloe walked up to her. "What's happening?"

"You're back. I guess let's get this interrogation over and done with," said Laurence, smiling coldly at the policeman.

The questioning went fast. They were asked about Beatrice and her relationship with Jean, and why Jean was home in the middle of the day. After writing down a few more things, the policeman got up.

"Thank you for your help. The bedroom has been cleaned up, and we have everything we need. Since Beatrice confessed there will be no investigation. You might both have to testify in court." He stiffly turned to Laurence. "I'm very sorry about what happened. If you wish we can now take you to see your father."

Laurence's face became white and her hands balled into fists. She took a deep breath. "Yes, I'd like to see him."

"I'll come with you," said Chloe.

"No," answered Laurence abruptly. "Sorry...I'd rather go alone." Laurence looked at Chloe, her clear blue eyes filled with sadness. She squeezed Chloe's shoulder. "I have to do that alone," said Laurence, looking to Chloe for understanding.

"I'll wait here."

"Thank you," said Laurence before walking out.

① ① ①

Once Laurence left, Chloe was left alone in the house. The silence gave her chills, and she walked around the main floor, scared of going upstairs for fear of what she would find. After a few moments of aimlessly walking around the family room, she directed her steps toward the stairs. She took each step slowly; the top of the stairs had never looked so uninviting. At the top of the stairs, she looked toward Jean and Beatrice's bedroom door. Chloe slowly walked up to it and opened it. She stepped inside the brightly illuminated bedroom and gasped. Everything looked the same, as if yesterday's tragedy had not happened. A book lay open on a night table with Jean's glasses beside it, his robe was negligently thrown on the bed and one of his suits hung from the dresser, still sporting the tag from the dry cleaners. Chloe walked carefully across the room and picked up a picture frame with Jean and Beatrice holding hands on a beach. "They look so happy…what happened?" asked Chloe to herself aloud. She put the picture back in its place and walked out. "It's hard to believe someone got killed in this room yesterday." Chloe shook her head sadly and walked down the dark corridor to her bedroom.

As soon as she crossed her doorstep, the doorbell rang. "Damn, who is that?" She rushed downstairs and opened the door to the mailman. He handed her a large envelope in her name.

"Merci," she said before closing the door. Chloe rushed back to her room and sat on her bed as she tore open the envelope. She reached inside and retrieved another envelope containing pictures. Memories of sending out a roll of films to be developed a few weeks back came back to her. With trembling hands, she opened it. The first picture was of Clément and Laurence playing with legos. Chloe slowly put the picture on the bed and closed her eyes, remembering the next picture she took. She took a deep breath and opened her eyes; there was Jean with Clément in his arms laying on the couch. A sob escaped Chloe, and she abruptly put the pictures down. She slowly got herself back under control and stood, deciding to hit the shower and hoping it would relieve the enormous heartache she felt at the moment.

① ① ①

Hours went by, and Laurence had still not come home. Chloe went to pick up Clément and returned to a empty house. As she got ready to call Jean's office to check if Laurence had been there, the front door opened and Laurence came in. She looked exhausted and her eyes bore a coldness that made Chloe shiver. Clément rushed to her, screaming her name. She picked him up without saying a word and sat on the couch holding him.

Her stiff appearance stopped Chloe from asking any questions, and she waited patiently for Laurence to speak. Clément, not understanding why Laurence would not answer his questions or come play with him, got off her lap and started playing with his favorite red fire truck.

Laurence briefly looked at him, and once she was sure his attention was on his truck, she spoke. "The funeral is on Thursday. On Wednesday I have to meet with my dad's lawyer to read his will. I spent the afternoon with his partner discussing what was to happen to the business. Technically, until the will is read, we have no idea what my dad would have wanted in this case."

Their eyes met for the first time since Laurence had walked in. "Is there anything I can do?" asked Chloe softly.

"No. I'm going to go upstairs to change and shower." Before Chloe had time to say anything, Laurence was already halfway up the stairs.

"Arghhh," yelled Chloe, getting up abruptly. "Why won't you let me in?" she yelled to the space where Laurence stood a few moments ago.

① ① ①

Laurence only came out of her room when she heard Clément and Chloe coming upstairs.

"I'll get him ready for the night," she said as she followed them into Clément's bedroom.

"Fine," answered Chloe, kissing Clément good night and leaving the room. She stomped back into her room and plunked herself on her bed. *I know she is hurting, but she is driving me crazy*, thought Chloe. A few minutes later, she heard Laurence's voice coming out of the baby monitor. She got up to turn it off, not wanting to intrude on Laurence and Clément's privacy, but what she heard stopped her.

"Sweetheart, I have to talk to you," said Laurence.

"Okay," giggled Clément.

Chloe heard Laurence take a deep breath. "I want to talk to you about papa."

"Papa come home?" asked Clément.

"No, he isn't coming home."

"I want him," said Clément, his little voice almost angry.

"Something happened, Clément, and I know you're too young to understand, but…" Laurence's voice cracked slightly. "Papa isn't coming home for a very long time. Chloe and I are going to take care of you now. It'll be fun, you'll see. I'll live here all the time, and we'll have so much fun."

Chloe heard Clément's voice break into a scream. "I want papa," he cried.

"I know, I know, sweetheart…so do I," said Laurence softly. A shuffling noise resembling bed sheets followed, and Laurence started singing. Chloe turned the monitor off and went back to her bed.

She waited for Laurence to come to her room after putting Clément to bed, but 11 o'clock came and went and she was still alone in her room. She decided that Laurence must need some time alone and with a heavy heart got ready for bed. She had just turned the light off and settled in when a light knock at the door startled her.

"Come in," she called, her heart racing.

Laurence entered the moon lit room and stopped after taking a few steps. They stared at each other, the moonlight barely giving them enough light to discern each other's face. Chloe got out of bed and walked to Laurence, stopping an arm's length away.

"One day you told me that you only wanted the truth from me. Do you still want that?" asked Laurence, breaking the silence.

"Yes, I do," answered Chloe honestly.

"I can't do it, Chloe. I'm not strong enough to handle everything. I have nothing…what kind of role model am I going to be for Clément? I need you so badly right now because I really feel like taking the first train out of here and never coming back…"

"You can do it, Laurence. You've gone through so much. You're strong. I believe in you….not a good role model for Clément? Are you kidding? His eyes light up when he sees you, he thinks you have all the answers." Chloe took a breath and laid her hand on Laurence's chest. "Reach inside yourself Lo…I know you have it in you."

"I love you," said Laurence suddenly.

"I lov…" Her words were cut off by Laurence's lips. Her kiss was demanding, almost fierce, as if her need to be with Chloe could never be satisfied.

"Promise me you won't leave me," asked Laurence between kisses, her voice almost begging.

"I'm here. I'm not going anywhere."

"No, promise me," begged Laurence, backing up and laying Chloe down on the bed. Tears flowed freely from her eyes as she went back to Chloe's lips. "Please," she pleaded, lifting Chloe's night shirt and running her hand on her bare skin.

"I promise," answered Chloe, understanding Laurence's need to know that someone else she loved wasn't going to go away.

"I can't lose you too," said Laurence's sobs racking her body. She could not get close enough to Chloe, her need to be held and loved almost overwhelming. "Please love me," she asked, her voice filled with tears. Chloe sat up and rolled Laurence on her back and kissed Laurence deeply, trying to convey her love through this one kiss. She kissed Laurence's tears away and took her face between her hands. "I love you," she said, before losing herself in Laurence. She poured every ounce of love she had for Laurence into her lovemaking, and at the end when Laurence sobbed in her arms, she promised her again that she'd always be there for her.

Chapter 18

Chloe slept very little, her mind too preoccupied by the events of the past few days and anticipating the ones to come. She got up before dawn, giving up on sleep. She carefully untangled herself from Laurence, kissed her lightly on the forehead, and left the room.

"6 o'clock. This is crazy!" she exclaimed, checking the clock while entering the kitchen. "Maybe I'll make them an American breakfast…good idea, at least it'll keep me busy." She proceeded to make pancakes from scratch. "Okay, how many grams in a cup? …damn, why can't they just use the same system as us?" said Chloe with frustration, trying to convert the measurements. She finally decided to just eyeball everything and see if it would work.

By 6:30, she had a large batch of pancakes ready. She set the table for three and got out the jam and Nutella. "That'll have to do since they've never heard of syrup in this country," smiled Chloe proudly, looking at the table and admiring her finished work.

"Are you talking to yourself?" asked an amused voice.

Chloe looked up and smiled at the sight of Laurence in the doorway, wearing only boxer shorts and a tank top. "Yeah, I do that sometimes. Keeps me sane," she smiled, walking towards Laurence. "How did you sleep?"

"Very well. I feel rested and ready to deal with whatever else comes up today," said Laurence, tenderly running her hand over Chloe's arm. Laurence's deep blue eyes met Chloe. "Chloe, about last night, I...."

"You don't have to apologize..."

"I wasn't going to," interrupted Laurence with a smile. She seriously looked into Chloe's eyes. "I was going to thank you. You give me strength. The fact that you believe in me makes me believe in myself. Thank you."

"You're welcome," answered Chloe, blushing.

Laurence drew her in for a hug and lightly kissed her on the forehead. "What did you cook? Smells good."

"I don't know if it's good, though; I sort of had to guess the measurements," explained Chloe, showing the measuring cup to Laurence.

Laurence laughed heartily. "Cups and grams, right?"

"Yeah, it's a pain." Chloe looked at the clock, which indicated 6:45. "Should we wake up Clément so he can have breakfast with us?"

"I think so. I'll go get him." She left, but not before briefly squeezing Chloe's shoulder as she passed. Once she reached the doorway, she turned around. "Would you come with me today?"

"To meet with the lawyer?"

"Yes. I don't know if you're going to be allowed in the room with us, but I'd like to know you are close by," said Laurence seriously.

"Of course I'll come," she smiled.

A smile lit Laurence's face, and for the first time since Jean's death, she looked happy. "Thanks. I'll go get the monster now." Chloe nodded and watched Laurence leave.

A few moments later, small foot steps were heard running toward the kitchen, and Clément came barging in. "C'oe," He called, running toward her.

She picked him up and hugged him briefly. "Good morning, little man," she smiled, sitting him down at the table. Laurence took her seat and Chloe brought the pancakes to the table. "All right. Those are called pancakes. You usually it them with syrup, but since we are in France, and nobody knows what syrup is, we'll have to eat them with something else." She sat down, grabbed a pancake, put it on Clément's plate and cut it in three pieces. "Do you want jam or Nutella on it?" she asked Clément.

"Nute'a ," said Clément happily. Chloe spread the chocolate paste on his pancake and grabbed one for herself.

"It's pretty good," said Laurence, chewing on one delightedly.
"You like it?"
"Yes, they are like crêpes, but bigger."
"I never had craps," said Chloe, spreading strawberry jam on hers.
"We had them at the brasserie with Tony. And they're not 'craps'! Crêpes – sort of rhymes with 'pep'," repeated Laurence, purposely enunciating every syllable to show Chloe the difference.
"Oh, that's what those were. That's what I said. Craps."
"I give up," laughed Laurence, finishing her plate and getting up to get the orange juice. She poured some for the three of them and sat back down. "We should probably get moving. We have to get ready, drop Clément at school and go."
"What time is the meeting?" asked Chloe, getting up and putting her plate in the dishwasher.
"More," interrupted Clément, his little arms reaching for the plate containing the remaining pancakes.
"One more, and we have to get rolling," said Chloe. "And Clément, the food goes in your mouth, not on your face," she smiled, looking at Clément, who had chocolate spread all the way up to his ears.
"Meeting is at 10. I tell you what. Why don't you go get ready? I'll clean up this mess and bathe him, and when you're out you can keep an eye on him."
"Are you sure you don't want help cleaning?"
"You cook, I clean. Fine by me," smiled Laurence. She grabbed Chloe's chin and drew her in for a kiss. Chloe barely brushed her lips on hers and withdrew.
"Lo, not in front of Clément," smiled Chloe.
"Why not? First of all, he doesn't care. Look at him, he is too busy, eating and wiping his hands all over his face. Second of all, I don't want to hide." She got up and kissed Chloe briefly on the lips. "Come on, go get ready," she laughed at Chloe's surprised expression.
"Do I have to dress up?"
"I honestly don't know. I'm going to…just don't wear jeans."
"I can do that. I'll be out in a few."
Half an hour later, Chloe walked down the corridor to Clément's room. She wore a pair of beige slacks, a green sweater and black shoes. "Will this do?" she asked, referring to her clothes. Laurence turned around and smiled at the sight of Chloe. "You look beautiful," she

said tenderly. "Clément, come back here," she called to Clément who had taken advantage of her moment of inattention to run to his toys. "I don't know how you do it every morning."

Chloe laughed. "Why don't you go shower and get dressed? I'll take care of him."

"Good idea," answered Laurence, handing Clément's clothes to Chloe.

Chloe looked briefly at the clothes. "Side note for you. No overalls for school. He can't go to the bathroom by himself with those. Stick to sweatpants or pants with an elastic around the waist." She explained, going to Clément's dresser and getting out a pair of blue sweat pants.

"Got it. Okay, I'll see you in a few minutes."

By 8:30, Chloe took Clément downstairs and sent him to the playroom. While keeping an eye on him, she picked up the phone and dialed her dad's office number.

"Hi dad, I know it's only 3:30 in the morning for you, but I thought I'd leave you a message on your voice mail at work, since this week is going to be very busy, and I don't know when I'll have time to call. Everything is going very well here, I'll try again next week…." She turned around at the sound of Laurence coming down the stairs and stopped in awe. Laurence was wearing a light blue business suit. The skirt stopped one or two inches above her knees, making her legs seem even longer. She wore her hair loose and had added a touch of makeup, accentuating her piercing blue eyes. "…okay, bye dad…love you," she hung up the phone and walked up to Laurence. "You look great. Is blue an appropriate color, though?"

"Instead of black?" Chloe nodded. "It will do for today. We have to wear black tomorrow for the funeral though," she said, her voice cracking slightly.

Chloe rose up onto her tiptoes and kissed Laurence. "You look stunning."

Laurence smiled. "Shall we get going?"

① ① ①

They piled into Jean's Mercedes and dropped Clément at school. Chloe waited for Laurence in the car while she walked Clément to his classroom. Laurence stormed back to the car with an angry expression on her face. She jerked the car door open and flopped herself on the driver seat.

"What's wrong?" asked Chloe, concerned.

"This group of women was obviously talking about us when we walked by, so I stopped and asked them if I could answer any questions for them. They started apologizing all over the place and telling me how sorry they were, and what a tragedy.... I lost it."

"What did you say?" asked Chloe, half amused, half concerned at Laurence's anger.

"I told them to mind their own business, and that they really didn't give a damn, but it only gave them something to talk about...I just made sure Clément will never get invited to anyone's birthday party ever again," smiled Laurence dryly, relaxing a little. "Okay, let's go."

① ① ①

They drove to Paris, and Laurence guided the car through fancy streets with old renovated buildings. BMWs and Porsches were parked on the sidewalks and old women walking poodles could be seen strolling down the sidewalks. Laurence parked the car in front of a large red building.

"We're meeting him at my dad's office," she explained as they stepped out. She opened the front door and they walked into a large hallway. A man in his fifties came to greet them.

"Chloe, this is Bernard, my father's business partner."

"Bonjour," said Chloe, shaking his hand. Bernard had deep brown eyes, a balding head, and a beard that was turning gray. He was slightly shorter than Laurence. He showed them into a waiting room. The room had couches that reminded Chloe of the ones inside Versailles, and paintings with golden frames hung on the wall. Bernard offered them coffee, but they both declined. Shortly after, the bell rang and an older man came in. He looked much older than Bernard and wore a dark business suit. He smiled paternally at Laurence and lightly kissed her on the cheek. Laurence spoke briefly in French with the two of them and turned to Chloe.

"We shouldn't be long. Are you sure you're okay here by yourself?"

"I'll be fine," answered Chloe, smiling encouragingly to Laurence.

Laurence nodded, took a deep breath and repeated, "We shouldn't be long."

Indeed, 45 minutes later, Chloe heard them coming out of what she assumed must have been Bernard's office. The front door opened and closed and Laurence returned to the waiting room. She looked as if she had grown ten years older in the short amount of time she had been gone. Her face was serious, her forehead wrinkled and her eyes unreadable.

"Are you finished?" asked Chloe, getting up.

"Yes…I need some fresh air…walk with me," asked Laurence, absently looking at Chloe.

"Sure."

They walked down the street in silence. The sky was cloudy, but the temperature was not as cold as yesterday. "Let's go there," said Laurence, pointing at a park ahead of them.

They walked past the gates and went to sit on a bench. The park was almost deserted, except for a few joggers and a mother dragging her screaming child behind her.

Chloe waited patiently for Laurence to speak. After staring at a tree for a few minutes, she couldn't remain silent anymore. "What's the name of this park?"

"Parc Monceau," answered Laurence. She turned to face Chloe. "I don't know how my dad managed it, but he changed his will a few weeks back. Beatrice gets absolutely nothing. Clément and I get his money, his business, and his houses."

"Houses?"

"Yes, we have a beach house in Bretagne and a house in Dordogne, plus he had apartments scattered all over Paris that are rented, and of course the Versailles house."

"Wow," said Chloe, surprised.

Laurence sighed. "We each get half and half, and I'm responsible for Clément's money until he turns 18." She passed her hand through her hair. "Bernard is going to buy my dad's half of the business from us…I don't want to take over." She stopped talking and stared ahead, lost in her thoughts.

"Lo, what are you going to do with the Versailles house?" asked Chloe, softly.

"Keep it…Clément has been through so much I don't want to force him to adapt to something else."

"It might not be the right time to speak about that, but what about school?"

"I'm not going back."

"What?" exclaimed Chloe.

"I'm not going back," repeated Laurence, her tone of voice implying that the topic was closed. But Chloe wasn't going to let it go that easily.

"What do you mean you're not going back? Lo, this is ridiculous. You are a month away from graduation...come on. Don't you think your dad would have wanted you to finish?"

Laurence looked at Chloe with a defeated look. "If I go back, Chloe, you are going to have to take care of Clément twenty-four hours a day...it's a little bit much."

"Stop worrying about me. He goes to school, and I'm sure Madame Cambier would be happy to help once in a while. She seems very fond of him. Lo, don't throw away your dreams."

"I don't know what my dreams are anymore," said Laurence sadly.

Chloe brushed a strand of hair behind Laurence's ear and took hold of her hand. "One more month, Lo...don't throw it away," pleaded Chloe.

Laurence nodded. She then laughed sarcastically. "You know I'm filthy rich now." She paused and sadness took the place of sarcasm. "So why do I feel so empty?" she said softly.

Chloe scooted closer and kissed her on the cheek. She brought their joined hands to her lips and kissed Laurence's knuckles. "I love you."

A slight smile appeared on Laurence's face. "I know," she said, getting up and letting go of Chloe's hand. "We should probably get back; I want to clean out my dad's office."

"Okay," said Chloe, following Laurence out.

① ① ①

Jean's office was on the second floor. A large oak desk stood in the middle of the room and a large leather chair and numerous shelves with books completed the room. Laurence dropped the empty boxes she had picked up downstairs and walked around the desk.

"You know that yesterday was the first time I had ever been to his office," said Laurence, absently passing her hand over the desk. A picture of Laurence and Clément stood next to the computer and behind the chair on the shelves was the picture of a woman who looked really familiar. Chloe walked closer.

"This is a picture of your mother," she said softly. She had previously only seen her in paintings. The resemblance between Laurence and her mother in this picture was striking. Laurence snapped the picture from the shelf and put it in one of the boxes along with the picture of her and Clément.

"He really loved her...you know, it never even occurred to me that he must have been hurting really badly when she died." She sat at the desk and opened a drawer. "I'm only taking the personal things. The rest stays here. Do me a favor, can you start packing the books in a box?" she said while going through the drawer.

"Sure," said Chloe, picking up a box and starting to stack books into it. A few minutes went by, each of them absorbed in their task. "Lo, look at this," said Chloe, holding a book with a white cover. "It's a picture album."

Laurence turned the chair around and extended her hand. Chloe handed the album to her and went to stand behind her. Laurence slowly opened it. The first page was a marriage certificate with a picture of Jean and Laurence's mother on their wedding day. Laurence wanted to close the album and stop the memories of her parents from rushing back, but she kept on turning the pages. Page after page told the story of her parents' life, her birth, her childhood... She turned one more page and stopped. There was the death announcement of her mother in the local paper. "Damn, papa, why did you keep all of that?" she mumbled, tears in her voice. Chloe was slowly massaging her shoulders, giving her the strength to continue. She turned to the next page and couldn't stop the gasp that escaped her lips. There facing them was a picture of her and Clément at the hospital; "December 7th 1997" was neatly written under it. "I had no idea he took pictures," said Laurence aloud.

"Go ahead, continue," said Chloe, encouraging her. Laurence turned the page and stopped. There was Clément's birth certificate. It read "mother: Laurence Glairon; father: unknown."

"Lo, he never recognized Clément."

Laurence didn't answer but instead closed the album and dropped it in the box. "I don't think there's anything else. Let's go."

They carried the boxes to the car and drove back to Versailles. "Are you hungry?" asked Laurence, driving the car into the expressway lane.

"I'm getting there," answered Chloe.

"There are a couple of good chain restaurants on the way, we'll stop there."

"Okay."

① ① ①

Laurence was very quiet for the rest of the day, only talking when spoken to. She dealt with the last minute arrangements for the funeral and spent the rest of the day playing with Clément. Chloe decided not to take offense and instead took advantage of the time off to write letters and finish her book. They had leftovers for dinner and Chloe went to the library while Laurence got Clément ready for the night. She was engrossed in *Madame Bovary* when she heard Laurence enter the room.

"Hi," said Laurence softly, sitting on the arm of Chloe's chair. "What are you reading?"

"*Madame Bovary*. I have been reading it for months. It's hard since I have to use the dictionary every ten words. Is he sleeping?"

"Yes," answered Laurence, lightly rubbing Chloe's neck. "I don't want Clément to be at the funeral tomorrow."

"Lo, don't you think he needs to be? It would provide some kind of closure for him."

"No, I'll ask Madame Cambier if she can look after him."

"Lo, Jean was his father, I think he…"

"Topic is closed, he is not going. He is two, Chloe. He doesn't realize what's going on. I don't want to traumatize him."

Chloe sighed. "I don't agree, but he is your son," she said, closing her book and getting up. "I'm going up to my room." She left, leaving Laurence standing behind.

"Chloe wait up," called Laurence, but Chloe was already gone. Laurence passed her hand through her hair in frustration, and walked upstairs. She walked into Chloe's room without knocking. "Why did you leave so suddenly?" she asked Chloe, who was standing at the window.

"I'm tired and frustrated. I just want to be alone right now."

"No," said Laurence, crossing the arms on her chest.

"What do you mean, 'no'?" asked Chloe, incredulous.

"I'm not leaving until you tell me what's bothering you, and why you are upset with me."

Chloe sighed, walked to her desk and sat on it. "I'm just being selfish, okay? No big deal."

"What did I do?"

"Nothing, really. Your reactions are normal because of what you're going through, but it's frustrating for me to never know what mood you're going to be from one minute to the next." Chloe got up and started pacing. "Take this afternoon, for example. I know that discovering this album and its implications was hard for you, but instead of talking you shut me out…I don't know, I'm probably just tired."

"I haven't been very easy to deal with lately, huh?"

Chloe stopped her pacing. "No, you haven't, but it's okay. You're going through a lot, and you shouldn't have to worry about me. As I was saying, I'm just tired…I'll be fine."

"No, you're right. I shouldn't ignore you and expect you to be okay with it…"

"It's okay, Lo…"

Laurence interrupted Chloe by putting her fingers over her lips. "Chloe, you and Clément are the only people alive that I love. I can't afford to lose you because I'm neglecting you. I'm sorry. I'll try to be better or at least tell you if I don't feel like talking."

"Thank you," said Chloe, tenderly kissing Laurence's hand.

Laurence smiled and stepped forward to kiss Chloe. They melted against each other, their argument forgotten for the moment, the only important thing each other and the way their hearts beat faster every time one of them whispered words of love.

Chapter 19

Jean's funeral was very brief, but deeply moving. Jean's friends and co-workers came to express their condolences. Bernard, who also happened to have been Jean's closest friend, gave the eulogy. Chloe watched Laurence during Bernard's speech. Laurence stood tall in her black suit, her hair was pulled back, and her eyes stared blankly ahead of her, her face expressionless. Chloe discreetly slid her hand into Laurence's and squeezed it to show support, but her squeeze was left unanswered; Laurence's hand stayed cold and unmoving in Chloe's. Chloe withdrew her hand and tried to remain focused on the speaker, but her eyes kept coming back to Laurence's cold face, and every time she caught a glance of Laurence's obvious attempts to retain control, her heart ached.

After the funeral, a short reception was held at the house. There again, Laurence remained polite and calm, her walk almost robotic. She thanked people when spoken to, and she forced a light smile on her face to reassure everyone. Once everyone left, she thanked the people she had hired to cater and serve the food and walked them to the door. As she closed the door, she turned to Chloe, who had followed her to the entrance.

"We should probably go get Clément from next door now," she said flatly.

"He can wait a few minutes. How are you feeling?" she asked, lightly rubbing her fingers up and down Laurence's arm.

"Relieved," she answered, walking back to the family room, sitting down and taking off her shoes. "Damn, no one should be allowed to wear high heels. Their true purpose must be to torture women."

Chloe looked at Laurence, not buying her 'everything is fine' attitude. "What do you mean relieved?"

Laurence sighed. "Somehow, today provided closure for me. For the past few days I have felt in a daze, sort of a nightmare, as if I was going to wake up and everything would be back to normal. But, it's not, Chloe. It's real. He is gone, and I have to move on." She got up and walked to the stairs. "I'm going to go change and get Clément." She turned and went up a few steps before Chloe caught up with her.

Chloe went up one step higher than Laurence and turned to face her. Their eyes met, Chloe's still red from the tears she shed earlier, Laurence's dry, questioning. Chloe didn't say anything, but instead stared at Laurence. After a few moments, she tenderly kissed Laurence and broke the silence. "You don't have to pretend to be all right in front of me, Lo."

"I know, and I'm not...." She stopped, and the tears held back all day long threatened to fall. "I can't mourn him forever. I have Clément to take care of. I'm not going to lie and pretend it didn't happen, but I have too much resting on my shoulders now to go hide in a corner and cry." Chloe nodded and stepped aside to let Laurence by.

① ① ①

On Friday, they were sitting on the couch watching yet another episode of *Sesame Street* with Clément when the doorbell rang. Chloe got up and looked through the kitchen window to see who was at the door. "A man and a woman wearing dark business suits. No idea who they are."

Laurence got up and sighed. "Let's see what they want." She opened the door. "Puis-je vous aider?" The man handed her a business card.

"Who is it?" asked Chloe, coming behind her.

"We are from social services. I am Philippe Garnier and this is my co-worker Linda Leclerc," the man said with a perfect English accent. "Can we come in?"

"I thought we weren't going to get a visit for another two weeks," said Chloe, looking at Laurence and then back at the social services workers.

"Can we come in?" asked the man again.

Laurence nodded and stepped aside. "Sure, please come in. Clément is watching TV, but I'm sure he'll be happy to draw or play with one of you," said Laurence sarcastically.

"That won't be necessary," answered Philippe Garnier. "Is there a room where we can sit down and talk?" he asked as he stepped in, followed by his co-worker.

Laurence nodded and led them to the dining room. Clément stood on the couch, curious as to who these strangers were.

"I should probably go and stay with him, or he's going to come and want to be part of the discussion," said Chloe.

"He is fine. Stay, you take care of Clément more than I do. He's watching *Sesame*, nothing can take him away from that," smiled Laurence.

"You're right," answered Chloe, sitting down at the table.

"Why did they assign new people?" asked Laurence, looking coldly at Philippe Garnier. She had for quite a while been annoyed with social services' constant visits, and this sudden change irritated her.

"We're not here to assess the child's behavior, we are here to discuss his placement into a foster family."

"What?" yelled Chloe and Laurence at the same time.

Linda Leclerc, trying to defuse the tension building up in the room, intervened. "We were told that Clément's father was killed and his mother is in jail."

"Yes, but we are here," said Laurence coldly.

"Mademoiselle Glairon, we know from your file that you don't live here, and Mademoiselle...." Philippe Garnier stopped and looked at Chloe.

"Jones," she said.

"Yes, and Miss Jones is only an au pair. She can't be expected to work 24 hours a day while you're away. This is a very simple procedure. We place Clément with a foster family until you are finished with your schooling. Then we assess the situation and see if you are fit to be his guardian."

Laurence got up abruptly, her eyes black with rage. "Get out of my house right now," she said fuming, her voice a low growl.

"Mademoiselle Glairon, you're not helping your case by not cooperating. We already have a history of violence in our files with the mother; please understand that we are only looking after the child's well-being."

"His name is Clément," yelled Laurence, slamming her fist against the wooden table. "Get out," she repeated.

Chloe, who until now had been too choked by the change of events to react, regained her senses and laid her hand on Laurence's back to calm her. "Sir, can we please have five minutes alone?" she asked politely. Philippe Garnier nodded, and Chloe pushed Laurence toward the family room. She briefly looked at Clément, who was still watching his show undisturbed. He looked at them and started to get up. "Stay here, sweetheart. We'll be in the next room." Clément flopped back on the couch and brought his attention back to the TV. Chloe dragged Laurence into the library.

"I can't believe those bastards," said Laurence angrily as soon as Chloe shut the door.

"Lo, slow down. The only way they are allowed to take Clément away is if both of his parents are unable to raise him, and the living relatives are not fit to take care of him, right?"

"What's your point, Chloe?" She suddenly stopped pacing as the truth dawned on her. She grabbed Chloe by the shoulders. "I'm legally his mother…I got so angry that I didn't think about that. Let me run upstairs and get the birth certificate," said Laurence, her face relieved. Chloe smiled and watched Laurence hurry upstairs.

Chloe walked back to the dining room. "Laurence is getting something upstairs, she'll be right back."

They both nodded. Philippe Garnier was taking notes, and his coworker waited patiently. A few minutes later, Laurence walked back into the room. She sat down and stared coldly at Philippe Garnier. "Clément's mother is not in jail, Monsieur Garnier," she said frostily, throwing the birth certificate across the table. He picked it up and stared at it.

"Why weren't we aware of that?" he asked, business-like.

"Enough questions," answered Laurence, her voice carrying an angry tone. "I think you should leave now," she said, getting up. Philippe Garnier hesitantly stood up, leaving the certificate on the table. "You don't seem very sure, Monsieur Garnier. He is my son. Doesn't the law say that as long as one of the parents is alive and has never committed any crimes or acts of violence, he or she is automatically granted the child's custody?" Laurence looked at Philippe Garnier, and smiled coldly. "You can't even argue that I'm not financially secure because I'm sure you know that Clément and I were the only inheritors of my father's fortune. Trust me, money is never going to be a question for Clément. Now, please may I escort you out?"

"Mademoiselle Glairon, we came here to execute an order. This new matter of Clément being your son will have to be taken in front of the judge. Until then, Clément will remain in a foster home. Now if you'll excuse me, we have other business to attend to. If you would be kind enough to pack a bag for Clément and inform him of what's happening, I would like to get going."

Laurence's face had turned pale. "My son is not going anywhere with you."

"I would hate to involve the police in this matter," said Monsieur Garnier coldly.

Chloe intervened again. "How do you explain to a two year old that he's going to go and live with some strangers for a while? Come on, Monsieur Garnier, don't you have a heart? Don't you have children?"

"My private life is of no concern to you." He walked past Laurence and stepped into the family room. "Shall we proceed?" He walked toward Clément and picked him up abruptly. In a fraction of a second Laurence reached Monsieur Garnier and snatched Clément out of his arms. She quickly gave him to Chloe and walked menacingly toward Monsieur Garnier.

"Don't you ever, ever, touch my child again," she growled, closing in on him.

Chloe, who was trying to comfort Clément, watched the situation helplessly. She glanced with panic toward Linda Leclerc, begging her with her eyes to do something before the situation got out of hand. She spoke up as Laurence reached for Garnier's collar.

"That's enough," she said, stopping Laurence with her voice.

Laurence turned her head toward her and spat, "If this bastard ever comes near my child again without my authorization, I won't answer for my actions." She slowly stepped away and tried to regain control of her emotions. Philippe Garnier straightened his tie and released a relieved sigh. As he got ready to speak, Linda Leclerc interrupted.

"I understand your anger, but please understand that we're only doing our job. This is standard procedure. I know it sounds silly and dumb, but until a judge says so, and recognizes the certificate as real, Clément has to come with us." She looked to see if she was getting through to Laurence. "I'm sure that this matter can be resolved by tomorrow."

Clément started crying. "I don't want to go with her," he sobbed, pointing at Linda.

"Take as long as you want. We'll wait outside." She smiled sympathetically at them, motioned for her co-worker to follow her, and left.

Laurence turned to Chloe, her eyes wide with terror and tears. "Come here, sweetheart." She grabbed him and hugged him tight against her chest. "Shuh...no need to cry. It's all right. Everything is going to be all right." She looked at Chloe intensely, tears streaming down her face. She put Clément down and wiped her tears quickly. "What about you go in the playroom for a little while. I have to talk to Chloe, and you know how grown up talk can be really boring."

Clément wiped his tears with the back of his hand and nodded. Laurence watched him leave the room with a heavy heart. As he turned the corner, she turned to Chloe. "No one is taking my son." Her shaky voice belied her uncertainty to the truth of her statement.

Chloe wished for an instant that she hadn't opened the door when the bell rang. "Lo, I don't want to give them Clément either...I...I don't know what to do. We're trapped. They have the law on their side. If we comply, we can probably call a lawyer immediately and have this matter settled by morning. If we don't, they can make our life a living hell."

"I'm calling Bernard."

"Your dad's business partner?" Laurence nodded and rushed to the library, quickly checking on Clément as she walked through the family room. "What about the other guy I met the day you had your dad's will read? He is a lawyer, isn't he?"

"George? Yes, but we need someone who specializes in this kind of thing." Laurence picked up the phone and dialed. She seemed to have regained control, the dry tears on her cheeks the only reminder of her previous state of mind.

"What did he say?" asked Chloe anxiously once Laurence hung up the phone.

"He gave me someone's name and number." She looked at her watch and frowned. "Shit, almost 5, hopefully this guy is still in his office."

Chloe left Laurence to her phone call and went back to Clément in the playroom. She found him lying on his stomach playing with his fire trucks. "Hi sweetie, what are you up to?"

"Playing with tuks!" smiled Clément, his eyes shining.

"Good, good," she answered, distracted, while sitting next to him on the floor. She had barely sat down when Laurence's head appeared through the door. Chloe got up. "I'll be right back," she told Clément, who barely looked at her as she passed by him.

"Were you able to talk to him?" A quick look at Laurence's eyes gave her the answer to her next question. "That's not good, huh?"

Laurence shook her head and passed her hand through her hair nervously. "He said that they're being assholes, but there is nothing we can do about it. They came here with one purpose and even if they're making a mistake, they still have to follow through."

"Damn fucking bureaucracy," said Chloe angrily. "What now?"

"Child cases always go to the same court, and he's very familiar with it. He's going to do some sort of appeal so we get to keep Clément until the case can get to court."

"This is insane! There isn't anything to bug a judge about. You've got the birth certificate."

"I know." Laurence sat on the couch and grabbed her head between her hands. "Arghh..." she yelled as someone knocked at the door.

"Let me get that," jumped Chloe. She quickly ran to the door and opened it. "I thought you told us to take our time," she barked impatiently at the sign of Linda Leclerc standing at the door.

"Miss..."

"Jones," said Chloe, annoyed at the social worker's hesitation.

"Miss Jones, believe me, I really wish you could take longer, but we've already been waiting for twenty minutes. Monsieur Garnier is getting impatient and is talking about getting the police. I'm sorry."

Chloe looked at the woman standing in front of her. She could see that this was a part of her job she didn't like to do. "Please give us fifteen minutes." Linda Leclerc nodded and walked back to the parked car on the side of the road.

"Lo, we have to make a decision now," she said loudly as she ran back to the family room. She found Laurence still sitting on the couch.

Laurence got up slowly. "You pack a bag for him. I'll go talk to him." She walked to the playroom with defeat.

Chloe looked at Laurence's defeated form and tried to control the tears pooling in her eyes. "We'll get through this," she said aloud, trying to reassure herself.

"Hi," said Laurence, as she walked into the playroom. Clément looked up and called her over.

"Read to me," he asked, handing her a colorful book.

Laurence sighed and sat next to him. "What about we talk for a while." Clément, as if understanding the seriousness of the situation, stood up and sat on her lap. "You know Chloe and I love you very much, right?" Clément nodded. Laurence tightened her grip around his small body. "I'm going to have to ask you to be really brave right now." She stopped looking for the words. "Tonight Chloe and I have to go somewhere very important and Madame Cambier is not here either, so we thought it would be great if you'd go and spend the night in a place where there are lots of other children. Wouldn't that be fun?"

"I don't want to," answered Clément, crossing his arms in front of his chest.

"Sweetheart, please don't make it more difficult," whispered Laurence, unable to hold her tears. "I promise you I'll come get you tomorrow. You know I'd never leave you. I love you."

Clément turned and looked at her. Her tears panicked him and he started crying loudly, repeating, "I don't want to go, I don't want to go!"

Laurence got up, still holding him and walked out of the playroom. Chloe was waiting for them in the family room. "I've got everything," she said, holding a bag.

Laurence nodded, not trusting her voice. She picked up Clément's jacket and tried to put it on, but Clément would have none of it. He yelled and kicked, refusing to cooperate. Chloe had never seen him in such a state. She tried to comfort him with soothing words, but they only served to fuel his anger.

"Let's do it now, while I still have the courage," said Laurence, opening the door and walking into the December cold.

Linda Leclerc had gotten put of the car and held the door open. Upon seeing Monsieur Garnier sitting in the car, Clément clung to Laurence's neck, refusing to let go. "Lo, Lo, please," he cried.

Laurence managed to remove his arms with difficulty. She handed Clément to Linda, who rushed into the car. "You and I both know how deeply scarred he's going to be by this experience. You call that looking after a child's well-being?" She then got on her knees to be at eye level with Clément. "Pumpkin, don't cry. I love you. I promise you I'll come get you tomorrow. I promise." She closed the door on Clément's screams, and sorrowfully watched the car drive away.

Chapter 20

Laurence watched the car turn left at the next street and disappear from sight. She balled her hands into fists and kicked the gate in anger. Chloe, who had stayed inside, came rushing out, calling Laurence. "Laurence, I think the lawyer is on the phone."

Laurence nodded and bolted inside, forcing Chloe to jump quickly out of the way.

"What did he say?" asked Chloe anxiously after Laurence hung up.

Laurence walked up to the window. Dusk was slowly setting, and the streetlights came on as Laurence turned slowly toward Chloe. "It's Friday night past 5 o'clock. He can't do anything until Monday."

"What?"

"You heard me," Laurence whispered before turning back toward the window. She closed her eyes and leaned her forehead against the window.

Chloe came slowly behind Laurence and hesitantly wrapped her arms around her midriff and laid her head on Laurence's back. "You know that it's only a matter of time. You are his mother, we have the cer…"

"I know," interrupted Laurence, her voice bearing a defeated tone. She removed Chloe's arms from around her waist and stepped away.

"I need to be alone for a while." She looked into Chloe's eyes. "It has nothing to do with you…it's how I cope."

"I understand," nodded Chloe, her tone sincere.

"Thanks." Laurence slowly walked away, grabbed a jacket in the entrance, and stepped into the evening cold.

①　　①　　①

She walked, head down, not feeling the biting cold of this late winter night. Her walk took her past Clément's school and she sat down on a bench facing it. For the first time since she had left the house, she took in her surroundings. She realized that a light rain had started to fall and was slowly soaking her. She shivered slightly and blew on her cold hands. She had mindlessly grabbed her denim jacket instead of her winter coat and the light fabric proved ineffective against the rain. She passed her hand through her wet hair and carelessly tucked it behind her ear. The street was busy with people hurrying under large umbrellas, their breath visible under the freezing rain. She covered her face with her hand and sighed heavily. Tears pooled in her eyes, mixing with the rain running down her face. A shiver ran down her spine and she slowly got up and started walking back. Her brain tried to find a solution to the current situation, but no matter how hard she tried, she couldn't come up with anything consequential.

"There's got to be a way," she said aloud, kicking the sidewalk angrily. The rain started falling more heavily, dripping down her face uncontrollably, forcing her to walk head down and speed up her walk.

Once she reached the house, her clothes had stopped giving her any kind of protection against the rain. She rushed inside and stripped down to her soaked jeans and tank top.

Chloe, who had been pacing in the living room, came to meet Laurence. "You're back," she said, taking in Laurence's shivering form. "You're soaked." She stepped close to Laurence and rubbed her arms to warm her up.

"It's okay." Laurence took a step back. "We might not be able to do anything legally until Monday, but there's got to be a way for us to find out where they took him." She walked past Chloe and made her way to the library and to one of the cabinets where she kept her personal papers. She hastily opened the top drawer and took a folder out. "I've kept social services papers in this thing," she said to Chloe who had just walked in behind her. "Here, this is where the center is. Come on, let's go." She didn't wait for Chloe to answer and rushed past her.

"Lo, wait! You have to change first." Chloe grabbed Laurence by the arm to slow her down. "I'm as eager as you are, but you won't be any good to Clément if you get sick. You're soaked, your hands are freezing and you lips are blue from the cold. Go change."

Laurence sighed. "Chloe, let go of me. I'm not a child, I know what I'm doing." She shook her arm free, grabbed her car keys on the entertainment center, walked to the entrance and put a pair of tennis shoes on.

"Fine, have it your way, but at least put this on." Chloe handed her a sweat jacket Laurence always left hanging behind the door in the library. The room often got drafty and cold because of its high cathedral ceiling, and Laurence had taken the habit of wearing the jacket while doing paperwork.

Laurence snatched the jacket from Chloe's hand and sighed for the second time in a few minutes. "Fine," she said, giving up the fight. She quickly removed her wet tank top, put the jacket on and added an extra jacket to her layers. "Let's go." She bolted for the car.

"You know where it is?" asked Chloe, putting her seat belt on.

Laurence nodded and started the car before rapidly directing it into the street. She kept her eyes focused on the road, her face tight and severe. Once outside of Versailles, she followed the sign toward St. Clou and stopped in front of a large white building on the edge of the town.

"Lo, wait...wait. Hear me out."

"Chloe, not now..."

"What's your plan of action? You can't rush in there, crack some heads and expect to get some answers. It's after 7 and it's Friday night. Chances are no one will be able to answer our questions."

"Chloe, all I know is that my son was taken by two people who work here. That's enough for me. Someone in there has to be able to give me some answers. I don't care how I get the answers." Her eyes had turned black and her patience was wearing thin.

Chloe grasped Laurence's hand. "I love you, and I love Clément. Let's not do something stupid that might forsake the chances we have to get him back."

"I don't intend to. You coming or not?" Laurence freed her hand from Chloe's and rushed up the stairs to the entrance. She rang the bell and waited only a few seconds before repeating her action. After five tries, she turned the knob, but the door was locked. "I'm not going anywhere until somebody answers this damn door."

Chloe looked at Laurence, who was now knocking on the door and ringing the bell at the same time. She shook her head sadly. "Lo, it's no use. Come on, we'll get some answers on Monday."

"No!" yelled Laurence, losing the little control she had left. "They've got my son, and he must be panicked, thinking I abandoned him." She rang the bell again. "Open the door!" she yelled. As she reached for the bell one more time, the door opened to reveal Linda Leclerc.

She looked puzzled at the sight of Laurence and Chloe standing on the stairs. "Mademoiselle Glairon. May I ask what you're doing here?"

"I want to see my son." Laurence took one step forward, but was stopped by the social worker.

After a brief moment of deliberation, she sighed and motioned for them to follow her. They walked down a large white corridor with flowery rugs covering the wooden floor. She directed them into a small office with two desks and walked to the one on the furthest side. She sat and indicated for Laurence and Chloe to sit down.

"First of all, let me apologize for the way we handled things earlier. It is never easy to take a child away, especially in your case. If it was up to me I wouldn't have taken Clément, but sadly enough I don't make the law. Each case should be taken separately. We came because Clément's apparent mother is now a murderer and his apparent father is deceased. It's standard procedure. We take the child away until we can decide which remaining family member is the most fit to take care of him. The fact that you're his real mother is a complication that needs to be confirmed. It's important for you to understand that." She stopped and looked at Laurence, who was being unusually quiet. Laurence stared at Leclerc, but not a word came out of her mouth.

Chloe felt uneasy at the silence but spoke first. "Can you tell us where Clément is?"

"I'm sorry, but I'm not..."

"Please," whispered Laurence, interrupting. She looked at the social worker and got up, slowly walking to the window. "Clément was taken away from me by my father. He didn't think I was capable of raising a child at the time...I guess he was right. For the past two years of my life I had to watch Clément call another woman mommy. A woman who I knew didn't return his love, a woman who, every chance she got, physically abused him. When my father died, I promised him I would be here for him always. I try to keep my promises." Laurence walked back to her chair. "I want to know where my son is, Mademoiselle Leclerc. I'm not contesting what you're doing. I just want to know where he is. It's a simple question."

Leclerc looked at the young woman sitting in front of her. Her love and worry for the child was evident and her voice rang true. "We have a temporary foster home on the other side of the building. We keep children there who are in limbo between trials or foster families. That's where Clément is."

"How is he?" asked Chloe.

"Last time I checked, he was watching TV with the other children."

"Take me to him." Laurence got up, her stance strong, her body language powerful.

"I can't. I am not allowed to and it wouldn't be good mentally for Clément."

Laurence laughed sarcastically. "Good mentally for Clément! What do you know about what's good for him or not? You just came storming in and took him away from the people who matter the most to him. Cut the crap, would you?" Laurence's voice had risen and Chloe could see that her patience was running out.

"Mademoiselle Leclerc, can I have a word alone with Laurence?"

Leclerc looked at Chloe, whom she had almost forgotten during the heated discussion, and nodded. "I'll wait for you in the corridor. Please don't be too long."

Chloe watched her leave and turned to Laurence who was angrily staring at her. "Don't give me that look, Lo. Sit down," she said with a firm voice. Laurence sat on the edge of the desk. "Lo, my dad always says, if you can't beat them, join them."

"Chloe, I don't have time for riddles. Get to the point."

"Fine." She got up and came closer to Laurence, her short height bringing her to Laurence's eye level. "Lo, it's no use getting upset with this woman." She briefly motioned toward the corridor where Linda Leclerc was waiting. "She's only doing her job. Let's show her we understand that, instead of insulting her." Chloe brought her hand to Laurence's cheek and lightly rubbed it. "Lo, whether you see Clément or not, we won't be allowed to take him home. It could be even worse for him to have to go through this trauma twice in one day. Think about him, please." She looked pleadingly into Laurence's eyes. Laurence dropped her head and sighed. "Let her in," she said softly.

Chloe squeezed Laurence's hand and went to open the door.

"Is there a place where we can see him without being seen? I want to make sure he is all right."

Leclerc met Chloe's gaze and almost imperceptibly nodded, silently thanking her for the part she had surely played in Laurence's change of attitude. "Yes, if he is still in the TV room, you might be able to peep through the door."

She directed them toward a large wooden staircase. They followed the muffled sounds of children playing with the TV in the background. They stopped in front of an oak door, and Leclerc opened it slightly. She took a quick look inside and turned to Laurence and Chloe. "If you keep the door mostly closed he won't be able to see you." Laurence stepped to the opening and scanned the room for Clément. She spotted him lying on his stomach drawing on a large white sheet of paper. In front of him was another child in the same position, also meticulously drawing on the other side of the white sheet of paper. Clément's ebony hair and the other child's bright red hair lightly mixed and touched as they leaned more into their drawing. Laurence stepped back and indicated for Chloe to take a look.

"Thank you," she said sincerely. She felt slightly reassured that Clément was well taken care of. Chloe soundlessly closed the door and also thanked Linda Leclerc.

"We'll be back on Monday first thing with our lawyer."

"It should only be a routine procedure," said Leclerc, escorting them out. They walked in silence to the car.

"He seemed to be all right," said Laurence, more as a question than a statement.

"Yes, he did." Chloe sat in the car and shut the door. She couldn't make out Laurence's current state of mind and it worried her.

Laurence started the car and drove them back to Versailles in silence. They walked back into the house, still not having spoken a word.

"Lo, are you all right?" asked Chloe concerned and also wanting to break the silence.

"I'm fine."

"Talk to me." She took her by the hand and sat her on the couch.

"There is nothing to say." Laurence reached for the remote and turned the TV on. They mindlessly watched a game show, each lost in her own thoughts. Around 11, Laurence got up. "I'm going to bed." She went upstairs without looking back. Chloe turned the TV off and followed her. She walked past Clément's room, and its darkness and silence made her heart twitch.

Their bedroom door was open and from the sounds of water coming from the bathroom, Laurence was evidently in the shower. Chloe undressed, put on a pair of shorts and t-shirt, lifted the covers and propped herself against a pillow.

In the bathroom, Laurence stood in the stall, her forehead against the marble, water streaming down her body. She let herself slide down against the wall into a sitting position and hugged her knees to her chest. Sobs racked her body, and she buried her face in her hands, letting despair take over.

Chapter 21

The weekend went by excruciatingly slowly. Laurence spoke very little, spending her time lost in her thoughts. Chloe tried to get through to her, but after a few unsuccessful attempts, she gave up. Laurence ate little, not even tasting her food, and moved around like a robot. Her nights were sleepless.

When Monday morning arrived and the phone rang, Chloe let out a relieved sigh at the break in the monotony. "Who was it?"

"The lawyer." A smile lit Laurence's face for the first time. "I don't know how in the world he pulled it off, but we have a hearing at 10."

"Great. Let's get ready." They hurried through the shower and by 9 o'clock were on the road.

"We're going to his office first. It's not too far."

Indeed, they drove for less than ten minutes before Laurence parked in front of an office building. His office was on the third floor. In the elevator Laurence was fidgeting with her sleeve, nervousness apparent on her face. Chloe noticed it, but opted against saying anything. She was still taken aback by Laurence's distance throughout the weekend, and she didn't know what was appropriate anymore. In the corridor leading to the lawyer's office, sounds of printers spitting out paper, microwaves beeping, and fingers running across keyboards could be heard. Laurence stopped in front of suite 23 and smiled nervously at Chloe. Before knocking at the door she briefly squeezed Chloe's shoulder. "Thanks for coming with me."

"I...thanks," mumbled Chloe, surprised by Laurence's affection.

A man in his fifties came to greet them. He wore a gray suit and a navy blue tie. The side of his jacket was slightly wrinkled from sitting in his chair since the wee hours. He smiled at Laurence and Chloe, and his genuine, reassuring smile made Chloe like him instantly. They sat in two big leather chairs facing his desk. Laurence handed the birth certificate to him. He took a brief look and smiled before speaking. Chloe was somewhat surprised when the words coming out of his mouth were French. She tried to follow the conversation, but gave up after the first sentence.

"What's happening?" she asked to Laurence.

"Monsieur Riviére thinks we should have Clément back by tonight. He is making a few phone calls right now and then we go for the hearing."

"Seems easy enough."

Monsieur Riviére hung up and stood. He again spoke briefly to Laurence, smiled at Chloe, and escorted them to the door. "The hearing is at the courthouse of St. Cloud."

The drive to the courthouse was short, and Laurence was more relaxed and had regained some of her confidence.

"Lo, wouldn't it be better if I waited for you outside? I mean, I don't understand anything that is being said anyway."

"I'm sorry. I know the language barrier is tough, but I'd like you by my side...that is, if you want to."

Chloe smiled brightly, and felt a heavy load slowly lifting from her heart. "Of course I want to be by your side."

Laurence nodded, brushed Chloe's cheek briefly with the back of her hand, and walked inside the courthouse.

In the hearing room, Philippe Garnier stood talking to an older man. Laurence's back stiffened at his appearance, but she politely shook his hand and sat down.

The hearing started with Philippe Garnier giving his version of what happened on Friday. Monsieur Riviére didn't feel the need to counter, but instead took the birth certificate out of his briefcase and handed it to the judge. Chloe's eyes were going back and forth between the three men. The judge then asked a brief question of Philippe Garnier, which, from his answer, Chloe guessed was, "What argument would you have against Miss Glairon getting her son back?" Philippe Garnier broke into a long tirade, from which Chloe understood only a few words such as "school," "busy," and "temper." The judge then shook his head and turned toward Monsieur Riviére for a counterargument. Once their lawyer had finished speaking, the judge spoke for a few minutes, smiled at Laurence, and got up.

Monsieur Riviére shook Laurence's hand. Laurence had a bright smile on her face once she turned to Chloe. "We won."

"I got that," she smiled. "What did the judge say?"

"Being too busy has never been grounds enough for anyone to take a child away from his mother. He ruled against social services."

Philippe Garnier closed his briefcase and glared venomously at them.

He walked past her and turned. "Mademoiselle Glairon, you might be legally this child's mother, but I still think you're not fit to raise him because of your schedule. I'll appeal this case."

"And then what, Monsieur Garnier? By the time you process the paperwork, I'll be out of school. Then where is your case?" She didn't wait for an answer and walked out the door followed by Chloe. They thanked Monsieur Riviére and walked back to their car.

"How are we getting Clément back?"

"We just have to go and pick him up. I guess they're going to call to let them know. I don't care how they do it. I'm getting my son back," she said with a smile. She sat in the car and let out a heavy, relieved sigh. "Let's go."

①   ①   ①

They only had to ring the bell once before the door opened. As on Friday, Linda Leclerc greeted them, but this time she wore a large smile. "Congratulations," she said sincerely.

"Thanks. Where is he?" asked Laurence, antsy.

"In the playroom upstairs. I'll go get him. You and Mademoiselle Jones wait here."

Chloe smiled at the social worker and nodded along with Laurence.

"I'm nervous." Laurence paced back and forth. "What if he is mad at us?"

"Lo, don't jump to conclusions. Let's wait and see. Actually, the wait is over." She pointed toward Leclerc, who was walking down the stairs holding Clément's hand. The social worker let go of his hand and handed him his bag. Clément stopped at the bottom of the steps. He looked at Laurence and Chloe but didn't move. Chloe stood back, knowing it was something Laurence and Clément had to work out themselves.

Laurence took a few steps toward Clément, stopped and knelt at eye level with him. His eyes filled up with tears as she opened her arms to invite him in. He let go of the bag and ran to her, burying his face in her neck. "I want to go home," he said with a teary hiccup while wiping his runny nose on the back of his hand. Laurence smiled tenderly at the sight and brought him back into the safety of her arms.

"You bet," she said, standing up and walking out.

It took a few days for Clément to get back to normal. He followed Laurence and Chloe everywhere, refused to be left alone in a room, and crept into their bed at night. They showed patience and love toward him, slowly giving him back his confidence. The following Monday, they both walked him to school for the first time since the tumultuous events of the previous week. They had just gotten back home when Clément's teacher called asking them to come back and pick him up. Clément had not stopped crying since they had left and he was refusing to move from the corner where he was hiding. Laurence drove there in a hurry. She tried calming Clément with soothing words.

"Pumpkin, this is school. Remember? You go and play with your friends during the day and you come home at night."

"No," he cried, hugging Laurence tight.

His teacher, aware of the past week's events, suggested that Laurence stay with him until he felt comfortable. So for the next few days, Chloe and Laurence took turns staying in the classroom with him. Never too close, but always somewhere where he could see them. He gradually went from checking every five minutes to see if they were still in the room to ignoring them. Eventually they both decided he was ready to get back to normal. The following day Laurence walked him to school and explained to him that today he had to be a big boy because she couldn't stay, but she would be back in the afternoon to bring him home. He cried a little, but his teacher said that his tears dried up shortly after she left.

Two weeks later, Clément turned three, and they took him to Euro Disney to celebrate. Life was settling down slowly. Chloe decided not to go home for Christmas, and, surprisingly, persuading her dad was easier than she expected. Laurence finished school on December 17th, and they left Clément with Madame Cambier overnight to make the trip to Lille to clean out her apartment. Chloe had her dad send her a University of Maryland sweatshirt as a present for Laurence's graduation. Christmas was coming, and every street was decorated, lampposts had bows around them, window shops had extravagant Christmas trees, and the streets resonated with Christmas music. Laurence and Chloe bought a very tall Christmas tree while Clément was in school and waited for him to decorate it. Clément seemed to have forgotten his misadventures and was growing to be a very happy and loving child, his fear of water long gone, the scars on his ankles the only reminders of his terrible night. He asked a few times for Jean, but the constant affection and attention he received from Laurence and Chloe seemed to be filling the gap.

On Christmas morning, Clément woke up very early as if sensing something special. He called for Laurence from his bed.

"It better be later than it feels," she grunted, hearing Clément over the monitor and burying her face in her pillow.

"5:30," said Chloe, yawning. "I'll go get him."

"No, I'll get up also…after all, it's Christmas morning."

They trudged sleepily to Clément's room. "Good morning. Clément. Do you know what time it is?" asked Chloe, smiling at Clément who was happily jumping on his bed. Laurence picked him up and they all went downstairs. At the bottom of the stairs, Clément wiggled out of Laurence's arms and ran towards the Christmas tree. Dozens of presents lay underneath, wrapped in bright and colorful shiny paper. Clément screamed excitedly, grabbed a present, and started to tear the paper off.

"Wait, wait," said Laurence, taking the present from his hands. "This one is not for you. Here is one for you," she handed him a big rectangular box wrapped with bright red paper, and handed the already half unwrapped present to Chloe. "This is for you."

"In that case, let me give you one of yours." She reached into the pile and retrieved one of Laurence's presents.

For the next hour, the only noises in the room were of paper being ripped, boxes being opened, exclamations of joy, and hugs being exchanged. After Clément opened his last present, Chloe looked around the room. Shredded paper lay everywhere, and piles of toys surrounded Clément, who was at the moment happily emptying a box of Legos. She looked at her pile and smiled; Laurence had really overdone it. It seemed to Chloe that every time she had told Laurence she would like something throughout the past month, Laurence had taken notes and gotten it for her. Chloe looked at Laurence, who was going through a Washington DC picture book that Chloe gave her, and smiled contently.

"Wow, museums are free in DC," exclaimed Laurence, reading the captions.

"Yes, they are…would that persuade you to come visit?" teased Chloe.

Laurence looked up and closed the book. "Are you thinking of going back?" asked Laurence seriously.

"Not any time soon, but what about when my year is over?"

"It's not for a long time, right?" questioned Laurence.

"Right."

"Then we have time to think about it," said Laurence, dismissing the subject. "I have something else for you," she said, getting up. "I'll be right back." She took the steps three by three, and was back in no time carrying something under her arm. She handed it to Chloe. "Here, open it."

Chloe looked at Laurence and tore the present open to reveal a very old version of *Les Fleurs du Mal*. "Holy cow, Lo! This one is even older than the one in your dad's library."

"Open it."

Chloe opened the book slowly, afraid of damaging it. On the first page was a dedication written in faded ink. "*Pour mon Impératrice, ce livre parle de mon mal de vivre et des tourments de mon cœur. Charles-Pierre Baudelaire.*" Chloe looked up at Laurence, excitement and disbelief in her eyes. "Is that book really signed by Baudelaire?"

Laurence nodded with a smile. "This is the first version of it before he got ordered by Napoleon to change some of his poems. I guess he attacked religion too much for the Empire's taste. Anyway, this book was sent to Eugenie, Napoleon's w—"

"Wife," finished Chloe. "Lo, this is a piece of history…how did you get it? Am I allowed to keep it?"

"Of course it's yours. How I got it? Are you forgetting that my dad was an antique dealer?" smiled Laurence, scooting closer to Chloe, and tenderly caressing her hair. "Merry Christmas."

"Thank you," said Chloe sincerely, while looking into Laurence's eyes. She carefully put the book down and tenderly kissed Laurence. "So far it's been an amazing Christmas," she said, gently caressing Laurence's cheeks with her lips. "I feel that my presents are so inadequate compared to what you gave me."

"Chloe, look at me," said Laurence, bringing Chloe to face her. "Do you see me? Do you see the smile I have on my face?"

"Well, yeah, but..."

"No, listen to me. If it weren't for you, I wouldn't have had the courage to pull through everything that has happened lately. If I'm here in this room with you, and Clément is not in some foster family, but here enjoying Christmas with his family, it's because of you. Nothing I can ever give you can measure up to what you've done for me."

Chloe looked at her with misty eyes and buried herself in Laurence's neck. Laurence put her arms around her and drew her into her lap, tenderly kissed her hair, and held her tight against her chest. Outside, snow started to fall, and Versailles was slowly waking up.

Chapter 22

A few nights after Christmas day, Chloe woke up in the middle of the night and found herself alone in bed.

"Lo," she called, turning the light on and scanning the room. Not getting an answer, she got out of bed. The cold wooden floor made her shiver, and she grabbed her discarded robe on the floor and put it on. The bathroom door was open but no light came from it. *She must have gone to check on Clément,* she thought, opening the door and walking out. Chloe walked silently down the dark corridor, but as she was about to turn towards Clément's bedroom, her eyes caught lights coming from under Laurence's bedroom door. Chloe lightly tapped on the door. She waited a few seconds for an answer, and slowly opened the door. Laurence was standing in front of her easel, her back to Chloe. Open tubes of paint lay scattered on the floor, two blank canvasses had been thrown across the room, and another one lay with its surface torn at Laurence's feet.

"Lo?" called Chloe softly while coming up on her side. "What are you doing? It's the middle of the night. Come back to bed."

Laurence didn't respond, but instead turned her head suddenly toward Chloe and flashed her a dark glare. She picked up the canvas she had been working on and threw it across the room. Instinctively Chloe took one step back. "Arghh," yelled Laurence, pushing the easel and making it fall. Chloe jumped at the loud impact of the easel on the floor.

"Laurence, what is your problem? You're going to wake up Clément. Come on, speak to me here," said Chloe, trying to calm Laurence.

"I can't do it Chloe, I can't paint anymore," answered Laurence, frustrated. She passed her hand through her hair in anger and walked away.

"Lo, please calm down and come sit here," said Chloe, petting the bed and sitting down. She had not seen Laurence so angry since the time Beatrice refused to bring Clément home before Laurence had to leave.

"I don't want to sit down," said Laurence angrily. "Talking about it is not going to help. The last time I had this kind of block was after my mother's death, and it took me a long time to be able to recapture the drive." Laurence kicked one of the discarded canvases on the floor.

Chloe got up, frustrated. "Fine, have it your way. Maybe talking is not the key, but it can help you remember how you got over it last time…remember, you told me about it, your shrink asked you to draw a happy memory of your mother…"

"I just said I don't want to talk about it," said Laurence with a growl. She kicked the canvas once more. "Wouldn't help anyway. The last time I was young and was having trouble getting over my mother's death…I'm fine now, I've accepted that my dad is gone. I don't know what the freaking problem is." She picked up one of her brushes that had fallen along with the easel and looked at it with eyes darkened with anger and broke it in two.

Chloe walked up to Laurence impulsively, and snatched the broken pieces from her hand. "You're right, there is nothing to talk about if you're going to keep up these tantrums of yours." She laid the broken pieces down on a table and walked to the door. "But let me tell you one thing. If you'll stop lying to yourself for only five minutes, pretending that everything is all right and that you don't miss your dad, than maybe you'll realize what the cause of all of this is…" Chloe put up her hand to stop Laurence from interrupting. "Let me finish. I know you say everything is fine, and it's all because of me, right? I give you strength…well, Laurence, I'm very flattered, but I'd rather see you admit that you miss your dad than you counting on me to get you through everything. It's just not healthy." She stepped out of the room and held the door open for a few moments. "I'll be in our room," she said before closing the door. She walked back to their room and turned the knob with a shaky hand, surprised at the anger and frustration she felt, and disturbed by another feeling creeping in: fear.

She waited hours for Laurence to come, but dawn filtered through the blinds and she still lay alone in bed. Around 6:30, she heard the sound of Laurence's motorcycle and ran to the window, only to catch a glimpse of Laurence driving away. Before she had time to react, Clément called over the monitor. She looked one last time down to the street where morning rush hour traffic had started to form, and left for Clément's room.

Morning went by without Laurence coming back. Chloe played with Clément, who was on Christmas vacation, and tried to keep him busy, but her mind was preoccupied and she was worried. Around lunchtime, the phone rang, and she rushed to pick it up.

"Allo."

"Hi sweetheart, it's dad."

"Oh, hi Dad," she said with disappointment in her voice.

"Well, you don't seem too excited to hear from me," commented her dad.

"Sorry, I'm just busy. What's happening? I spoke to you a few days ago."

"I've been thinking. I know you couldn't come back home for Christmas, so I was thinking that I might come visit for a week or two."

"I don't know… I guess that would be great."

"You don't seem too convinced. Is everything all right? The family you're staying with is still treating you nicely, aren't they?"

"Yes, dad, don't worry about it. I have to talk to them, but I'm sure they'd love to have you over."

"Great, it's settled then. I'm thinking of coming at the end of January. Talk to them and call me back."

"I'll do that."

"Okay, bye sweetheart. I love you."

"Love you too, Dad."

"Damn," she said while hanging up the phone. "How am I going to explain to him what happened? What about my relationship with Laurence? Damn," she repeated, walking back to Clément, who was playing with his fire trucks.

Morning slowly gave way to afternoon and afternoon to evening, and there was still no sign of Laurence. By 8 o'clock, she was worried sick and thinking of calling the police and checking the hospitals. Putting Clément to bed was not easy, and he started crying and asking for Laurence.

"Come on babe, don't cry…she'll be back really soon. You'll see her tomorrow, I promise." She tenderly rocked Clément in her arms and rubbed his back for comfort. Clément's tears soon stopped and changed into whimpers. "Shuh," she kept whispering in his ears. After a while, her soothing was rewarded, and Clément fell asleep in her arms. She held him for a little while longer, and gently put him down on his bed.

She walked out and left the door ajar, her mind going through places where Laurence could be. *Tony's house…yeah, but I don't have the number. Her friends in Lille?* It suddenly dawned on her that Laurence must have run to a place were she felt safe. She remembered the words spoken by Laurence a few months back when showing her the hideout underneath the castle. "I come here when I need to think," Laurence had said. *That's got to be where she is.* Feeling slightly better at the idea that she might know where Laurence was, Chloe settled on the couch and turned the TV on.

"As usual, nothing on," she spoke aloud, but her only answer was silence. She flipped once more through the channels and turned the TV off. As the TV clicked off, the door opened and Laurence came in. Chloe jumped to her feet and tried not to laugh at the sight of Laurence standing in the hallway covered with mud from head to toe. Chloe wiped the smile off her face and regained seriousness.

"I don't know if I should be mad or laugh right now, Lo," she said sadly. "I was worried about you all day."

Laurence's eye carried a sad expression. "I'm sorry. I had to think." She took off her jacket and dropped it in a corner to be picked up and washed later, and she removed her muddy boots. "I…I went to the cemetery today…I should have done it earlier…I miss him, Chloe, I really do. Thank you for helping me come to terms with that." Chloe smiled at her. "Another thing, I love you and don't you ever doubt me again when I say that you give me strength…"

"I never did, I was just trying to shake things up this morning, make you realize certain things. That's it. I would have done it some other way, but you were too mad to listen to reason, so I figured that was the best way to go. I'm sorry."

"No, I'm glad you did it. Are we okay?" Laurence asked unsure.

"Yes, we are," Chloe stepped close to Laurence. "We have another problem, though."

"What is it?" asked Laurence, looking intensely into Chloe's eyes.

"My dad wants to come visit."

"So, where is the problem? I'd love to meet him."

Chloe sighed and walked away, sitting down on the couch. "I haven't told him any of the last few months' events."

"Does he know about us?" asked Laurence, already knowing the answer from Chloe's body language. "You haven't told him, haven't you?"

Chloe shook her head no. "I don't want to hide it, though. If he comes I'll tell him."

"When does he want to come over?"

"End of January."

"Then we have time to think about how to explain things to him." She extended her hand to Chloe. "Come upstairs with me...I really have to take a shower."

Chloe reached for Laurence's hand. "How did you get so muddy anyway?"

"I spent the afternoon in our hideout. Remember the puddle? I fell in it." Chloe chuckled. "Are you making fun of me?" she asked jokingly, grabbing Chloe's hand and yanking her to her feet and straight into her arms.

"You should see yourself," laughed Chloe.

"Oh, really," smiled Laurence, tightening her arms around Chloe's waist and rubbing her muddy cheeks against Chloe's

"Lo, stop it," said Chloe between laughs.

The cheek rubbing turned into kissing, and Chloe forgot about the mud covering Laurence's clothes and stepped as close to her as she could. Laurence broke the kiss and tenderly nipped on Chloe's lips. "How about you join me in the shower?" she whispered sensually into Chloe's ear, sending shivers down her spine.

Chloe swallowed with difficulty. "Lead the way," she said, taking Laurence's hand.

① ① ①

Chloe's father gave them January 29th as his date of arrival. A few weeks before, Laurence had found a job as a part-time reporter for a local newspaper. She had told Chloe that she intended on working even if she didn't need the money. "I can't stay home all day, I'll go crazy, and I'll for sure drive you crazy," she had explained. So, on this cold morning of January, Chloe took a cab to the airport to go pick up her dad. The traffic was really bad on the expressway, and she arrived at Charles de Gaulle half an hour late. *Hopefully he's still waiting where we told him to*, she thought while pushing her way through the crowd of people. She spotted him waiting impatiently, his eyes glued on his watch. Robert Jones was a man in his late 40s with blond hair and clear eyes, who hated lateness and had never had any patience for it. She smiled to herself, and waved at him. "Dad," she called, walking to him.

"There you are. You're late. I was getting worried," he answered, hugging her. "You look great."

"Thanks, Dad. Sorry about that, the traffic was awful. I took a cab up here, but I don't think he waited, so let's go hail another one." She picked up one of his suitcases and showed him the way. They chatted all the way back to Versailles. Chloe had asked the cab driver to take them through Paris, and she pointed out some of the monuments.

"You're happy here, aren't you?" asked her dad with a smile.

"Why are you asking that?" asked Chloe, as the cab pulled in front of the gate.

"You have this huge smile on your face when you describe things," he answered, getting out.

"I love it here," she answered simply while dialing in the code to open the gate. She walked through the courtyard, opened the front door and stepped in.

"No one is home?" asked her dad, putting his suitcases down.

"No. Laurence is working and Clément is at school."

"What about…what's their names again, Beatrice and Jean?"

Chloe picked up one of the suitcases suddenly. "…let me show you to your room, and I'll give you a tour of the house." They had chosen one of the guestrooms next to Clément's room. She opened the bedroom door, stepped in and dropped the suitcase on the bed. "This is where you sleep." Her dad walked in and looked around.

"This is great. They're antique dealers, right?"

"Right," answered Chloe quickly. "The bathroom is over there," she said gesturing toward a far door. "Would you like to rest for a while? You must be jetlagged."

"No, I'm all right. I'm so happy to see you. We have so much catching up to do. I brought you something." He opened up one of his bags and retrieved a plastic bag. Chloe opened the bag and smiled.

"Peanut butter and maple syrup. Thanks," she said laughing.

"I have something else." He looked through his suitcase and took out a present. "Merry Christmas. I would have sent it you, but I was afraid it would get lost."

Chloe picked up the present. "It's heavy." She ripped the paper. "Dad, this is too much," she exclaimed, staring at a laptop.

"It's so hard to get in touch with you, I figured that if you could get e-mail, then it would make communication easier," he smiled.

"Thank you," she said, hugging him.

She gave him a tour of the house and then they settled in the library to talk. She tried to dodge the question about Beatrice and Jean, but finally gave up and spilled out the story.

"You are kidding me, right?" said her dad, getting up and pacing.

Chloe sighed. "No. I didn't tell you because I didn't want you to worry. It was hard on everyone, but everything is okay now."

"This madwoman could come back any time. This is a dangerous place to stay…" He walked up to Chloe and grabbed her by the wrist. "Come on. You are packing up, and we're leaving," he said, bringing Chloe to her feet.

"Dad, calm down. I'm not going anywhere," she said angrily. "I like it here, and I was never in any danger. The way you're reacting is exactly why I didn't tell you sooner." She yanked her wrist free of his grip.

The last sentence seemed to affect him because he stepped back. "I think I'm going to go rest for a while. I'm staying for a week. If at the end of the week, I think you're not safe here, you're coming home with me."

"Fair enough," she answered, deciding not to argue. As her dad made his way upstairs, the phone rang.

"Allo."

"It's me. How is everything going?"

"I told him about what happened. He is convinced that I'm in danger."

"That's not good."

"No, it's not. I calmed him down. If we can make it to the end of the week, we'll be okay."

"You can tell me more about what happened after I get home. I have to go. I'll pick up Clément on my way home. See you then."

"Okay. I love you," answered Chloe before hanging up.

① ① ①

Around 3: 30, Laurence and Clément came back home. Clément ran to Chloe's arms with a drawing in his hand. He gave her the drawing. "Is that for me?" she asked, looking at it. Clément nodded.

"He drew it at school...pretty good, isn't it? I think he takes after his mother," smiled Laurence proudly.

The drawing was of three stick figures. The tallest one stood on the left with black hair, the smallest one in the middle with black hair and the medium one on the right with yellow hair. They were connected as if holding hands. "This is a picture of us, isn't it?" smiled Chloe. "Thank you, sweetheart," she said, kissing Clément on the cheek. She turned to see her dad standing in the doorway.

"Lo, this is my dad, Robert. Dad, this is Laurence and Clément," she explained.

Her dad politely shook Laurence's hand and smiled at Clément. Clément looked at Robert and grabbed his hand.

"Play with me?" he asked sweetly.

Robert couldn't help but smile, and he nodded. "Sure, show me the way."

After seeing them turning the corner toward the playroom, Laurence took hold of Chloe's hand and lightly kissed it. "You see, it's not going so bad."

"So far...he doesn't know about us yet."

"You know I'd understand if you don't want to tell him. We can just behave for a week," she smiled.

"I don't want to bluntly tell him, but I want him to figure it out."

"Okay, it's your call."

① ① ①

They went out for dinner, and Robert and Laurence chatted amiably about differences between life in France and the United States, jobs, sports, and pretty much anything else that crossed their minds. Robert seemed to relax a little and Chloe felt relieved. After coming back, Laurence excused herself and went to put Clément to bed while Chloe hung out with her dad downstairs.

"She is nice," said her dad, speaking of Laurence. "Strikingly beautiful though—she must have lots of men chasing her," he joked.

"Dad!" reprimanded Chloe.

"What about you? Any lucky French man?"

"Well, I have someone."

"I hope I get to meet him before I go. This is a really beautiful house," commented Robert, his eyes scanning the room.

"You already have," answered Chloe, ignoring the comment on the house.

"What do you mean?" asked her dad, not understanding.

"Dad, you know sometimes I wish you wouldn't ask so many questions," sighed Chloe. "You've met her, not him. It's Laurence." She looked at him intently and waited for his reaction. Robert looked at her, speechless. "Dad, I'm sorry. I never intended to lay everything on you the first day, but you asked for it...and I don't want lie to you."

Robert stood up. "Are there going to be any more major surprises, or are you done now?" He slowly removed his glasses and tucked them into the pocket of his shirt. "I think I'm going to retire for the night. I honestly don't know what to say."

"Dad, wait! Please say something," she said, her eyes pleading.

Robert sighed and looked at his daughter. "I just need to think for a while."

"Dad, this is important to me. Please don't shut me out."

Robert smiled sadly. "It's going to take some time to get used to it. As I said, I need to think for a while."

"Okay," whispered Chloe in defeat.

"Good night." He kissed the top of her head.

"Good night," Chloe answered as she watched her father walk away.

Laurence and Robert crossed paths on the stairs, and he cordially wished her good night. "He is going up already?" asked Laurence, coming down the rest of the steps.

"He knows about us."

"You told him?" asked Laurence incredulously. She sat next to Chloe on the couch.

"I had to. He basically asked if I had met anyone here, and when I told him I had, he said that he would like to meet him!"

"He didn't seem too upset just now."

"He is confused. What a mess!" She laid her head on Laurence's shoulder and closed her eyes. "I'm exhausted. Today has been emotionally draining to me. Can we go up?"

"Sure." Laurence got up and walked upstairs holding Chloe's hand. Once they got to the bedroom, she engulfed her in her arms. "Thanks for not lying to your dad about us."

"I couldn't do it, Lo," she said, holding Laurence tight. "Hopefully, he'll understand."

"I hope so," answered Laurence, kissing the top of Chloe's hair.

①   ①   ①

The rest of the week actually went very smoothly. Robert seemed to enjoy his stay, and he had warmed up to Laurence. One evening as Chloe was giving Clément a bath, Robert went into the study where he knew Laurence had disappeared shortly after dinner. She was at a table surrounded with papers.

"Balancing the checkbook?" he asked.

"Something like that," answered Laurence. "Chloe is upstairs. She should be finished shortly."

"I know. I wanted to talk to you."

Laurence's heart sped up a notch. "All right," she said politely. "What's on your mind?"

"You and my daughter…you are…"

"Yes, romantically involved." Laurence couldn't help smiling at Robert's attempt at finding the politically correct word.

"Right," he said regaining his composure. "Chloe is my only daughter. I want her to be happy, and to be honest with you, I think she really is happy with you."

"I love her very much."

"I don't doubt that you do. I'd like you to think of her future, though. She can't stay here forever and take care of Clément. She is really bright, and she has a great future in front of her. Have you thought about what will happen once her year is over?"

Laurence looked at Chloe's father. She knew he was only being a protective father, but his scolding tone of voice annoyed her slightly. "That is for her to decide, not you, and not me. She is an adult capable of making her own decisions."

"And no matter what she decides, will you accept it?"

"To the best of my abilities. I love her, and I won't lie to you and tell you that I want her to leave at the end of the year because I don't. But that is her decision."

Robert nodded and politely wished her good night, wondering why his lawyer's tactics didn't seem to be working on Laurence.

The night before his departure, Robert asked one last time what Chloe had in mind at the end of her year, hoping she would have a more precise answer.

"I don't know, dad. I told you already that I haven't thought that far ahead yet. I have a few more months to think about it." She looked at her father, wishing he would stop quizzing her.

Robert, who so far had accepted Chloe's vague answer, this time refused to give up. "Chloe, you seem very happy here, but you can't be an au pair forever. What about your visa? It expires at the end of the year, and then what? Don't you want to come home and finish your studies?"

"I don't know," repeated Chloe.

"You should think about it seriously," answered her father. "Don't get me wrong, I like Laurence. I think she is a good person, and she really cares about you. I can't say that it's the kind of relationship I had always dreamt of for you, but I'm okay with it. I'm also happy you could be here for her with everything she's been through, but don't throw away your future. That's the only thing I'm saying."

Chloe looked at her dad, happy he had finally accepted her relationship with Laurence, and also disturbed by the truth in his words. "I'll think about it."

"Good, that's all I can ask."

His plane left early the following morning. They took a cab to the airport. Chloe told her dad goodbye, waited for the plane to take off, and took the metro back home. His last words were still on her mind. "Think of your future." She shook the memory from her mind and concentrated on not missing her stop.

Chapter 23

The Friday after her father left, Chloe was at home waiting for Laurence to return after picking up Clément from school. Light snow was falling outside and the roads were slowly being covered with the white crystals. She was starting to worry when the door opened and Laurence stepped in, her black hair covered with snowflakes, and her cheeks red from the cold. She removed her boots and unzipped her coat.

"It's freezing outside," she commented as she hung up her coat.

"Where is Clément?" asked Chloe, coming to greet Laurence.

"I dropped him at Madame Cambier's house." She walked into the kitchen and poured water into the kettle. "Do you want some tea?"

"No, thanks. Why did you drop him at Madame Cambier's?" Chloe opened the cupboard. "English Breakfast or citrus…we really have to go grocery shopping."

"English Breakfast." Laurence came up to Chloe and wrapped her arms around her and spoke tenderly in her ear. "Do you have any idea what the date is today?"

"No, not really, I know we're in February. Why?"

Laurence chuckled and kissed Chloe on the cheek. "Go check the calendar while I check on the water."

Chloe left the kitchen, confused, and walked to the library where she knew a post office calendar hung on the wall. The calendar still showed November, and it obviously hadn't been touched since Jean's death. She lifted the pages and scanned through the month of February. "Friday...Friday...oh boy, I can't believe I missed that," she said aloud, her finger pointing to February 14th. She walked back to the kitchen, embarrassed and mad at herself for not remembering a day like Valentine's Day. "Lo, I'm sorry...I haven't been paying attention to the date, I just know if it's Monday or Sunday or...I'm sorry."

Laurence's smile illuminated her face as she removed the water from the stove. She poured the warm liquid into her cup and reached for a spoon in the drawer. "It's okay, I really hadn't given it much thought either. It just dawned on me yesterday that today was Valentine's. I thought we could improvise and spend the evening together." She stirred her tea and brought it up to her lips, sipping it slowly.

"How long do we have before we have to pick up Clément?"

"Until tomorrow around noon."

"You're kidding!" Chloe was incredulous. As much as she deeply loved Clément, she had sometimes wished she and Laurence could escape for an evening, or spend the night without having to plug in the monitor.

"No, I'm not." Laurence smiled warmly and put her cup down. She drew Chloe into her arms and kissed her lightly on the top of her hair. "Happy Valentine's," she said tenderly.

Chloe sighed and tightened her grip on Laurence's waist. "I feel so stupid for forgetting about it." Her voice was muffled by Laurence's shirt.

"Don't be. I tell you what. Go ahead and change, and I'm taking you for a night on the town." Laurence's blue eyes twinkled with happiness.

"It's snowing, isn't it going to be a problem?"

Laurence chuckled. "Your dad explained to me that in Washington everything becomes a mess with only one inch of snow." She finished her tea and put her cup in the sink. "Don't worry about it...we know how to drive in France."

"Hey, I take offense to that." Chloe tried to look offended, but a smile broke across her face.

Laurence laughed at Chloe's almost-pout. "Wipe that smirk off your face. We both know that Washington drivers are supposed to be the worst...hey, I'm quoting your dad."

"Coming from someone who lives in a country where the speed limit is never respected, and where driving on a sidewalk to pass traffic doesn't seem to be against the rules, I still think we're better drivers than you guys are."

Laurence's laugh resonated through the high-ceilinged room. "Yeah, yeah...come on, go change, this argument is not bringing us anywhere." She kissed Chloe and gently slapped her bottom.

"Hey," protested Chloe, trying to get out of the way. "Giving up so soon, huh?" she teased. "I guess I rest my case." She playfully stuck her tongue out at Laurence, who opened her mouth as if to speak, but reconsidered before anything came out. Chloe turned around seductively and winked at Laurence over her shoulder. "I'll go change now."

① ① ①

An hour later, they were both ready and walking out into the cold winter evening.

"Where are we going?" asked Chloe, buckling herself in.

"I thought we could go to a bistro café I know really well. We don't have reservations, but I know the owner so it shouldn't be a problem."

They drove through Versailles in the direction of the expressway. Laurence had turned the seat warmer on, and Chloe relaxed slowly into her seat as the heat spread through her body. Large flakes of snow hit the windshield as the car sped onto the expressway.

They ate in a nicely decorated café. As Laurence had promised, they had no trouble getting a table. They ordered some onion soup to start with and a bottle of white wine. As the waiter poured some wine into Chloe's glass, Laurence looked at Chloe lovingly. She wore a pair of black slacks and a green cashmere turtleneck that beautifully matched her eyes, her hair was up in a ponytail, and she had added a touch of gloss lipstick. Chloe glanced up and smiled seductively.

"You're staring at me," she said flirtatiously, her voice a sensual whisper.

Laurence broke her reverie. "You look beautiful." Their eyes met, and they held their gaze for a few moments. The noise of the restaurant was forgotten, and each was only aware of the other's presence.

Chloe broke the gaze, her cheeks flushed.

"You still make me blush after all these months," she smiled, taking hold of Laurence's hand across the table and lightly stroking it. She released it as the waiter came back with their soup.

They ate mostly in silence, enjoying each other's companionship.

"I'm stuffed," stated Chloe, pushing her dessert plate away.

"Yeah, three pieces of chocolate cake will do that to you. Are you ready to go?"

"Sure. Are we going home?"

"No. I thought we could go dancing. The last time we went you got sick, and I never got to dance with you." Laurence dropped money on the table and got up, offering her hand to Chloe.

"We danced in your apartment, remember?"

"I sure do. We don't have to go if you don't want to."

"No, let's go. Which club do you have in mind?"

"It's around Les Halles. It's called Troubadour. They have good music if I remember right." She thanked the waiter on her way out, and waved goodbye to the owner who was standing in a corner. He smiled at her and nodded at Chloe.

They parked the car a few blocks away from the nightclub. The snow had stopped falling and the air was crisp, giving the night an extra layer of cold. They walked with their hands deep inside their pockets and their faces down, trying to avoid the February wind.

The nightclub was different from the one they had gone to a few months ago. It stretched out on one floor, sofas surrounded the dance floor, and a bar stood in the corner. The smell of smoke and perfume assaulted them as they opened the door. The dance floor was crowded with a wave of people moving to the sounds of Ricky Martin. Laurence directed Chloe toward the end of the room, and motioned for her to sit on one of the couches. "I'll go get us something to drink. What do you want?"

"What are you having?"

"Don't know. Nothing too strong."

"Just get me whatever you're having."

"Okay." She kissed Chloe briefly and left for the bar.

Chloe watched her leave, her hips swiveling gently, and her tall form breaking through the crowd easily. She smiled to herself and settled comfortably against the couch. As she watched couples move sensually against each other on the dance floor, her heart swelled with happiness at the thought of Laurence. A chill ran down her spine and she felt herself being watched. She slowly turned her head, and caught Laurence moving back toward her, drinks in hand, her eyes glued on Chloe. Laurence handed Chloe her drink and sat down next to her.

"What were you thinking about?" she smiled, gently brushing a loose strand of hair back behind Chloe's ear.

"You," answered Chloe, tenderly kissing Laurence's cheek. "Thank you for making this evening so special. What kind of drink did you bring back?"

"Gin and tonic…Wait, it's not over yet. Want to dance?"

"I'd love to." She put her glass down on the coffee table and got up. Laurence linked her fingers through Chloe's and led the way to the dance floor. They started dancing to a fast beat, and Laurence drew Chloe closer to her.

"Lo, I don't mind, but are you sure it's okay? I mean…it doesn't seem to be a gay club." She had to almost yell in Laurence's ear to make herself heard.

Laurence laughed and mouthed, "Mixed."

Chloe smiled and relaxed. They danced to a few more songs and walked back to their drinks. Chloe picked hers up and took a big sip. "Boy, you call that not strong," she coughed.

"Technically it's not. Trust me, these drinks are really watered down." She drank from hers and sat down. "Are you having fun?"

"I love it. Even the music is pretty good."

"Yeah, I like it." She finished her drink in one gulp and turned to face Chloe. "Would it have bothered you if this club hadn't been a mixed club?"

"What do you mean?" She took another sip of her drink and let the beverage slowly slide down her throat.

"I mean, would you have kept your distance from me?"

"Probably at first," she answered honestly. "But I couldn't have lasted very long." Laurence's smile was worth any sacrifices such a situation would have brought. "Lo, being openly out is still scary to me, but I don't want you to think I'm ashamed of our relationship."

"I know." Laurence brought her face down close to Chloe's and their lips barely brushed. "Happy Valentine's Day. I love you."

"I know." She brought Laurence's lips in contact with hers and smiled through her kiss.

"I'll go get us another drink," said Laurence, reluctantly taking her lips away.

"No, let me do that. Do you want the same thing?"

"Actually, I'd like a Coke...I have to be able to drive back, but go ahead and have another one."

Chloe smiled and left. Walking through the crowd was harder for her than it had been for Laurence because of her smaller height, but she ordered the drinks and made her way back without difficulties. She spotted Laurence in conversation with a man dressed in bleached jeans and a white t-shirt. His hand was nonchalantly placed behind Laurence's back, but before his gesture had time to upset Chloe, Laurence took a step aside, putting a slight distance between her and the stranger. She walked to the couch and handed Laurence her drink.

"Chloe, this is Michael. Michael, this is Chloe."

"Hello," said Michael with a white smile, lightly shaking Chloe's hand. "I heard you are American."

"Yes, I am."

"Very good. Where exactly are you from?" His eyes had barely left Laurence as he spoke to Chloe, his gaze sweeping up and down her body, envy slightly clouding his eyes.

"Washington D.C."

Michael ignored her answer and sat next to Laurence, then whispered something in her ear and got up. "Chloe, nice to meet you." He looked at Laurence one more time and left them.

"What was that about?" she asked, sitting down.

"Phantom from the past." Laurence seemed to have gone into her own world, her eyes staring ahead blankly.

"Lo, who was he?" Not getting an answer, she gently grasped Laurence's face and turned it toward her. "Lo?"

Laurence's eyes focused slowly on Chloe. "He was one of the guys I used to hang out with when I lived in Paris. We dated for a while."

Chloe didn't need to ask to know that Laurence was referring to the time before she had Clément, the time during which drugs and alcohol had been some of her favorite hobbies. "Lo, what did he tell you before he left?"

"He asked me if I wanted to leave with him…just for old time's sake."

Chloe's blood boiled and her eyes flashed with anger, quickly scanning the room in search of Michael. "I'm going to go tell him what I think of him." She got up angrily, only to be stopped by Laurence.

"Please don't. It's useless. I don't want him to ruin our evening. Dance with me?"

Chloe sighed and quickly passed her hand through her bangs.

"Sure," she answered, trying to bring her temper back under control. The DJ was playing slow songs in the honor of Valentine's Day, and they started dancing to the rhythm, wrapped up in each other's arms. Laurence tightened her grip on Chloe and brought her as close as possible. She gently rubbed her hands up and down her back and tenderly bent to kiss her. Time seemed to stop as they gently deepened their kiss. A familiar song came up, and after the first few notes, Chloe broke the kiss. "Lo, this is this song we danced to in your apartment."

"I know, I requested it earlier." She picked up the slow rhythm, her hips softly waving against Chloe's. Chloe buried her face in Laurence's shirt and deeply inhaled the familiar fresh scent of Laurence's perfume as if to commit it to memory. They stayed on the dance floor until the rhythm changed back to a more rapid one. "We should probably get going. We have to drive back to Versailles."

"I'm ready when you are."

"Then let's go now." They made their way through the crowd to the coat check, and as they put their coats on Michael appeared. He went straight to Laurence and stood close to her.

"T'es prête?" His arrogance was almost too much for Chloe to bear.

Laurence looked at him coldly and pushed him aside. She grabbed Chloe's hand and brutally turned to Michael. Her eyes were dark with anger, leaving no doubts in anyone's mind that one more move from Michael would release the beast in her. Michael stepped back, and Laurence threw one more deadly gaze toward him before walking out, dragging Chloe behind her. They walked quickly back down the street, Laurence's strides long and determined.

"Hey, Lo, slow down. You've got longer legs than I do." Chloe stopped and tried to catch her breath, hoping that her plea had reached Laurence and that she would slow down.

"Sorry."

"That's okay. I just hate running to keep up with you." This sentence brought a smile to Laurence's lips.

"I'm sorry. This guy really upset me."

"I know, but somehow you managed to scare him away without even breaking any bones. Pretty good," she said jokingly.

"You're right." She linked her fingers with Chloe's and kissed her knuckles. "Come on, let's go."

Chloe fell asleep on the way back home. The warmth of the seat, and Laurence's smooth, controlled driving gently lured her to sleep.

"Chloe, wake up. Come on sweetheart." Chloe opened her eyes, her mind still foggy with sleep, and registered her surroundings.

"Lo, we're not home."

"Not really, but sort of. Come on." She stepped out and opened the trunk of the car, reaching for a duffel bag. She took out a flashlight and locked the car.

"Are we going to the hide out?" Laurence nodded, and walked down the street toward the line of trees. "Lo, come on. Not tonight, it's freezing out here, I don't want to spend the night among the ghosts of Versailles, please." Chloe's eyes were almost begging.

"I promise you, it'll be worth it. You coming?" She extended her hand, and Chloe grabbed it with sigh.

"Fine."

They walked down the hill and entered the tunnel through the usual path. The walk to the room seemed to Chloe to take hours. She jumped at every sound and kept less than an inch between her and Laurence. They finally walked into the first room and Laurence lit a few candles. Their room was the same as they left it, and as the first time it took Chloe's breath away. "Lo, I had forgotten how beautiful it is." Laurence smiled and dropped the duffel bag on the table.

"Are you cold?" she asked, opening the bag.

"Yes, a little."

"I brought extra blankets, plus we still have plenty from last time. We should be just fine."

"Lo, I don't want to break the mood, but why do you want to spend the night here?"

Laurence walked to Chloe and pulled her toward her. She seemed to be searching for words, but her eyes suddenly sparkled and she spoke. "I brought you here tonight because this is the place where I first realized I was in love with you. This first day when I showed you this place…I can't explain it, something happened inside me, and I realized that if I was to spend the rest of my life with anyone, I wanted it to be with you." She stepped away from Chloe and reached inside her coat pocket, taking out a small box. "This is for you." Chloe took the box with shaky hands and opened it. Inside was a gold band ringed with diamonds. It was thin, very simple, and took Chloe's breath away.

"Lo, this is beautiful. I don't know if…"

"Wait…I don't expect anything. You don't have to make a lifetime commitment to me because you accept it. It's a sign of my love for you." Laurence's blue eyes looked deeply into Chloe's, baring her soul.

"Thank you." She rolled the ring between her fingers, admiring it, the diamonds shining in the candlelight.

"I tell you what. You put it on the right hand, and when you're ready for it you can switch it to the left one. No pressure." Laurence took the ring and slipped it on Chloe's finger. Chloe looked at Laurence, words not enough to describe how she felt.

"I love you," she said simply.

"I know." Laurence smiled and drew Chloe in her arms. "I just don't want to push you. I know you are confused about what's going to happen once your visa expires. This is a token of my love for you. No matter what you decide, I'll stand by you."

Chloe stepped out of Laurence's arms and drew her in for a kiss, sensual and loving. "Let's go to bed."

They settled into the makeshift bedroom, removed their clothing and slid under the covers. "Cold?" asked Laurence, when she felt Chloe shiver.

"A little." Laurence got up and ran to get the extra blankets, and rushed back under the covers. "Now I'm the one that's freezing." He teeth were chattering and shivers ran down her spine. Chloe sat up and spread the blankets over them. She tenderly drew Laurence against her chest and rubbed her back. "Warmer?"

"Much," answered Laurence, burying her face in Chloe's neck and slowly closing her eyes.

Before sleep claimed them, Chloe whispered. "You lied…you set me up, this evening was planned." Her only answer was Laurence's low chuckle.

①   ①   ①

Winter slowly gave way to spring, the trees started blooming and the grass turned green again. They spent long hours in the park, relaxing under the sun or playing with Clément. Clément was becoming a very independent little boy who wanted to do everything by himself. His speech patterns had improved, and from time to time he was able to pronounce Ls. Chloe couldn't help seeing the strong resemblance between mother and son everyday. Their stubbornness, short temper, and need for independence were comically similar, and Chloe found herself using the same argument techniques with Clément than she used with Laurence. They talked about plans for the future, but nothing concrete could be set until Chloe knew what was going to happen once her visa expired. The phantom of uncertainty hung over them, but they both tried to ignore it and enjoy every moment together as if it was going to be the last.

One afternoon in late June, Laurence came home from work, kicked off her heels, and shed her summer jacket. "Hello? Is anybody home?" She walked into the family room and found Chloe sitting on the couch staring at the TV screen. Chloe turned her head briefly toward Laurence and dropped her gaze almost immediately. Laurence moved to Chloe, unexpected fear grabbing her stomach. "Hey, what's wrong? Is Clément okay?" She tried not to panic, but Chloe's strange attitude made it hard.

"Yeah, he's in the playroom, building one of his Lego forts." She looked up at Laurence. Her eyes were red and dark circles had formed under them.

"What's wrong?" she asked again, sitting down and gently rubbing Chloe's back. "Come on Chloe, what's the matter, you usually greet me with a smile when I come home." Laurence tried to lighten the mood by making a joke, but Chloe's face stayed serious. Suddenly Laurence jumped back and got up slowly, the answer to her question readable in Chloe's eyes. She kept her gaze fixed on Chloe, her eyes begging for it not to be true. She shook her head. "No…when did you make this decision?"

"This morning. I'm sorry. I tried to find every reason I could to stay here, but none worked. Lo, I can't be an au pair for the rest of my life. I have to finish up school…"

"Why can't you go to University here?" Laurence's voice was sad, almost pleading.

"Lo, we've been over that. My French is not good enough. I'll have to take French classes before being accepted...I'll lose another year. I'm sorry," she dropped her gaze, her voice almost a whisper. "You and Clément could come back to the States with me?"

"You know that's not possible..." Laurence breathed deeply, trying to keep her emotions under control. "When?"

"The end of August. My dad e-mailed me this morning...he said that going back to University of Maryland shouldn't be a problem since I had already been accepted."

"I see you've organized everything. How long have you been exchanging those little conspiracy e-mails with your dad?" Laurence's control slowly slipped away and anger filled her. "You know what? Why should I care, obviously you don't." Her voice cold, meaning to hurt.

"Lo, this is not fair."

"Oh, really...you dare to talk about fair," she laughed sarcastically. "What do I tell Clément? Sorry, you weren't important enough for her."

"Laurence, stop it!"

"No! What about all the I love you's, were they a lie? Tell me!" she yelled.

"You know very well that they were not." Chloe's voice broke and her eyes filled with tears. "I love you...I never lied about it."

Laurence flashed Chloe a dark look. "It doesn't really matter now, does it?" She walked past her, not stopping.

Chloe let the tears fall and her hands balled into fists. "Damn you, Laurence," she said between tears. She dragged herself upstairs and flopped on her bed, sobs racking her body.

Downstairs, Laurence sat next to Clément who, oblivious to the storm raging inside her, asked her to help him. She blindly picked up blocks and stacked them up together, her anger slowly faded, and the memory of what she had just told Chloe came rushing back. "I'm such a jerk." She banged her forehead with her hand and sighed. "All right, I know what I have to do." She got up and reached for the phone and dialed an all too familiar number.

"Allo, Madame Cambier. C'est Laurence. Est-ce que je peux vous donner Clément pour la soirée?"

"Mais bien sur."

"Okay, nous serons là dans cinq minutes."

Laurence hung up and turned to Clément. "Hey, sweetheart. Do you want to go and play with Madame Cambier?"

"Yeah!" yelled Clément happily, dropping his Legos and running out of the playroom. He had taken a real liking to Monsieur and Madame Cambier over the past few months and loved going to their house. They had a wooden train track that Clément absolutely loved to play with, and they treated him like their own, sometimes spoiling him a little too much. Laurence had thought of buying Clément the same train track, but Chloe had suggested she didn't. "If you get it for him, then it won't be special anymore when he goes over to their house." She had agreed, and indeed she always enjoyed hearing Clément talk to her about the train and how much fun he had with Monsieur Cambier building tracks.

She rang her next door neighbors' bell and watched Clément run into Monsieur Cambier's arms as soon as the door opened. She told Madame Cambier that she would pick him up around his bedtime and walked back to the house. Once inside, she climbed the steps to the first floor and rushed down the corridor to Chloe's room. She lightly tapped on the door and waited for an answer. Shortly after the door opened to reveal Chloe wearing a wary look. Her eyes were red and swollen, and she made no effort to hide her pain.

"Can I talk to you?" asked Laurence, her heart aching from seeing the damage she had done. Chloe didn't answer, but instead stepped aside and motioned for Laurence to walk in. Laurence took in the clothes lying on the bed, and the suitcases open. "What are you doing?"

"Packing. What does it look like?" answered Chloe, fatigue and slight sarcasm obvious in her voice.

Laurence sighed and thought for a minute about the best course of action to take to stop her. "I'm sorry…wait, no, that was lame." Chloe didn't look at Laurence and picked up a pile of sweaters lying on the bed, and stuffed it in one of her suitcase. "Chloe, please look at me." She grabbed Chloe by the shoulders and turned her to face her. "Please hear me out, okay?" She waited to read acceptance in Chloe's eyes before letting go. "Please don't go…don't leave now. I…I reacted selfishly and I know I hurt you. I'm worried about Clément; he has had so many changes in his life over the past year that I don't know how he is going to react to your departure…"

Chloe interrupted Laurence, her voice cold. "Did you ever stop and consider that this decision is tearing me apart, but I really don't have a choice? No, you judged me and accused me right away. I don't want to spend the last few months of my life in this country feeling guilty for something that is out of my control. Gosh, Laurence, don't you know by now how much I want to stay and be with you? I've gone over every possible solution a thousand times in my mind. I've even considered taking an intensive French course when I get back home, so I can ask for a transfer to a University here, but you didn't bother asking. No, as usual, you got pissed off first and asked questions later." Chloe stopped to regain control of her emotions. "I'm tired, Laurence. I'm tired of arguing about it, so I'm doing us both a favor…I'm checking out now." She turned back to her suitcase and grabbed another pile of clothes, stuffing it in angrily. Something shiny on the dresser grabbed Laurence's attention, and she realized that it was Chloe's ring. She picked it up and squeezed it in her hands, and as she did so Chloe turned around suddenly.

"Plus, Laurence, I've heard you apologize for your temper zillions of times…it doesn't cut it anymore. I'm tired of you not talking to me or scaring the shit out of me with your temper. I just can't…" Her words were muffled by Laurence's hand on her mouth, her eyes boring into Chloe's soul, pleading. She slowly removed her hand from Chloe's mouth and stepped back slightly, her eyes never leaving Chloe's. She softly reached for Chloe's hand and slipped the ring back on, and, getting no reaction, she looked up and her heart broke at the sight of tears falling down Chloe's pale face. Her eyes became watery, and she kicked herself inside for the hurt she had caused. Not a word had been spoken between them, but the emotions filling the room were strong, their eyes enough to express what they felt. Chloe lost it first.

"Laurence, you hurt me, you know?" she said with a sob.

"I know," whispered Laurence, taking one step toward Chloe, but not touching her.

"Why do you do that? Why?" Her question was left unanswered as Laurence stepped closer and tentatively wrapped her arms around Chloe. "I can't do that, Laurence…I can't do that anymore." Sobs racked her body, making her words almost inaudible.

"I love you, I love you so much," whispered Laurence, letting her tears fall, and tightening her grip on Chloe."

Chloe raised her tear-stained face to Laurence, and smiled through her tears. "Hopefully you do, otherwise I don't know why I'm staying with you."

Laurence laughed and buried her face into Chloe's hair, inhaling the smell of fresh vanilla shampoo. "I'm so sorry. I overreacted...I'm so sorry."

Chloe kissed Laurence's chin. "I overreacted too...we're even." Laurence smiled faintly and tenderly kissed Chloe's nose.

"We make such a pathetic team, don't we?"

Chloe nodded, her face buried against Laurence's chest. "Chloe, I promise you to try to think before reacting for now on. I know I've said that before, but I don't want you to leave me because of my temper. I promise I'll try harder."

Chloe nodded, looking deeply into Laurence's eyes. "That's all I can ask." They held each other for a long time, basking in each other's closeness.

① ① ①

The last month flew by. They tried to put away any hard feelings and enjoy what was left of their life together. Every day, the final date drew closer. Laurence quit her job shortly after Chloe's decision to go back. She argued that she wanted to spend every possible moment with Chloe. Deep inside Chloe welcomed this decision, even though she tried to convince Laurence not to throw away her career for her. "You're more important than any career," Laurence had answered.

Before they knew it, their last evening together arrived.

"Okay, I think I'm all packed," said Chloe, closing her last suitcase and turning to Laurence who was standing at the window.

Laurence smiled and extended her hand to Chloe. "Come here," she said softly. Chloe stepped toward Laurence and let herself be taken into a hug. "I can't believe that this is our last night together," whispered Laurence, her voice trembling. Their lips met tenderly. The kiss started as a reassurance, but quickly turned into passion. Hands started roaming against each other's bodies, tenderly brushing against bare skin, and fingers trailed down flat stomachs. Laurence slowly removed Chloe's shirt, exposing her skin to the warmth of the bedroom, and she slid her fingers over Chloe's back, eliciting a moan from Chloe. They gently broke their kiss and tried to regain their breath, eyes clouded with passion. Chloe dove back for Laurence's lips, the distance almost unbearable. Their bodies slid down against the wall to the cold hardwood floor, legs entwined together as their passion reached its peak.

① ① ①

At Charles de Gaulle Airport, boarding for Flight 64 to Washington D.C. was announced for the second time. Chloe let go of Laurence's hand and stood up. "I should go." As if understanding the urgency of the situation, Clément threw his arms around Chloe's legs. She picked him up and hugged him tight. "Don't forget about me, little man." She had promised herself that she would be strong and keep her tears for the airplane, but her emotions go the best of her, and tears spilled from her eyes. "Go on," she said putting him down. Her eyes locked with Laurence and she reached for her hands. "I really should go," she repeated, her voice tight with tears.

Laurence nodded and engulfed her in her arms. "I love you, Chloe." She hugged her tight, unwilling to let go. Chloe slowly extracted herself from Laurence's arms.

"I'll call you when I get there. I'll come back for Christmas. It'll be okay, right?"

Laurence smiled and fought tears that threatened to fall. "Go on, you're going to miss your plane." Chloe picked up her carry on, and ruffled Clément's hair and briefly kissed Laurence. "I'll call," she whispered, turning and walking away. She hadn't even taken a step when she was suddenly pulled back into Laurence's arms. Laurence grabbed her face and kissed her passionately. They melted into each other's kiss, oblivious to the stares from people walking by. The kiss ended, and Laurence stepped back. She wiped the tears from her eyes and picked up Clément. "Go now," she said softly.

Chloe made her way slowly toward the escalator, stepped onto the moving stairs, and turned to face Laurence. Their eyes met, and the connection didn't waver until the ceiling blocked their vision. Laurence continued to stare where Chloe had been only a few moments ago, unwilling to accept what had just happened.

"I want Chloe," whined Clément.

"So do I," whispered Laurence, turning around and walking slowly toward the exit. As she stepped outside, her last vestige of bravado left her, and she finally let the tears fall.

Other books by
Justice House
Publishing

Accidental Love, BL Miller
Accidental Love is a captivating story between Rose Grayson, a destitute, lonely, young woman, and Veronica Cartwright, head of a vast family empire and extraordinally rich. What happens when love is based on deception? Can it survive discovering the truth?
0-9677687-1-3 $17.99

The Deal, Maggie Ryan
Laura Kasdan is cruising along as the News Director at the number one television station in Dallas. When a momentary lapse of control almost costs her a stellar career, she makes a deal to save her job and keep a promise and moves to a smaller station, where she meets a charismatic reporter who promises to turn her well-ordered world upside down.   0-9677687-7-2 $17.99

Of Drag Kings and the Wheel of Fate, Susan Smith
Elvis isn t dead, he s just in Buffalo and he s a she. When Shakespearean scholar Rosalind meets Taryn, a young drag king, they invoke a karmic cycle that began with recorded history. Is their love strong enough to outwit fate and revise their destiny? *Of Drag Kings and the Wheel of Fate* is passion, mystery, and magic, just as you like it.   0-9677687-8-0 $17.99

Josie & Rebecca: The Western Chronicles,
BL Miller & Vada Foster
At the center of this story are two women; one a deadly gunslinger bitter from the injustices of her past, the other a gentle dreamer trying to escape the horrors of the present. Their destinies come together one fateful afternoon when the feared outlaw makes the choice to rescue a young woman in trouble. For her part, Josie Hunter considers the brief encounter at an end once the girl is safe, but Rebecca Cameron has other ideas....
0-9677687-3-X $17.99

Hurricane Watch, Melissa Good

Dar and Kerry are back and making their relationship permanent. But an ambitious new colleague threatens to divide them and out them. He wants Dar s head and her job, and is willing to use Kerry to get it. Can their home life survive the office power play?
0-9677687-6-4 $17.99

Lucifer Rising, Sharon Bowers

Lucifer Rising is a novel about love and fear. It is the story of fallen DEA angel Jude Lucien and the Miami Herald reporter determined to unearth Jude s secrets. When an apparently happenstance meeting introduces Jude to reporter Liz Gardener, the dark ex-agent is both intrigued and aroused by the young woman. A sniper shot intended for Jude strikes Liz, and the two women are thrown together in a race to discover who is intent on killing her. As their lives become more and more intertwined, Jude finds herself unexpected falling for the reporter, and Liz discovers that the agent-turned-drug-dealer is both more and less than she seems.

In eloquent language, author Sharon Bowers paints a dazzling portrait of a woman driven to the darkest extremes of the human condition-and the journey she makes to cross to the other side.
0-9677687-2-1 $17.99

Redemption, Susanne Beck

Redemption is the story of a young woman who finds out that the best things in life are often found in the last place you d look for them. Angel is a small-town girl who finds herself trapped within her worst nightmare, a state penitentiary. She finds inner strength, maturity, friendship and love while at the same time giving to others something she thought she d lost within herself: Hope. It is the story of how Angel rediscovers hope blazing within the piercing blue eyes of another inmate, Ice.   0-9677687-5-5 $17.99

Several Devils, K. Simpson

What do you do when you live in the most boring city in America, you hate your job, and you re celibate? Invoke a demon to shake things up, of course. Join Devlin Kerry on her devilishly funny deconstructive tour of guilt, fear, caffeine, and suburbia.
0-9677687-9-9 $14.99

Tristaine, Cate Culpepper
Tristaine focuses on the fierce love that develops among strong women facing a common evil. Jesstin is an Amazon from the village of Tristaine who has been imprisoned in the Clinic, a scientific research facility. Brenna, the young medic assigned to monitor Jess s health, becomes increasingly disturbed by the savage punishments her patient endures at the hands of the ambitious scientist Caster, and a bond grows between the two women. The struggle Brenna and Jess face in escaping the Clinic and Caster s determined pursuit deepens the connection between them. When they unite with three of Jess s Amazon sisters, the simple beauty of Tristaine s women-centered culture weaves through the plot, which moves toward a violent confrontation with Caster s posse.   0-9708874-0-X $14.99

Tropical Storm, Melissa Good
Tropical Storm... Enter the lives of two captivating characters and their world that hundreds of fans of Melissa Good s writing already know and love. Your heart will be touched by the realism of the story. Your senses will be affected by the electricity, your emotions caught up by the intensity. You will care about these characters before you are far into the story... and you will demand justice be done. 0-9677687-0-5 $17.99

A Year in Paris, Malaurie Barber
When student Chloe Jones becomes an au pair, all she s looking for is an interesting year abroad in Paris, but she gets more than she bargained for in the mysterious Glairon family. While caring for sweet little Clement, Chloe begins to care a great deal for his beautiful but haunted half sister, Laurence. But not even the most romantic city in the world can help these two when the family s secrets threaten to destroy them all.   0-9708874-1-8 $17.99

Above All, Honor, Radclyffe
Single-minded Secret Service Agent Cameron Roberts has one mission-to guard the daughter of the President of the United States at all cost. Her duty is her life, and is the only thing that keeps her from self-destructing under the unbearable weight of her own deep personal tragedy. She hasn t counted on the fact that Blair Powell, the beautiful, willful First Daughter, will do

anything in her power to escape the watchful eyes of her protectors, including seducing the agent in charge. Both women struggle with long-hidden secrets and dark passions as they are forced to confront their growing attraction admist the escalating danger drawing ever closer to Blair.

From the dark shadows of rough trade bars in Greenwich Village to the elite gallaries of Soho. Cameron must balance duty with desire and, ultimately, she must chose between love and honor.   0-9708874-1-8 $17.99

Blood Scent, Patty G. Henderson
A story of obsession
Love beyond the grave.

Blood°Scent takes the popular trappings of vampirism, romance and the gothic; bringing them together in a modern tale of a young woman s journey into the dark side of her soul.

Set in fictional Bayton Isle, off the coast of Maine, Samantha Barnes, a successful cover artist for romance novels, must come to terms with her manic depressive past and her obsessive desire to find true love even if it leads her to the grave itself.

When Samantha suddenly finds herself attracted to a woman with a mysterious and haunting past, she is whisked into a nightmare world of vampires, blood and murder. Thinking that she has finally found the perfect lover in Lara Karnov, the unholy pact she forges with the vampire nearly costs her the lives of those who love her most. °Samantha slowly discovers that the infamous Karnov Family is a savvy group of vampires surviving for centuries on the blood of those who served them. By the time Samantha comes to realize the truth, the trail of blood has taken a deadly turn.

The Countess Lara Karnov brings to vampire lore a new and surprising twist in an ending that will haunt you long after you ve put the book down.

Blood°Scent delivers a bold and daring look into our own darkest fears.   0-9708874-4-2 $14.99

Join the legacy of
Justice House Publishing

☐ **Above All, Honor**, Radclyffe
0-9708874-2-6 $17.99

☐ **Accidental Love**, BL Miller   0-9677687-1-3 $17.99

☐ **Blood Scent**, Patty G. Henderson
0-9708874-4-2 $14.99

☐ **The Deal**, Maggie Ryan   0-9677687-7-2 $17.99

☐ **Of Drag Kings and the Wheel of Fate**, Susan Smith   0-9677687-8-0 $17.99

☐ **Josie & Rebecca: The Western Chronicles**, BL Miller & Vada Foster   0-9677687-3-X $17.99

☐ **Hurricane Watch**, Melissa Good
0-9677687-6-4 $17.99
(Dar & Kerry Vol. 2, the sequel to **Tropical Storm**)

☐ **Lucifer Rising,** Sharon Bowers   0-9677687-2-1 $17.99

☐ **Redemption**, Susanne Beck   0-9677687-5-6 $17.99

☐ **Several Devils**, K. Simpson   0-9677687-9-9 $14.99

☐ **Tristaine**, Cate Culpepper   0-9708874-0-X $14.99

☐ **Tropical Storm**, Melissa Good   0-9677687-0-5 $17.99

☐ **A Year in Paris**, Malaurie Barber   0-9708874-4-2 $17.99

To order by mail send this page and a check or money order for the cover price(s) and $4.95 s/h for the first book (plus an additionall $1 per each additional title) to
Justice House Publishing (JHP), 3902 South 56th St, Tacoma, WA 98409. Delivery can take up to 6 weeks.

Name: _____

Street Address: _____

_____

City/State/Zip: _____

_____

Country: _____

Phone: _____

Email: _____

I have enclosed a check or money order in the amount of

$ _____

Please be sure to check the books you would like to order on the other side of this page.

Visit us on-line at www.justicehouse.com

Order our books at your local bookstore.